WITCHES OF WHEREWITHAL

ALEXANDRA SHARP

Rainbow Skull

For Gabe and Beatrice

Complacencies of the peignoir, and late
Coffee and oranges in a sunny chair,
And the green freedom of a cockatoo
Upon a rug mingle to dissipate
The holy hush of ancient sacrifice.
She dreams a little, and she feels the dark
Encroachment of that old catastrophe,
As a calm darkens among water-lights.

— WALLACE STEVENS, FROM "SUNDAY MORNING"

I

Salem, Massachusetts
The New World
1692

AMERICA HAD NEVER BEEN PARTICULARLY WELCOMING to a witch, even before the girls began to have their fits. But when writhing limbs whipped heads and eyes around in search of a source – then, for the first time, the real witches began to worry.

Until they remembered what they were capable of.

So on a gray-brown morning they traveled from up and down the coastline and from far inside the still-uncorrupted continent. They met at the high tide line, where a tracing of sea-debris scrawled over the sand. Already nervous and wary, they gathered, strangers to one another, and held hands loosely against a wind which threatened to toss them back into civilization or out to sea. Together they chose the sea.

No mere hysteria or paranoia brought them to this point of departure. They'd seen what would come, in dreams and visions which caused them to overturn cast-iron cauldrons of boiling soup on clean floors and cry out in the middle of solemn crowds. Branches so heavy with hanging bodies that feet, too late, brushed the earth. Rivers dammed by the accumulated guilty until the fields beyond went fallow and the rot in the water caused everyone not killed by association to grow deathly ill from disease. The women who gathered on the shoreline saw these things and knew them with the animal awareness that precedes natural disaster.

Most of them couldn't swim. Some were beginning to panic. Many had just gotten off a boat, by choice or by force, their legs still wobbly on solid ground. The thought of getting on another ship made a seasick feeling rise up in their throats.

But the ship was coming for them in the morning. *The Wherewithal.*

Not that they had any idea where to go. Their voices broke against each other: those who'd escaped enslavement and those who were wealthy; some of them servants and some indigenous to the continent.

"I only just got here three months ago!"

"I've been here for two thousand years."

Heads turned, eyes wide: "You have?" She didn't look much past sixteen years.

"Well, my family has been."

"I cannot see anything. Are we meant to see something?"

"Wait."

One wave rolled in much closer than the rest.

"We cannot wait any longer!"

"My dress is soaked through to the knees!"

"Wait!"

"Now! Look now, across the sea! See it now!"

Maybe everyone saw it at once. Maybe one grip after another tightened, numb fingers around barely-feeling ones. Maybe one person saw and everyone else was too scared to admit they hadn't. Until finally they saw, too.

There it was and there it would be if they survived long enough to find it: Lonely cliffs rising out of the waves in the North Atlantic Sea, far enough from everyone that it seemed the island's only desecration was bird shit and thorn bushes. There was ice, and there were green things, and there was a cold, clear river than ran between them, bringing new air to feed new life.

So that's where they were going.

2

**Island of Wherewithal
The Newer World
Late afternoon, December 1, 1947
14th year of the drought**

Waves crashed against the cliffs, with a roar and hiss as the ocean siphoned into the narrow valleys that spread like veins along the coastline. That water didn't touch the road where Theodora Ashe walked. No water had for a very long time, and when she lifted her hem it was only so the dust wouldn't dirty the black cloth.

She closed her eyes, knowing the path so well she could feel her way. The late afternoon sun came sideways over the horizon as she crested a rise and lit up the back of her eyelids. *Why worry?* For once, she wanted to enjoy the sea without thinking only of the salt. Maybe once she could have helped, but not for so long now. Perhaps it was time to well and truly give it up.

When a breeze blew her hair in front of her face like a veil, Theodora smiled and opened her eyes. The days were short and when night fell a billion stars would be revealed in a cloudless sky. The upside of no rain.

Maybe this is what peace feels like: time and familiarity. Boredom.

"Come, Diana," she said, and the whalehound, nearly five feet tall, bounded ahead to cover the remaining distance to the post office in a grey-brown blur. When the dog reached the little stone building she curled up beside the door, just enough out of reach that her heft wouldn't block the entrance but close enough, always, that she could smell Theodora.

At least Theodora assumed that was the idea. By the time she caught up Diana was already snoring.

Theodora pushed the door open and the bell above the doorframe tinkled. The Widow Green, head tilted toward the newspaper on the counter, didn't look up. Theodora's nostrils flared as she paused in the doorway.

Every damned time.

The old woman stood with hands clasped behind skirts that nearly but not quite obscured the oddity of her body: stooped back and crooked shoulders; lumps and protuberances; a riot of hair gone half-white. The result of some deep seismic activity years ago, it seemed, or an attempt to look as much like a character in a fairy story as possible.

Then there was the bird. Widow Green walked with a large green bird on her shoulder, whom Theodora always ignored. *A bit obvious, really.*

"Good afternoon, ma'am!" Theodora shouted.

Widow Green turned slowly, eyes wide like a fish coming up from the ocean, until the words found her wherever she'd gone. "Well, hello, Theodora." Widow Green always seemed somewhat surprised to see her, like she expected Theodora had anywhere else to be.

And she would talk you into the ground if given the chance, so now Theodora smiled politely without pausing in her errand. But Widow Green tapped the front page of *The Sentinel* with a gloved finger.

"It's happened. Did you see?"

Theodora looked down at the page despite herself, and stopped.

ISLAND OPENS HARBORS FOR FIRST TIME IN HISTORY
PEACE BRINGS OPPORTUNITY, SAYS GOVERNOR

She breathed out softly.

"I can't believe it either," the Widow said. "Trade. Books. Visitors! People thought to have vanished beyond the cliffs, gone to different shores, might finally return. Can you imagine?"

Yes, Theodora could imagine. People like her mother, if she felt like returning with as little notice as she'd given when she'd left. Or like Theodora's husband, if he were still alive after nine long years. If he felt like reappearing to clear her name of his murder. If she hadn't, in fact, murdered him.

But that was another matter, one Widow Green would be all too happy to pry into.

"I suppose that will keep them all busy in the city," Theodora said brightly and still too loud, as if volume could compensate for confidence. She smiled in a way she'd been practicing: as if she'd remembered she'd left the algae aglow but didn't want to be rude. Lots of visible teeth.

She nodded at the stack of mail in Widow Green's hand. "Looks as though you have quite a lot to keep you busy, too. I suppose we Widows must be good at correspondence, mustn't we?"

The older woman tensed her jaw. "It's an art form, isn't it? Not that you're a Widow, dear. Not fully. Henry's not quite dead yet."

Theodora blinked. Widow Green was better than she was at this, the managing of other people's expectations for how you'd act and what you'd say.

The Widow lived alone in the same cottage she'd shared with her husband long ago. But she didn't seem lonely. Wherewithal's widows were notorious for their thriving correspondence, letters shooting every which way through the subterranean tubes of the island's pneumatic post. Theirs was a whisper network – *loud whispers, heaven knew, but still* – that trafficked either in the island's most profound truths or its most asinine conspiracies theories, depending on who you asked.

Not that anyone asked Theodora, to join or for her opinion. She didn't get many letters at all, let alone from a cozy sorority of black-clad women. *Probably just recipes for tarts and tips for keeping slugs off your lettuces. Anecdotes about rosy-cheeked grandchildren and ungrateful children.*

Still. It would have been nice to be asked.

And she wasn't alone, not really: She lived at Ashe House, her mother's house, with her father and stepmother and half-siblings. But they were so preoccupied, the house so large and rambling, that Theodora could've wandered the estate for years without anyone paying much mind. It seemed to be working as far as the wider island was concerned. It had been years since anyone had sent a photographer around.

Now Theodora only smiled tightly at the Widow and went to her family's mail chute, its shining brass knob the size of a thimble, and took the smallest key from the chain at her neck. The Ashes were descended from the first ship to land and mostly this meant her father was in charge of local admin, or was meant to be. He regularly retrieved piles of unexciting, impersonal correspondence: bills and announcements, pending or passed legislation upon which Master Ashe had happily – or at least obliviously – ceded his vote to the majority. Theodora took today's pile from the tube and scanned it as she always did. She frowned at the last letter, a bill from Assembly for medical services rendered.

"Still nothing from Henry then?" Widow Green asked.

Bloody Lady of the Lake.

"No, no, nothing today! Still nothing." Theodora waved the letters above her head without turning.

"Hmm. Not terribly surprising, that," Widow Green said. "And what of your mother?"

Theodora closed her eyes briefly. *Is she doing a survey of everyone I've driven away? Still has a ways to go then.*

"Not a word! Lots to take care of, though!" she called over her shoulder. "Ashe family business, et cetera."

Her father was, by the kindest interpretations, benignly neglectful. Theodora had plenty to keep her busy answering his correspondence, handling his bills, signing his name to resolve petty grievances in town.

"Pity, pity," Widow Green said, halfway to another reverie. "Do you remember when you caused that tornado at your father's wedding? What a sight that was! Your mother would've known what to do."

Theodora felt her neck get hot.

"And what of that time you brought down lightening, opened up a vein of algae? Quite a geyser! Right before your mother left, wasn't it? That *was* you, wasn't it?"

"Who the bloody hell else would it have been," Theodora muttered. Everyone knew the story. *That was the whole damned problem.* Everyone knew everything about her, or so they thought. Theodora flipped through the same five envelopes, endlessly, beginning to see red.

The bell above the door rang once, and Theodora exhaled. She waited for it to ring again to signal she was alone, and stooped down before the package bin.

With the Solstice coming there were quite a few parcels. For the Ashes, bolts of fabric for her stepmother and washed-up rest-of-world bits and bobs Master Ashe had written for from the city antique shops.

Perhaps it would be just a little lonely, once her siblings had gone off to live their own lives. Once her father and stepmother had died and Theodora had grown old. She'd married so young, just barely eighteen. *I might live a very long time still*, she thought. She sighed and stood, turning back toward the door.

The Widow was staring daggers at her. Theodora nearly fell over onto her haunches.

The older woman held up a hand. "It's not over, child. They think it is and that's why they're opening the harbors. But it will only get more difficult, the longer you wait. People will only become more afraid." Her voice was sharper than Theodora had ever heard it. More tired, too. "Have you tried lately?"

A charge went up Theodora's spine. All her life, she'd gotten nosy questions from people who thought they knew her own hands better than she did. It had only gotten worse in the years since her mother, and then Henry, had gone.

Felt any twinges lately, Mistress Ashe? Do you know when the rains might return? A witch of the weather, aren't you, just like your mother? Just like your mother until she went mad and doomed us all to die of thirst?

No, she thought. *Actually I won't be lonely at all.*

Theodora stood up gracefully, all her energy concentrated on remaining calm. *Frigid Witch*, that had been one of the better headlines, and appropriately now she felt as though her veins had all gone frozen. "That's quite impertinent."

"I don't think it is, when so much depends upon it. But I suppose that means no?" The Widow didn't wait for a reply. "How long has it been since your mother left? Since Henry?"

Theodora folded her arms, tucking her useless hands away. She didn't like being reminded of how she could be helping the island, if she wasn't so dried up and useless. People still spoke of her mother with far more respect than they ever spoke of her. Her mother had been able to do something.

"Is this meant to be inspirational?"

The Widow Green arched an eyebrow so high it began to interfere with the hat.

"I'm not here to inspire you, child. Only to remind you. We have choices, we always do, even when it appears otherwise. Your mother made a choice, and I do not blame her for that. Henry did, too," the merest twitch of smile, "one way or another. And if I could do what you can," she added as she turned away, "hell, if anyone in my family had been able to do magic that I could ever recall, I'd make a choice. Something other than sitting and letting the world decide for me."

Night was falling quickly, and though the street was still dusty yellow the room had grown much darker. Glowing motes of algae began to dance up inside the frosted glass sconces.

Theodora squeezed the letters in her hand so hard she thought she might turn them to pulp.

"It's not a choice," she said tightly. "I'm unable. I haven't done anything at all, any magic, in nearly nine years, and I wish everyone would believe me when I tell them it's well and truly gone. I bled out of every finger trying. It's not a damned choice I've made! Magic was going anyway. Someone had to be last. A lot of good it does to have a mother who does magic when your mother leaves you – "

Widow Green raised one hand again, palm out, and Theodora's mouth stilled.

"Yes," the Widow said drily. "Pity. How people leave and things change."

Theodora leaned against the counter wearily. "I didn't ask to be the last one. It's not my job to educate them," she said, speaking mostly to herself.

Widow Green's face softened. "I know, child. But fools will always fill in the gaps of their understanding with fear. And just because other people have come to fear what you may do, doesn't mean you need be afraid, too." Widow Green looked at the sky as she stepped through the door. "You have correspondence, dear. Come through just now."

Theodora turned at the soft swoosh and thud of a newly arrived letter, and then heard the tinkle of the doorbell. When she looked back the retreating feathers of Widow Green's hat were just visible at the edge of the window.

But what if they're right, she wanted to ask. *What if they're right to fear me?*

Instead Theodora slammed her open palm against the counter so hard the old wood shook and the door to the post office blew open again. Diana ran inside as if summoned.

"Can't everyone leave me the bleeding hell alone?" she muttered as the pages of the newspapers turned over in the entering breeze.

Theodora remembered the letter.

Through the glass of the chute she could tell it was made of more expensive stuff than what usually came through. She'd become a connoisseur of such things. The letter was heavy; the paper nearly pebbled, like a tongue.

What an absurd comparison, she thought, and looked at the return address.

Theodora forgot about the Widow Green and witchcraft, about her mother and her husband and the drought and the wider world.

Not just because it was her own name on the address line. Theodora would have recognized John Dove's handwriting anywhere, even if it had been 100 years instead of nearly 10.

That bastard.

3

Wherewithal River
Southward from the Glacier
Nearly dinnertime, December 1, 1947

JOHN DOVE CURVED his body over the railing of the ship and looked down. He imagined a razor blade across his cheek. Maybe a scalpel. The ship was a jeweler carving blinding ice into facets of blue water. A painter dragging one color against the other all the way down the center of the island until the river below opened its fist and surged over the cliffs at the south end of Wherewithal.

It all made him feel a little sick. He pulled away from the edge, away from the churning ice.

Instead John looked to the receding horizon, the gentle slope of the glacier that was itself not gentle at all. The ice had been his home for nearly nine years, as much as any place had been since he'd more or less fled the south in a fit of heartbreak and adolescent self-indulgence. Aided by fierce, stifling familial pressure, of course.

The river water below was so clear John could see, past the froth of the breaking waves, lonely bits of bioluminescent algae that had come unmoored from the glacier and escaped his family's filters to journey with him downstream. John had considered not coming south at all this year. Staying over winter, ensconced in darkness and muffled sound, was more appealing each year. He'd thought this might be the one he actually did it. With the unspoken implication, of course, that he'd do the same for all the years to come. But that would have to wait a little longer.

His father had asked him to come home, and John had no idea what it might mean. John had tried not to think too much about it, since it made him feel a bit like a child. Like the walls were closing in and he'd done something quite terrible that no one would explain.

This year the river ice had come on early and this might be the last ship that made it to the city before the thaw. Perhaps his father had known that, as he always seemed to know all things: annoyingly, accurately, and in advance.

"Sir?"

John turned to find his valet a few feet behind. He wasn't used to having a valet; this had been another strange request from his father. A bequest. The valet was exceedingly polite and seemed good at his job. It was just that John had no need of a man to tell him when dinner was served or help him tie his tie. He had no need for a tie, at all, really, and the thought of having to put one on again when he reached the city made his throat start to constrict.

"Dinner is served, sir?"

John pulled at the scarf around his neck. "I'll be down to the mess in a bit." He turned back to the river. "Thank you, Ned."

"Sir, the captain has requested that you join him for dinner throughout our voyage?"

John leaned forward and let the metal bar press a cold line against his abdomen. He did wish Ned would take a firmer stance on things once in a while. Not his fault, of course. *Goes with the position. Not to mention mine.* "Has he now?"

"He has, sir. He's already at table?"

Back before they all kept quiet whenever he came around, John had heard some of the workers on the ice talking about how long you could survive under the water. Apparently if everything happened just right, your body would slow down and you could survive for quite a while. At the time it had seemed poetic, to become one with the cold. Now it just seemed like a relief. He slept terribly.

John wondered whether, if he jumped overboard, Ned would jump in after him. *Probably.* John twisted his head around. Without seeming to move Ned had come two steps closer.

"In that case I suppose there's nothing to do," John said, straightening and coming away from the edge. "Wouldn't want to get on the captain's bad side, eh?"

Ned dipped his head. "I have heard he has an excellent selection of dessert wines, sir?"

"Is that so?" John clapped Ned on the back, willing to take any opening he could get. If he was returning to a certain way of doing things, even for a little while, John was going to need allies. "I'll try to grab you a bottle when he's not looking."

"Quite all right, sir. Though thank you. There is also this, sir?" Ned produced a letter from deep within the folds of his wool coat. "It only just arrived."

John raised his eyebrows. "In the middle of the river? I hope you didn't swim out to get it, Ned."

Ned shook his head. "No sir. The mail was retrieved when we last stopped at a port. I believe you were sleeping, sir?"

John repressed a smile. "Yes, I do understand how the mail is delivered. That was what I call in my line of work a joke. Albeit it a very weak one."

"What is that, sir?" Ned asked.

"I'm afraid if I have to explain the joke it means I've utterly failed —"

Ned cleared his throat. "Your line of work. If you don't mind my inquiring?"

John's eyebrows went up. "Surprised my father didn't let you know. But then I suppose he'd have to tell me, too. Let's say I'm the one who tells the ice how best to get out of the way."

"How interesting, sir."

"Not the way I do it." John took the letter. "Anyway, thank you. I'll be in for dinner shortly."

Ned nodded and turned back inside. John looked down at the return address: Victoria White.

Right. His fiancée.

He'd met Victoria on a trip several years ago at a party thrown upon her father's appointment as Agricultural Minister. John had a suspicion he was being called home to finally make public the long-standing agreement between the families of Dove and White. Or at very least the longstanding consensus in the court of public opinion and editorial page and men's club, which is what really seemed to matter. John's father would say it was well past time that John marry. "Set an example!" he would boom at his son from across the room, without making eye contact. *Well-connected, no brothers, wide hips: What more could you want?* That was how he'd put it. *When her father dies, you'll take his spot easily.* Not that John wanted to be Agricultural Minister. Not that anyone had asked.

John was not at all comfortable with his ambitions and reputation – or Victoria's hips – being so summarily dispatched. But he supposed his father was right. Victoria was lovely, smart and pretty and with an affinity for politics well beyond his own. A perfect wife for a rising star. They wrote each other long letters full of anecdotes and intellectual riddles and completely devoid of romance and passion. Perhaps that was the perfect kind of political marriage, too.

So John would marry Victoria White. But then he was returning to the glacier, as soon after the Solstice as possible. He had a nice little cottage and hundreds of employees who did him the courtesy of talking about him only when he was entering or leaving a room.

He had a wide expanse of ice to contemplate and a box of sadly neglected painting supplies. Most important, he had an idea that the safest place for him, where he could cause the least damage if not undo his father's work mining the heart of the island out entirely, was alone, and cold, and dark for most hours of the day.

4

Ashe House
Evening, December 1, 1947

MAIN STREET WENT EAST from the village green out into what was, once, a springy countryside laced with deep ravines that connected to the river canyon and led in their labyrinthine way to the cliffs at the island's edge. Now there were only dry veins and empty arteries crisscrossing dry fields and meadows. What water ran down from the ice through the river itself ended up a sad trickle into the North Atlantic Sea.

The roads were dark by the time she left. *All the better*, Theodora thought as she hurried, head down, letter clutched hard inside her coat pocket. She didn't want to deal with anyone's questions and she knew she looked a fright, nearly running, sweat making her hair go every which way.

Even though there was no one around Theodora waited until she was beyond the village proper to rip open the letter. A very pregnant snowhorse and three bored wooly sheep, remnants all from an ancient ice bridge long since severed, looked on.

Theodora read the letter. Then she read it again, and again:

I need very much to speak with you. I've needed to for quite some time. Come to the city? Please.

I'll be arriving back from the glacier on the 2nd of the month.

Yours,
  John

She read it once more, then hitched up her skirt so she could walk faster.

Ashe House, long home to Theodora's mother's family and now home to Theodora's father and his, was at the top of a stepped hill of stony outcroppings. A tree-lined lane wound from the road up to the estate, if you could call it that. Two stone mermaids sat atop columns marking the entrance, their tails split to wrap like vines around the old stone. Their faces and scales had worn away long ago.

After Henry left Theodora had seen the house with new eyes, as if not just her illusions about marriage but about the entire world had been wiped clean: the foundation in disrepair; the grounds neglected and overgrown; the stewardship of the farms adjoining only an afterthought. Coming from one of the first families was meant to be an honor but also a burden. At least that was, Theodora gleaned, the original idea. In practice it often it ended up looking like it had with her own family: privilege and neglect, with little to justify the way things were except that they'd always been that way. *Challenge the status quo too much on a closed island and everyone's afraid you'll destroy the whole ecosystem.*

Theodora turned the lane and began to pick her way through the bramble. She knew her way by heart and normally would have made the trip up the hill in half-time, but today she stumbled and crashed, cursing and scaring away the crows. When she broke through the trees she could see, three hundred yards ahead through the tall pale grass that was at least four months past due for a trim, smoke coming up from the chimney. She frowned: someone was always home, puttering at projects. *Perhaps if I'm quiet* – she didn't finish the thought, lest she call them down upon her, and put her head down to go straight to her wing of the house.

Through a cloud of bumblebees and a swarm of butterflies, over two sunbathing cats, then nearly dizzy at the smell of her stepmother's flowers, overdue for harvesting for the – *was that still happening?* – parfumerie project Miranda had begun in the dry, bored heat of summer.

It'd been the hottest summer anyone could remember, but her stepmother nearly lived outside. She was much better with plants than with people, really. Despite having known her stepdaughter for going on 14 years she still treated Theodora as though she were a bulb mistakenly planted upside down: a thing of tender frustration and near hopelessness. Theodora could hear Miranda singing loudly from inside a hedge somewhere and ducked behind a rose bush so she wouldn't be seen.

Closer to the house a pool of brackish water (they'd ordered in ice for the Summer Solstice celebrations) lapped at cracked opalescent tiles, and bullfrogs perched on lily pads. At least a dozen open books were scattered on the patio stones, drying out from some plumbing catastrophe, and someone had left a very large and oddly patterned quilt hanging from the branches of the tree next to the front door, which had been left ajar.

The ancient rug in the entryway had gone half-cocked, and with one foot Theodora pushed it in place as she walked through. The family birds began to trill from the solarium and then someone began to play, very loudly, a recording of an overly shrill soprano.

Theodora didn't pause. She turned at the stained-glass window depicting a ship cresting a wave at dawn. Diana had beaten her here and pushed open the door to the western wing of the house with her snout. Theodora shut the door firmly behind them, giving it a shove with her shoulder to get the wood to fit the frame.

After her marriage – or rather, after her wedding – Theodora could have stayed in the house her husband had purchased. But it was large and strange and full of a household staff that whispered whenever she left a room, casting sidelong glances as she passed by in the hall. She'd only lasted a week before returning to her father's house and commandeering this wing. No one had used it since her mother had disappeared anyway.

Theodora reached the first closed door along the hallway and took out one of three keys she wore around her neck, even in sleep, even in the bath. This room had been her mother's library.

She flopped into the chair behind her desk and, for the first time since getting the damned letter, allowed herself to consider it fully.

Nine fucking years! What on earth was that smell? Maybe she had a cookbook that would help Marco with whatever he was cooking.

Had it really been nine years? She jumped up to pull a crusty volume from a low shelf. *Clams?*

She threw the book on a nearby chair and strode to the leaded glass windows. *No.* She couldn't. The last time she'd been to the city, three years ago, it had ended up all over the press. She'd become a bit of a spectacle, and it would only be worse now that the harbors were opening.

"The Widow Witch of the South," *The Sentinel* had called her then.

She hadn't any desire to give them more ammunition. Show her face only to raise suspicions again that she was some sort of savior. Or a murderer. A revolutionary. Whatever fit the current mood.

She nodded, resolved. *Whatever it is, John, I'm sure you can manage on your own. He's managed well enough without me these last years. Nine years!*

Theodora frowned out at the fields rolling away from the house toward the cliff edge. Small crystals, dense and still covered in places with lichen, glittered and absorbed the sunlight as they twisted, hanging in front of the windows. She swatted one away and went back to the old leather armchair.

For years she'd been waiting for some word from Henry. Without a body no one really knew what had become of him – herself included –

and Theodora held out hope for her own peace of mind if nothing else. So she checked the mail. And who should send a letter finally?

John.

That bastard!

It wasn't just that he'd gone away, or that he'd not written after her wedding – or more to the point, after what came next. It was also what he'd done with himself since.

What must have happened up there, digging his machines down to mine energy and light from the ice? *He must be a completely different person.* Chilled through, like his father.

But she couldn't picture him as anything other than the boy he'd been. Which made her think, of course, of the girl she'd been.

She looked around the room. As if someone therein might answer or at least commiserate, though of course there never was. By design.

It wasn't that she didn't trust her family. It was more that they wouldn't have noticed where they were walking and would have waltzed or wandered in and long ago taken over her space without any malicious intent at all. Safer and saner to keep the door locked when Theodora wasn't around.

But the room was very full. There were maps and globes of not only this island and this earth but of every continent and planet they knew of, supplemented with conjecture and folklore and legend. Delicate instruments balanced on bookshelves besides piles of dirt and chunks of precious metal. Books, a full wall with rogue shoots of paper springing up from inside each one. Seeds in copper trays; ancient bugs caught mid-metamorphosis in amber; prehistoric silver tools that were barely more than chipped stones. There were great hanging mobiles that illustrated every type of cloud, the patterns of lightening and the reverberations of thunder. Scarves draped across the ceiling mirrored the winds of the earth. Glass orbs filled with spiny plants and vines that fell to the tiled floor from pots hung fifteen feet up. Ladders everywhere, to reach books and storage or to allow her to rearrange the clouds.

This room, abandoned and left to molder by her father after her mother disappeared with no note or warning, had seemed the safest place after Henry disappeared, too.

Eventually some of the books picked up by the University would reenter circulation; some copied over and reprinted for sale by shabby little printer-booksellers in the city. But that took years, and it was easy to run out of things to read before the lava-like flow of volumes worked its way slowly throughout the island. Some books never even made it to the university, secreted away by Assembly. It was impossible to know what you might be missing, and quite infuriating.

Theodora's mother's books were different. They were all old, bound in hide and sometimes written on thin sheets of vellum rather than paper. Many had been written on the island, by hand in poor ink kept from fading only by the darkness of the rooms. Every so often, for reasons Theodora could never glean, her mother would pull her daughter from whatever she'd been doing and bring her quietly into the study. She'd page through a book as if double-checking, and then finally she'd hold the book out to Theodora.

"Would you like to practice together for a little while?" she'd ask. Theodora always felt that she could have said no, that her mother would have understood. That perhaps her mother wished she would say no. But she never did.

They would each try small versions of spells, side-by-side. It was difficult work, because the spells weren't their own: Records of other witches' work, done in other places and times, either here on Wherewithal or on some other land. That was what filled nearly all the books, though sometimes it took the form of stories and sometimes of poems, sometimes pictures or etchings.

To reinterpret and make the work their own took concentration, and Theodora and her mother would work silently, peacefully together until the light from outside grew too dim. Her mother never lit candles in her study. Then she'd gently put a hand on Theodora's shoulder and smile, and Theodora would know they were done.

After her mother had gone Theodora took the books off the shelves in a near frenzy, balancing crazily on a ladder, opening each one, looking for a clue or at least an apology. She'd found only spiders' webs and flowers pressed to dust inside the pages.

Now Theodora picked at the dark lace encircling her wrists. Her mother's books contained everything from ancient midwifery to hydraulics to Morse code, and to pass those first long lonely hours Theodora had thrown herself into reading with a fervor that bordered on mania. It wasn't that she'd been trying to lose herself in the books, though at times she'd come close, refusing to eat or speak to anyone who ventured to call through the crack beneath the door. No, she'd been looking for something, though she wasn't quite sure what. She was sure she hadn't found it, though.

Either that or she'd just got through all the books and gotten hungry. Eventually, Henry's cousin, her dear friend, Adelaide, sent her a whalehound puppy, the size and general appearance of a startled porcupine. The two of them started taking long walks around the canyons and along the edges of the cliffs, keeping most people at a distance. If Theodora had played into people's fears at first it was only because she was afraid that they might have all known something about her that she didn't.

But this room had become Theodora's sanctum. In one quick motion she pulled another key from her chain and unlocked the largest desk drawer in from of her.

She'd collected her own books to it over the years, the works of local writers and mapmakers, historians and philosophers and poor translations of water-logged volumes cast against the cliffs with the remains of shipwrecks. But not just books.

Inside the large hard-backed portfolio she retrieved was the story of who she'd become, or at least who people thought she was: news clippings from *The Sentinel*, gossip clippings from *The Flotsam & Jetsam*, sophomoric cartoons from the university rag, all tracing the sordid, highly embarrassing, highly suspect goings-on of the Widow Witch. Theodora flipped through to the back of the folder. Where she kept the clippings about John.

Of late all his mentions had been gossip and hearsay; anodyne quotes about lighthouses and irrigation no doubt crafted by his father's company men. Nothing at all about a trip to Mooring.

She slammed the drawer shut, beginning to wish someone from the rest of the family would barge in to take her mind off things.

Must be feeling quite dire then.

Theodora breathed deep: Marco was cooking, as usual, for a family dinner that would come two hours later than appropriate. Roberta, Miranda's child from her first marriage, was probably en route to an explosion in her chemistry lab, formerly known as the basement.

They were both blithe as their mother, Miranda. Theodora was, by design or comparison, the serious and moody one. Dark where the others were fair, which she found nearly as obvious as Widow Green's stupid bird.

Theodora checked the status of the moon, just risen. Master Ashe had left on a walk along the coast long before the sun was up, but he was always in plenty of time for dinner.

And Theodora? She was, in addition to being moody and gloomy, also simply *around*. In the absence of a clearly defined role in the family or much of a future to speak of, and in the presence of all those books, she'd become something of an expert on all sorts of things that no one else could be bothered to remember or learn. A solution to a problem with the rats in the attic, or the Latin term for Sulphur, or a definitive answer to whether or not the basil had gone bad.

She rubbed her hands against the green leather armrests, shiny with use, then carefully splayed her hands on the broad expanse of the desk. Fourteen years her mother had been gone; nearly nine since she'd taken over this room. Long enough to erase whatever fingerprints had been here before and replace them entirely with her own, but still her life revolved around waiting: for someone to come back or something to change.

"Useless," she muttered and pushed herself to standing. She slid John's letter into her skirt pocket as she left.

5

Wherewithal River
Dinner, December 1, 1947

THE CAPTAIN of the ship was a shy man. But he was also a heavy drinker of the purple-black ale they aged up north in great carved barrels of ice. After the first bottle, John was barely able to get a word in.

After the second, John learned to leap at pauses in the old man's speech. By the third, the two of them were laughing and crying and pounding the table.

"You are a young man, aren't you?" the Captain asked. The wood of the tabletop had begun to look like black dirt fresh after a storm, and John had been staring into it, remembering someplace he couldn't recall.

The question was asked jovially enough, but when John looked up to answer – *depends how they're defining young these days* – Captain Hillside was squinting into his glass as though it was a periscope, as if he'd forgotten he'd asked a question at all.

"Sir?" Maybe the captain really wasn't used to drinking this much after all. *It must be a lonely life here.* A little like his own. John tried to find the captain's downturned eyes.

"Surprised you haven't taken a wife," the Captain said. "Must be lining up for you. What with your ambitions for the island, your reputation as man who'll lead us into the future. That's the next step in these things, isn't it? How it's done?"

"It is," John said, with a smile that painted him the reluctant fiancé. *At least if you're interested in power and money and paperwork.*

It was, though, how these things – the lives of men like himself – generally went: Make a start in some profession; get noticed just enough to secure invites to the right sort of dinner parties; get strategically sat next to eligible young ladies; end up at the Magistrate's office signing papers six months later.

He sighed. "You know, Captain, while it's true I may have become something of the public face of Dove Holdings —"

"You must think us fools," the captain said, without changing his tone, without looking up. He nodded at his glass, then in one move took it up and gulped his ale.

When he finally looked at John his face was balled up in defense.

It wasn't the first time a conversation had turned this way, though John was still caught off guard each time. He always wondered how it wasn't more obvious, to Captain Hillside or anyone how much John disliked his lot in life.

John smiled into his drink. "Sir, I'm sorry, I don't believe I understand." He reached to cut a slice of the rock-hard bread they'd been served with the soup. "More bread?"

The captain gave a loud, barking laugh and grabbed the knife before John could reach it. John froze. "There will be no bread when you are done. There will be nothing here left for any of the people who work this ice. You're sucking the marrow of the place. But not just the glacier. It's the whole damn island you're destroying! Don't you understand?" He pounded his fist on the table as the ship knocked hard against ice and then lurched forward. "You know my father was a naval man but my mother, she was from here. From the glacier."

John was silent, trying not to stare at the man's grip on the knife, his fingers a breath away from the blade without the Captain seeming to notice.

"That entire side of the family," Hillside went on, not loosening his grip or breaking eye contact. John wondered if he'd be able to wrest it away. "As far back as you can go. Of course, my mother's gone now. But this," he waved the knife to encompass not only the ship but, John surmised, the whole ungoverned territory they were sailing from, "and these?" He pounded himself in the heart, then the head, so hard John flinched. "Part and parcel of each other. That's what I've got. Not your youth. Or your power or money. I've got connection to the place where I lay my head at night." And just as quickly as he'd grown fierce, he dropped the knife, poured himself more wine, and grabbed the entire heel of bread. He took a bite, breathing hard through it. "When I'm not sailing, that is," he shrugged.

Wonder how long he's been preparing that speech.

John picked up his fork and pushed at the last few scraggly, honey-soaked carrots on his plate. He had to accept that he'd spend his life explaining himself to men he had, without realizing it, alienated or ruined. Working on the ice was hard work that was sold as crucial and honorable. It was also terribly low-paying and involved the complete forfeiture of representation in Assembly for the workers. To the officials of Wherewithal, the ice was no-man's land, except plenty of men still lived there.

That was part of why he wanted to stay on the glacier. To acquit himself. To punish himself.

And after all John was very good at the part of the conversation that came next. "I suppose you're referring to the activities of my father's company," he said. Appeasement.

"Your father, yes." John had the feeling some other superlatives were amended to that in the captain's thoughts, if not his words. Which was fine. John had plenty of his own superlatives for his father. "I don't begrudge it you, either — we need the light from those damn bugs."

"Bioluminescent algae," John said. The science was a sticking point for him. It felt like the one thing he could insist upon.

When he first went to the ice to look after the company, John had thought he'd stay for a season. Maybe a year. But his father's aggressive tactics paid off, and the drillers found an untapped ore that nearly tripled output. Then things had changed so rapidly, or so it felt: His mother had died. His father had sold their house near the Ashes. Dove Holdings expanded exponentially. Theodora had gotten married.

No one quite knew where to put algae: Was it science, or energy, or mining? The same could have been said, for quite a while, about where to put the Doves. John felt very affectionate toward the algae itself, perhaps because it too had been shoved into an uncomfortable public role from which there seemed no return. These days the algae was more interesting than himself, he had to admit.

"Yeah, the algae-bugs," the captain agreed, tracing his finger along the edge of the bread knife.

Perhaps now's not the time to be a stickler for accuracy. But something stuck in his mind.

"What was that you said, about destroying the island in its entirety?" He tried to keep his voice light, though the words betrayed him.

Captain Hillside hesitated, a moment too long for John's taste. "Eh, I'm just getting carried away is all. The harbors opening and all. Assume you heard the news?"

John nodded.

"Well they'll only ramp up the work now, you know." He pointed the knife at John but the anger had gone out of his voice, and there was nearly a smile on his face. "You will, I mean."

John smiled tightly, relieved but not entirely convinced the captain wasn't still holding back. He didn't quite feel like getting stabbed, though.

John didn't know much about the company's involvement in the opening of the harbors, what deals they'd struck already with the wider world. It was above his pay grade, even as the founder's son. Maybe especially as the prodigal son, kept untarnished for whatever his father was planning for him.

It had been his idea, though, to give the technology to the world. Isolated as they were there had been signs, seen through telescopes, that all was not well in the wider world: shipping lanes repopulated with tankers, warplanes diverted overhead. And then there was the shrapnel and the debris tossed up against the cliffs, weighing down boats when it got caught up in nets. John had thought, stupidly, that their technology might be able to help. It had only been the seed of an idea, but it had been enough, apparently, to set things in motion.

So he could do this. All his life he'd been able to convince people to see his side of things, even when he wasn't sure they should.

But his hands shook as he brought the glass to his mouth. It was wrong, all of it, and the Captain was right. *Damn, now I'm drunk, as well.* He looked at the glass accusingly, and the purple of the ale bled into the green of the algae in the votives on the table behind it. The jagged blue line between them danced and disappeared as John spun the glass.

"I lost my mother," John said. He didn't know why he said it; if it was to win the Captain over to the company side or to just make sure the man didn't hate him. "A long time ago. That's why I came here."

He raised a brow. "She from the ice?"

"Oh no. She caught a chill standing in the shade. But she's why I came here, nonetheless. To heal, I suppose?" John smiled. "Sounds ridiculous when I say it out loud, all these years later."

He wasn't used to drinking this much, or perhaps when drinking alone there was just far less chance of sharing secrets. John cleared his throat and addressed the votive, still wary of looking the man in the face. But he was a real person, all of them were, and it was wrong to hide from them. Especially if he planned to live the rest of his life among them.

"I've found a home up here, is what I mean. I will raise the issue of enfranchisement when we get to Mooring. I promise no one is bent upon destroying a way of life, let alone an entire part of the country. We have mutual goals, Captain. It won't do me any good, after all, if you all start burning down the mines."

John heard a scoffing sound and looked up from the line of blue light. He was surprised when it wasn't his father seated across the weathered wooden table. Yes, he could do this. John leaned forward and folded his hands, much like his father would have.

Captain Hillside raised an eyebrow. John tapped the table and smiled.

"All this ice, melting? I'm a terrible swimmer."

Captain Hillside looked at him a long moment then slapped the table and laughed. He finally dropped the damn knife. "You're a right hardheaded bastard is what you are."

"That's what everyone says," John replied, smiling grimly. "If only."

6

Ashe House
Dinner, December 1, 1947

THEODORA SMILED DOWN into her potatoes. Her blue potatoes. They weren't bad – hardly anything Marco cooked was technically bad – but they were so very blue.

The table was set with all their best china and glassware — all of it by this point mismatched and chipped though her father kept reassuring them it was all quite rare and of great value. The table was more than two hundred years old, built by Theodora's great-great-great-great-great grandparents on her mother's side when they'd built this house, room by room as their farm had grown and the town had built up around them.

The sconces along the wall, each one the shape of a different bird, glowed with pale yellow algae and filled the hall with low, warm light. Long brocade curtains — nearly tapestries with their faded depictions of unicorns, forests, and sea voyages — had been drawn against the early dark. The rug was threadbare, but like everything else here it had been created long ago with care and skill and it still held the warmth from the day's sun.

Theodora's nose began to twitch with something hard and biting: The feel of metal against her tongue and the lingering buzz in a dark room after the light's has been covered up. That couldn't be from the potatoes, surely?

Roberta burst in holding out a dish full of electric blue shimmering something as though it was an offering, she some newfangled priestess. Theodora stared at her stepsister, whose face had gone blue in the glow.

"Roberta! You made that? How unstable is it?" In truth it took very little for Theodora to swell with pride at Roberta's scientific accomplishments, though to say that outright seemed to beg an experiment capable of leveling them all to the ground.

Anyway Roberta looked quite pleased with herself. "Not at all. And of course I didn't make it. It's algae. An unclassified type. I discovered it."

"Here?" Miranda asked, seeming slightly panicked. "Near the house?"

"By the Hills' farm. Do you know they haven't filled in that hole where the river rift collapsed?"

Theodora pursed her lips. "Truly? Someone should write a note – what am I saying? Roberta, I believe you've made quite a scientific breakthrough."

Her sister beamed. It made her look much younger than nineteen, which she knew, and she quickly tried to put on a more serious face. "Possibly," she said, sliding into her seat, putting the algae beside the bread plate. "Pending much research. Anyway hush up about it."

"Who'd hear us here?" Marco asked, seeming slightly nervous about the prospect of unknown spies.

"Well — no one. It's just — can you imagine what might happen? If they knew there was algae down here, as well? They came here once to look, you know. Twenty years ago or some such."

Theodora remembered quite well: They'd come to test the land, taking great ores up out of the earth, right before her mother left. "Not twenty. Not that long ago." She looked to their father, but he was worrying something from between his teeth. "I won't tell anyone," she said to Roberta, smiling. "Promise. But I'm quite impressed."

John was deep below the ice with that same algae. No, that wasn't right: He was sending her a letter, traveling to Mooring. He can't have changed so much, can he? If the people working for his father's company were anything like him, Roberta had nothing to worry about. Perhaps there were still beautiful things to be discovered. Or perhaps John had changed as much as she felt she had.

"Do you know that damned Mr. Salt from this summer was still lurking around? I swear he's following me, trying to swoop in. And now there'll be other men come, too, from Europe and the Americas. Academics," Roberta whispered with narrowed eyes, unable to take her own advice, as if academic wasn't what she would do as well, if women had been allowed. Women who weren't witches, that is.

Master Ashe coughed, the discussion having gone on without him for far too long.

"Well then," he began. "Have you heard anything from Henry, then, love?"

He asked it every Sunday dinner, but every time Theodora felt she needed a moment to keep from screaming: *Is this when it's traditional to mention the possible return of my estranged husband, after nearly nine years apart? After the salad but before the cheese, when everyone's had at least one cocktail to dull the awkwardness of dealing with the spinster daughter who insists on hanging about? Or should I wait until the dessert?*

But instead she looked down at her mourning clothes and smiled tightly. As she did every week.

Theodora looked past her skirts and studied the rug's pattern, interrupted only by Diana's dream-twitching paw, before she replied. This room was a comfort. The objects that filled it were friendly and they sighed at her in commiseration. It had never really been so bad to be here, not really.

"No news, Father."

"Hmm, well, yes." He began to cut his fish. "Pity that."

Marco and Miranda likewise began to eat. Roberta looked at Theodora and rolled her eyes, as she always did. *Well that's settled for another week, then. Pity he didn't ask about John! Then I'd have some news.* She began to eat.

It had been years, she realized with a small shock that made the food catch in her throat, since she'd been away from the family home for even a night. She went with Roberta up the coast or down a crevasse to help haul something back home, but no further.

At the other end of the table, her father coughed. The family paused.

"What is it, dear?" Miranda asked, benign and infinitely patient. To stay married to Master Ashe one had to be not just patient, but saint-like in her suffering.

Everyone waited, cutlery aloft, for a fiscal announcement, a proclamation of belt-tightening that her father would promptly forget once he found a new antique piece of naval equipment to polish and stack inside one of the stables.

"Well, Theodora." Everyone else exhaled. Theodora lost her appetite.

When Master Ashe had something innocuous to say he did it privately. When he had some unpleasant news to impart he did it with an audience, so he had to go through with it. He wasn't a bad man, really; he just had blinders on to the rest of the world. When he took them off he always seemed surprised and a bit frightened to realize he wasn't alone.

"Well, Theodora," he began again. "I'm selling the house."

"Oh Thomas. Now, truly? With the children here?" her stepmother murmured. But she said it to her plate; when her husband decided to make a pronouncement there was no stopping him.

"What? When?" Theodora asked, the words a croak in her throat. She looked around the table at the everyone's downcast eyes. She felt like the air had gone out of not just herself, but out of the room. Out of the world.

"You all knew?"

"Hmm, yes. Well." Her father began to cut his fish into very small pieces.

"Roberta?"

Her sister looked up with a bright red face. "I didn't know how to —"

Theodora slammed her fork down and everyone jumped. *Good. Feel something*, she thought.

"How dare you not consult me?" Theodora asked, carving out each word, her voice quivering. Better angry than crying. "Am I not a member of this family?" More than that – this house was her mother's house. Or had been, and if it belonged to any of them, it belonged to Theodora, perhaps not by law but certainly by all common decency.

They never spoke about her mother, though. It was a tacit agreement made soon after Marguerite Ashe had gone, and Theodora had respected it through the years, even when she burned to ask questions or wept from loneliness and guilt that it may have been her own fault.

But selling the house. That had not been part of any agreement.

"This is my mother's house, Father."

Master Ashe's knife scraped against the plate. "What? No. Well, Theodora. It is not yours. It is mine."

Theodora gripped the edges of the table, feeling as though she were at sea. How could she convince him? She needed time. She needed to think, to strategize, to do something.

But that was why he was ambushing her, she realized.

She tried to smile. Change tacks. Tried to make her voice sound strong and appeasing. "Why would you sell it though? You won't find a finer house or better land, I'm sure. Miranda, what of your gardens? Come now, Father, you're being quite silly." Theodora picked up a bite from her own plate and tried to chew, but her mouth was dry and the blue potatoes tasted like sawdust. She took a large swig of wine to wash it down, waiting for her father to respond.

"Oh, it's a burden, isn't it?" he said, gesturing around the room with his fork. "All this land and this old stonework always crumbling. Damned expensive, isn't it. You understand."

Theodora glanced at the little antique clock, another relic on the mantel. Certainly, he could pawn some knickknacks still.

"To be honest we've already had an offer. They're interested in surveying the land for more mining. It seems we might have an ore," he added proudly

"What?" said Roberta, moving her algae closer.

"And obviously you know what this means."

"I do not," said Theodora, and her voice sounded very far away.

Master Ashe looked pained, but mostly a little desperate at his daughter not taking the hint. Theodora looked around the table once more, desperate for some clue to soften whatever blow was coming, but no one would look at her.

"We'll need you to go, Theodora," he said, mouth full of food so that the words came jumbled. But clear enough to make Theodora's heart nearly stop.

"You want me to leave?" She was still holding out hope. But the look of relief on her father's face dashed that all away.

"Not want," he said. "No, no, no. But you understand! Even with the sale and a portion of the algae profits money won't be flowing as it once was. And you do take up quite a bit of space with your odds and ends, don't you? We can't just have you here forever." He smiled tightly around the table and picked up his knife. "It'll be good. A fresh start. Exciting things for all of us, really. Good? Good. I'm glad we had this talk."

He began to cut his fish again, carefully extracting the bones and putting them in a little pile just off the side of his plate.

Theodora felt like roof had fallen in, why it might as well have. She felt absurdly like laughing.

"Talk?" Theodora's voice was low and tight but controlled. "You have summarily dispatched my home with barely a word from myself, and you call that a talk?" Something clicked. "Is this about the inheritance?"

When Henry was declared dead on the Solstice, nine years after he went missing, Theodora would come into quite a bit of land and money. Quite a bit, or she would have if she wanted it, or had ever made any noise at all about claiming it. As if enough people didn't think she killed him already.

Her father huffed and threw up his hands.

"Oh Theodora! Honestly!" He pursed his lips at her. "You've made it quite clear that you're going to be stubborn on that count. Plus, you could never pay me what the Doves are paying me."

Theodora's stomach dropped further.

"Though you'd be doing her a favor, you know," Master Ashe went on, pointing down the table with his knife. "Electra Martin's not fit to run that land, will run it into the sea soon enough. You could sell it, too. I'm sure Assembly would look more kindly upon you if you sold it to them for development. To be sure why anyone would want the responsibility is beyond me. Let alone a woman!"

"Let alone," said Roberta through clenched teeth.

Theodora knew Master Ashe wasn't nearly so skeptical of women ruling as he was of anyone actually seeking out that sort of burden. He simply couldn't fathom giving up pre-dawn rambles or weeks spent deep inside dusty volumes for the expectations and obligations that came with power and responsibility. *As if*, she'd always thought, *were he to allow just the smallest bit of obligation to sneak in, the floodgates would open and he'd be crushed under the weight of expectation.*

It had been that way for all of Theodora's life. It made her crazy, though she supposed it had kept him safe.

"I will not take everything from his mother," Theodora said tightly. "She's lost enough." She steeled herself, gripping the table hard. "As have I. You cannot do this to me, Father."

Her father had stopped mid-bite when she began to talk, and now as his face went red, she worried he was choking. But then he banged his fist upon the table, the point of the knife straight up in the air. A saucer jumped onto the rug at the impact, but no one moved to get it.

"Nine years! You've had nine fucking years, Theodora! You couldn't stay a witch or get a husband in that time, and now, somehow, I'm to blame in all this?"

Her stepmother reached out a hand and placed it over his clenched fist, her fingers around the blade so the knife stopped shaking in the air. Master Ashe was still staring down the table at Theodora, and Theodora felt the blood surging through her body. She'd never seen him this angry.

"Come now," he said, and just as quickly as it had come on his anger was blown away by exasperation. And that's how he's sounded for years, she realized, like he just can't be bothered. He shook his hand lightly free of his wife's and went back to his fish. "Be reasonable, Theodora."

She remembered something he'd said. "What did you mean, 'Assembly will look more kindly on me'?"

"Yes. Well. You don't have to worry about where to live once we've gone," her father said. "I've just had a letter from Assembly. You've a cottage being built for you. Upriver."

"Upriver?" she said, as if that was the most worrisome part. "A cottage? Whatever for? Why?"

He waved his knife like he was shooing away a fly. "Eh, you know, because of your – your history. I take it with the borders opening it's thought prudent to keep you somewhere you can be guarded. I should've thought you'd like it, being so solitary and such a nervous sort. I take it there'll be some sort of guardian to watch over you. Or guard. Something like that."

"But you'll always be welcome in our home," her stepmother said, before Theodora could form any words or thoughts at all. Miranda leaned forward and extended her other hand across the tablecloth. "For visits. Anytime, dear."

Theodora recoiled in her seat. She pushed back from the table. "Thank you. That's very kind. To share your home."

A look of pure embarrassment passed over Miranda's face. "I didn't mean –"

Theodora held up a hand, palm out. By now she was nearly vibrating with anger.

"Ted." Roberta was staring at her. Everyone was staring at her except Master Ashe, who was still determinedly cutting his vegetables.

Theodora stood up fast. She didn't know what made her say it. The house, her father, Widow Green. John. Damn them all.

"Perhaps I should run off to the mountains then?"

Master Ashe looked up, mouth half-full of food. *Huzzah finally got him to stop eating at least.*

The mountains cut the island horizontally just as the river cut its length. Forests on either side of the range were full of life, but the mountains themselves were barren, sheer cliffs. Weather swirled around their summits, but – at least lately – never deigned to roll down into the valleys below. It had taken decades to blast through the rail line that connected the north and the south, and near a hundred men had died doing it. Theodora couldn't imagine finding any kind of refuge or purchase there, unless your goal was to turn into rock yourself. But apparently it was possible, for women of a particular, peculiar persuasion.

Women like her mother. The mountains were as far as they'd traced her when she'd left without any note or sign. But the trail had gone into the rock. Straight into it.

"You? What? That's absurd!" He started to shake his head, hands shaking as he pulled loose from Miranda. "No, you couldn't, you wouldn't be able to – you're no longer a witch, then, are you? No. No. Never like her. No, never."

"Maybe I am. Maybe I've just been waiting for the right time."

She said it so quiet she barely heard herself. But it had its effect. Everyone's mouth fell open just a little. *Some satisfaction that.*

Finally, Marco spoke.

"Don't leave before dessert, Theodora?" he asked quietly. His voice still had a note of panic to it, and when Theodora looked over to him his eyes were huge. Damn it. He was only six.

"I'm sure it's delicious," she said to him, and her voice cracked. "But obviously it's time for me to go. Come, Diana." As the dog stood her skull hit the table with a thunk that shook the crystal and the porcelain both.

7

The Atlantic Ocean
Dates and points lost

It's one thing to see a place in your mind, even to see it in many minds at once. It's another thing entirely to have a map. They did not have a map.

One of them was married to a sea captain. So everyone packed what they could carry, either woke their children in the night or cried and let their children sleep, and the group took sail two days after meeting on the beach.

Some of them had already travelled far to get to this point, and by now this felt like just a little farther. Some had to force their feet forward with every step. Only a few decided not to escape with the others, not believing things could truly get as bad as the others feared, or not believing anywhere else would be better.

Rain, sometimes sleet, had been falling steadily since the night before their launch. That was good for keeping the people of the nearest town from noticing but bad for everything else. As soon as they began to wade out into the water toward the dinghies, waves crashing into bare legs and layered wool alike, the adults all quiet and grim, the rain seemed of little consequence when compared to the terror of the sea. Only the babies, who knew nothing except cold and being held too tight in fear, cried.

They sailed for months, aiming northeast. They took turns as lookout posted high in the crow's nest, in mild weather and during storms which either crept up over tortuous hours or materialized all at once directly above the ship's deck. Between the weather and the many children aboard someone was always throwing up or shitting, until no matter what magic was worked the place still stank worse than dead fish.

Magic couldn't save everyone, either. The sea was bigger than any one of them, bigger than all of them put together.

They sailed for months. They knew that much by the moon, but otherwise they stopped counting days. Once they found the place they'd seen together, time could begin again.

8

Ashe House
After dinner, December 1, 1947

It was a long walk from the dining room back to Theodora's part of the house. What she'd been thinking of as her part of the house. She glanced at an old and precarious vase and considered sending it crashing to the ground. Instead she stopped, lifted her hands and examined them slowly, front and back.

She tried to see them as someone else's hands, someone who might be able to do something useful and good with them. Make it rain, or stop up the algae so the land could retreat back into peace and neglect.

Maybe her mother's hands. Maybe her own, when she was younger. Theodora glanced at the vase, filled partway with water. Maybe she could do it, make water into something bigger than itself. A system, a storm. It had come so easily once –

She let her hands drop. It had been too long.

The house's entryway had its own atmosphere: warmer and drier than anywhere else in the house. She breathed it in and tapped Diana lightly on the haunches to send her bounding ahead back into their wing. This was what had always been so good about living here: Close enough to her family to keep an eye on them, but far enough away not to be driven completely crazy. Apparently they didn't feel the same.

She went past the study, then a storage closet she'd converted into a second library, and a storeroom full of half-dead plants and arid soil samples. The walls and the ceiling of the hallway were swollen and lumpy with moisture, scratched and singed and smoke-stained. Her mother's work. Her own attempts.

The bedroom was different. Theodora didn't work here. She didn't spend much time here at all, other than in bed – her marriage bed, in fact, dragged by a team of icehorses when it became clear Henry wasn't returning anytime soon. It had been his gift to Theodora, a grand and hand-crafted thing the size of a lifeboat, made from the wood of the forest at the base of the mountains. It took the entire family a week to figure out how to fit it through the doorway.

At night Theodora spread her arms and legs out with room to spare, and after the pain of being alone faded she found she liked the freedom to toss and turn as she pleased. Except for being a very large, physical embodiment of her failure as a wife and a woman, it wasn't a bad place to sleep.

Theodora undressed and pulled on old and soft pajamas. She ran her hands down her legs to stretch her tired back and, truthfully, to delight as she did every night in the feeling of wearing pants. Perhaps at some point the tide of fashion would change on the island.

"Quite a wave that would be," she said to Diana, sleeping next to her on a pile of dirty laundry, as she climbed into bed.

I wonder if I can take it with me, she thought, and squeezed her eyes shut tight, gripping the sheets hard in her fists. Or, if her mother had been able to turn into stone, than surely Theodora should have been able to do the same. To become part of the stones and mortar of this very old house, to weather away peacefully until she was just gravel and dust.

Unfortunately, that was yet another area where Theodora's magic was of completely no use. It wouldn't have been helpful even if she still had it really, as transmutation was never really her bag. At age eight she'd turned a loaf of bread into a very large hailstone, but that was about it.

But she breathed out and let her eyes relax. Her father had been wrong: There was a little magic left in her, not her own, and just a little, but there nonetheless. Something of her mother.

Theodora never had trouble falling asleep, no matter if her husband had abandoned her, or the entire island was gossiping about her. No matter if her father had just thrown her out. Sleep came like a riptide, so strong it made her hesitate sometimes to close her eyes unless she felt truly ready.

Marguerite Ashe had been a witch of the weather, too, so Theodora had no idea why or how she'd always had the gift of putting people to sleep. Not in a murderous way. Like a lullaby that always worked, a tea that soothed the stomach and the mind. Several strong cocktails. Marguerite had done it with a song. She wasn't even a very good singer; Theodora remembered her mother's voice raspy and whispering on notes another woman might have pierced or harmonized. But Marguerite was just that good of a witch.

Theodora closed her eyes and – she never knew if, truly, she was choosing to do it – began to remember the melody. Part prayer chant, part song, her mother's magic, or at least a crumb of it left behind. Theodora had never tried it on anyone else. She was afraid the song would stop working, and sometimes it felt like all she had.

The familiar heaviness lapped. A sense of being in two places at once. And with the part of her brain that was still awake and in bed she tacked a wish onto the end of her whispers: For the sake of all that's good, Teddy, dream about something else tonight. Be original.

Nine years on, the dream of her wedding night still came far too often. Tonight was no different.

Festivities were winding down: older relatives nodded off at cleared tables; small children ran with late-night energy around the periphery. The food, none of it good, was nearly gone. Her friends clustered at tables near the exit. Adelaide held court over a gaggle of admirers. John was not there, of course.

She could never wake herself up, either.

In the dream the barn beside the river seemed endless, walls and ceiling hidden in such blackness they might as well have been the sky.

John wasn't there but she searched for him in the crowd, stepping over crushed flower petals and overturned cups of punch. *Maybe he'll have the courtesy to finally show up.* Did she always look for him as much as she was looking for him tonight? She couldn't recall. But he wasn't there and now no one else was either. Only the giant, starless ceiling, and Henry.

She turned to him in bed.

Sometimes he was gone almost as soon as she saw him, and then she was waiting by the window late in the afternoon the next day – *utterly ridiculous, how long I stood there.* Sometimes she was with the brusque, mustachioed detective sent down from the city.

Tonight she and Henry were in bed.

For all that Theodora had worried about it, it hadn't been bad. Not that she had much to compare it to, but no one had been injured or run screaming from the room. Perhaps that would have been better, in retrospect.

On their wedding night she'd turned herself soft and demure, batted her eyelashes and undressed slowly as her husband sat on the bed. She and Henry had always had an almost formal courtship, full of what seemed now like foolish philosophical talk and withheld touch. Now that there was nothing left to withhold Theodora began to wonder if their love – was that what it was, truly? – could stand up to flesh and bone.

Theodora thought Henry was everything she ought to be: serious and intellectual, idealistic and dedicated to bettering the world. He'd settle for nothing less than radical change, and though Theodora hadn't been entirely sure how that change would occur, the idea of something entirely new had seemed bracing and right.

Before Henry proposed, before John wrote to say he wouldn't be coming down again and would instead be going to the glacier to run his father's business, marriage had seemed foolish. Theodora knew that someone always bore the brunt of it. In that, at least, she'd not been wrong.

And Henry was lovely, slim and tall with sandy hair and fine features. Much lovelier than herself, she knew. And John was gone.

Henry stared as she let her wedding dress fall. At that moment, she'd considered reaching out and touching his cheek, making them both stop and talk, making him laugh as she always could. But her dress fell too quickly, and instead Henry reached out and put a hand on the curve of her waist.

Henry did seem to enjoy what followed. It wasn't terrible for Theodora, either, not really. She'd been jabbed by an elbow or other appendage several times, but she only panicked once or twice and managed to bite her lip when it hurt the most. One day they'd make it enjoyable. Maybe even beautiful.

Afterwards they faced each other on the giant bed, breathless and close. He kissed her again, softly on the cheek.

"Ridiculous, isn't it?" she said, so quickly she wasn't quite sure what she was referring to.

He smiled. "Quite ridiculous."

Relief felt a bit like adrenaline. Theodora grinned madly back, so happy was she to see the man she thought she knew. This was why they were good together: Henry saw only the work to be done, the pain to be relieved; she could show him the joy in doing that work together. She made him smile.

That's why she'd chosen this wedding gift for him. Miranda had seemed politely horrified when Theodora had brought up the possibility: "You are the gift, Theodora!" So Theodora hadn't told anyone else, not even Adelaide.

Henry had seen her do magic, of course. She made bits and bobs of thunderstorms and sunlight to punctuate conversation the way other people waved their hands. But that was before Henry walked her home from the summer solstice festival and their steps had grown slower until finally they stopped beneath the lightening-struck tree at the edge of her family's property.

Since then doing magic for Henry seemed both childish and very important, like she had one chance to get it right and otherwise she'd ruin things entirely.

But she'd been practicing. She needed the energy of a storm

without the snow itself (which she figured would be a bit unpleasant on one's wedding bed). She had to hold the moonlight and the air just so to make sure all the colors were sharply demarcated and bold. A moonbow. The perfect union of time and place and nighttime element. What could be better, to give to your new husband?

Theodora scrambled to her feet on the mattress, unsteady above him. She lifted her hands above her head, biting her lip in concentration, feeling the reflected glow of the sun coalesce at the base of each finger –

Henry grabbed her leg. "Please," he said. "Not now."

She looked down at him, confused and half-annoyed at the disruption, the energy making her hands ache with nowhere to go. "I want to do something for you, Henry," she said, but even as she spoke she was being tugged gently and insistently back to earth. "Whatever is wrong?" she asked when she was kneeling beside him.

"I'm very tired," he said. "Let's get some sleep?"

She cocked her head at him. "But this is –"

"I don't have any energy for anything else tonight, Theodora."

Her face fell. She hadn't realized that her magic required energy of anyone else.

"Of course," she said, and tried to smile. "Maybe in the morning?"

He scanned her face one last time and nodded, as if they'd decided something of far greater importance than whether or not to go to sleep.

He rolled over. "Turn down the lights?"

She walked around the room, twisted each tiny knobs that closed the lamp shutters and dampen the glow of the algae. Then she got back into bed, facing her new husband's back.

She whispered to the subtle points of his spine: "I'm sorry if – "

He snored softly. She stopped talking. The dream lost its thread:

Awake in an empty bed, an empty house. No note, no explanation. Standing by the window and waiting. Staring down at her hands which wouldn't stop clenching and unclenching, which seemed to be acting all on their own. Henry's spine again, those delicate bones like a bird's. A rage building inside of her until her palms burned with the need to do something, anything to relieve the pressure building up inside her veins. Crying, alone, catching a glimpse of something horrible in the mirror and then realizing it was her own face.

Theodora woke shivering and sweaty, though not surprised. It was nearly boring by now. Or would have been if she knew what really happened nine years ago. She was no longer sure at all, so convincing and insistent were the dreams, so murky had the time just after her wedding been. All she had was memory, and Theodora was no longer at all sure which memories were real. Whether her husband had vanished, or if she'd vanished him. Killed him.

The cliffs were scoured, climbers going down into the deepest cracks; the rocks combed by every fisherman who could be spared, daring as close as they might with the waves crashing around them. Diana had gone out every day on the urging of her mistress, searching for a scent. But there was nothing and people began to talk. Who else could make a man disappear like that, besides a witch?

They still talked, too, when there were papers to be sold or someone remembered that there was a former witch in their midst who should've been able to stop the drought once and for all.

Just how deeply had she slept on her wedding night? People talked in their sleep, or walked – could she have magicked in hers? Created a tornado in her bedroom in place of the gift she'd meant to create, and spun her husband out into the night? Drowned him in a peculiar, concentrated storm and dried the water with the rays of the early morning sun? Or taken the sun and burned him until there was nothing left but ashes easily taken care of by an open window and a cooperating breeze?

She'd had a lot of time to think of every horrifying, terrible thing she might have done. She was quite good at imagining, unfortunately. But try as she might to recreate the sensations in her fingertips, Theodora couldn't remember.

But she hadn't made a conscious choice to stop doing magic. Instead, there was a gradual waning of herself over time, until when she did try again she found she was unable to do any of the things that used to come without thinking.

She cursed her younger, stupider, more innocent self, who'd taken it all for granted. Making rainbows zigzag across Adelaide as they sat through another tedious luncheon; catching John in a rainstorm and then in the next moment making the air around him so warm that his hair puffed up to twice its size. Creating a cloud around herself when she felt dreamy and wanted to be alone on long walks down to the cliffs. These were things that seemed natural to her all her young life.

Fully awake Theodora glanced out the window: Still hours before dawn. But she swung her feet over the edge and nudged Diana awake. The mighty dog whined and turned over on her back.

What good is sleep if there's no peace to be had in it? What good is a bed without a home to put it in? What good is all the notoriety of a witch without any power to show for it?

Except perhaps being thought a witch was still good for something.

"Let's go," Theodora whispered to the whalehound. It wouldn't do to wait any longer.

If they wanted a witch, she would give them one.

9

Ashe House
Late afternoon, August 1, 1933

"Why are you here?"

In the open doorway, backlit by the sun so she could barely see him, Henry Martin opened his mouth. Theodora frowned. She knew it hadn't been a polite way to greet someone who'd come to your home and that was partly why she'd said it. She wanted nothing to do with further comings and goings from her house. Even if the person who'd come was a boy, about her age with a sharp profile and hair that caught the sunlight and an outfit much nicer than what most boys could be bothered to wear.

Even so. She deepened her frown to compensate for her thoughts.

"Are you the witch whose mother made the storm?" he asked. "I'm Henry Martin. I'm Adelaide's cousin. Is it true you're the last witch now?"

Now it was Theodora's mouth that fell open.

Yes, when her mother had gone a storm had begun, one that lasted for weeks, and not in the usual sense of rain that comes and lingers, ebbing and growing stronger in turn. Not a monsoon, either, though it was near as much rain. This was a storm: wind, lightening, thunder, and rain that sometimes became hail and other times turned into snow. Snow! The entire island flooded. Homes were plunged underwater. Wild animals suddenly revealed an ability to climb trees and scale walls, as if they'd been waiting for this moment. They said in Mooring it looked like an ancient city some of them knew of, where boats sailed down streets and alleyways.

When it ended and the water receded, everyone was just grateful, and so it took much longer than it should have to notice that the rain did not return. Still hadn't, months later, beyond some freakish middle-of-the-night soakings that dried fast in the sun. Sometimes you could smell rain, if you woke up early enough, but otherwise it was as though all the rain had spent itself at once, never to return.

All that was true, but people didn't tend to bring it up with Theodora. As if she was dry as the earth had become, and would splinter and blow away like dust if anything disturbed her.

Except this boy on her doorstep just had. She couldn't tell if he didn't care at all or if he cared much more, and more rightly, than anyone else. *I'd like to find out, though.*

"Yes," she said, thrusting out a hand. "All that. I'm Theodora. Would you like to come in?"

10

Wherewithal River
Sometime after midnight, December 2, 1947

THE ONLY SOUND was the cracking of ice and the slow churn of near-frozen water.

The wine had calmed his body but not his mind, and after John fell into bed still in his clothes, he lay awake repeating what the captain had said as they parted:

"Young man, I will tell you the cold is not much for healing. It'll numb you and it'll keep you, but perhaps it's good you're going south for a while."

John never slept well, always slightly fuzzy around the edges and half in a dream when he was out of bed. Worse still, when he did sleep he dreamed of made-up landscapes that, when he woke, his fingers itched to paint. They always came out terribly, murky and derivative. Eventually he'd given up trying.

But tonight was different. Tonight he couldn't tell if he wanted to dive off the ship and swim back north or to hop ice floes all the way to

Mooring just so he could get everything over with as soon as possible. Or perhaps, as seemed most actually likely, just sink to the very bottom of the river along with all the frozen creatures that lurked there.

John stretched his hand out to the small table bolted in the center of the room and picked up the stack of mail that been retrieved along with Victoria's letter. He tossed the reports and business plans to the floor to read later and glanced at the cover page of the '48 business plan: "Peace is an Opportunity: Expanding the Reach and Output of Dove Bioluminescence Energy Co. Abroad"

The damned company changes its name every two weeks.

He got the newspaper every day on the ice and read it front to back: Politicians gave speeches about increasing trade, about creating an army of the island's own, about the benefits of tourism in the face of continuing drought. Convert the cliffside gardens and farming plots into hotels and resorts. Give idling farmers new work as miners and factory workers. Look into the future – look to the horizon, is what they really meant, and the ships and planes that would now being to arrive – with eagerness and adaptability instead of fear. It wasn't the 17th century anymore, after all.

Indeed. John wasn't opposed to the future. Not as a concept, anyway. But the heady pace of development. The desperation. It wasn't that he was such a believer in the old ways, fishing and isolation. Both made him feel sweaty and useless. It was that he wanted to believe there was a way forward that didn't feel so raw and ripped up from everything that had come before. That wasn't literally ripping the ground apart in a way he wasn't sure could ever be put back again.

Ironic that his business was with pickaxes and explosives.

And those articles, to his increasing embarrassment and something else, something like shame, often mentioned him by name. *John Dove* was an idea of the future, the boy – he took umbrage at that, but yes, it made for good marketing – at the helm of the company that would secure Wherewithal a place on the world stage.

He didn't know how the devil they were supposed to ship even more down this small, ice-choked river. The captain would have something to say about that, surely, not that it mattered what the old man thought. Or what John thought. Dove Holdings was like one of the drills that bored down into the ice, taking forever to get going but then damned hard to stop without getting oneself killed.

He tossed the report onto the floor and picked up the newspaper. He squinted in the dim light, the glow of stars against ice through the windows. Breathless news of diplomats and businessmen sailing and flying over the oceans, already coming here to make plans and deals. Waiting wasn't how fortunes got made, it seemed.

John rolled over to face the wall and jammed the newspaper beneath his pillow for extra padding. The water lulled him to sleep.

11

The Atlantic Ocean
Dates and points lost

THROUGH THEIR CONVERSATIONS with each other the vision of the island became clearer. Sometimes no words were spoken, sometimes it was just mutual imagining.

Theirs was a piecework, patchwork kind of witchery. It took many days on the sea before the refugees began to trust one another to share who they'd been or what they knew beyond the magic they'd shared on the beach. They'd been brought together by a desire to survive, but little besides magic united them. Appearance and experience varied widely: Some on the ship were White Europeans, some were native to the Americas, and some had been brought enslaved from Africa and other points east.

Some were better at prophecy, some could tell you truthfully what had happened to you years before. Witches of farming, of storms, of rivers and lakes; witches who could heal and ones who could cook so well it might as well have been magic. Witches of formulas and potions, of language both human and animal, of fabric and woodwork and metallurgy.

Control wasn't the right word for what they did: Each had an intimate relationship with the elements, one that unveiled atoms and molecules, high hidden winds and hot pressure systems waiting for their cue. Like dancing with a partner, some said, or a being truly listened to. Or sex when it was good. There were as many types of magic as there were people but no matter the form, you couldn't make something from nothing.

Once they began to share it was still a gradual revealing, and traditions began to bleed into each other like water-logged words on a page. Some magic fell away entirely, ill at ease off the land. But some new, though weak, abilities emerged: solid things could become vapor and salt fell from the sky in flakes that clumped on the deck and looked like snow. They were never hungry, though they quickly grew tired of fish and the seaplants that loosed themselves from the ocean floor and floated up to be caught in witches' nets.

The new language of shared magic they spoke was reinforced, nearly daily, by visions of the island. Partly they recalled it for reassurance that they hadn't, like those girls in Salem, experienced a collective hallucination – at least not a false one. But also they sat each day, in pairs or small groups, and discussed what they'd seen on the beach because otherwise they were all afraid they'd never actually find it. Every conversation was a search for a clue, some hidden coordinates in the sea or arrangement of stars that could guide them home.

12

The Meteor, en route to the City of Mooring
Morning, December 2, 1947

THERE WAS no one else in the train car, just Diana snoring on the green leather seat across the aisle, but still Theodora felt self-conscious. They'd left before dawn, arrived at the fishing village station with the sun. Diana scared the ticket agent so much he'd spilled his tea across all the untorn tickets, and Theodora was so jumpy she'd practically yelled at the poor man when she told him her destination.

She'd left a note for her family on the study door, though she wasn't sure when Roberta would notice she was gone. Not for hours, maybe. A day if her work was going well.

She sat up straighter and closed her eyes. When she opened them again they were high along the west side of the island, above the bowl of what was once the agricultural valley.

The cliffs dropped so precipitously beside her that the ocean looked far away, the water still and calm. In reality it slammed against the cliff sides and narrow inlets, sprayed salt water and minerals and deposited small creatures and plants that would cling and grow as they had for — how long? Millenia, certainly. *Very tenacious, that marine life.*

At least it had been. If the drought kept up perhaps this would be the end, and Theodora was glad she couldn't see the withering vertical gardens along the crevasses, or the dusty fields farther inland.

She needed to smell the earth, suddenly, and Theodora shoved the window up with some trouble. Both she and Diana arched their noses up as the salty air rushed in, followed quickly by a gust of dirt. Theodora began to cough and wheeze as the train's shadow passed over a field of lurid green.

An unnatural color, Theodora thought. Families who were rich enough could ship down enough ice from the north to water their fields and charge whatever they would. It worked out well for the ones who could do it, and for people like John.

She hadn't stopped thinking about it: *What the devil could he want? What could he possibly need?* Certainly if he was in trouble of some sort he'd have more helpful, or at least more socially acceptable, people around to sort it out? Unless it was magic he was after.

She nearly laughed aloud. Well, he'd get it then, or at least as good an impression as she could manage. And she'd get to ask him to make his family stop drilling in the south. Ask him as convincingly as she was able to

The grass outside turned dusty again. She turned from the window and splayed her long fingers, her wide palms.

If the only way she could inherit her mother's home was to be a witch, than a witch she would be. Most people still thought she was once, despite her best efforts, anyway. She would go see John, but not as some lovesick girl come running: As a witch who could use his newfound status and pull to achieve her own ends.

It was high time she looked out for herself, if everyone around her was just going to run away anyway. And if playing this part made John Dove just the slightest bit remorseful at the way he'd left things, well – so much the better.

Her hands started to ache as the pressure changed and they plunged into the forest at the base of the mountain. She clenched and cracked them without relief. In truth this was about all she could manage these days: aching bones at pressure systems, a walking old wives' tale.

Great job you'll be seducing John, she thought, and laughed out loud, her nerves getting the best of her. Diana grumbled at her feet.

"Beg your pardon," she said to the dog.

The door to the car banged open as the train took a hard curve, and a conductor walked in on seasoned sea legs. He was tall and wide, all muscle, and he stopped beside her, blocking the aisle entirely. Theodora realized her hands were still in the air and quickly folded them. Out of long habit and instinct when in public she tilted her chin so the brim of her hat cast a shadow over her eyes.

At times people treated her, as the last witch, with undue deference that verged on adulation, and while that was mortifying it was the other type of reaction she could no longer bear: The people who muttered under their breath when she passed or shouted obscenities from their windows. Upstart widow witch. Witch-bitch. Dried-up hag. Murderess. She'd been spat on, she'd had mud – let's call it mud, why not be generous – thrown in her face.

The worst of it was she could never tell which reaction was coming. If the beatific child walking up to her would be holding roses or a doll stabbed in effigy. It wasn't just the gossip columnists who kept her tucked away at home.

"Is there something I may do for you?" she asked the dusty floor of the train car.

"D'you know that the mountains are full of subterranean tunnels, dearie?"

Theodora looked up sharply but the man wasn't looking at her, was instead bent halfway over and squinting out her window.

"Yes," she said, momentarily startled out of her wariness. "I've a bit of a side interest in geology. Mining."

In the south the river had long ago carved the slot canyons into the landscape, so she wasn't surprised to hear the same formations occurred in the mountain. She'd read that caverns existed elsewhere so large they had their own weather, and she craned her neck to glimpse the top of the coming range through the trees.

The man was now several inches above her face, nearly bent over double, but he didn't seem to have recognized her. She exhaled a little; maybe she could get to Mooring without having to play the part of a witch just yet. On the floor Diana rolled onto her back for a scratch. Her paws tickled his stomach, and he gestured with one hand out the window as he began to pat her with the other.

"Yes, my brother-in-law is a water-tester. He was assigned to the southern edge of the mountains, where the water goes underground, you see? Ah there we are, yes, see that?"

The train was curving sharply inland and he pointed where the river came into view. A jumble of temporary buildings gave way to stone structures and fearsome machines, the latter just now being rolled into place.

"They must've been at work all night," Theodora said.

"And all day, and all the night before, and on and on," he said. "They don't stop. Truly a marvel of the modern age. They're preparing to blow out the mountain, you see, part of it that is, to gain better access to those caverns."

"To what end?" The trees were thinning and they were close enough to see the small bits of thorny shrubs clinging to the white cliff face.

"Algae, of course. My brother-in-law – his name is Harold – says there's not much this far south but some still makes it here. Especially now that the water's so low. It's time to strike." He laughed. "Maybe they'll finally find your mother, eh? Or your man?"

Theodora felt a familiar chill break out all along her skin.

"Perhaps," she said carefully, tipping her hat lower once more. She swallowed hard. *Now or never, Theodora.* "But shan't it disrupt the river? Especially when the water comes back? I imagine the mountain will flood then."

He looked down at her with a skeptical face. "Nah! Flood with money mayhaps! In fact Harold says he has a job lined up for me there. Giving my notice end of next week. Unless you know something the rest of us don't then, love?" He seemed near to laughing.

That did it.

She slowed her breathing and slowed her hands as she let his question linger in the air and opened up the bag upon her lap. With ceremony and infinite slowness she extracted her ticket and, snapping the fingers of her other hand, brought Diana up to sit at her full height so that the conductor was nudged unceremoniously backward and away. Theodora looked up once more from beneath her brim.

"I wish you the best of luck, sir," she said, unfurling the ticket toward him so she felt a bit more like a magician than a witch. Oh well, time to practice still. "You shall need it, inside the mountain when the winds change. As I assure you, they shall."

She raised an eyebrow as he took her ticket from her. Perhaps that's not obvious enough? Theodora arched her eyebrow even higher. How did Widow Green do it? Damn it all. She took one finger and placed it on the side of her nose, full of import and hoping that the ticket taker would infer what he liked, and that he fell on the side of magical nostalgia rather than rage.

He stared at her for a long moment before breaking into a huge grin. "Rain?"

She smiled and raised one finger to her lips.

"Oh! Thank you, ma'am! What news, then! The wife will be excited to hear. You know," he leaned down again, though giving her much more room now, and continuing conspiratorially, "I didn't much like the idea of going to work in the mines. Harold's a right idiot, sometimes, you know."

By that point the conductor was largely talking to himself, moving back down through the empty rows and out into the next car. When the door banged shut behind him Theodora swiveled in her seat to look out the window once more.

Theodora sat back, catching her breath. She'd started it, then. She felt strangely lightheaded. Light-bodied. She smiled again, giddy with nerves and something else she couldn't place, and looked out the window just as the train passed into the mountain. A hulking piece of machinery was being readied to claw into the mountain. Writ large on its side were two words:

Dove Holdings.

The train shot into the dark of the mountain.

Then again, I suppose this might have been an absolutely terrible idea.

13

The Atlantic Ocean
Dates and points lost

A GIRL on the ship lost her parents to the waves. She took to hiding in the dampest, smelliest corners of the ship, and came above deck only at night when there was only a skeleton crew about. No one besides the captain and his wife knew how to sail a ship anyway, so the sailing came down to a few witches concentrating very hard, urging the wind and the sails to work together with the promise of rest and reward (left very vague) for both later on.

The little girl scurried between hiding spots when the older people had their backs turned, and it became a game she played with herself: If she was unseen she was safe. If she was unseen she might have been powerful, for all anyone knew, including herself. She moved her hands and pretended to pull the moon-lit waves up and down and felt the ship heave and roll with her magic.

Then it began to hail. Cold the girl could manage, even though she had grown up very warm in the colony that she'd taken for her name;

rain she could outlast in a small cave beneath a pile of oiled tarps. But hail was aggressive and intrusive and confusing, so the child escaped belowdecks, where the adults were yelling.

Lamplight glowed from the captain's quarters, and she stopped outside the door. Warm air from the press of heated bodies flowed into the passageway and she huddled inside it.

"It is a sign we should never have left!"

"Bah, sign! The only sign is that we should have brought a navigator."

"Or a map that wasn't so full of monsters we have to change course every third day!"

"No one is following a map."

"We left so many behind!"

"Maps?"

"People!"

"If they didn't come when called, what could we do?"

"Maybe they didn't hear," said very quietly, so the girl had to lean toward the door. "It's hard for some people to hear. Some of them were very young."

"It's not just those like us – what about the others? The innocents taking the fall."

"Should we have taken the fall instead? What good would that do?"

"What good do we do here? Wandering the sea, close to starving, going mad! Some swept overboard and we can't even save them."

The child shut her eyes.

"We'll bring the others, someday. We'll make things right."

"Bring them where!"

"What would you have us do? Give up? Toss ourselves into the sea? Go back?"

She turned from the doorway and wandered back above, where she realized she'd put her hands over her ears and forgotten to take them away. The hail had stopped but the deck was nearly deserted.

With her ears covered she heard only a deep, rhythmic whooshing sound that comforted her deeply. She shut her eyes and started to walk toward the railing; she'd gained her sea legs with the ease of a naturally nimble child, and with her senses muted it was even easier to anticipate the roll of the ship and the swells of the sea.

She'd always been an imaginative child but this was the first time she really began to wonder what it had been like for her mother and her father, as they went overboard. Did they stay together, or were they torn immediately apart? Did they look back at her one last time? How long were they in the water, cold and lost, before they died? Perhaps it had happened all at once. She didn't know what drowning was like. She couldn't swim.

But maybe they were saved by mermaids. Maybe they were living under the sea with fish for pets and beds made out of seaweed and shells. Maybe they were waiting for her.

Her hands fell down to hover over the railing before she let them lightly rest on the wood. Her face scrunched up: Cold and damp and rough, like everything here. Moldy and smelling of vomit.

The child breathed sea air as the wind blew mist against her face. She clung so hard her skin was pierced with splinters. But she didn't notice. She kept holding on, imagining the mermaids.

When she opened her eyes, she saw the cliffs of a distant island rising up from the waves.

14

Wherewithal River
Before dawn, December 2, 1947

A CAT WAS LICKING John's face. He'd let his beard grow in and now a cat — or something, someone — was roughly licking the hair. There was a low constant scratching in time with his breath, the smell of paper and ink.

He opened his eyes and saw in place of a cat the newspaper he'd jammed beneath his pillow, its pages all wriggled loose and crumpled between his cheek and the wall. He pulled his head back and rubbed his eyes, hoping he didn't now have a headline printed backwards across his forehead. His eyes focused on an interior page and he saw it, a few column inches below the fold:

Widow Witch of the South Nears End of Mourning
Henry Martin to Be Declared Dead at Solstice

Assembly debates distribution of assets before unprecedented consolidation of power

There was a photo, one John recognized even though it had been done after he'd left. She looked the same as the last time he'd seen her, only in the picture she wore a wedding dress. By that point he'd been halfway to the ice. At least they'd cut Henry out of the wedding portrait. *Small mercies.*

The article was the usual mix of gossip and panic: Did Theodora still have her powers? If she did why wasn't she using them? And if she didn't well what was wrong with her, anyway?

More than that, though. He'd heard the talk: That she'd killed him to get his money, or in a fit of jealous rage, or just because she felt like it. As if Theodora would ever do anything so poorly planned.

And as much as John didn't understand what in the world Theodora had seen in Henry in the first place – besides political power, and a fortune, and a sort of figure-on-a-classical-urn beauty that John found quite outdated – John knew as well as he knew himself that she could never kill anyone. Especially not silly, quiet, thoughtful Henry. It wasn't her fault the fool had run off the day after the wedding.

"Idiots and asses," he muttered. The light through the porthole was still the icy blue of early morning but he swung his legs over the edge of the mattress. The boat moved more swiftly now, the sound of crunching ice gone silent. Perhaps he ought to finally shave off the beard. In theory it was to keep his cheeks warm; in truth, he hoped it made him look a bit more heroic.

But first he turned back and pulled loose Theodora's page of the paper. He folded it into a square the size and shape of his handkerchief and slid it neatly into his breast pocket.

15

Dove Townhouse (fmr. residence of Esperanza Dove, née Esperanza Snow)
City of Mooring
Very late, December 2, 1947

THEODORA AND DIANA slipped inside after walking, stately and serene, around the block three times. *Case the joint. Wasn't that the term of art?* She'd read it in some water-swollen book Adelaide had sent down from the city.

It hadn't been hard to get past the housekeeper, who seemed so nervous at John's imminent arrival that she kept opening the front door and then remembering to go beat a rug or close a curtain or straighten a doily, but not to lock the door behind her.

The rest of the house, what little she'd seen as she tiptoed down the hallway, reminded Theodora strongly of the late Mrs. Dove: Well-maintained and thoughtfully designed for the utmost comfort, bones and architecture buried under flowers and artwork. A safe place for John.

His study was at the corner of the house farthest from the stairs and the parlor, closest to the bustle of the small park across the street. The room that would have the best light, come morning.

And a locked door, though she couldn't very well fault him for that. Theodora frowned and pulled a long silver pin from her hair. She jammed it into the lock, hoping force would compensate for skill. *Forget weather. This would be a useful talent.* The problem was that Theodora was very unused to attempting entry into places; she had much more practice keeping other people out. Seconds passed. Sweat began to gather between her breasts.

There was a battering-ram noise, and the door swung open, sending Theodora sprawling into the study on her hands and knees. Besides her Diana padded softly in, giving her head a soft shake to clear the impact.

"Thank you," Theodora said, righting herself. "A little warning next time, please." The lock hadn't been wrenched out of the woodwork entirely by the dog's skull, thankfully. *How auspicious.*

Theodora brushed herself off and, as her eyes adjusted to the light, smiled with recognition. Framed paintings covered the walls, jumbled atop one another up to the ceiling. They were all beautiful, even if none of them were John's.

She wondered if perhaps all this intrigue was a bit silly. Surely the housekeeper would have been happy, if a bit flustered, to show Theodora in and prepare her something warm to drink. *He did invite me, after all!* But that was just the point: After all this time John had made the first move, and Theodora didn't intend to let him have the upper hand any longer.

She arranged herself in a chair in the corner, backed by tall windows. The moonlight was bright behind her, and she was turned away from the door. She didn't want to give him a heart attack, but a small shock would be fine. *He deserves that much.* Her dress was equal parts velvet and satin, so that the light glinted in some places and was absorbed in others. Her hair was piled on top of her head, and there was a scarf wrapped up and behind it like the collar of a queen. That was partly because it was so damned cold. *It was always so cold in the city. Even more so this year.*

Everything she wore, of course, was black.

She spent the first half hour planning what she would say and how it would go. The second half hour she spent hoping she hadn't made a terrible mistake. Now she had to go to the bathroom. *Perhaps I got the day wrong?*

Theodora put her hand on top of Diana's head, her fingers barely spanning the space between the dog's ears. Diana whimpered, wanting to lay down, but Theodora scratched her in an attempt at appeasement. It would be much more dramatic if the hound was sitting up at her full height.

"Sorry, girl, appearances matter," she whispered.

Of course it wouldn't be dramatic at all if John never flipping came home.

Theodora wished she could relax, too, or that she'd at least picked a more comfortable chair to look imposing in. *Eventually he had to come home, didn't he?* Perhaps he'd changed enough that his study was no longer the place he'd return to. She glanced out at the moon. If the night started to lighten she'd have to leave soon regardless, if only to save the housekeeper from a heart attack upon finding her and the dog. Diana had that effect on people.

Hell, perhaps I have that effect on people.

John paused with his key in the study door, staring down at the dark green carpet gone mossy with age. The hallway lights glowed faintly blue. Mrs. Meadows had lit the lamps for him. *She's done too much for me to never be here to appreciate it.* He resolved to let her go, help her find a position that was less lonely.

Damn it, John. That was his father talking. He would set her up with a well-funded retirement instead.

The study had once been his art studio and it was, of all the rooms in the house, the one that felt most like his own. There were still bits of paint splattered under some of the chairs, hidden from the housekeeper. He hesitated still, wondering if he should just go up to bed. *But maybe I'll sleep on the couch in here tonight. Or every night.* Who was to say no? It was his house, after all. Or at least his father's house. Most important, it had been his mother's.

Diana snored loudly, and Theodora bolted upright. The dog had unorthodox methods for protecting her mistress – namely in that she usually did so without waking up – but she was rarely wrong. In the hallway there was a sound of stamping feet and the shaking off of a coat. She didn't hear the housekeeper. It must be very late indeed.

Footsteps approached quickly down the hall, and Theodora panicked: *What if he went straight to bed? What if he didn't and came in the room? Damn your parlor tricks and your theatrics*, she said to herself. *He invited me. He wrote to me. There must be some reason. After all this time.*

Then she dared to think it: *What if everything is the way it once was between us?*

The footfalls paused outside the door, and a key began to turn in the lock. Theodora tried to make herself look as dark and stern and magical as possible. *If I sit up any more I'll be levitating.*

The doorknob turned, and the door swung open inwards, and she was faced with John Dove for the first time in nearly a decade.

"Fuck all, Teddy!" John took two long steps backwards into the hall. He caught himself on the doorknob only to swing wildly and widely to the floor.

Theodora jumped up.

She took two steps herself and stopped. He was already righting himself, glancing at her with wide – *damn all, was he frightened?* – eyes.

"Teddy?" he gasped, half-bent.

Theodora's lips pursed. "No one calls me that now, John."

John unfolded to his full height and smiled his thin crooked smile. "Apologies, my good Mistress Ashe-Martin."

"Oh, John, really, do shut up. Are you all right? I'm sorry I startled you, I thought –" What had she thought exactly? That he would wrap her up in his arms, drop to a knee and, well if not solve all her problems then at least present her with a much more interesting set of them?

Shit. Perhaps that was what I'd thought.

"It's a grand surprise," he said, coming forward with arms outstretched, pulling up short as she stepped away. He smoothly put his hands in his pockets. "I didn't mean to be impertinent."

She rolled her eyes. "Teddy's fine." Her palms had started to sweat and she pressed them flat against her skirt. She looked down, trying not to smile. *Exhaustion, clearly.*

John noticed Diana, still snoring. "Madame," he said, tipping his head.

"She's extremely loyal." *Why do I sound as though I'm apologizing?* "I mean, I'm sure she would be if a threat ever to arise. She appears to be quite a fearsome warrior when she's dreaming. Nowhere else really. She's a very good friend."

Why on earth are we talking about the dog? John wondered. The whalehound woofed softly and flopped over on her back. He was afraid to look back at Theodora, that if he did maybe he'd wake up.

So instead he kept staring at the dog. "Must be excellent bloodlines," he murmured absurdly. *John, you utter bastard. As though she'd come to the city to enter the non-sporting division kennel show. Perhaps she had? God, what if it really was about the dog?*

John appeared to be having a very complex inner dialogue about Diana, and Theodora took the opportunity to glance up at him. Unfortunately, John had turned into a beautiful man. There was no other word for it.

He'd grown taller, though he hadn't filled out much. But he'd opened up. *He's bloomed,* she thought. She immediately rolled her eyes at herself for thinking it, but she was having trouble looking away from his face, his shoulders, the line of his trench coat. His shoulders were broader and he held his chin high, maybe a touch too high, as though he was trying to see everything from above. Not with arrogance, but like he wanted to see all the patterns because he was a bit amused by them. She fought back a smile again. Of course he would look at the world like an artist still.

And he'd grown his hair out. *I always said it would look better that way.*

He hadn't thought it was possible but time had made Theodora look even more regal. Of course hardly anyone looked possessed and self-assured when in the throes of puberty, but if anyone had it was Teddy. Always standing up straighter than everyone else with her hair piled on top of her head like a crown. Always serious, even about the most frivolous things: What to have for lunch; how best to sneak into his father's office to plunder his pens and inks; what sorts of sordid fantasies Henry might be daydreaming as he sat in his family's garden each afternoon with an open book before him.

Of course now John knew the latter at least, and it made Teddy's seriousness in considering the matter seem both appropriate and highly embarrassing to John. Henry had been dreaming of Theodora. Which made two of them. The crucial difference being that Theodora had been dreaming of Henry, too.

"Why did you ask me to come?" she said softly while he was still looking at the dog. John looked up, startled from pretending he could have the upper hand.

"What do you mean? I didn't ask you to come, Teddy. I was about to ask why you're here."

Theodora cocked her head and raised her arm partway. Something passed across her face, between panic and a deep disappointment. "But you wrote me – " she began, and John noticed the letter in her hand.

Diana jumped up. They both turned to her as she sprang towards them, and instinct made them both lunge away.

"Girl, no!" Theodora said. "Sit. Stay! John is quite safe, I assure you." But the dog slammed straight into them both, and the three of them hit the wall beside the fireplace.

Her words were swallowed up by the sound of shattering glass. Something hard and metal hit the floor before them. The world burst into noise and heat, and the two former friends and large whalehound were tangled up in darkness and the smell of blood and fire.

16

Ashe House
Afternoon, June 21, 1936 – Summer Solstice

"And then a house falls on her!"

"How the hell does a house fall on her?" Theodora asked.

"It's a metaphor," Henry said. "For domesticity and misogyny. Clearly."

"No, it's a real house!" Adelaide replied, waving the book in the air. "It's hilarious."

"Oh. That's actually quite stupid, then," said Henry, and he leaned back on his elbows on the grass. It was blazing hot in the early afternoon and everyone had lost all hope of any more motivation before the evening's solstice festivities began.

"There's a wizard, too," Adelaide said. "You'd probably like that part, Henry. He's full of hot air."

"Aunt and Uncle could get you any book on the island, Addy, or near to it," he said, lying back in the grass and folding his hands behind his head. "Shouldn't you take advantage of that with something more substantial?"

"There's more than one way to take advantage," she said lightly, but then she threw the book at his stomach with some force, and excellent aim.

"Oof!" Henry rolled over on top of the book and then kept going down the hill, ending up far from them.

A true jumble of titles ended up in Wherewithal's shops via intermittent and unreliable off-cliff trade, and after Assembly and the university picked through everything for the rare or noteworthy or dangerous. From the remainder Adelaide's parents would buy her any book she chose. Adelaide's parents would buy her anything at all as long as she kept going to society dinners and dazzling as many people as possible with her innocent face and her wicked-beyond-her-years tongue. But Adelaide, who loved beautiful things and stories and was quite good at dazzling, hated to be reminded of the bargains she'd made.

"Henry come back!" Theodora called. "I wish he wouldn't take things so personally," she said, looking after him.

"Melodramatic, more like," Adelaide replied.

"Anyway the book sounds horrifying," Theodora said, turning back. "Why must there always be an evil witch?" She paused. "Is that really what people think of us, do you think?"

"Of us? I don't think anyone thinks of us," Adelaide sighed. "Of you? Of witches? I'm not sure, really. There's a good witch, too, you know."

"That's worse! Good, bad. Is there an in-between witch? A witch of complicated morality?"

"The hero is a little girl. She has a lovely small dog, too."

"That's something, I suppose. May I borrow it when you're through? Keep abreast of my reputation?"

"I'll probably be done tonight if you want to come over later."

"Brilliant. That'll give me a reason to escape Father. He just received this horrible giant pushing device that sucks things up with a tremendous noise and he's been out in the garden gathering slugs with it for days."

"You'll have to bring me a book in exchange."

Theodora pouted. "Must I truly?"

Adelaide pulled loose a clump of grass and let it rain down over her face. "You've got all those books right there, you've got to share," she said lazily, knowing she'd get her way.

"They're not 'right there,' they're in her dusty office and I catch a chill every time I go in there."

Adelaide's cocked half a grin. "If you bring a me that book on the vapors I was looking at last time I'll be able to fix you right up."

"Why don't we just go in now and get it?"

"Mum and dad told me not to go into your house anymore because you're a 'terrible and corrupting influence'."

Theodora sighed. "You'd better make a list and I'll just bring you a stack. Oh!" Her face brightened. "Is your father around? Could I use the telescope a while?"

Adelaide waved her hand through the air. "He's somewhere but no matter, we can sneak by. It won't be dark until quite late, though."

"It's not the sky I want to see tonight, it's the clouds." Theodora sat up suddenly and shielded her eyes. "Oh look, there's John finally! I thought he was getting in on the first train. John, hello! John!"

"Save us from Henry's lectures!" Adelaide called to John, who was now jogging up the hill to them. He leapt neatly over Henry.

"Sir," he said as they crossed paths. Henry's hand shot briefly to his forehead in a salute.

"Hello, stranger," Theodora beamed at John as he flopped down beside her, then turned to frown at Adelaide. "And be nice. Henry's not lecturing, he's just committed to his causes. Oh but Henry," she called down the hill, "do come back, you're being ridiculous!"

A hundred yards away Henry lifted Adelaide's book above his head to shield against the sun and began to read.

"How was your trip down?" Adelaide asked John.

"Old Archie came with me, so it was far too long," he said. "I heard quite a bit about the potential applications of algae to the transportation sector; how I'm so lucky to have gotten out of the countryside; and oh by the way, John, have you befriended the Governor's son at school yet?"

"The Governor's son is such a bore," said Adelaide.

"That's what I told Archie," John said, with a grin. "Actually I said that he was a bore who did not look kindly on the upstart sons of merchants who were trying to needle their way into power, but my father seemed unconvinced."

"I'm sorry," said Theodora, studying John's face. "At least the transportation bit sounds interesting? Anyway we're very glad you're here. Will you finish that painting from last time?" she asked him. "I've been staring at it half-finished in my room for too long, it's starting to make me feel unsettled. I almost took up a paintbrush myself just to give the mountains a sense of completion."

"Oh please, don't let her do that," Adelaide said drowsily. "She has no sense for color."

John laughed, unbuttoning his cuffs and stretching out his legs. "Teddy has a keen eye for perspective. And you might have to finish it." He winced slightly and looked away. "I'm not sure I'll have time this visit, unfortunately."

"Has something happened?" Theodora asked. "You only just got here," she added, trying not to sound too sad about it. She knew he couldn't control his own schedule, it was just that things were so much more interesting with him around.

"Just until the late train. Mother didn't come down. If Archie didn't have to fire his port foreman I'm not sure we would have come at all."

"You're not staying for the party?" Theodora exclaimed, unable to keep the hurt from her voice. She tried to collect herself. "Oh please stay. That is, I'd just hoped – I do understand, though."

The smallest hint of smile played on John's mouth. "Well. Maybe," he said. "Maybe I can convince Archie that I can be trusted to take the dawn train tomorrow."

"Hooray," Theodora said, and he looked to see her face but she'd already lain back into darker shadow.

Instead John nodded down the hillside. "I don't think he likes me, you know."

"Your father?" Adelaide asked, looking nearly asleep. "He hates everyone, honestly."

"No, Henry."

"He does isolates himself," Theodora said thoughtfully. She sat up, cracking her fingers. "I'll fix that."

"Oh hooray! Make it hail on him, Ted." Adelaide sighed a little melodramatically, and continued speaking, mostly to herself. "I'd make a marvelous witch. Doesn't seem quite fair you're the only one can do it anymore."

"Would you mind a breeze, while you're at it?" John asked, settling in to watch her work.

"That's the idea," she said, with a grin. She raised her hands in front of her face, then crossed them loosely over each other and positioned herself so she could just see Henry through the latticework. With both hands at once she began to knead at the air, like a cat in blankets.

Almost immediately a wind begin to pick up. Down the hill the pages flipped forward out of Henry's fingers so he lost his place, and for a moment he frowned, confused. Then one side of his mouth curled up and the book flew from his hands entirely and spiraled up into the air on a gust headed back toward them.

"There," Theodora said, only half paying attention as the book continued through the air like an unsteady bird, dipping and soaring before landing heavily in front of Adelaide.

"Very nicely done, Ted," Adelaide said, picking it up. "Not a single ripped page this time."

Theodora folded her hands neatly, a proud smile on her face, and turned to John. "But of course he doesn't hate you. He's jealous of you," she said matter-of-factly.

John's eyebrows shot up and he laughed a little too loudly. "Jealous! I'll have to ask him which it is, the horrible father or the stifling future or the dying mother."

"John," Adelaide said softly in the silence that followed. "Is it that bad then?"

John only shrugged.

Theodora reached out and put her hand on top of his. John stared down at their fingers, half-buried together in the green grass so no one could have seen even if they'd been looking. He turned his hand over so their palms met, and with the slightest pressure she gripped his fingers in her own. He looked up at her, surprised. "Thank you," he said very softly, and opened his mouth to say something more.

"Hello you all," Henry said, standing in front of them so he blocked the sun and they were all able to look up for once without squinting. Theodora and John pulled their hands apart so quickly that later neither could tell who'd been first to move.

"Decided to be sociable, have you?" Theodora said, smiling.

"Only because you made such a convincing argument for it," he said, and swept his arm out to her as part of an elaborate, old-fashioned bow. "Care to join me for a pre-dinner swiping of the buffet table?" He held out a hand and Theodora blushed and rolled her eyes before letting herself be pulled to standing.

"See," John said as he flopped back onto the earth, "how could he ever be jealous of me?"

17

Outerbridge Estate
Arboretum District
City of Mooring
Sometime after midnight, December 3, 1947

SHE SHOOK her head as she walked, trying to clear the ringing. But her whole body was ringing. She'd waited with him until she heard the bells of the fire service clanging down the road and then, having checked his breath for the dozenth time, grabbed her bag, called to Diana, and set off through the hole in the wall.

Hell's bells, the housekeeper. Theodora shut her eyes, willing the old woman to have left for the evening, that she hadn't been hit by debris, that the floors hadn't collapsed under her.

Theodora's step faltered, and she nearly went straight back to John's.

But no. It wouldn't help anyone heal to have her found by his side, bloody hands on his chest.

She walked fast through the dark streets, head down and her shoes clicking too loudly against the cobblestones. Adelaide's house wasn't far, she told herself again and again in time with her steps, and Diana would keep her safe.

Everything felt crystalline, etched by adrenaline but ready to shatter, and she tried to commit everything to a deeper part of memory. It had definitely been a bomb; she remembered now glass shattering, plus the dog's warning, and then an outward explosion. Not a small explosion, either.

Someone was trying to kill John. *Why would anyone want to kill John? I mean besides me*, she thought, *when he's being particularly annoying. Or charming.*

But that was entirely different. John had always been loved by everyone, everywhere he went. Moreover, according to what she'd read the growth of his family's business had made his reputation grow in tandem. She took it he was viewed as something like a savior.

She kept going south, past the Mineral Museum and the City Gardens, eventually arriving in Adelaide's part of town, where everyone stayed hidden behind their chauffeured cars and their umbrellas and their high fences. She didn't think anyone saw her arrive, breathless and soaked through with sweat, though she made a loud enough fuss with the butler that eventually Adelaide came herself.

"Holy hell, Teddy, you look like an absolute beast!" she'd exclaimed, as she pulled Theodora into the house and wrapped her up in a hug. "Come inside this instant. Roger, get the dog a steak, would you please?"

Now they sat in a very pink room in the wing of the house that Adelaide shared with her husband, the Chief Magistrate, and their three boys. Adelaide filled Theodora's glass.

"Thank you." She wrapped her hands around the glass to stop them from shaking. "I thought John had died. I thought Diana had died. I couldn't do anything – I couldn't – "

Adelaide put a hand to Theodora's knee, which had started to jump and bounce. "Teddy, you're safe here. I'll make sure of it."

Theodora took a deep breath. "Thank you," she said again.

Adelaide shook her head. "But on top of all that to learn John never invited you at all!"

Theodora recognized the flawless balancing of death threats and social faux pas as quintessentially Adelaide, even if they'd never specifically had to deal with bombings before. "Yes, but I suppose under the circumstances—"

"I don't know what his motives could possibly be. It's quite, quite strange. Thrilling, too, honestly." Adelaide leaned very close to Theodora. "Is the drink working? Would you like something stronger?"

"It's helping wonderfully, thank you." Theodora didn't know what they were drinking, but it made her feel calm for the first time since the bomb had gone off and warm for the first time since she'd arrived in the city. Diana was asleep once more at her feet.

"You'll let me know? I might just –" Adelaide held up one finger, then pulled a pearl-and-opal inlaid box from the pocket of her dressing gown. She opened its tiny clasp with her tiny fingers, and removed two tiny pills. She swallowed them with more of the drink.

"Adelaide, what are those? Are you unwell?"

She waved a hand. "I'm marvelous."

Theodora's eyebrow went up.

"Oh, everyone takes something in the city. A little of one thing, a little of another," Adelaide said. "Otherwise it's too grating, living here. You wouldn't know, out there in the bucolic countryside." Adelaide sighed loudly. "I'm so jealous, truly."

"You should visit then," Theodora said. "I'm dreadfully lonely you know." She meant it in jest but was surprised how serious her voice sounded. Adelaide didn't seem to notice.

"Well that shan't be a problem for either of us now, I think," Adelaide said, smiling as if they were children again having a sleepover. "We do need to come up with a story for you though," she added, tapping her lip with one finger.

Theodora knew there was no escape from gossip, and that soon enough everyone would not only know that Mistress Theodora Ashe-Martin had arrived in the city, but that she'd been at John Dove's house late at night when a bomb went off. That she'd run off to the most home of the most sociable woman in the city immediately thereafter.

Theodora flopped against the side of the couch. *John! Stupid, still-beautiful, John. Who could ever want to kill him?*

A fire crackled behind them, and Theodora was beginning to feel very tired. It had been such a long day, and it was only the beginning. Her mother's magic lapped at the back of her eyes, pulling her down into sleep as a defense.

"Adelaide, I need your help." She shook her head to clear it. "I need to be a witch again."

Adelaide gasped, delighted, and clapped her hands. Then her brow furrowed. She opened her mouth, then hesitated, and finally put on a very serious face. She took Theodora's hands in her own.

"Yes. Of course. Whatever you need. I'm delighted. I've missed you so."

Theodora smiled, relieved. She realized that she'd been afraid Adelaide wouldn't want to help, or wouldn't understand. That seemed so foolish now. "Addy. Thank you."

"Besides, I'm so bored, Theodora, you have no idea, it's terrible." Adelaide laid back, putting on a very dramatic pout. Then she clapped her hands. "And now we have a plot to solve and a deception to plan!"

They were the same age, summer neighbors since they were babies and Adelaide's parents had bought a home in the south for vacation. But it was remarkable, sometimes, how much her friend could seem both very much a child and so much more worldly than Theodora.

Adelaide was focusing very hard on Theodora's face, her eyes a little glassy. *Maybe that was due to the hour? Or the fire?* "I know you worry, about the people in the city, about your position, about what you can do, but I'll make sure no one causes a fuss. I'll take you around, only to the best places, the best people. Very discreet, I promise," she added conspiratorially. Theodora could see the social plans taking shape behind her friend's curls, even as Adelaide had begun to gently sway forward and back.

"Adelaide, I can't wait to see the boys. Are they all quite giants by now?"

Adelaide's body tensed a little, but her eyes softened. "They may be," she said.

Theodora cocked her head. "What? Are they well?"

"I'm sure they're fine. My dear husband took them off with him when he went out on business. Did I not mention?"

"You did not," Theodora said carefully. "How long ago?"

"Oh, a month? Perhaps two."

"Two months!"

"Hmm. Yes, I had a letter from them last week. I do miss them," she added, with a sudden thickness to her voice.

The Magistrate was an ass. Theodora had disliked him since before she'd met him, when Adelaide had written shortly after Henry disappeared: *I'm to be married, too!* As if that was meant to be some consolation, as if Theodora wasn't proof that young women ought to extend the stay of their engagement just a little while longer. *He says I'm his muse*, the letter went on, *and he's to have a brilliant career in the law!* Why a magistrate would ever need a muse, Theodora didn't know, and nothing in the years since indicated that the man had used Adelaide for anything other than sons and dinner parties.

But she didn't think he'd had ever taken the children away before, and while Adelaide had always loved a drink or four, the drugs were a new development.

"When are they coming back?"

Adelaide shut her eyes and shook her head. "Eventually, I'm sure. He doesn't tell me much. I think he likes the element of surprise. Don't worry about John, though," she said, opening her eyes again. "I'm sure he's not at all cold and vicious, like his father." Adelaide nodded vigorously over the top of her glass, her eyes now definitely gone unfocused.

Theodora looked away, out the tall windows bordering the street. The curtains hadn't been pulled closed and though it was very dark and the glass too thick to permit sound she felt in her belly that the wind had picked up. *I hate the wind.* Goosebumps prickled her forearms.

"Oh, and have you heard?" Adelaide went on. "I hear he's to be engaged to Victoria White."

Now Theodora felt like the wind was inside her belly. That a great wide open empty space had opened up just under her ribcage.

Certainly that was only because of how it upset her plan. Convincing him to help a notorious widow-murderess-witch — she was thinking of herself here, of course — had seemed somehow reasonable. Or at least possible. But if he not only hadn't asked her to come, but was also as good as engaged —

"Is that so?" she said, afraid to say more unless her voice gave her away.

When she looked back she saw Adelaide had fallen asleep still holding her half-empty glass upright. Theodora took it and placed it on the table, and tucked her friend in under a warm knitted blanket. In sleep Adelaide looked more worried than she had all evening, and Theodora had to resist the urge to smooth the creases between her friend's eyes.

"Goodnight, Addy," she whispered. "All things considered, it's very good to see you again."

18

**George Law's Apartment
University District
City of Mooring
Morning, December 3, 1947**

JOHN FELL HEAVILY into the armchair next to the fireplace as George Law threw more moss on the flame. *Should've gotten into the moss industry,* John thought, staring into the fire as it smoked thickly with the new fuel. *Could have spent the last years mired in a cozy bog. Not a growth industry. Romantic, though.*

John held his hands out to warm them, and saw that he was shaking.

"I think you're in shock, sir," George said, handing him a cup of tea. John took it with both hands and took a sip. He winced: more whiskey than tea. He took a longer sip.

"It's very good to see you, sir," George went on, "even if these were not the circumstances you or I had planned." He sat down in the chair opposite. John had gone from his own house to the hospital, riding in the back of the ambulatory wagon with Mrs. Meadows.

His housekeeper had been just leaving when the bomb went off, having waited for John to be settled. Now she had a face full of broken glass to show for her loyalty.

After her daughter arrived to sit bedside, and John had promised every sort of medical aid imaginable, he'd gone to find George in The Broken Ladder. His friend was asleep and ink-stained in his usual far corner booth.

Latent academic impulses were probably why he and George Law had become such friends. George was a professor now but when he'd shown up at John's ice office three years ago he'd been a student, come to study the movement of the glacier. He'd ended up staying for two years, doing research until eventually he had to return to finish his degree. It'd been very quiet since he'd gone.

"I had a bad feeling about coming back, George, but I just thought it was my father's damned cryptic letter." John shook his head. "But a bomb? Why? They must have been waiting there all night. And the worst of it is it can't have been a coincidence that Teddy was there. She could have been —"

"Theodora?" George broke in. "Theodora Ashe-Martin?"

John needed a refill already. He nodded.

George's eyes got wide. "And she came to see you?"

"Apparently so. I don't know which was more surprising, the bomb or seeing her."

George squinted at him. "What have you been up to on the ice? I leave you alone for a minute, it seems, and —"

"No, no," John interrupted. "You left and everything got more boring. And, you know, with Teddy, it's not good at all. She thinks I wrote her a letter asking her to come meet me. A forgery, I'd imagine by the same damned person who tried to blow me up. Blow us up. But the letter was burned up in the blaze."

"You're sure you didn't write it?"

John set his jaw and thrust his glass out for more whiskey and tea. "I think I'd recall. We haven't spoken in years! Not that I haven't wanted to, but no. Not now."

"Not with Victoria?"

"Not with many things, George. We've both gone on with our lives. She married, for heaven's sake!"

George shrugged and handed John back his glass. "For a day. I could tell you held a torch for her, is all. And she could be quite an ally, depending. Or enemy."

"Depending on what?"

"Oh which way the wind blows. Which way you want it to blow. If people weren't mad enough that her mother caused the drought, half of them are still furious Theodora hasn't fixed it. But there's a sizable portion who're mad she hasn't wed and popped out wee witches to repopulate the island."

"I am aware."

"And the other half –"

"Don't be cute, George."

" – are afraid she will get her powers back, or worse that she already has them and really has been hiding all these years, and that she'll upset this brilliant military-industrial future we've got heading out way."

At that John sat up. "She's owed everything she wants!"

George ignored him. "Not to mention how many people are eager to get their hands on the land around the cliffs these days."

"Land that should be hers."

George nodded. "But of course you knew that. Your father's one of them."

John slumped back into his seat, staring into the fire. His chair creaked loudly.

"Sure this isn't kindling, as well?" John asked, tapping the arm.

"Budgetary measures, sir. The life of an academic."

"An academic with half a dozen Assembly contracts."

"Don't change the subject. You cared for her once."

He was drunk enough not to be distracted by John's charms as he'd once been, or maybe John had overestimated how charming he actually was.

I've been spending too much time with people who depend on me for pay.

John tried to make his voice light. "We were friends. What do you mean?"

"I hear things," George said. "People talk."

"Which people?"

Now George did break eye contact. "Adelaide Outerbridge."

"Mistress of the Courts?" John asked, a slightly disbelieving grin on his face. Adelaide was married to the Chief Magistrate and, not that it gained her much besides invitations to parties, had the title to go with it. She was also Theodora's best friend and she definitely did not run in shabby academic circles.

"She wasn't always that," George said, frowning. "Just Adelaide once."

You cad. "Yes, I knew her as Adelaide, too."

George looked up sharply and John held out his hands. "She's – well she's Henry Martin's cousin. We all knew each other."

"Ah. Right." George poked the fire so sparks flew upward. "Sorry."

"I'm sure that's where Theodora went after the bomb. She didn't wait long after." When he woke up on the floor he thought maybe he'd dreamed her ever being there at all but there were giant sooty paw prints all over the floor. "Do you think you could find out if she's there?" he asked. "I need to – I'd like to make sure she's all right."

George nodded. "Already sent a letter over. Waiting to hear back. Adelaide sometimes needs some time."

The corner of John's mouth went up. "So to you she's still just Adelaide?"

George frowned. "Sometimes."

John grinned to see his friend look so like a schoolboy in love. "How often?"

"Not nearly as often as I'd like, unfortunately. For about a year now, though."

"Egad man, a year!"

"We were talking about you, John, and about Mistress Ashe-Martin. Or Teddy, isn't that what you call her? When you two were young and in love?"

"Don't call her that. She hates it." John threw back the rest of his drink. "And we weren't in love." *Technically true*, John thought. *There was no "we" in what we had.*

19

The Flotsam & Jetsam
THIS WEEK'S NUPTIALS
Union of Master Thomas Ashe and Mistress Miranda Lake, née Bloom
June 12, 1934 edition

(ASHE HOUSE, SOUTHERN DISTRICT)—The wedding of Master Thomas Ashe and Mistress Miranda Lake was by all accounts to be a lively and largely joyous affair. After the sturm-und-drang disappearance of the first Mistress Ashe – the Witch Marguerite (Headwaters) – a cloud of infamy by association had settled upon the bucolic Ashe House along Wherewithal's southeastern coast. But with a whirlwind courtship and an elaborate springtime garden wedding party, it appeared the skies were finally clearing. If it all happened a bit fast, who could blame the newly minted Ashes? The erstwhile Mistress Lake had a daughter from her first marriage, to a canyon farmer who fell through the cracks five years earlier. And the only child of Marguerite and Master Ashe needs, of course, no introduction.

What was our last witch up to during the festivities? She spent most of the day on the margins. At least until she got into an argument with her father and created a tornado in the kitchen.

The cause of her upset was not unknown. One moment the couple was walking down the aisle to the applause of invited guests, including a number of local and city luminaries; the next moment a great crashing erupted from the kitchen of the manor house. Those who arrived first upon the scene described nearly all the china broken and the girl herself cut and bleeding in two dozen places, standing in the midst of a huge windstorm which threatened to tear down not only the house but, witnesses described, to level the entire neighborhood if allowed to progress.

Luckily Master Ashe, undoubtably an expert at such matters from dealings with his ex-wife and now their daughter, knew what to do immediately. He fought grave injury, fending off a metal teapot that came perilously close to his skull, to enter the eye of the storm where he took his only child into his arms and held her quite tightly. After several moments, the storm began to die down. At which point Master Ashe quickly scanned his daughter for signs, it would seem, of continued mania, before ushering her away from the prying eyes of attendees.

The family was able to borrow china from neighbors to allow the reception to proceed, and the remainder of the day and evening were said to go off without a hitch – so to speak. The Witch Theodora Ashe, it should come as no surprise, was not heard or seen from again that day or night.

20

Outerbridge Estate
Late morning, December 3, 1947

Theodora woke under the weight of a whalehound across her legs, the sun bright through the windows. Diana stretched and pawed at the pale silk comforter, and then snored softly. It'd been years since they'd slept in this late.

Even if John hadn't sent the letter, even if he was engaged, maybe we should stay. For a little while. It's not as though it changed anything regarding the real reason she'd come: Very soon she'd still have no home to go back to. Then there was the matter of Adelaide, and how she holding up. And the bomb. And John.

On second thought, perhaps better to stay in bed.

"Good morning, love!" Adelaide burst into the room looking like the sun, in a golden dress and a bright smile. "Good afternoon, really. I didn't think I'd ever say that Theodora Ashe slept later than me."

Theodora wondered how she did it after the drinking and the pills. *Maybe there are other pills for the morning?*

Adelaide sat down heavily on Theodora's feet. Diana grunted. "I've planned a very exciting day for us, Teddy."

"Adelaide I was just nearly killed. Shouldn't that be enough excitement?"

Adelaide waved her hand. "Quite the wrong kind. Don't you realize what this is?" Her eyes were huge.

"I'm afraid to ask."

"It's your coming out! Your debut. You've been in hiding, after all."

"I haven't been, Adelaide." Theodora pulled her knees up close and frowned. Her eyes felt hot, and she didn't want to look as weak as she felt. She tried to sit up, though she it was hard when she was so weighted down by dog. "Merely containing the zone of my impact."

"Well that's no way to show everyone how witchy you are, now is it? You have to make a splash, my dear."

Theodora pursed her lips. "Was the bomb not splashy enough then?"

"It would have been, had you not left the scene of the crime immediately!" Adelaide clucked her tongue, as if Theodora should have written first to get a second opinion before fleeing.

Well perhaps I should have. But that's why I'm here now.

Theodora braced herself and gave Diana a gentle shove to try to return feeling to her lower portion. "All right. What do you have in store for me then?"

Adelaide smiled, much more gentle now, and took her hand. "I've made us appointments at the dressmaker's, and it would mean so much to me if you'd let me buy you a new wardrobe. Now Theodora, this is a much better way to spend my husband's money than what he'd chose for me," she added, when Theodora began to protest. "Please, Ted. I really am so bored, and I miss you so much. Let me do this. I'm good at this. At playing pretend."

There was a note in Adelaide's voice that reminded Theodora again of the missing boys, and so she smiled and squeezed Adelaide's hand back. "Fine. I'm in your hands."

21

Boston Post-Tribune
A Closer Look this Sunday:
"Mystery Island" is Back in the News
By Marian Blake, Society Pages
January 19, 1940

(BOSTON)—Some nautical ne'er-do-wells for you this week, dear readers. Nautical – and magical?

Captain Bryan Bridgewater of the *USS Brighton* received no quarter or communication late last week during an attempted encounter with isolated "Wherewithal Island" in the North Atlantic Sea. Capt. Bridgewater attempted to flag aid but the *Brighton* was forced to continue onto Norway, where the ship received mechanical support. Despite their ill treatment by the islanders –*Wherewithalians* – all American sailors aboard the ship are present and accounted for as of this writing.

Your intrepid columnist was reminded of the highly unusual and largely unknown history of this mysterious island, and so decided to take ... *A Closer Look*.

Wherewithal Island, long a favored but mysterious stopping point for ships lost or in distress, does not officially exist. But it is real, a three-quarter-mile-high rock outcropping the approximate the size of our U.S. states of Virginia, North Carolina, and South Carolina.

My dear readers may recall the 1933 polar flight of famed aviatress Millie "Golden Girl" Gillingham, which gave the world its first aerial accounts of the island. Miss Gillingham described an arid landscape nonetheless divided north to south by a glacial river. The island is divided horizontally by a substantial mountain range.

To the shock of the international community, she also reported what appeared to be a thriving city, evidence of extensive agricultural undertakings, and advanced fishery.

The discovery created, for a time, speculation around the island. You may remember, dear reader, the 1934 Rogers and Astaire clunker, *A Ship to Ol' Wherewithal*. Or semi-popular children's toy, "Wherie" the Mermaid?

A study, led jointly by the USGS, the U.S. Navy, and the Columbia University Anthropology Department, was undertaken to investigate the potential diplomatic and trade benefits of contacting the island. A short report issued in 1936 by that task force, *Possible Uses of Island "Wherewithal" and Claims to Sovereignty*, revealed only stranger findings: The island has no electricity, but is lit by a "dull blue-green glow" of varying intensity. Stranger still, a train line yet appears to run throughout the island, its power source also unknown, and considerable mining has altered the structure of the sizable glacier at the island's northern end. And what – dare I say *magical* – substance are they mining?

Speculation was further fueled by the long-standing mythology associated with the island among barnacle-encrusted sailor types. In the grand seafaring tradition of mermaid sightings and many-limbed cephalopodic foe, reports from as far back as the 17th century claim the island was founded by witches – and that the practice of magic continues still.

"There's a time you'd get to the rocks around Wherewit'al – not close, mind yer, it's treacherous, but that's how they want it," said ret. sea captain Martin Smythe, a self-styled "Wherewithal historian."

Capt. Smythe was reached for comment at the Clam and Dagger Pub in Derby, RI. "But there was time they'd come to greet ya in little boats, having spotted ya from their great stone lookouts tucked away in them cracks, and they'd come out to yer boat and they'd do magic on the deck, to fix ya up. Little bits a' tricks and whatnot, but damned if it didn't plug up holes when they needa a pluggin'. Beg yer pardon, ma'am."

Despite a push by the U.S. government and assorted allies to broach the surface, ships were unable to penetrate this rocky fortress. Parachuting was deemed too dangerous on an island riven with deep cliffs in its southern portion and frozen ground in the north, whose inhabitants, witches or no, have chosen to remain apart from the modern world these many centuries.

Without further fuel to feed the fire, popular sentiment shifted: Who would want anything to do with a heap of rock populated by the inbred descendants of delusional colonials? The U.S. government's official statement remains that "the island known colloquially as Wherewithal does not exist."

I pressed Capt. Smythe as to why the "Wherewithalians" may have turned their back on the *Brighton*, especially in such times as these when the world is on the brink of great and terrible war – perhaps they are nefarious allies of Germany or Russia? Smythe gave this answer:

"Nah, that's [rubbish] and [malarkey]. They're a good sort of people. Helpful. And they look all kinds a-ways, so I can't tink they'd hate any particular sort. But they always were very scared-seeming. And it wouldn't be the first time they turned their backs. Back in the Great War, the same ting happened to ships that'd stop by. Wouldn't get no quarter."

Capt. Bridgewater reported sightings of an unusual accumulation of debris and metal parts washed up upon the rocks surrounding the island. He ventured that an increase of oceanic travel and the increasing use of metal tools may give the islanders some clue as to the state of the world.

Not enough of a clue, it seems, to shift their sentiments towards helping sailors in need.

So is the so-called "Wherewithal Island" the long-sought Valhalla?

An icy Amazon run by frigid women? Your intrepid columnist has a different theory, one that's less the stuff of science fictional stories or mariners' tales. Perhaps this mystery island is full not of witches or mythological beasts, but people very like you or I, who are simply terrified of what the world has become, or of what it once was to them.

For now the truth remains shrouded in mist beyond rocky shoals, guarded by wary eyes in cliffside watchtowers that glow with unknown light. Someday perhaps the wider world will prove too great a temptation for the citizens of Wherewithal Island. Or the responsibility we all feel to our fellows will become too great.

Until next Sunday, dear readers, when we'll take *A Closer Look* at the politics of starlet Loretta Manchester: Red Menace Mistress or Triple Threat Patriot?

22

Dove House
Assembly District
City of Mooring
Evening, December 3, 1947

"Sir?"

John stood in the doorway of his father's bedroom, barely able to see. The shades were drawn against the morning and Master Dove was a small, still outline in the center of a vast bed. Someone was knitting in the darkest corner of the room. She didn't look up, or at least not that John could see, and her needles clicked faster than he knew human hands could go.

His feet felt frozen to the floor. He'd never seen his father like this. Not anything close: The last time they'd seen each other Archibald Dove had held court over a shadowy room of politicians, loudly and commandingly telling them how Dove Holdings would continue to supply the nation's water supply. John had slipped out and caught the next ship north. Now his father looked half the man he had been, but the worse sign was that John was being allowed to see it. Archibald was not a man who let his guard down without excellent cause.

"Son?"

John leapt forward as if shot. "Yes, yes, I'm here. Good grief, why didn't you tell me? Why didn't anyone tell me?" He sounded gruff and loud, but only because that was how they'd always spoken to each other. In the stuffy room, full of blankets and whatever sickness this was, he sounded as though he was yelling. John pulled up short at his father's bedside, resisting the urge to take the old man's hand. "I'm sorry. How are you feeling? What may I do?"

Archibald only waved a hand.

"You're here, aren't you?" he asked. "That's all I require. I'm taking care of the rest, boy."

Archibald had never had time for the opinions of other people, even when they happened to agree with him. *At least that much hadn't changed.*

"What on earth happened?"

"Age, mostly." Archibald coughed. "Sometimes things become precarious enough it only takes one small push to tip everything into total failure."

John didn't know what to make of that particular diagnosis. Archibald just seemed, as he said, very old. There was a pharmacy's worth on the bed table: pill bottles, syrups, and syringes. John glanced at the nurse and lowered himself gingerly into a chair, as if everything in the room might collapse.

"I didn't know," John said, feeling grossly inadequate. *That hasn't changed either.* "Are you in pain?"

Archibald shrugged and winced. "Yes, but I have to fight them for it." He nodded at the nurse. "They keep trying to drug me into oblivion. What of you, though, son? I heard there was a bombing at your mother's house."

"That's what they tell me, yes. I was a bit blitzed by it." John didn't know if anyone else knew about Theodora being there, or more to the point, whether his father knew. Mr. Dove had never been Theodora's greatest ally. He'd found her frivolous, a distraction. "I was lucky," John said, "to have been standing at the opposite end of the room."

Archibald didn't blink. "Have the police told you anything?"

"Not yet. The house is a bit banged up, though."

His father nodded. Better for both of them if no mention was made of where John was staying. Even if this sudden illness made their conversation flow a little easier, neither of them wanted to share a roof.

"How is the ice?" his father asked.

John's eyebrows went up. "Didn't you get my last report? And don't you – you know – just know?" The foremen sent daily missives to the city, and some of the workers were paid to report, as well.

"Yes, but I'd like to hear it from your mouth."

"Ah. Well," John considered. *How was the ice? Beautiful, mostly. Cold. Glowing, occasionally.* He cleared his throat. "Output is steady. Though they tell me we're nearing the bottom of the ore on six of the red lines. We'll need to send a team out again to scout." John turned his palms up. "The workers seem satisfied with their wages, but turnover's still too high. Being under the ice takes a toll."

The nurse stood and, still not looking at John, began a series of ministrations upon Mr. Dove. His father lifted his arms and turned his neck without being told; he moved delicately and thanked the nurse sincerely when she smoothed down his pillow. John sat back in his chair and watched it like he was at the theater, not quite following the plot.

As the nurse left the bedside and sat back down John's father turned to him. "Time to push outward then. Still virgin land north."

"Yes. But that land's not ours," John said, as the clicking of knitting needles recommenced. He was surprised she wasn't making sparks. "People live on that ice. The families of many of our workers, in fact."

Mr. Dove turned his own palms upward on the bed. "And what do they have now? Frozen water? They have nothing, John. And imagine what they could have, working for us. Much better lives. Money. A future as part of the engine of this island. Tell me, John, do you believe they would want that? You know them better than I do."

Not as well as I should, John thought, but he was distracted by his father's sincerity in asking for his opinion. "They will take the jobs, yes. But I worry that's only because they really won't have another choice, short of leaving their homes entirely."

"The island depends upon the ice," Archibald said, like doing simple math. "And very soon the future will depend on it, too, of not just ourselves but of the world. No one in Mooring'll be voting against more mining, not with money flowing in now from the wider world."

"That's another point, father: we're altering the entire landscape. Did you know the tunnel roofs are already quite weak in places? We're wading into very deep waters if we extend the tunnels without great caution."

"Ha!" his father barked, seeming delighted at something. The nurse jumped at her knitting, though she didn't look up. *Almost reassuring, seeing Archibald cackle.* "That's just it, John: It's not deep water, it's ice! Like stone. It's a fact. It's only for us to take advantage of it. They're not children up there. You have to let them make up their own minds." Another nurse came in. Noticing her, John's father prepared to turn over.

John took that as his cue, and stood.

"Before you go, son – I was meant to attend a dinner tomorrow night, at the Governor's. You'll go for me, as I'm in no condition."

John opened his mouth to protest, then saw the pale blue outline of veins in his father's thin forearms as he moved. He did look like such an old man, for the first time in John's life.

"Of course, sir," he said.

23

Merchants' District
City of Mooring
Afternoon, December 4, 1947

"Don't you love the cold?" Adelaide asked, rubbing her hands together as though she about to enjoy something delicious. They were in the covered back of a coach headed through town.

"Not unless it brings rain, or snow, or something other than numb feet," Theodora grumbled. Her fingers were numb, as were her toes, and she longed for the days when she'd been able to raise the temperature around herself just by wanting it.

They'd spent the last 24 hours sequestered in Adelaide's house, since Theodora told Adelaide she needed time to recover from her travel and the bombing. Really she was just petrified of what came next.

Going public. Playacting a witch. Potentially seeing John again. Shopping with Adelaide.

Now Adelaide turned toward her and pouted. "You mustn't let it take over your life, Ted. You mustn't lose sight of what beauty there is amid the current circumstances. Hasn't the drought taught you that? Though I do hate to think of how it must look down there, all parched and shriveling." She shuddered, then waggled her fingers in the air at Theodora. "Nothing you can do about it then?"

Theodora glanced at the chauffeur and raised her eyebrows. Adelaide tapped lightly on the partition. "Ralph, dear? Do you mind?"

Theodora watched the muscles in his shoulder bunch as he began to turn an unseen crank to roll the glass all the way up.

"Nothing's working. Nothing's been working for a long time," Theodora whispered. "I can still tell what the weather's going to be, but what old farmer's wife doesn't feel the weather in her bones?"

Adelaide leaned closer. "How long is long?"

Theodora had known Adelaide since they were children, even before she'd known Henry or John. She'd seen Theodora do more magic than practically anyone.

Theodora mumbled into the folds of her scarf.

"What?" Adelaide said, much too loudly.

Theodora held up nine fingers. "Years. Nearly."

"Nine years?" Adelaide gasped. Theodora flinched. "Apologies, but God's Wounds, Ted, why haven't you said anything? Have you been to a doctor?" She dropped her voice once more. "Does that mean it was when Henry disappeared? Is it shock?" She grabbed Theodora's knee a trifle too hard. "I always assumed you would have told me, but – did he do something to you?"

Theodora shook her head. "He didn't have time, did he? What could he have done in a night?"

"Hmm, well," Adelaide sniffed. "But no doctor then?"

"There aren't really doctors for that sort of thing, are there? Besides I'm sure they'd tell me it's all in my head."

Adelaide began to tap her fingers against her leg. "There's no one else down there? No old farmer's wife?"

Theodora shook her head.

"I might have some literature that can help."

"Really?"

"Don't seem so shocked. You know I was going to be a doctor. For a little while at least. I like to keep up on what's happening."

Theodora was momentarily distracted from her own troubles. "That's so wonderful Addy! I'm so glad that you do. I'll admit I was a bit afraid, seeing you last –"

Adelaide brushed her words away. "A silly pastime for a silly woman," she said, sing-song. "But I'll see what I can find. In the meantime," she clapped her hands together, "I'm so glad we're going dress shopping! I had no idea things were so dire, but now it's especially important that you make an impact."

Theodora was aware that the impact Adelaide meant was almost wholly sartorial. But she also was beginning to suspect that Adelaide's plans for her did not include a quiet life lived in seclusion at the ancestral home.

"Let's not get carried away." Theodora toyed with a trim of lace halfway down her skirt. "I want to convince them I'm a witch, not make them worried I'm going to burn the Assembly hall down. Besides, I think black rather suits me."

It had come to seem that there were great depths to the absence of color: If you stared into it long enough you could see very far into the future or the past. But Theodora had always been intimidated by Adelaide's sense of fashion, and her natural way of commanding a room with a swirl of her skirts.

"It's ghastly," Adelaide said, waving a hand. "You make everyone feel like they've done something wrong when you enter the room. Oh good, here we are."

Theodora didn't have time to be annoyed; the door opened from outside and they were ushered under cover of umbrella into the already-open doorway of a skinny stone building with a small brass sign above its door: "Oiseau Gowns and Outfitting, est. 1765."

They were on a residential street and inside seemed much more a home than a business, with cheery wallpaper depicting pastoral scenes and elegant family portraits on the walls. An assistant led them down a long entryway, past an abundance of sitting rooms. *Perhaps it was more like a salon*, Theodora thought, feeling slightly optimistic, *where women gathered to discuss philosophy and magic.* She'd heard about places like that existing, years ago.

The proprietress greeted them from a doorway at the end of the hall, standing between thick, drawn-apart curtains. "Such a pleasure to see you again, Mistress Outerbridge! And your friend," she added in rather more hushed tones. Theodora might almost have said *reverent*. Then she took Theodora's hand as though it was the softest silk, the rarest feather, and pressed their palms together. "Please do trust me, my dearest," she said.

Hildegarde Oiseau was about the same age as Theodora and Adelaide and she kept clasping her hands whenever she looked at them – especially at Theodora. She winked ostentatiously at them both and turned to bring them into her showroom.

Adelaide might be doing rather too good a job so far, Theodora thought.

Hildegarde signaled to her assistant to raise a curtain, revealing two dozen models attired in black garments and arranged like a rainbow seen through a storm: silk blouses; full skirts that hovered above satin high heels; tight draped silk dresses that pooled on the floor; feathered turbans and small lace caps; suits with pinched waists and shining buttons; fur-lined capes that somehow seemed to fan out in the nonexistent wind of the room.

Adelaide cooed and rushed to run her hands over the colors; the models moved fluidly around her hands, seeming used to this kind of thing. "I did tell myself this trip was for Ted, but it will be very difficult to contain myself, Mistress Hildegarde."

"Yes, they're very beautiful," Theodora said, not moving any closer. The styles were all so new: Short skirts shown with heels that looked suitable for tap-dancing on the stage; tops with plunging backs and exposed shoulders and capelets on top. "Is this really what people are wearing now?"

"They will be, as soon as I get done with them." Hildegarde rubbed her hands together. "As soon as the harbors were opened I gathered all the scraps of information I'd collected over the years, bits of magazines and photographs, and hybridized it all for our specific proclivities and expectations. And then tailored it all for you, my dear," she added.

Reflected in Hildegarde's shining eyes Theodora saw her own image, blown up on the cover of newspapers and running through newsreels.

Theodora smiled back and hugged herself. *Perhaps this had been a mistake.*

But then Hildegarde lurched forward and clutched again at Theodora's hands. "It's such an honor to be dressing you, Mistress Ashe-Martin. You must know. Your status is so important to all us women here in the city. To all of us on the island. The fact you still have your powers –" she paused as if overcome. "I want you to look as beautiful as possible when the world takes notice. In an Oiseau gown, of course," she added, letting go with one hand to add in a flourish.

Hildegarde and Adelaide both stared at Theodora with something close to pride, and not a little bit of expectation.

"You did this so quickly, for me? For the world?" Theodora asked, her voice sounding very thin.

Adelaide nearly hopped up and down. "Come, Ted, get out of those things."

From nowhere three other saleswomen appeared, one with drinks and a plate of cheese who left the drinks and took the cheese away nearly as soon as it had appeared. The two others silently approached Theodora like war submarines, fingers out to unzip and unbutton all her defenses.

She felt a rush of panic: If she ran, where could she go? But then everything went black as her dress was pulled unceremoniously, but gently, over her head. Someone began to unroll her stockings and yet more hands slid her feet from her boots. It was strangely comforting.

Theodora heard a rip and realized she wouldn't be wearing this outfit again.

Hours later Theodora and Adelaide laughed as the carriage drove through the quiet streets close by Adelaide's house. There was barely enough room for the both of them, with all the garment bags and hat boxes and shoe boxes. Hildegarde had given them the rest of the sparkling wine — not that there'd been much left— and Theodora was having a very hard time holding her glass upright as the car pulled up slowly to the curb.

"Isn't it so lovely, how you have a coach with crystal glasses and its own tiny icebox?" she asked.

"Yes, I suppose I'm very lucky," Adelaide said, but she sounded very bored. "The Magistrate got an entire crate of things on the first ship in, I'll have to show you: chocolate bars and rubber balls, some sort of moving image device, butter. Cow meat! I tried to explain that no one here eats meat, we hardly have space in the cellar, but the porter sent over from the ship seemed to find that the height of hilarity."

"Did you try it?"

Adelaide nodded and made a face. "I tried to get it over with as fast as possible," she said, laughing, and then turned away as if she didn't want to think of it anymore. She stared out the window at the park across the street from her home. "It's like living inside a jewel box, isn't it? Or a genie's lamp."

Theodora leaned over Adelaide heavily to look out the window. The Common Gardens had high metal gates with sharp tops, but it was easy enough to see the dense topiaries inside, the imported flowers, the soaring greenhouse. The plants made their own atmosphere, and the mist around the greenhouse gave the impression the world inside the gates was covered in tiny diamonds. It looked like a castle in a fairy tale, the kind of place a queen would be banished to live out her days.

Theodora sighed very dramatically. *That was rather loud*, she thought.

"I wish I was a plant," she said.

"Darling, you are squishing me. Whatever do you mean?"

"Then I could really do it. Make the island whole again."

Adelaide stopped squirming to get out from under Theodora, and turned her head to look at her instead. Theodora turned, too, and their noses bumped. She started giggling.

"Oh for pity's sake," Adelaide said, but she was smiling. "You are so much better than a plant, my darling. Don't give up hope quite yet." Her voice got a little more serious, and she leaned back a little so that she could look Theodora squarely in the eyes. "There's still time to make things whole again. All right, dear?"

Theodora tried to make her face very serious, though her lips kept twitching up absurdly. "I do not understand in the slightest, but I will trust you. Because you are the greatest jewel of them all, my love," Theodora said, and awkwardly cradled friend's face, one hand still gripping the flute.

"Thank you," Adelaide said, looking amused once more. At some point they'd come to a stop, and from the other side of the car the chauffeur opened the door, and the pink-grey dusk entered the car.

"Come now," Adelaide said, and quickly slid out past Theodora, letting the chauffeur take her hand. Theodora followed unsteadily. She was halfway up the marble steps to the front door when several lights exploded in her face. She immediately thought of the bomb, and reached out blindly for Adelaide.

"Theodora!"

"Mistress Witch!"

"'Widow Witch flies north', eh?"

Theodora turned only to be blinded again as the flashbulbs went off. There must have been five or six photographers; far too many for Ralph, who was trying to wrestle them all simultaneously to the ground. Theodora realized she was still holding a half-empty glass of wine in her hand, and lifted it up began to take aim. *The least I can do to help the poor man*, she thought.

As the glass took flight, the wine arching out behind it in an exaggerated arc, several hands took hold of her from behind. Theodora watched the outside world disappear below as she was lifted into the sanctum of Adelaide's entryway.

24

Between the University and Assembly
City of Mooring
Early evening, December 5, 1947

"THANK you again for coming with me," John said, breathless.

"Wouldn't have missed it."

Here was Mooring: bisected by the river curling to the north until it disappeared around a hill, disappearing to the south in the near-black forest that bordered the warehouses and the factories. To the east of the river there were houses, first the oldest neighborhoods that had emerged cautiously out of the woods. As the streets moved north the houses grew grander, one-story labyrinths that crawled around elaborate fenced-in gardens full of cultivated hothouse hybrids.

The University campus was further north on that side of the city, the houses genteelly separated from it by city greenhouses. Then the University proper, with the schools of Archaeology, Healing, Geology, Astronomy, and Botanical Arts. Above those, the warren of streets and pubs where the students and the professors lived. Finally, the Great

Library, atop a rocky outcropping that overlooked the meadows and the river as it receded. Fishing villages along its banks beyond, though these days most of the fishers had turned to ice-harvesting and algae-shipping.

Along the city's east bank, meadows again, but also shops and businesses up against the rocks. Assembly and all its departments further south, then severe new homes built up by the merchants.

John and George ran out into traffic, dodging carriages and a man on a bike. John wasn't used to this much traffic, or any traffic that wasn't slow-moving drill trucks pulled by shaggy icehorses, though it was nice not to have to dodge the antlers. He wasn't sure what his friend's excuse was. George had been in some upper atmosphere all afternoon, ever since John had invited him to the dinner at the PM's.

"So it's in honor of the Ag Minister?" George asked.

"Seems like it," John said.

He smiled sideways at John as they maneuvered around a town caller reciting the evening's news to a small crowd from atop an overturned fruit carton. "Victoria should be there then, eh?"

John nodded and groaned inwardly. Then felt terrible for groaning, even inaudibly. A few hours ago he'd sent Victoria a note to let her know he'd be attending but should have let her know days ago. *Should have been to see her already.*

He should have done many things, but since seeing Theodora he really couldn't think about anything else. He should have found *her* already. He'd been an idiot to let himself be buried in paperwork, though of course it hadn't been all accidental. Since they were children he'd always assumed that if Theodora wanted him she'd find him, and so he'd been hesitant for years. Then Henry had stepped into that void and now Theodora was in this public mess of name-calling and power-hungry politicians.

"Holy hell," George said, stopping in front of a newsstand. The proprietor looked up, seemed bored by them both, and went back to his cigar.

"What now? Holy hell."

Mistress Theodora Ashe-Martin Arrives in City Amidst Opening of International Trade
An End To Crippling Drought?
Or Beginning Of Nation's Nefarious Co-operation With Foreign Powers?
Our Editors Say "Get Back On Your Broomstick and Get Out!"

Beneath the headline was a photo of Teddy, looking both surprised and like an avenging angel. She held a champagne flute like a bolt of lightning and the look in her eyes was such that John nearly braced for it to be thrown in his own face.

"Guess it's out now, then?" George asked.

John nodded again. He wondered what she was doing right now. If she was all right.

25

Outerbridge Estate
Evening, December 5, 1947

"Can't you wear something from Oiseau? No? Perhaps? Maybe let's just try it on and see, shall we."

Adelaide had recovered fully from the swarm of publicity on the doorstep but Theodora had not. She was in fact a little annoyed at her friend, who seemed to be relishing the excuse to embrace a more public persona, not only for Theodora and not only for very specific aims, but also for herself. In fact in her less charitable moments Theodora suspected that perhaps the photographers weren't so unplanned at all, that her friend might have thought the photo opp worth the shock and surprise.

Adelaide thrust a knee-length off-shoulder number at her.

"Adelaide, my current dresses fit fine. They're much more appropriate. I'll just bring these new ones home with me when I go back."

"Oh brilliant, when you'll be tucked back in the countryside to molder for eternity, with no one will appreciate them at all." Adelaide flounced down on a seat, managing not to spill a drop of her cocktail. Theodora wished she could move like that. She wished the mention of moldering didn't set her stomach roiling with the truth of it. She pursed her lips.

"That's rather ungenerous of you, Addy. People do pay attention to these things in the country, even if we must adjust for practicality. You do have to be able to farm, and scale cliffs, and harvest. Can you imagine someone rappelling down the side of a valley dressed in those heels?"

"You do a lot of cliff-scaling, then?" Adelaide asked.

"That's not the point, it's about adhering to time-honored traditions of widowhood and not appearing to ask for more than –"

"I think I could manage it," Adelaide said with a laugh. "I like heights very much, actually." She turned back to Theodora's closet.

The thought of home made Theodora queasy. There might be questions tonight at the Governor's: what her plans were for Henry's inheritance, what actions might be taken in face of the drought. What actions Theodora planned to take, and why she'd waited so long.

She rubbed her hands. For a very rich man, the Magistrate certainly kept his house cold.

Or perhaps worse: What if there weren't questions? As much as she'd worried about being able to convince them she was still a witch, the prospect of sitting down with people who might actually be able to help and having them ignore her ideas and her thoughts was nearly painful.

"No sequins," Theodora said, folding her arms.

"Fine then wear this one, please," Adelaide said quickly, as if she'd expected that, and held up a dress that Theodora didn't recognize.

"What have you done now?" Theodora asked, but she took the garment from Adelaide lovingly, like it was a small creature. It was as soft and friendly as one: One of her own dresses tailored with soft wintery accents even as it had been shortened and most of the sleeves removed.

"You can't argue with that, can you?" Adelaide asked, happy like a child who knows they've gotten away with something. "Oh go, put it on. Think of it not like showing off, think of it as the first performance of your new political career."

"I'm not a politician, Addy."

"That's right. You're something else, entirely."

26

Governor's House
Cocktail hour, December 5, 1947

JOHN AND GEORGE crossed Assembly Bridge on foot, silent and braced against the wind. Not nearly so bad as up North, John thought, but still he wished that George had taken him up on his offer to get a coach.

"Not on the company dime anymore, no thank you," George had said.

Not that John was thinking much of the cold. He thought only about Theodora as they stepped onto the river promenade, as they made their way the short distance to the Governor's gate, gave their names and were let up the stairs.

"Good evening, sirs," said the butler as he took their coats. "The party is having drinks in the library, if you would care to go through."

And how am I dealing with my fixation? By schmoozing.

George went first and John followed, still thinking about his failures and only half-seeing the rare volumes displayed on the walls, the framed illuminated pages. The room was nearly full; it appeared they were rather late. And so he was completely unprepared when he walked into the library and the crowds, like clouds providing a glimpse of the day that might have been, parted for a moment, and Theodora appeared before him.

She was on the second floor of the library, over to the side and lit by pinpricks of warm white algae-light lining the balcony floor. Above a sea of colored dresses and against the backdrop of the brown-red bookshelves she stood out like an etching. *Those damned mourning blacks. Damned if they don't suit her.*

As he stared Teddy turned to look down at him, and for a moment they saw each other.

"John!"

John looked away to see Adelaide Outerbridge standing two feet from him. Her eyes were huge and she held two glasses of wine. On her face was a shadow of the look she'd given the newspaper photographers: Annoyance and the already-spinning wheels of recalibration.

"Hello, Mistress Outerbridge," John said, and turned to George, who stood agape between them. *George is truly in over his head.* "I don't know if you know my good friend, Mr. Law?" John asked Adelaide. "He's a bright rising star at the university, where he lectures in Northern Geology."

George shot him a look that only made it harder for John not to laugh.

"Hello, Adelaide," George muttered. "John invited me last minute. Didn't know you'd be here."

But Adelaide, society spouse that she was — *hardly an adequate use of her skills*, John had always thought — simply appraised him with a look of cool, distant delight on her face, and held out her hand to be chastely kissed. Then she turned back to John.

They had known each other their whole lives, seeing each other just often enough to check their own growth and attempts at maturation through each other's eyes. But it had been several years, and looking at her now John realized with a start that they had turned into some new edition of their parents. At least Adelaide had: Dignified and worldly, looking as ever completely at home wherever she was, whether among the rich and the powerful or farm animals and tall grass.

"John! How lovely to see you. How long has it been? Too long, surely." Adelaide leaned forward, still holding her two glasses, to kiss John quickly on both cheeks.

She slipped one glass into John's hand, and whispered against his cheek: "Did you see her? She's upstairs. You really ought to see her. Terrible that you haven't yet, honestly."

Then Adelaide moved her newly freed hand forward, ever so slowly, and pinched John very hard on the ear.

John yelped and then, glancing around to make sure no one had noticed, grinned sheepishly at her.

"Thanks for the reminder."

He turned sharply to go find Teddy. As he left he was vaguely aware Adelaide and George had each taken one half-step closer to each other.

Theodora watched him walk in behind George Law. Adelaide had known he'd be coming, of course, and had warned her.

He looked up at her almost immediately, almost as if someone had tipped him off to where she'd be. Too fast for her to look away and pretend she hadn't been staring at the entranceway. She hadn't meant to stand there waiting, really, her feet had just sort of led her to this spot on the balcony, with a perfect view.

A second after their eyes met Adelaide exclaimed something and John looked away. Theodora stepped back into the shadow of the shelves and laid her hand on Diana's head to steady herself.

She wasn't hiding. At least that's not all she was doing. She was looking at the Governor's library, thousands of volumes of island history, untouched for decades by the looks of them. She ran her fingers over their spines, leaving a trail in the dust.

"Do me a damned bit better if I was a witch of small talk," she muttered to herself.

"I'm sorry?"

Theodora jumped as a young woman ducked her head out from behind the next shelf. Victoria White had an open, smiling face and lovely hair, curled and piled up on top of her head.

"Oh, nothing!" Theodora sang out, too loud for the space or for the distance between them. "Just my old mind going," she said, and laughed too loud. *You're supposed to be the witch, Teddy, not her. Try to look at least a little imposing.*

Victoria stuck out her hand and began to speak in a rush.

"You're Mistress Ashe-Martin, aren't you? It's such a pleasure, I've heard so much about you. I can't believe you're here, actually," she added. "In the room. With me."

Theodora was a bit taken aback by Victoria's giddiness, though she could see why John liked her: Not merely the only daughter of the politician responsible for feeding the nation, Victoria was beautiful and, it seemed, extremely friendly. Also startlingly young. *Good for him,* Theodora thought. *Good for both of them. Yes, good for him.*

"It's a pleasure to meet you as well, Miss White," Theodora said. "Your reputation precedes you."

Victoria cocked her head, still smiling but looking confused. "What do you –"

"Teddy."

Theodora spun around and Victoria stepped out further into the aisle to look around her, where the voice had come from.

"And Victoria," John said, eyes going very wide.

He froze a smile on his face. *He's gotten very good at that. The politician's inability to be surprised.* Her own face always gave her away.

"John!" Victoria said, clapping her hands together.

"Hello to all of us!" Theodora said.

"Do you two know each other?" Victoria asked. She'd taken several steps toward John, who was advancing much more slowly, and stopped now to look from one of them to the other with a broad grin. At her question Theodora turned to John with one raised eyebrow.

"Yes. We were friends. As children," John said.

"Some time ago," said Theodora. "That's all."

"Hmm," said John, laughing nervously. "Is that all?"

The space on the balcony had gotten very stuffy, and John seemed not to know what to do with his hands. Theodora wondered if she could jump over the edge of the balcony and survive. *This is ridiculous. It's not as if John and I have done anything wrong.*

But was this, the way they were acting right now, something in itself?

Victoria, luckily, didn't seem to notice any of it. She leapt forward to take John's hands in her own, forgetting the famous Mistress Ashe-Martin long enough that Theodora could slip behind a large potted fern nearly as tall as she was and then to the landing. She made it down the stairs in seconds.

"Theodora Ashe!" Victoria whispered to John as soon as they were alone. She squeezed his hands, her eyes bright. Then she smacked John lightly on the arm. "I can't believe you never told me you know her! She's a legend, John."

There were many things John and Victoria hadn't talked about over the course of their lengthy correspondence: plans for their wedding; their not-insignificant age difference; their feelings on children or where to live or John's propensity for spending nearly all his time marooned, alone, on the ice.

Theodora Ashe was another thing they hadn't discussed.

"Erm, sorry," John said.

He wasn't sure why he and Victoria had never addressed their mutual future, but he'd certainly allowed himself to be carried along on the tide of other people's expectations. It made John's father happy – or as close as he came to it – to think them as good as betrothed. And John liked to think Victoria's father, Agricultural Minister White, liked him well enough to consider him a suitable match for his only child.

"Could you get me her autograph?" Victoria asked, bringing John back to himself.

"What? Well, I suppose so," he began, before noticing the smirk on Victoria's face. "Oh shut up," he said, and laughed, releasing her hands and offering her his arm.

She began to lead him toward the stairs, nudging him playfully with her shoulder. "You looked more starry-eyed than me for a moment. I couldn't resist."

John really did like Victoria. She was lovely, intelligent, and had lost her own mother long ago. She also seemed to find many of the trappings of society ridiculous, though not so much that she'd ever buck them entirely. Just like John.

The eyes of the crowd below turned up to steal glances as they descended the curving stairwell. Victoria, dressed in a dark purple dress that swirled and kicked out with each step, was more than equal to the attention. She kept up conversation with him about all that he'd missed in Mooring, all the while nodding and offering smiles to the people below. *She's better at it than I am*, he thought. *Perhaps she actually enjoys it.*

Jewel tones seemed to be in vogue this season; the crowd parting to embrace them as they reached the floor was full of reds and golds and blues. But try as he might to concentrate as Victoria filled him on the latest scandals and petty grievances of their mutual acquaintances, he couldn't stop himself searching for Theodora's black dress in the crowd.

27

North Atlantic Ocean
Dates and points lost

THE PROBLEM WITH A COLLECTIVE VISION, a shining beacon, an image of inspiration and hope, is that it's short on logistics. The witches at sea had realized this already, what with the aimless wandering around the Atlantic and its environs for the last hard, cold (but sometimes very hot) months.

When the child saw the cliffs and raised the alarm, there were tears, emphatic nods, cautious and then jubilant glances at one's neighbor to confirm that this was not, in fact, a mirage. Like seeing a color for the first time that you've only heard described: *Is that blue? Do you think so? Yes, if we agree why not let's call it so.*

But the cliffs were higher than anyone had anticipated, the waves that crashed against them harder and larger. The landscape, such as it could be seen at this remove, appeared scrubby where it was not barren.

They sailed around the island for a week, keeping good distance in case of shallows or unfriendly inhabitants. In the case of the latter, what would the witches do? They were nearly out of food, their magic, even the kind that belonged to the sea, was weakened from so much uncertainty and rootlessness.

But they saw no one besides massive pale gray seals that yelled at them from a distance and strange orange-beaked birds which decided the ship looked like a good place to shit, and who could blame them at this point. The ship did not run aground and by the time they came back to the wrinkled cliffs that made up the island's southern face, everyone was eager to get onto land, come what may. No one had gotten any better smelling.

"I still can't swim."

"I am terrified of heights. You shall have to blindfold me to get me up there."

"I am nine months now with child, and I will not have this babe be born drenched in saltwater and bird shit."

"We will drop anchor here," the captain's wife said, "and take a small party in to find the best route up."

The captain's wife was very stern and very tall and she could sing in birdsong. No one really wanted to argue with her. It was good to have a plan of action, at any rate, rather than more bobbing about in the sea, so a group was selected and the advance party set out.

"Perhaps something with a shoreline, next time, eh?" one of them muttered as they came closer. No one laughed, but they shivered and nodded their heads: *Yes, if there was a next time, ought to pick a better place.* Of course if they went about this right, there need never be a next time. There would only have to be this place. That alone kept them rowing against the current.

As they paddled closer the cliffside grew up before them. The waves crashed against sharp peaks of rocks which had long ago cleaved from the island, each covered with slime and a few hardy, lonely plants. Their little boat tossed and heaved in the chop. It took everyone working together – calling to the wind and the waves, steering and paddling and shouting directions in a constant stream of curses – to angle in close to the rocky wall without catastrophe, and even still hands and bodies were bloodied, used as bulwarks.

But when they got close enough everything went very calm.

"What happened?" The woman's voice boomed out so loud in the silence that everyone. Another woman laughed, a little hysterical. And the boat continued on into the cliffside without their help, the island having taken them in.

Striations in the rock created the illusion that the cliff was an unbroken line, but there were countless inlets and crevices of varying sizes all along its length. Their boat was pulled by a swift, sure current as though they'd been deep inland on a quiet stream. Perhaps that's where they were headed; when they dipped their oars they found it was nearly impossible to arrest their own progress. No one felt like fighting anyway. Everyone felt like taking their first deep breaths in what felt like months. Like a spell, though no one would take credit.

It was also the smell. Green. Green like dyes that hadn't yet been created, green like money that hadn't been printed, green like the very bottom of a swamp in the middle of a forest at twilight under a green moon. A little moldy, very damp. Like things would grow. The walls of the canyon were covered with plants: vines as thick as forearms, moss three fingers deep.

Vegetation covered the cliff walls from the water line – peering over the edge they could see the green extended into the water – up to a little sliver of blue sky, interrupted by passing clouds. They passed flowers the size of a baby's head, and leaves that dipped in the center like two cupped palms together.

"Fresh water," the captain's wife said, tipping her mouth to the point of one such leaf. "Everyone drink."

For a moment or much longer they forgot about the sea and everyone back on the ship anxiously waiting to hear their report.

Soon they were hopelessly lost. The current carried them deeper into the island, down sudden hairpin turns and farther canyons. There didn't seem to be any reason behind the route; maybe it was shifts in the weight of the boat, or the tides, or the moon. *Had several hours passed?* No one was sure how long ago the sun had dipped below the edge of the land above them but for some time they'd been coursing through a nighttime green-and-blue world. Lit from below. The water was so clear it seemed to glow, and the glow stretched up into the air.

Anyone of them could have stepped easily from the boat and grabbed hold of a vine, taken a step up and began to climb the canyon walls. That's how narrow the space was, and how craggy the dark gray rock. Almost like steps, though of course none of them dared try it. They all thought it.

The water grew choppier and their surroundings harder to parse, and the occupants of the boat realized they hadn't been going deeper into the island at all, only twisting up and down and around in a network of rivers and streams and caverns. They were coming out again, just a little farther from where they'd gone in.

"We can stay here, can't we? For a little while?" the girl asked.

Everyone turned to look at her, sitting in the center of the boat where it was thought she'd be safest. Everyone turned to the captain's wife.

She didn't have any authority. They'd have to hold a vote, or rather her husband would, since it was his boat and that seemed to be the way these things were done. But she looked at the child, thin with hunger of several different sorts and as cold and scared as the rest of them, though with less armor to prevent it all from bleeding through.

"Yes," the captain's wife said. "Of course we'll stay here."

28

Governor's House
Dinner, December 5, 1947

"What a truly splendid demonstration of our fine island-nation's position amongst the constellation of luminaries that make up our times."

All the heads around the table benignly smiled and murmured at the Governor. They'd already had the cheese and the first fish course, and the Governor was taking advantage of the kelp course being served to give his speech. John managed to forget, every time, that the man was like this. In the newspapers the Governor's manner came across as less ridiculous, like you'd accidentally started reading the text of a flowery play from the century before.

"Master White, our venerable Agricultural Minister and keeper of the staff of the chaff of metaphorical wheat – really more a relative of seaweed, in our case – that has throughout our history grown so nobly on our cliffsides, and which we shall grow again."

John glanced at Theodora. She was staring down at her plate with wide eyes, her forehead propped up on her hand. He remembered once, when they were teenagers, his father had repeated verbatim from the local magistrate something truly fatuous about the island's public education system. Something about how it was a waste of public funds to send girls even for primary schooling, since without witchcraft what was the point of women at all?

Theodora had not been pleased. It had shown.

John looked down at his plate to rid the smile from his face, the memory of that pompous ass from his mind. The red-headed man sitting next to him muttered, sounding as though he was holding his breath.

"What the hell is this?" The man poked at the green-brown vegetation, cunningly spun into the shape of a little nest.

"It's a palate cleanser," John whispered back. "Mind you stretch your jaw a bit, it can be tough at first."

"When's the meat?" The man had gotten his fork stuck in the kelp now.

"Oh, I'm afraid we don't go in for that here," John said. "I take it that's a bit unusual?"

"This better be worth it," the man muttered again, and John realized that he was no longer – if he ever had been – part of the conversation. He also realized that Barrow was saying his name.

"Master Dove, though we are of course saddened to hear of your father's ongoing illness, we are pleased to learn of his continued resilience, and delighted to have your company with us tonight. May it, unlike said illness, linger." John hesitated, trying to parse the tenor of what the Governor had said, before smiling and dipping his head in an appropriately vague manner.

Governor Barrow sat at the top of the table; then John; the American in search of meat; Adelaide; an official from England; Mistress Barrow; Lydia Barnswallow, one of the leading lights of Wherewithal's stage; an Englishman; George; Theodora; a Russian; Victoria; a woman from Cuba; Horace Barnswallow, Lydia's paramour onstage and off; and finally the Agricultural Minister. John hadn't caught any of visiting dignitaries' names, though he wasn't sure any of them had been given.

"And welcome to the wife of our illustrious Court Magistrate, Madame Adelaide Outerbridge."

Adelaide raised one eyebrow, smiling, sipping her drink.

"And of course our honored guests from the East and the West." The Governor looked on the brink of elaborating, but the men all around him smiled without their teeth, and he swallowed his words.

"Yes, yes, and of course," Governor Barrow went on, "I feel I do no disservice to the rest when I say that Mistress Barrow and I are truly delighted – and not a little flabbergasted – to have Mistress Theodora Ashe-Martin dining with us tonight."

Theodora's head shot up, a large red mark where her palm had been and a bit of hair pushed straight up from her forehead.

"Truly your reputation precedes you, my dear," the Governor laughed, and all the men from far away laughed. The Cuban woman sat back in her seat, assessing. Theodora blushed and opened her mouth to speak.

"I'm sure you know," the Governor said, turning to each of the foreign guests in turn, "about our very interesting history?" They each stared back at him, revealing nothing. "Yes, yes, quite, exactly," he said. "Founded by witches! And their kin. Really a novelty item now, a footnote, you know. Good for tourism, perhaps?" He cleared his throat. "Witches may inherit, though. And serve, should they wish. Whereas women, yes, may not. Meant to do a bit for parity, you see. Guarantee those early men a say. And this one here, what ho! Would stand to come into quite a bit if she wanted. Suffice it to say her situation has inspired not a little bit of speculation here in the Assembly! Besides all the, you know." He waggled his fingers at her and approximated a chuckle.

He was speaking so fast he swayed a bit and had to brace himself upon the table. *He's terrified*, John thought suddenly.

"Mistress Ashe-Martin is sitting on some very potentially lucrative land, twice over. Should she want the burden," he added, with a very obvious wink towards her.

John wanted to strangle the man with kelp.

She felt like a pig at market. Everyone at the table was staring at her. Theodora fixated on the sconce on the wall above the Governor's head, and willed herself into a hole in the ground.

"But Mistress Ashe-Martin we are so thrilled you are here, as a show of goodwill and solidarity and all that!" The Governor lightly banged one fist into the other. "To go confidently into our mutually beneficial future!"

Theodora noticed that some of the nameless faces around the table had started to shift in their seats and angle themselves so they became obscured in the shadow of the algae-lights. *That's why they're here, of course.* Limitless energy, endless light. Funny how the closer they got to it the more their faces were obscured.

"Yes, well, at any rate. To Mistress Theodora Ashe-Martin!" Barrow raised his glass to her and, before anyone had time to chime in, brought it to his lips and drained it.

Theodora did the same.

The Governor smiled and opened his mouth once more. "And so —"

She pushed her chair back loudly, and stood.

"I am so happy to be here," she said, with more force than she'd intended, mostly so that she'd have the courage to get it out, "and to serve my island, with the fullness of my power. My powers."

Governor Barrow stood with his mouth open.

Theodora took a sip and smoothed her skirts as she sat. "You may go on. I'm finished."

There was a hush around the table which was, Theodora thought, the loudest hush she'd ever heard. She rather liked the effect.

John stifled a laugh.

Barrow coughed. "Well then. Plenty of time for talking after supper, eh, men? And ma'am," he said, nodding toward Cuba. "Let us recommence eating!"

The Governor sat and from an invisible door behind him four footmen entered with shining silver dishes that they unveiled dramatically at the left of each visiting dignitary – each except Theodora, John noted.

Everyone made noises over the local specialties dressed up for what John was beginning to realize must be quite an occasion: There was whole blue trout, and salted eel, and purple potatoes, and fresh wild denuded thornvine. At the latter everyone gasped.

"Where did you get those?" Theodora asked, very serious.

Mistress Barrow clapped her hands and leaned toward Theodora, eager to share. "Chef paid top dollar for them this morning at the market. This was the entire supply! Don't they look lovely?"

John knew enough of what was going on to know that this particular vegetable hadn't been exported from the south for years, because of the drought. If someone was selling them here it meant a black market had started up. People were getting more desperate.

Theodora caught John staring at her. She turned back to the Governor's wife.

"Exceptionally lovely," she said. "I loved them growing up."

"I don't believe we've ever been introduced."

Theodora was glad for an excuse to turn aside; the Russian on the other side of her had been explaining his version of the proper technique for eating the fish. When she turned away to look at George Law she saw he was making a very subtle, very ridiculous fish face himself.

She snorted into her plate.

"Mistress Martin," the fish-explainer said, deadly serious and rather like he was in the mood for a duel to defend her honor, "are you quite all right?"

"Yes, yes, thank you," she replied, hiding her face in her napkin. George was pretending to be busy with the salt cellar.

"That was shockingly immature," she said quietly to him once the Russian had been reassured. "My thanks, though I'm afraid you nearly caused a diplomatic incident."

"Apologies, Mistress Ashe-Martin. Though I do wonder if any sort of geopolitical drama could be entered into with a man without a name. Who's to say he even really exists? Perhaps he has only recently been conjured."

He asked it so academically that Theodora glanced over to see that the man hadn't actually disappeared for want of an audience. He was still there. But George Law had a point.

"Sometimes I do feel," Theodora said, "that I am an unwitting actor in a play. Something written to challenge the audience's trust of the author." She knew that George was a friend of John's and she'd almost forgotten what it was like to talk to someone like this: Honestly, and like an adult.

"I feel that way most of the time," George said. "Though it's not terribly comforting to hear you say that, Mistress Ashe-Martin. Aren't you the main character?"

"Theodora, please."

George poked at his eel. "I do feel as though I know you already. From that one, mostly." He nodded his head at John, who was trying very hard to follow along with whatever the Governor was saying to Adelaide. "I also hear that you're a very powerful, very talented witch, and have come to Mooring to make your mark on the world." On the other side of her the Russian paused, just for a moment, in his new conversation.

Theodora speared a bit of food on her food and examined it. "Have you heard all that then? A bit presumptuous of you, isn't it Mr. Law, to discuss my private affairs at the table? And not behind my back, at that?"

George only shrugged. "It's not illegal, is it, to discuss witchcraft for the public good? Not quite, not yet. And I have interests, even as a bit player in this play. My survival mostly, but also the survival of the island and its people. In these times we need people with talent to reveal themselves, Mistress Ashe-Martin. Theodora."

She opened her mouth, ready to say something arch and leading in reply. But nothing came. *Damn if I wouldn't have revealed myself if I had something to reveal*, she thought. *Instead I'm playacting, and to what end?* But play she must if she wanted a home to go back to, and she bit the food off her fork, delicately, to buy herself a moment.

But then, and for the first time, George turned to look at her squarely. "My apologies," he said, and she saw that he truly was. "I've had too much to drink and being here," he glanced across the table at Adelaide, "makes me feel like I have nothing to lose and everything to gain. I begin to speak as if I'm in a play myself, and quite a self-serious one at that."

He smiled sheepishly and Theodora saw in an instant what John liked about this George Law.

She smiled back at him. "I do empathize. Though I feel as though there's always more to lose."

He stared at her a second longer before looking away. "Perhaps. You're new to the city. So is John, for all practical purposes. And I know none of how your – your business, works." He fluttered his fingers next to his steak knife. "But these fellows here," George's voice went even lower, "are not here for just for trade relations and wooing our dear friend, Mr. Dove, for algae contracts." He shook his head, frustrated. "They are here for access. They are here for control."

Theodora glanced about at the strangers around the table and frowned. "What access? How do you know all this?"

George's face went blank. "I work at the university," he shrugged as if that was explanation. "Most people do not take me seriously, but I pay attention. Moreover, like a fool, I care what happens to this island. I always have."

"And it is bad to care?" Theodora asked it lightly, but found she really wanted to know the answer.

"About your home and its place in the world? I don't believe it's wrong to care, no. Do you care, Theodora?"

She ignored his question. "Access to what, Mr. Law?"

He cleared his throat a little and smiled at someone across the table. "Everything." His smile became grim. "The whole island. We didn't simply open the harbors because we thought it might be helpful for the drought. We did it because we realized a lot of very powerful nations might need something we could offer, at this particular moment in history, especially. Not just Dove Holdings, not just military outposts on the cliffs and weapons testing on the ice."

Theodora's mouth went dry; she gulped her ale so she wouldn't choke. But George wasn't finished.

"These powerful people," he said, keeping his voice low so only she could hear the disdain dripping from it, "they love out-of-the-way islands full of people at a desperate moment in their history. So it's not so much the contracts I'm worried about, though they're a treacherous step, as I'm concerned about –"

"Colonization?" Her voice sounded hollow, like she was very far away.

"Precisely. Or occupation, more like. And that man over there," he nodded at Barrow, "is aware that on an island running out of water with half its industry going down the drain, political fortunes can be saved by timely partnerships with powerful people bearing the promise of jobs."

"You can't think that we'd actually accept that! To come under someone else's power." All around her the visitors were picking at their food, making a good diplomatic show of understanding how to eat the food, with various degrees of success.

"Depends how it's worded. Dove Holdings has made their reputation convincing people that laboring underground is the path to riches."

Theodora thought of the train conductor. She glanced down the table at John, animatedly telling a story to the couples on either side of him. "You sound critical of him," she said, and realized her own voice sounded defensive.

"Oh no, it's just that he's far too trusting. A bit willfully naïve, perhaps, about his own father's intentions. You know it was John's idea, to offer up the algae?"

She nodded. Everyone knew. *Very like John, of course.*

"But did you know he wanted to do just that: Offer it, free of charge? 'A gift to humanity,' those were the actual words he used. We talked about it quite a bit on the glacier," George said. He shook his head. "I knew that'd never happen, that he'd be steamrolled by his father. And by Assembly, who took so damned long arguing whether or not to do it the war was over by the time we could be of any use. I won't be too damned late to the party next time, whether I'm invited or not!"

He looked sideways at Theodora and gave her a crooked smile.

"Sorry," he said, lowering his voice. "I hate being left out is all. I'm sure you understand?"

Theodora dipped her head graciously, more to avoid the question than anything else. Did she want to be included? No one had ever really asked, least of all herself.

"Yes, well," he said. "Perhaps we're all guilty of underestimating the role we play."

Theodora frowned. "You're very knowledgeable, Master Law. But you're not subtle."

George stifled a laugh and picked up his glass. "You'd be surprised, Theodora."

At the sound of silver against crystal they all looked up. The Agricultural Minister, a large man in every sense, stood beaming down at them.

"Good evening, friends old and new. Delicious food, my dear, delicious," he said to Mistress Barrow, and then turned to Theodora. "It is an especial delight to meet the famed Mistress Ashe-Martin, as well. I hope to learn more about you than mere reputation. To work with you, if you'll have me. To help us survive, and then some." He looked around the table at them all. "I believe that's why we're all here today, isn't it? To thrive?"

Theodora stared back at him for a moment, startled. One of the island's top officials, looking to her for counsel, or at the very least for an endorsement: *Perhaps this is my coming-out, after all.* Beyond that, though, she was surprised by the look of sincerity on his face. By the way he seemed to really care about the island, and to assume that she did, too.

"I knew your mother, too," he went on, bringing her back abruptly to the table. "Rather, I met her once. A very formidable woman, very. We could use more like her these days."

She blinked rapidly. *Don't ask about her, don't ask, don't ask. Not the time. Maybe, though, soon –*

She lifted her glass to him. "Thank you, Minister White. I look forward to discussing the future of our island with you. I wish to serve not just the people, but also the land, the ice, the cliffs, the sea. Like the vow our forebears took when we first came here."

The Ag Minister looked only mildly surprised. Mostly, she thought, he looked pleased. "With witchcraft, too, may I hope?"

It was so warm in the room. She reached for her glass, refilled almost automatically, and brought it nearly to her lips. She glanced around the table and caught John's eye for the briefest moment.

The room grew hotter.

Wait, she thought. *Make them wait.*

Holding her drink in the cup of her palm she tried to smile as though she had a secret. *Which I suppose I do.* She glanced at John; he was watching her. They all were.

"Of course," she said, "with witchcraft." She turned to the shadowy figures around her and raised her glass. "Welcome to Wherewithal."

Somewhere along the table crystal shattered. At first it seemed like an overzealous call for attention and everyone looked to the Governor. But he was looking at Minister White.

The Ag Minister stood up even taller. His eyes went wide, and then he fell, hard, onto the table and then off of it, taking with him an uncut shank of eel and landing in the lap of the Governor. Barrow grunted, and when he wrenched his hand out from under the Minister his fingers were covered in blood. Theodora thought at first that it was from the food.

Then Victoria White screamed.

John was at Minister White's head, struggling to hold it upright even as the man had fallen to the floor, as if the problem were drowning instead of bleeding, as if he were not already clearly dead.

Half of them jumped to the Minister's side. The other half jumped under the table.

Except Theodora: She sat like a statue, staring not at the Minister, but at the bright red hand of the Governor, which he waved about so wildly that later all the dinner guests would find red constellations of blood across their own hands and faces. He turned away at a cry from Victoria, and when he looked back Theodora had vanished.

The bullet had come through the window and by the time anyone thought to go outside the streets were deserted. The gun must have come in on a ship, though. There had been no such things on Wherewithal before.

John stayed with the others until the constabulary and ambulance arrived, helping Victoria into the back. She looked so young, like a soldier fresh to the field.

"I'll come to the hospital!" he called out to her, and though she nodded she didn't take her eyes off her father, clutching one of his hands in both of hers and holding it to her heart.

The double doors shut and the bell began to clang as the icehorses burst out into the street. John bent over double, feeling like he could outrun it with the adrenaline pumping through his chest.

Instead he pivoted in the center of the street. He would get to the hospital. But he wasn't going to desert Theodora again.

For a third time, he said to himself as he began to run.

"But Teddy, you really have to stop doing this," John muttered, his breath puffing out in the cold as he crossed the bridge. *If she kept fleeing the scene of the crime people were going to start to talk. Keep talking, more accurately.*

John slowed to a stop across the river. He assumed she'd gone west, away from the Assembly buildings and back toward Adelaide's. But he had no idea what route she'd take, or if that was even where she was headed.

He could still see the lights outside the Governor's house, the sconces opened wide and the detectives' lanterns glowing, when he turned. The press would arrive any moment.

The river was green and grey and white. Flags on the bridge posts snapped, and some would surely tear before the night was over.

Then the wind stilled. John smelled fresh water. Warmth.

But when he looked up at the star-filled sky there were no clouds, no rain. He sniffed the air, feeling like Theodora's dog, and as he found the source of the smell he found something else as well.

"Holy hell," he breathed out.

The first time he and Theodora argued, not one of the childish fights that had blown through constantly and quickly while they were growing up, but a real argument, they'd been sixteen or seventeen.

Soon before he went away. It was at her parents' annual solstice party, when it seemed everyone from the surrounding area passed through Ashe House. At night there had been a roast and dancing that spilled onto the patio, down the steps, into the grass.

At some point during the dancing, after too much liquor, he'd said something foolish. He couldn't recall what he'd said, perhaps he hadn't even known at the time. But Theodora had disappeared in an instant while his back was turned, and when he noticed her absence the shock was strong and bracing. It was the first time he realized how much he took her presence for granted.

John had gone after her, calling out her name in the dark. He wandered further from the crowd, passing couples at the outskirts, lights strung up in the giant trees dotting the property. Eventually he found the fog and then he'd found her.

Now a low current of fog ran south along the riverbank, very low to the ground. The lick of its tail, closest to him, was already beginning to dissipate, and he ran to catch it. The tendrils wound around his ankles, warm and wet.

John ran after the fog, down into the park. When it started to thin a little, threatening to disappear into the river, he ran faster. He was almost where the park met the forest when the fog ended. Across the water there were markets and banks; warehouses and factories, some of them his own. But the trees here, fed by the river which was fed by the glacier, were high and thick enough that he could pretend none of that was there at all. Nothing except for Theodora, sitting on a boulder with her dog beside her, for all the world as though she'd been out for a stroll.

29

River Park
City of Mooring
Night, December 5, 1947

Theodora saw John coming.

More than that, she felt him as that damned fog spun out behind her and thickened each time she took a step. She'd felt him the second the fog wrapped around his legs.

She hadn't thought about where she was going, only that she must run away. It was well and good to want the world to think she was a witch, but not if would make her the prime suspect in a murder. Again.

So she'd run as soon as she could get her legs to move once more, while the rest of the dinner party guests were trying to stop the bleeding. And then before she'd known what was happening there it was: magic, seeping from every part of her.

She'd wanted to cry when she realized it. *Why now, finally, after all this time?* But even then she hadn't stopped running. Especially not then. Magic would only make her look more guilty.

Though running doesn't exactly make you look innocent, you ninny.

When John entered the fog it brought her back to herself. She'd been in a panic, barely seeing, and he made the edges of the world seem real again. She realized Diana was beside her, that they should cut down into the riverside park to avoid being seen. No one would be there now except other lovers.

Lovers. I meant lovers.

When Theodora arrived at the small circle of rocks, surrounding a rose garden all clipped for the winter, she'd been so out of breath she'd had no choice but to stop. Plus it was evident by then, by the warm current running back through the fog and all over her skin, that John was going to catch up to her. So she arranged herself as artfully as possible, told Diana to stay and try not to fall asleep, and waited.

And now John was here. And coming closer.

She composed her face. *He will not catch me off-guard for a third time in so many days.* She sat up taller on the very cold boulder. Diana was cooperating, looking regal in the dissipating mist.

"Good girl," Theodora whispered. Diana sneezed.

John stopped several feet away and tipped his hat to them. So ridiculous, and so like him, to have managed to keep it on while in pursuit. "Good evening, Teddy," he said. *At least he's out of breath.* "Just wanted to make sure you're all right?"

She was not all right. She'd just seen a man murdered and then run halfway across town for fear of being thought the murderer. She was shaking beneath her skirts, though she couldn't tell if that was because of the cold or shock.

"I'm quite fine, thank you," she said.

"Oh," John replied, and she was glad to see that for once he was the one unsteadied, at least until she had to look away from the concern on his face. At her feet, Diana's tail began to thump heavily.

"Would you rather I leave you alone then?" he asked.

Would I?

"I only left because I didn't want to be photographed," she said, in lieu of answering.

He nodded. "I understand."

"And also because –" For a horrifying moment Theodora thought she might cry. "Is Victoria all right?"

John shook his head. "No."

They were silent for a long moment, leaning a little bit towards the space between them without noticing they were doing it. He looked so warm after running, steam was nearly coming off him.

"Why would anyone –" Theodora began, the words rushing out.

"I have no idea," John said. He pounded one fist into the other palm. "I haven't been paying enough attention, Teddy! The politics. This damned city."

She slumped on the rock. "I haven't either. Not nearly enough attention. I've been trying to help my family." *Help myself, really.* "And all the while people have been making plans for me, using my name for their causes, it seems. I can't believe the Governor – and then even poor Minister White –" Theodora shivered violently.

John slid out of his jacket and held it out. "Please?" She hesitated but took it from him; it was warm inside, the silk lining nearly hot. He was only two feet away now, how had that happened? Diana whined, wanting attention.

Theodora slid down from the rock suddenly and John took a step forward to support her. She held out a hand, nearly a warning, and he stopped.

"I need to be going," she said. "Back to Adelaide's. She'll be worried."

"Please," he said again. "Don't go yet."

Theodora threw up her hands, exasperated. "Especially right now, do you think it wise we're seen together? Do you think it'll help your career to be seen with me, John?" He opened his mouth to protest, but she pretended not to notice. "I need to – I don't know what I need to do! Everything's gone wrong. People are being murdered, John!"

"I know," he said. "Do you think I don't realize?"

"I'm sorry," she said, and pulled his jacket closer.

He took a step closer, and then another. "Let me help you."

He really did, she was sure. He would do whatever she asked, never mind that she'd come here with a mind toward taking advantage of him.

Truly, the man was infuriating.

"Nine years, John!" she burst out. "Nine damned years! Not a word? What the devil were you thinking?"

John took a step back, and for a moment she thought he might actually spin about and run away. Then he raised his eyebrows.

"I could say the same to you, couldn't I?"

She crossed her arms. "I'm not the one who left!"

"I'm not the one who got married! To Henry. Of all people."

She looked away, and pursed her lips. *Was I supposed to wait for you?* She looked back at him from the corner of her eye, and her face softened. "But your mother – I am so sorry."

John jammed his hands in his pockets. "Thank you," he said tightly. "I wasn't there. I can't believe I left her like that."

His face looked so open and so pained. "John," she said again. "I'm so sorry."

He shrugged and put on something like the smile she'd seen him give the other people at the dinner party. "I meant what I said: I want to help you navigate this situation, whatever it is."

Theodora sighed. "Oh, John. Too much time has passed. We're on opposite sides of the aisle, don't you think? Opposing poles, nearly literally. You're the vanguard: You're the reason they opened the borders. You're bringing us water and I'm the dried-up witch everyone's afraid of."

"That's rubbish, and you know it. All of that."

"Tell your father that, John," she said. "He's mentioned in those articles, the ones about the end of witchery and the beginning of our new modern future. So are you."

She thought of his study, full of artwork but none of it his own. The suit he wore to look exactly like every other upright businessman. He'd never wanted to end up that way and it made her ache, to see how much his life had followed the rutted road his father had ground into the earth.

"Teddy, that's not me! Don't accuse me of being him." He spoke so plaintively, desperate to be different from his father. She saw the boy she remembered. In her fingertips something twitched of the girl she'd been once, too.

"I know, I know – I'm sorry."

"I think he might be changing," John said, and laughed grimly. "Or at the very least dying."

I've never seen him look so sad.

"We should talk about how someone is trying to kill you," she said. *Dammit, Teddy.*

John's eyes grew wide and he barked out a laugh. "What? Me! Teddy, don't be ridiculous. Why would someone want to kill me? They're trying to kill you!"

Theodora threw up her arms. "Honestly, John! You have no idea the effect you have on people. Your importance to this island. But never mind that: a bomb went off in your own home!"

"Where you'd been invited!" he yelled, looking, if she wasn't incorrect, just a little amused. "What about you, Teddy? If anyone has no idea the effect they have on people…." He looked up at the sky, then took a deep breath and took a world-spanning step final toward her. Diana stood up, nose held high and pointed toward John's chin.

John sidestepped her neatly. They were so close, she could feel his breath on her face. Diana shoved her nose into his sternum.

"Me?" Theodora said, ignoring the dog as it began to nuzzle a footlong snout into John's pocket. *Why does my voice sound so strange, so breathless?* "How absurd, why would anyone want to kill me? I'm the past, John. The only reason anyone ever thinks of me at all anymore is as a novelty. My presence is a party trick to impress guests."

She thought of the magic she'd once been able to do, and for the first time in so long she felt its absence not with resignation, but like a hunger.

"I'm no threat to anyone," she said still more softly.

"Maybe they see something in you that you don't see in yourself," John said.

Theodora inhaled sharply, and a little bit of the fog rose up in front of her. "Don't you dare tell me I don't know myself, John Dove."

John looked down. "I'm sorry. I didn't mean it like that, I – I only meant that I think you'd be a wonderful threat, if you ever wanted to try. But maybe you're right. Maybe it doesn't matter what either of us want. Maybe it only matters how the world sees us."

Both their faces were shining now from the moisture of their voices. It was almost like they were inside a cloud and for a moment Theodora felt herself dissipating, dissolving into it.

She cocked her head. "Do you really believe that, John? That what you want matters so little?"

"Teddy," he breathed out. He leaned forward, as if he trusted the fog would catch him.

Maybe I could catch him, she thought. *Or maybe he'd never stop falling.*

"Maybe you're right," she said, and snapped herself back into focus. Her voice was crisp, and John shifted back on his heels. Diana finally pulled a forgotten candy from John's pocket and began to loudly eat through the paper wrapper. "I've spent the last nearly nine years hoping that if I just kept my head down everyone would leave me alone. And that doesn't seem to be the case? Whether they're trying to kill you or get to me, it seems they want us both involved."

Theodora rubbed the bridge of her nose. Creating the fog, whether she'd meant to or not, had exhausted her, and now she fought a yawn that could have split her face in two. She wished she could conjure up a swift wind to carry her home and then tuck her in.

Out of practice, she thought absently.

John looked away, staring at something far off. "You're right," he said, finally. "Perhaps it doesn't matter which one of us they're trying to kill. Only that we both survive. At least 'til the solstice?" he added, with a laugh. "I've got a boat ticket back."

Theodora took a deep breath of the night air. *'Til the solstice.* She could keep him alive. She could convince him to help her have a home to go back to. She could be a witch, until then.

And if someone really was trying to kill her – better not to die with unfinished business.

She stuck out her hand. "At least 'til then. Let's both survive, at least 'til then."

30

The Waters Just Beyond Wherewithal
Dates lost, est. early 18th century

THE ADVANCE PARTY returned to the ship and reported what they'd seen.

First there was the matter of getting everyone and everything up the sheer cliff faces –so helpful once they were all atop them, but problematic currently. The tools they'd brought were lightweight and rusted. Ropes had long ago been taxed to their fraying point, and many of the people on the ship were weak with hunger. The prospect of scaling a slippery, weed-crusted wall while proprietary birds shat from on high and curious insects skittered over your hands was not entirely appealing. For a moment there was only the sound of the waves.

"I can work with wood," one woman said. She'd travelled farther than any of the rest of them, having been forced across the ocean once before.

"We haven't any wood!"

"What about the ship?"

"We can't use the ship!"

"What the hell else are we going to use it for?"

She had a point, they all had to admit. Even if destroying the ship really meant no way back.

"And if we're trying to stay hidden it won't do to leave a giant ship docked off the coast, now will it?"

That decided it.

The ship pulled up tight and close against the island, much nearer than would have been considered safe in other circumstances. The women helped the wood-worker-woman build a ladder. They calmed the waters, strengthened the sickly and quieted the children, asked the birds to circumvent the area and made the insects lazy. They asked the sun to shine hotter to dry up the lichen and the moss and give them purchase. Their belongings were secreted away into bags that were much too small.

The men began to tear apart the ailing, battered boat, even as they all still stood on it. The weather was turning despite the shaft of sunlight shining down on them, and waves crashed against them. The men formed a chain and delicately passed planks to the wood-worker-woman.

The wood-worker-woman took each green-stained and slick plank in her hand, examined it front, back, and sideways, and hurled it like a spear off the prow of the ship. The planks landed on the cliff face as though they were being drawn home, and a ladder began to form in switchbacks and small bridges across the crevasse.

Before it was finished they began to shuttle the youngest and weakest up, as men balanced on the rock wall prying timbers apart with bleeding hands and women clung to the rock wall with necks craned up to catch anyone who slipped. At the end it was the wood-worker-woman and one young man who was the strongest swimmer, and then they went up, too.

When they were all up one of the women set fire to the ladder.

The southern bit of the island was a maze of canyons, and though it was dark by the time they'd all reached the top no one felt it was safe to rest. A little before dawn they came to the remains of a river. It flowed from the north and fell over the cliffs. The soil was dense and wet.

"Promising," said the captain.

"And uncanny," his wife said, but she smiled and took his hand.

31

City of Mooring
December 6, 1947

EVERYONE WALKED around reading the papers, casting suspicious glances at each other over the top of the newsprint. The shooter had not been found and the latest rumor was that the Agricultural Minister's seat had been switched at the last moment with John Dove's. Everyone agreed the boy wonder, the ice heir, had been the real target all along.

No one could remember when there'd been a murder last – certainly never by a gunshot through a window at a state dinner – and there were some who said it was a sign, that opening the borders had been wrong. A crime against the island.

Some said it was because the Widow Witch had come up. Everyone knew Theodora had been there.

There were no photos this time, but that was all the worse: People were free to imagine what she might have looked like, how she might have cackled over the corpse or controlled the bullet with a twist of her fingers. *The Sentinel* ran editorial cartoons in quick succession and when George told John that several of them ended up spiked through the wrought iron gate outside Adelaide's home, John ran out with his boots unlaced to buy every copy he saw. He burned them in the fireplace and the apartment smelled of ink and smoke for days.

It grew even colder: Pipes burst, and the streets turned to ice. It was not uncommon to see a woman's brilliant plaid skirts splayed out as she spun on her backside, or a man's wool trousers pushed up above the knees displaying bright orange socks as he tried to maintain some dignity.

The children loved it. They threw even more water on the sidewalks and donned skates.

Archibald sent reams of documentation for him to read and John spent a week reading through it all, or at least glancing at it, or at least turning the pages. He listened to the radio nearly all day long, and read all he could: underground pamphlets and student papers and last week's news newly shipped over from the continents on the ships which, already, were beginning to clog the waters just beyond the rocks. Everything about the war was worse than he could have imagined.

The Sentinel was breathless with news of those ships and with updates on the Widow Witch: The police had interviewed her at the Court Magistrate's house; the police were awaiting further evidence. The police had no other suspects and no other leads.

32

George Law's Apartment
After lunch, December 8, 1947

As JOHN SAT by the fireplace in George's apartment he felt his brain beginning to thaw. He'd spent too long isolated by his money and his family, tucked away with a job in the ice, far away from the drought. Thinking himself apart from everything, marking time in a ledger. The world began to take on some of its old color and heft. That was good, because he wanted to not sound an idiot when he talked to Theodora.

"Take a break from business," George told him after several days of returning from a day at classes – and the bar – to find John in the same spot he'd left him. "Your art's suffering."

"It would have to exist to suffer," John muttered without looking up.

John had written to the art store in town to stock up on supplies, as he always did when he was in town. But the paper, ink, and paint sat in the corner, beneath the steep angled ceiling of George's top-floor apartment. Picking up a paintbrush still seemed too frivolous. Or tempting.

"Then take another kind of break," George said, stirring up the moss in the grate with a sharp metal poker. "See Theodora?"

John did put his papers down. It was pointless, after all, to offer to help her if he never actually spoke to her.

He sent Theodora a note asking if they might meet. George didn't have his own chute, so John sent it through the public line in the pub downstairs with a bunch of tipsy university students surrounding him. *A bit sordid*, he thought. But a bit thrilling, too, like he was a student himself in love for the first time.

He was so nervous someone would intercept her reply he nursed a drink for three hours, leaping up every time there was another soft whoosh and thud of a letter coming in. He was beginning to think that perhaps his note had been misdirected, or a mole had eaten it. *Perhaps a pack of highly evolved, malicious earthworms?* Or, of course, she had just decided never to speak to him again.

When her reply finally came, he opened it right there in the pub, standing up:

Shall we meet at the Navigators' Club to discuss this cat-and-mouse game?

Signed, yours,
   a wicked black cat

John couldn't think of many places less appropriate for them to meet. He and his father had been members for several years and apparently they'd hired an excellent new chef ("Top-notch dolphin," George had said, in passing), but that was about all to recommend it. Only men were allowed membership and though the Club did admit entrance to women they were not necessarily – no, John was fairly positive they were not – the sort of women Theodora wanted to be confused with.

Unless she did? Gods, he wasn't sure of anything, truly.

There weren't many courtesans in Mooring. At least there weren't many who would call themselves such, but a thriving underground economy existed nonetheless. Most of the women were widows.

How about the Aurora? he wrote back, elbowing aside a drunken student who appeared to have gotten lost looking over John's right shoulder. The Aurora Luncheon Society was a big, bright spot atop Mooring's department store and it had been the height of fashion when his mother was a child. Now it was mostly populated by well-off ice distributors and hydraulic engineers who were terrified of getting on the Doves' bad side. They'd never gossip about John or Theodora. Or at the very least they'd do it discreetly. *Or I can come to Adelaide's,* he added hastily. *Hell, she could come to George's. The pub would be better.*

He put the letter in the chute, checked it had gotten off, and went upstairs to George's. Halfway up the stairs he stopped.

"Wicked black cat?" he said aloud.

The Navigators', she'd replied the next morning. *I've always wanted to see it from the inside. And I've heard they're very discreet. See you at 1.*

"Do you think she doesn't realize –?" he asked George, showing him the notes.

"It sounds like she understands perfectly," George replied, seeming vaguely amused. "She's right, they are very discreet."

Trying to change her mind seemed a good way to have the whole thing called off, and it was already nearly eleven. John picked up his coat.

"I'll come," George said.

"Why do you need to come? We don't need a chaperone, George."

"The sol meuniere. And I'm your alibi, obviously," George said, seeming willfully oblivious about how much John wanted to go it alone. "I'll get dressed. Won't be a moment."

"I thought you hated these people," John muttered.

"I don't hate them," George called from his bedroom. "I dislike many of them – yourself excluded, of course – but I have a real esteem for the founders. They believed in science and humanity and exploration. Check, check, check. And they're all dead now."

"Ah. Crucial point."

33

Navigators' Club
Assembly District
Afternoon, December 9, 1947

THE DOOR OPENED on an entryway bathed in warm red from lamps filled to the brim with algae suspension. It smelled of sweat and the necessity of removing layers, and of the various vegetal matter being smoked by the members.

"It's hot as Hades," John said under his breath to George as the butler took their coats.

"Keeps the elderly limber," George said, nodding his head toward the men seated in high-backed armchairs in the lounge. "Though ice might be more prudent at this stage. Get me when you're through?" At that he clapped John on the shoulder and strode off across the club, to where John had no idea.

John had reserved a private room. He made his way across the lounge, nodding to his father's associates. Archibald was still housebound. *Perhaps a little better than when I arrived?* He seemed so changed from how John had known him before, so willing to engage his son in – *well, in conversation for one thing* – that it was hard to tell what the state of his health truly was.

Not that there ever would have been much chance of stumbling upon the elder Dove at the Navigators'. Archibald Dove, keenly aware of all things at all times, knew what people thought of him: that he was a cold, ruthless merchant whose ice kept the island from withering away entirely, but who'd made plenty of enemies along the way.

That was at least partly, John knew, why his father had kept him sequestered on the ice. It kept John untarnished in public opinion. It kept him pure, and positioned for bigger, better things. *Preserved.*

Almost enough to give me a complex, too, really.

John swung open the door of their private room. Theodora sat on the window seat, peering through the blinds, Diana on the floor. Theodora hadn't heard him enter, it seemed, and John was struck by how at ease she looked, how fascinated by the world below. He was struck, too, by how ill-at-ease she seemed with him, by comparison.

Algae burned in the grate and it made her skin and hair glow in a way that made the trappings of the club seem much more modern. Like everything was done knowingly, with a wink and a crooked grin. *She was right: She does fit in here.* But at the same time she looked like some alien queen come here to study the customs of Earth. (*And find a mate,* he thought, then cursed himself.)

"Hello again." He nodded to the dog. "And Diana, good afternoon."

Theodora turned, smiling, as if she'd known he was there all along, and was already reaching across the table for the pitcher of ale as he slid into the banquette beside her. Her own glass was already half-empty.

"How have you been, John?"

"Exhausted." He laughed, realizing how true it was. "Attempts on your life take a toll, it seems. But I'm still alive, so I shan't complain."

Theodora smiled, and her glow erupted into something more brilliant that reached down into John's body and sparked a flint.

"Let's keep it that way, shall we?"

She reached to the seat next to her and pulled up a heavy folder, and then another and another until she'd stacked them as high as the ale bottle. "I knew a bit about the politicians because, well, they're always talking about me. Adelaide's been helping me fill in the bits I didn't know. I need your help with the businessmen. The money. It's usually the money, I've found, that makes people the most willing to act irrationally."

She looked as lively as he'd ever seen her: working like this, having a mission, was good for her. John thought briefly to the stack of art supplies moldering in the corner of George's apartment.

He raised his eyebrows at the stack. "I'll tell you what I can, but I'm not sure how much more help you need at this point."

She shook her head. "No, no, I've been so out of touch," she went on.

"Come now. It worked brilliantly the other night," he said, smiling warmly.

She looked confused. "What did?"

"The – the touch? Witchery? The fog?"

Fuck. He'd misunderstood, and she looked in a complete panic.

But then she recovered, somewhat. The ease had left her and she went a little farther away from him once more.

"Oh yes. That. I do that all the time. You know." She picked up her glass and brought it to her mouth. "Fog," she said before draining the rest of the beer.

John considered how much to ask. He had assumed all these years that the drought was beyond her ken, that she hadn't been able to generate enough water or change the course of weather systems that swirled in huge from across the Atlantic. Nothing about her seemed not strong enough, though.

Theodora put her glass down with force and turned to him with a challenge in her eye.

"Well then let's get started," he said.

She smiled and pushed the papers closer toward him. "Come see," she said.

They annotated margins and scribbled outlines. A man came in to turn up the lamps on the wall and stoke the fire. The ale bottle emptied, and then another.

It was surprising and – he was embarrassed to admit – a bit flattering to realize the scope of his influence. Or the scope of influence that his absence might create, which was very nearly the same.

They started on the ice and moved down: workers at the mines; the captain of the ship who'd brought him here; Ned the butler was ruled out since he didn't seem the type to get his hands dirty. There were at least five prominent families who stood to gain from the removal of Dove Holdings' heir; men who would like to extend their influence and their investments into algae and ice mining.

None of the foreign visitors who'd been at the Governor's dinner seemed to still be in Mooring ,but none of whom could be found on departing ships' passenger lists, either. Three widowed sister from adjacent holdings along the cliffs in the south, who'd entwined themselves already with foreign investments and might be eager to extend contracts in the absence of a strong domestic player, were added to the list.

And that was just John. It turned out there were a lot of people who might want one or both of them dead.

"Perhaps we should discuss anyone you may have inadvertently angered?" John asked, carefully. "Anyone who's lobbied to create a guardianship of the south, perhaps?" There'd been talk of taking over administration of the cliff farms, as though the drought were a failure of the people who lived there. He meant, too, that Theodora had always had something of a temper. A righteous one, for sure, but he'd been on the wrong end of it enough times to know –

"Like you, for instance?"

Right. Good luck with that then. "Oh. I suppose hadn't thought of that," he began lightly. "Should I – hmm – should I add myself then?"

"John!" Theodora laughed. "I'm joking. You truly are the most selfless man," she added, smiling sideways at him.

He felt his face go hot. "Right. Yes. Sorry. Damn it, Theodora," he said, starting to laugh, and she laughed harder.

In Mooring the most likely suspects seemed the Ministers for Trade,

Botany, and Women. They'd all have their power and investments upset if Theodora consolidated Henry's land with her own family's, or if she pushed for more water rather than more development and used her status as a witch as leverage.

And of course if she ended the drought much of the reason for international expansion dried up instead.

Theodora went quiet for the first time since they'd begun, and John bit his lip. Sitting here, working with her so closely, he could forget that their interests really were at odds, at least in her mind.

"I hope you know," he began, "that I never intended to disrupt the land –"

"You're blowing up the mountain" she said sharply.

He sighed. "We are trying to do it in as ecologically sensitive –"

"And as quickly as possible," she said, sharply again but also sad. *Disappointed.*

Why the devil am I defending this? he thought.

He leaned back heavily against the seat, pulling one leg up to turn more fully toward her. "You're right. I've been arguing the same thing, to no avail. I don't know why I'm giving you my father's answer for it. I'm not happy about the speed of it, and I'm not sure what to do."

Theodora was watching him, no judgment in her eyes.

"Perhaps I've been ignoring the severity of the situation," he said. "Or what I might do about it."

She put a hand on his knee, in as chaste a manner as possible that did absolutely nothing to keep a thrill from running up his leg. "I've been guilty of that, too, haven't I," she said. "I think," she said slowly, "that what must matter for both of us is what we do from now on. To not look back."

John swallowed hard. Her hand was still on his knee. He nodded. "I believe you're right. Shall we keep going?" His voice was dry.

"I'd like to. It's been so long without anyone understanding really," her voice faded and she turned back to the table. She lifted her hand to pick up her pen, and he felt the absence of her touch like a sudden hunger. "But perhaps we'll be of more use to the island generally if neither of us is dead?"

"Right," he said, trying to recover. "So any other enemies, then?"

"I have been spat at several times," Theodora said.

"Spat at!" *I'll murder them myself.*

She waved her hand. "It's harmless. If quite rude. More eccentric than psychotic. I rather doubt any of the spitters have the means to put together a bomb, anyway. It'd have to be someone with wealth, and access to materials and we've already listed all those."

"That's all, then," he said. "Just an in-depth analysis of who might be trying to kill one of us."

"Nothing to it," she said, smiling a little grimly. "Are you hungry?"

John worried for a moment that she could read everything on his face, before realizing what she meant.

"Starving. Late lunch?"

"Let's," Theodora said, "I'll fetch the attendant."

John watched her disappear around the doorway, then looked back at their pages.

What have we forgotten? Or rather, who?

There was a caution and a wariness to her now that hadn't always been there. How close he'd come to ending up on the wrong side of those walls, and could still. It was painful, and damned enraging. Because Theodora, since they'd been young, had only ever wanted to do good.

To think people once came here once to escape from persecution.

Theodora came back, hands full of food and drink, and used her hip to shut the door behind her. John felt the warmth of her presence spread over his entire body; perhaps that was what made him notice that frost had gathered around the windowpanes. It reminded him of being in the north. *How beautiful it had been to live there*, he realized for the first time, *but also how much better it was to have Theodora with him in the cold.*

"Welcome back," he said as she slid next to him. *Was she closer than before? Yes. Perhaps?*

He had to calm down.

"It's good to be back," she said, as she began to pour out two glasses. She lowered her head and squinted at them to make sure they were exactly even, and he felt the warmth in his stomach burn a bit like a fire. "In the city, too."

"Is it?" he said, a bit surprised. "I thought you hated Mooring."

"You're one to talk," she said, taking a sip. "How long have you been on the glacier?"

"Hard at work," he said, picking up his glass and tipping it to her. "Hard at work hiding. But truly, aren't you just itching to get back home?"

John, you utter fool, he thought.

Theodora considered her reply, and he couldn't read her face. "I am. I mean that was the plan. Is the plan," she said. "But it's nice to see everyone," she added, and looked deep into her glass. "It's especially nice to see you, John."

He felt as though he could have burst out into a song-and-dance number on the tabletop.

Tell her, tell her, tell her! Tell her you hesitated, tell her you were a fool boy, tell her you always took her for granted only because you couldn't imagine a world in which the two of you weren't together.

She glanced up at him with bright eyes. John picked up his drink. He took a long swallow to steel his nerves.

"But I do think we should speak about Henry," she said. He nearly choked.

"Erm?" he got out, thumping his chest.

"It's so important to me, that you know, John – "

Perhaps this what it's like to be drawn and quartered.

"— that you know I didn't actually kill him." Theodora smiled, bright and ever so nervous, and he wanted to take her in her arms and kiss her right then and there.

But she was still staring at him. Asking for his trust.

"Yes, Teddy," he said, as serious as he could be. "I know that. Have always known that. I swear it."

She exhaled loudly and drained the last of her drink. "Gods' wounds, that's good to hear!"

"Teddy, do you –"

"Think Henry might be behind this?" she tapped her fingers against the table, looking away from him. John's words caught in his throat.

"What? Henry?" he said, so caught off-guard he nearly laughed. He supposed Henry's philosophical leanings did put him at odds with Dove Holdings – that the glacier was sacred, that mining was destroying not just the island but the people who lived on it.

Damn it. I agree with bloody Henry.

"Perhaps we should add him to the list, just to be safe?" she asked.

It did make a sort of sense. Henry had always been a radical, and was one of the few people who would think to connect Theodora with himself. He didn't like to think it possible of the skinny, bookish boy that he'd known — but then he didn't like to think many things possible of Henry Martin which were, quite obviously, very much true. Like that he was the one Theodora had wanted, above all others.

"But isn't," he said, picking out his words carefully, "and as I said I do not you're not the cause, but isn't it still safe to say that—"

"Henry is dead? There was never a body, John," she said, and he heard the tightness in her voice as she said it.

"Yes, of course not," he replied quickly. "Sorry."

he scrawled *Henry Martin* on the list. John even hated seeing the ease with which she wrote it. *You're jealous of a dead man. Maybe dead. Definitely undeserving.*

He tried to smile. "Though if I'm honest Henry seemed much more the type to write a stern letter. I always thought he was just waiting for the right moment to corner me for a heart-to-heart, rather than an assault."

Unless Henry knew, of course. Unless he knew more than John had known until quite recently: That John still loved Theodora and always had.

Theodora put the pen down and smiled up at him as brightly as she could manage: Speaking of Henry with John seemed sacrilegious, though she couldn't quite tell who she was offending. "Anyone else then?"

John shook his head.

"Me either. Not George Law, surely. You're living with him so he'd have done it by now even if he was a truly terrible assassin. And I doubt that Adelaide has designs on our lives. Unless she's been dressing me for the funeral pyre this whole time."

Theodora didn't know why she'd been so set on meeting at the Navigators' Club. *A fit of pique*, Adelaide had called it, seeming delighted. It had been the decision of a moment to dash it off in her reply to John, but from the start it had felt completely right to be here. Like she'd passed through a door into a realm where things actually were accomplished rather than just talked about. Even if that door had been around back, in an alley, just past a pile of manure from the stables across the way. Adelaide had told her about the women's entrance – the "widows' walk," they called it.

Theodora suddenly became conscious of the flush in her cheeks, and the way the edges of the room seemed a little fuzzier than the hour or the worn down algae embers should have warranted. John was very close to her now; her dress against his leg, his leg nearly against her own. He seemed so very real after so long away. So very fragile.

She smoothed her skirts and then her hair back into place. "I'm afraid I've kept you too long?"

John looked like he'd woken from a trance. "What? Teddy, no. I want to help you."

"It doesn't all need to be done tonight," she said, beginning to straighten up their cups and plates. She didn't know what to do with her hands suddenly. "It's nearly dinner, and I don't want you to exert yourself overmuch. Look it's past five already," she said, nodding to the ancient clock on the mantle, an ornate and patchwork piece that must have crashed against the cliffs two hundred years ago at least.

John opened his mouth. *He has a beautiful mouth, doesn't he?*

She stood up so fast she nearly upset the table, though it was nailed down like in a ship's mess. "A lot to think about, yes? A lot to sort through. I could use to be alone for a little while. We'll meet again, though," she added, unable to keep the nervousness from her voice. "Won't we?"

It was a damned tricky business keeping him at just the right distance away; she'd spent years doing it when they were younger, and look how that turned out.

"I promise if you do?" He was smiling but still sitting down, staring up at her with calm eyes. Like he really would wait for her.

"Promise," she said, raising an eyebrow, trying to sound coy. *I need you, John*, she added in her mind.

They stayed like that for a long moment, until John shook his head as if he'd just awoken. "I did tell George I'd meet him. He might be waiting. Or getting into trouble. Anyway I believe I'm meant to leave first."

John actually blushed, and Theodora fought a smile.

"George was here?" she asked.

"Yes, why?"

"Adelaide insisted on accompanying me, and said she'd wait at the bookstore on the corner. I'd assumed she'd left by now, but —"

"Hmm."

"You know then? About the affair? Apparently it's been going on for months. Or had been."

"Yes, I did hear about that part."

"Harmless?" Theodora asked. She felt a bit like they were talking about their children.

John shrugged. "Is anything?"

"I suppose not," Theodora said. "What's the alternative, though, I suppose?"

John stood and banged his knee hard against the table edge. Theodora sat.

"I'll wait until you leave," she said.

"Hmm? Yes. Funny business." He tried to extricate himself and banged against the table again. Theodora pursed her lips not to laugh. She hadn't seen him this flustered in –

Her smile fell away.

"Just the way things are done, I suppose," she said, and folded her hands on her lap. "We'll be in touch? My best to Victoria."

"What? Oh. Yes." He was backing out of the room. "I will. Good-night, Teddy." Finally he turned, just before slamming his head against a sconce.

Theodora stared as the door closed. She took up her drink and leaned against the banquette. Someone would come get her when it was safe, when John was clear of the building and the hallways weren't too full.

Once it had seemed like such a relief, to no longer be the subject of anyone's attention or fear. It was different, though, sitting in this building full of people who had never questioned that they might act, or that they might be allowed to speak and have anyone listen.

The steward would be in soon. He'd ask, kindly, if there was anything else she needed, when really he meant was there anything else she was needed for. Then she'd make her way down the narrow stairwell in the back.

But until then she'd sit here, and reminisce about the last time John Dove had seemed so flustered in her presence.

John collected his hat and coat from the doorman.

"Mr. Law left approximately an hour ago, sir."

John paused with his hat held just above his head.

"Yes, of course he did." *Well good for him.* John smashed the hat down on his head with unexpected force. "Mistress Ashe is to have the room as long as she likes."

The butler nodded and made a small note on a sheaf of paper hanging from the wall. It seemed members left women sitting in reserved rooms for quiet exits all the time. *What a club I've joined.*

John took the steps three at a time, half-hoping he'd slip on the ice and fall flat on his ass, just to punish himself for his own inability to make a damned decision. He used the cloud his breath made as a fog to obscure his face and ignore several navigators coming in for a late drink. As he continued down the sidewalk he was aware something was wrong but unsure what it was. Something other than Teddy. Other than himself.

At the corner he stopped.

"Ice?" he said aloud. What the devil.

He looked up to the club and found the window where he and

Teddy had sat. There, on the window ledge, were piles of fluffy white snow. It was snowing still.

And silhouetted in the window was Teddy in profile, raising a glass to her mouth.

34

Southern Departments, headed north on foot
Very early, December 23, 1938

THEODORA HAD TRIED to do magic for him last night. He was sure it would've been beautiful. He hoped she'd still do it for him when he got back.

Unless she murders me first for leaving.

In the quiet dawn, halfway across a field gone fallow for the winter, Henry smacked himself hard with the palm of his hand against his temple. *This had been a terrible plan. Terrible. It had seemed so romantic at the time, when he'd thought about it far too much in the lead-up to his wedding!* Because what did you get a witch who had everything?

You got her the one thing she didn't have: a mother.

Henry knew how he came across: Overly serious, overly quiet, overly concerned with abstract notions and ideals instead of, say, how to keep a farm running or how much sleep one needed not to go slightly batty.

Theodora had never seen him that way. She'd seen that there was a real, breathing person underneath all the things that made his brain run in circles. And she'd been willing to indulge all those circles, too, and pull him out of them when necessary.

Still he worried that maybe everyone was right after all. Maybe he was all talk. Then what better way to prove himself a man of action than to leave in the dark of his wedding night on a quest, a real, damned quest, to bring back his wife's long-lost mother? From what Theodora had told him, Henry didn't believe the island's second-to-last witch had abandoned her daughter. Henry believed that Marguerite Ashe knew something the rest of them didn't, about the mountains and what was happening below the surface after all this earth-forsaken mining had been eating away at the island for years.

Something must have happened to her inside the mountain. Henry was going to get her out. That was why he hadn't let Theodora do magic for him last night. It was going to be a gift and, well – it wouldn't be right to not give anything in return. How would it look to her if he sat there naked and empty-handed as she dazzled and performed and did things he could only dream of doing?

She thought magic was all she had to offer. At some level that must have to do with her mother going missing. This would make them equals, too, and he wanted above all a marriage of equals.

There you go again, he thought, *psychoanalyzing*. He shook his head and stamped his feet against the cold.

Did it really matter why he was going? Even if it was to prove to himself he was worthy of her? Even if his own interests and unquenchable desire for the truth made the discovery of whatever information Marguerite Ashe might have about the island of utmost, paramount, unavoidable interest?

What mattered was that he brought Theodora's mother home.

Assuming she was still alive. Assuming he was able to defeat whatever an actual, fully grown, incredibly powerful witch hadn't been able to defeat in the first place.

Assuming Theodora didn't refuse to speak to him ever again and run off north into the arms of John Dove.

Henry smacked himself in the head again as he crested a rise and the sliver of moon faded from view. It really had been the most terrible idea. But he was here now, standing beside a scarecrow guarding nothing, amid a field of rotting potatoes, half a mile from a solid wall of rock that had its own peculiar, angry ecosystem.

Except it mustn't be solid. It must have an opening somewhere, because they'd traced Marguerite here years ago and then no further. And if Henry was ethereal and absent-minded, if he was idealistic and he was radical, well then: *who better to find a way to walk into a wall of solid rock?*

35

Outerbridge Estate
Night, December 9, 1947

THEODORA OPENED the door to Adelaide's house and ran directly into George.

They both grunted and Theodora nearly upset a vase. George recovered and took several steps neatly sideways, like a dancer in a show. It seemed George was also good at repressing his reactions.

"Hello, Mr. Law," Theodora said, smoothing her hair. She'd walked the riverside path after leaving the Navigators', and the moisture in the air had given her a halo.

"Hello, Mistress Ashe-Martin," George said, already walking past her. He barely looked up as he moved quickly across the threshold and down the steps.

She watched him go then turned inside.

Adelaide always maintained a skeleton staff when her husband was away. Theodora wandered through the near-empty house with its half-lit lights glowing green and blue off the white-painted stone walls. The hallways were too wide, the ceilings too tall, designed for display rather than living.

Adelaide's wing was a little warmer. Her footsteps were hushed by thick carpets; the walls were painted pale lavender and hung with paintings that reminded Theodora of lying in the grass as a child, feeling the earth spin beneath her. Washes of color and far-off perspectives.

When Theodora got to Adelaide's open bedroom door all she could see was one hand extending past the side of a chaise lounge, swinging a nearly empty martini glass. Theodora leaned against the doorframe and sighed loudly.

"Oh don't, please, darling," Adelaide said without turning. "Let's not spoil what little fun I'm afforded." Her voice had an edge, not only from the booze. Theodora straightened and walked over to her. Adelaide had been crying.

Theodora dropped to her knees. "What is it? Is it George? What did he do to you?" Theodora's elbow knocked into something metallic; a vial tipped over on the glass table behind her and knocked into a needle that had been discarded carelessly and was dampening a stack of mail.

She looked back at Adelaide, whose eyelids fluttered.

"What has he done?" Theodora asked, her entire body tense. *I can still catch him.*

Adelaide had enough of her senses remaining to roll her eyes. In fact, she didn't seem far gone at all, or at least was enough used to this sort of thing to pull herself together.

She shook her head delicately, like a bird in a bath, and sat up with exaggerated grace. "Oh stop it, Ted. George hasn't done anything at all." Some part of Adelaide remembered she'd been crying, and tears began to roll down her cheeks once more even as her veneer didn't crack. "In fact that's why we were arguing. That's why he's gone. He said he can't – how did he put it – he can't watch me do this to myself."

She tried to laugh and took a sip from her empty glass. "Do it to myself!" she spat, anger distorting her features. "I said he should come away with me, then, finally. But of course he said no. Again. Said that he couldn't support me. Couldn't take me away from my entire life. My life! But he's afraid, Ted. That's all, scared and pathetic. He doesn't love me as much as I love him at all." She cracked and the last words came out as a wail. Adelaide fell forward into Theodora's arms, and Theodora only just managed not to fall over.

"Oh darling," Theodora said, holding on tight, trying to keep them both up. "I'm so sorry. I had no idea. Poor George," she murmured, looking back out the doorway, and Adelaide pulled away.

"Poor George!" Her eyes were barely focused but in that moment Theodora still felt a little afraid of her friend's anger. Her power and intelligence, and the way she knew half as well again as anyone else how the world really worked.

"Not poor George," Theodora said quickly, pulling them both to their feet. She began to lead Adelaide toward the bed. "Poor both of you. Poor you, mostly, really. Obviously. Shall I get us some water?"

Adelaide nodded. "And champagne?" An over-bright smile lit her face. "Come sleep in bed with me and we'll talk. I want to hear how your day with John went!"

"Of course, Addy. You lie down. Be right back."

When Theodora returned with a pitcher of water and a sturdy glass, Adelaide had fallen asleep with her heels still on, both of them dangling over the edge from her toes. Theodora gathered her up onto the bed, dampened the light, then climbed into bed beside her. She lay a hand on her friend's skinny leg and listened to Adelaide's steady breath. *That was good, at least.*

"Ted?" Adelaide's eyes were still closed but her face was lit up like she was at a dinner party. She sounded faintly amused.

"Yes?" Theodora whispered, leaning closer.

"You've got a letter." Adelaide gestured with a lazy finger toward the drugs. "They want you to come state your case, darling. So very unusual, I'm sure everyone will be there, even the people with the good spots already booked at the springs. It means it's working, darling! But really it's a testament to you. You are a testament, darling. Really highly unusual," she murmured, and then she was gone again.

Theodora watched Adelaide for a long moment, half-expecting some new string of vocabulary to pour forth. But her breathing grew deep, and Theodora extricated herself from the bed.

A floodgate of correspondence had opened to her since coming to Mooring, and Theodora found the usual: Requests for interviews from *The Sentinel* and the *Mirror & Candle*, the portrait magazine; but also from several newly arrived foreign reporters. Death threats accusing her of malicious witchcraft, or at the very least nefarious feminine wiles, against the proud and heroic John Dove. Or against the mysterious young Henry Martin, whom the letter writers seemed to recall in only very vague terms, except for their certainty that he must have been cut down at the start of a glorious career by the Widow Witch.

She got some fan mail, too.

Adelaide insisted they send all the notes to the Magistrate's office for analysis. They'd yet to hear anything back.

There were invitations to luncheon, too. Even if Theodora might be a murderess she was also very good social currency.

She pushed them all to the side, unopened. At the bottom of the stack, pockmarked with whatever was making its way through Adelaide's system, was a thick card in the mint green of Assembly correspondence:

The presence of Mistress Ashe is requested at the closing of the autumn session of the minister's government, 8am, December 10.

Theodora turned the paper over but there was nothing more. She supposed when one was requested to Assembly chambers, there was only one response. *A full day to prepare, at least.*

She tossed the paper on the table, then crawled under the blanket next to Adelaide. It was early still but she was so tired. Overwhelmed, really. Sleep would be a respite.

Maybe Adelaide would be more receptive to talking in the morning. It seemed they had more than Theodora's political future to discuss. As Theodora fell asleep she wondered whether all her life would be dictated by missives from unseen men, sending paper airplanes determining her fate down from the darkness and the rafters.

36

Archibald Ashe's Townhouse
Assembly District
City of Mooring
Before breakfast, December 10, 1947

W<small>HEN HE RETURNED FROM THE</small> N<small>AVIGATORS</small>' the landlady gave him the message: Archibald Dove requested, if one could call it that, John's presence at his bedside first thing tomorrow.

John wanted to help Theodora any way that he could. He wanted to help her even more than he wanted to help himself. *I never did have a great sense of self-preservation*, he thought, *so why start now?*

So that strengthened his resolve as he lifted his knuckles to knock on his father's door the next morning. It was still dark out and bitingly cold, and John's hand stung after he rapped.

He was going to help her, no matter how much her needs ran counter to his family's goals. *Damn Archie's legacy. Damn my own, blighted, political future.* If things kept going the way they had been, he'd be dead before Solstice anyway. *Henry wasn't the only one who got to be a martyr.*

He was chuckling darkly to himself when the butler opened the door. The man, ageless since John was a child, raised an eyebrow but said nothing as he turned and led the way.

The door to Archibald's room was open, and inside a new nurse backed away with bent head to reveal John's father, sunk still deeper into a sea of blankets. Archibald reviewed a sheaf of papers on a lap table with a slight smile on his face and though John hated himself for it, all he could think was that illness might have mellowed his father for the better.

"Hello John," his father said, barely audible. John smoothed his coat and strode inside. He took up a position between two chairs and folded his arms. *Do not be swayed*, he told himself. *So he's an old man, that doesn't mean he's not a self-righteous ass. He's just an old one.*

Archibald looked up and smiled. Not warmly, exactly, but not sarcastically either. "Do sit, boy. You'll tire me out standing."

Caught off-guard, John sat.

Archibald had never looked well, not even in photos from youth. He was a pallid man, looking as though he had eaten not quite enough of something that was right on the cusp on being spoiled. But for all that, for the first time John remembered his father seemed vulnerable.

"How are you feeling?" John asked.

Archibald returned to his work. "Determined. Lots to do to get ready."

John waited, unsure if his father was awaiting a business opportunity or death, or if he'd found some way to make them one and the same.

"You wanted to see me?" John asked finally.

Archibald put down his pen. Another nurse materialized with coffee and a pastry. John had never known his father to eat pastry — had he ever eaten breakfast at all, before? — but now the old man took an over-large bite, flakes of dough falling onto the desk and jam smearing his fingers. He didn't finish chewing before beginning to speak.

"I called you here because I'd like you to attend the closing of Assembly tomorrow. As a representative of the family."

John's mouth fell open slightly. It was tantamount to abdication. Archibald took another bite and lurid orange spilled on his chin. "Yes, I know. Bet you thought it wouldn't happen until I was in the grave. But I'm near enough."

"I –"

"Don't get excited. I'm still here. You've been working hard, and my name – our name –has not suffered for it. You must claim what is past due."

John tensed and relaxed all at once, recognizing the father he knew. "And what would that be?"

"This drought is like a war. A tragic opportunity. Do you know I've had six new contracts just this week for ice? Three for algae to go overseas. We're on triple shifts."

John opened his mouth but his father held up a hand.

"Tell me, what would our workers be doing up there, if not for us? Eating algae and digging in the dirt? What would the ice be doing, for that matter?"

John laughed drily. "Ice needn't have a utility, Father."

Archibald assessed the page before him. Then he signed with a flourish and grimaced – *perhaps that was meant to be a smile, damned if I've ever been able to tell* – up at his son. "Perhaps. But John, what a tragedy. To not become the fullest manifestation of what you could have been. Don't you believe so?

John opened his mouth again, and though his father didn't go on, John didn't know what to say. This wasn't how they spoke to each other: Thoughtfully, philosophically; opportunistically, yes, but still. *Where was this while I was growing up? This man I could have dealt with. Or known at all.*

"It's not so much the ice I'm worried about, father," John said carefully, after a moment. "Nor myself, if I may be so bold. It's the entire landscape we're altering. Very quickly, without quite knowing what we might be changing. It's rather thin ice, you know," he said, and tried to laugh.

"The places where the ice is thin is where it's easiest to drill, boy."

Archibald shook his head and then said, talking mostly to himself, "I would have thought you'd realized by now. Assembly opens at 8:30 a.m. tomorrow. I'd not be late if I were you."

"Father, I –"

Archibald was taken by a violent coughing fit, his thin body doubled over at an angle, his head thrown back with each hack.

"Father! Nurse?" John yelled, jumping up.

With calm and militaristic detachment, the nurse rose and began to slap Archibald's back with what John found to be alarming force. The old man's face went red, then white, and John felt his own skin go clammy with panic. John stood, mouth open. *Damn it, he thought, make an effort!* The nurse began to inject something into his father's neck. Whatever was in the syringe glowed in the darkened room.

After a moment, wiping phlegm from his lips and chin, the fit passed. Archibald let himself be slid further down into the bed and rolled, with some effort, onto his side so he face away from his son. He shooed the woman away. John watched her retreat from the corner of his eye. Mostly he was concentrating on his father's arm, where the large vein throbbed a quickly dissipating neon blue.

"Algae!" his father said, as though he heard his son. Archibald slapped the injection site so hard John winced, with more force than he'd shown all evening. "Seems to be working, doesn't it? Hasn't killed me yet, at least." He settled deeper down, and the nurse threw a doily over the lamp to soften the glow of the same algae now coursing through his father's veins.

"I'll expect a report on the session tomorrow," Archibald said, and John realized he was being dismissed.

"I'll be there," he said, resigned, though it had never really been a question.

"Then we must talk about the engagement," his father said faintly, sounding half-asleep. "To Vicky White."

37

Outerbridge Estate
Too early, December 10, 1947

ADELAIDE WAS DECIDING when to open her eyes. She'd been awake for several minutes but it was of the utmost importance to time the actual opening of one's eyes in the morning very precisely. Especially when one was fond of spending evenings the way that Adelaide, increasingly, spent hers.

If she mistimed it or – devil forbid – sat up too quickly, the effects could be truly catastrophic. She stretched out her fingers and wiggled her toes on the silk sheets, taking up as much room as possible, testing if anything was aching. This was one advantage of a husband who, having in quick succession procured three boys via your reproductive system, henceforth wanted very little to do with you: Great expanses of covers and sheets and pillows, all to oneself.

It was, Adelaide thought, *very possibly the only advantage.*

She rolled out of bed and crossed the room to the window that overlooked the rock garden. She'd had it built there, an expanse of grey and white, last winter after the boys had gone. *An excellent way of pretending that no time was passing at all.*

She opened the curtains just a hair, leaning back so the light didn't crash in upon her, but the sun was already behind the house. *Noon. Not terribly bad at all.* She worked her jaw, and smiled a little at herself. *Well done, actually, Addy.*

Then she remembered Theodora's letter, come late last evening.

"Shit!" In quick order she threw open the curtains to force herself into wakefulness and strode to her dressing room. *We all must sacrifice in times like these,* she thought as she tied on a long silk dressing gown and hurried down a hallway that swayed like the deck of a ship.

Theodora was eating lunch in the solarium, or at least pretending to. Music warbled from the radio and Theodora stared into the center of a large potted fern, an uneaten triangle of sandwich held loosely in one hand.

Adelaide dropped the stack of newspapers she'd gathered from the butler. The crash on the table had the intended effect, though it didn't help Adelaide's headache.

"I believe it's well past time to outline our strategy for Assembly," Adelaide said.

Theodora raised one eyebrow. "Isn't it my strategy?"

Adelaide sighed inwardly. *Someday Theodora would well and fully lose her temper, and it would be a beautiful thing to behold.*

For now, Adelaide could only wave her hand dismissively and sit down across the table, tucking her feet beneath her. A bird swooped overhead on its way toward an upper window left ajar. "Dearest, you have no idea what it'll be like to sit in on an Assembly session. But," Adelaide smiled proudly, "as soon as I saw the letter yesterday – well, I have rather a network, you know –"

"Of whom?"

Adelaide's jaw clenched. "Wives, of course. Who do you think opens all the mail in this damned city?" Of course, not all the other wives were entirely aware they were part of a clandestine information-gathering system, but no matter. The ones who loved to gossip got some enjoyment from sharing secrets with the Magistrate's wife. Others – Jameelah Pine and Charity Sands came to mind, and perhaps Fan Thorn if she wasn't too busy running the tapestry circle she took entirely too seriously – understood that information was as good as currency. Better than, if your husband held the purse strings. "You're meant to give a statement, declaring intent and ability. That's why they've invited you: So you can put them all at ease once and for all."

Theodora frowned at her sandwich.

"It's good, dearest! It means our plot is working!" Adelaide settled deeper into her seat cushion. "It means the Ministers are worried, and that's the first step to being scared, and that's – " she paused dramatically as she raised a cup of tea " – the final step before they do what you want."

Theodora spoke to her sandwich: "Or before they string you up."

Adelaide rolled her eyes, though only because Theodora wasn't looking. "Trust me. Will you? Please?" Adelaide clasped her hands together and did her best pout.

Theodora finally looked at her and smiled, a little wistful. "Addy," she said, slowly.

Adelaide put her teacup down with force. "No."

"It's just – do you think this is all still wise?" Theodora asked in a rush. "Someone is trying to kill John! Trying very hard! And now they're calling me in front of them, when I haven't had nearly long enough to, to –" She waved her sandwich in the air, her eyes frantic. Adelaide was close to losing her entirely.

Damn John Dove's recent propensity for nearly dying.

"Well yes, that is true," she said slowly. "But why would his survival depend upon you sacrificing – "

"I mean what's the point, really? It's just a house, after all."

Adelaide wanted to scream. *What's the point? What's the bleeding point? Power, and freedom, and magic, and love, you ninny! It was ever so much more than a house, as if a house and a home weren't enough to get worked about all on their own! But to have the chance to inherit, to speak before the men who made the laws, to advocate for oneself –*

"Besides, Adelaide, you're married to the Court Magistrate," Theodora said, startling Adelaide back with her own unfortunate marital situation. She leaned forward to take Adelaide's hand. "You know how things work. But things will get better for women eventually. I'm sure."

All their lives, Adelaide had been trying to impress her older, witchier, wiser friend. Trying to keep up or outdo, even going so far, though she'd never say it aloud, as to rush into marriage when it seemed Theodora had done the same. But Theodora possessed a weight and a command of the world that Adelaide never would, and Adelaide had accepted that long ago.

But she also understood how the world could look at you a certain way, for so long, that you started to live inside their version of your own life. How gestures and decisions that seemed to everyone else foolish, silly things could be the difference between losing yourself entirely and holding on a little longer because at least you deciding something, anything for yourself.

Theodora had to keep acting the witch. If the Assembly – but moreover the press, the population at large – believed witchery was still possible, maybe it would crack open the door for every other ordinary woman.

For herself. Adelaide had realized long ago that what some people might call selfishness was in fact merely survival.

She'd barely known him at all, just a few dances and chance meetings. The power he held as a Deputy Magistrate, in charge of ruling on a quarter of the complaints on the island, had seemed vague and exciting and of relatively little practical importance. She had understood even less the scope of his ambition to become the highest judge on Wherewithal, the man who made every final decision.

Adelaide understood her husband very well now. She didn't want *better*. She wanted a revolution. Getting this for Theodora, that's how it would start.

"Ted," she said simply. Adelaide tried to erase all the pretense and all the affect from her features, all the things that she'd gotten so good at, so Theodora would know that she really meant what she said. *Funny how even sincerity took work.* "You need a home. You need someplace to be safe. You deserve that. Can't you see that? Can't you believe it?"

Theodora fidgeted in her chair, mouth pursed and brow furrowed, like she was attempting to solve a particularly difficult equation. Adelaide realized that she was the equation.

Finally Theodora cracked a smile. "Thank you, Addy. Let's keep going. But I do need your help."

Adelaide felt her whole body relax and she covered her exhale by pretending to blow on her tea. The steam wafted across the table between them to mix with the humidity in the room.

All she needed was a start. An opening to convince Theodora to take what was hers. "My dear, that's what I'm here for," she said.

This is a start.

38

Assembly Hall
Closing Session before Solstice Break
Morning, December 11, 1947

THEODORA FIDGETED with the black velvet buttons of her suit. They were entirely decorative; the black boucle jacket was cinched tight around her waist with an internal network of bones and wire and clasps. *They may need to bury me in it.*

She tugged her hat a little lower over her eyes and tried to quiet the tapping of her heel against the stone floor. Beside her Adelaide was having a very loud, very animated conversation with the minister for roads about the best way to the hot springs.

"You have a secret route, don't you?" she yelled. Minister Beechwood sat below them and halfway across the cavernous hall. "Something underground, you old fox?" She gave an exaggerated wink to be seen across the space then spoke out of the corner of her mouth to Theodora: "That would explain why he's got the best pool reserved each time I go, spread out like he's bleeding Neptune."

Theodora smiled, distracted and only half-listening. She was very glad that Adelaide seemed entirely recovered from when she'd found her two nights prior. All their lives Theodora had spent half her time worried sick about Adelaide and half her time amazed at her friend's gumption and ability to recover. It was just that Theodora didn't have quite the time to concentrate on that now.

Beechwood had a jolly if overly red face – *too much time at the springs, clearly* – and waggled his finger at Adelaide before he tucked his tails and sat down.

Yesterday she and Adelaide had pored over the newspapers so that Theodora could memorize the faces she'd be speaking to, but everyone looked older or skinnier or shorter in person. *Damn men's ability to change their facial hair*, she thought as she tried to place them. But nary a seat was empty: Ministers for Scholarship & Research; Botany, Fossils, Hydraulics; Roads, Hygiene & Plumbing; Public Information, Trade, Law & Prophecy; History; and Women. All except Agriculture, of course, and there was a vacuum in the crowd where all the other men kept their distance from his empty chair, with its yellow sash, as if death was catching.

Adelaide lowered herself into her seat and turned to Theodora as though they were alone at tea instead of in the gallery around the central theater of Assembly, with all the women and other non-essential persons. Below them the ministers were separated from the men of state – businessmen and visiting dignitaries – by a low stone gate, all facing the Governor's dais at the front of the room. A small boy was posted at the gate below, and he fidgeted with his black coat. He seemed extremely nervous, and possibly like he was in desperate need of a toilet. Theodora commiserated.

"Did you miss John?" Adelaide asked lightly.

Theodora's ears went hot. "What? Miss him? Honestly, Adelaide. You know how we left it. Or rather how he left it. Me. Left me. And I am a widow! After all this time, I've no idea why you thought this was the time to —"

Adelaide laid a hand on Theodora's knee. "I meant, did you see him? He has just walked into the gallery. I thought perhaps you'd been too distracted to notice."

Theodora shot her head around. It wasn't hard to find him: so tall and with his hat still on, and a scrum of men gathered about him at the gate. But she'd always been able to find him in a crowd anyway.

The ministers and the under-ministers and the visiting dignitaries alike plucked at his sleeves to get his attention, like he was a star of the stage. Even from this distance Theodora could tell John was overwhelmed, turning every way at once. But he was smiling.

Theodora didn't take her eyes off him but pulled her hat even lower as the Governor banged his gavel against the stone podium. The plinth had been found here more than three hundred years ago just a few hundred yards from the river, and they'd built the hall around it. Apparently while installing the mail chutes some years ago, they'd been unable to find its end beneath the earth.

Theodora wondered when they'd call her down to speak at the podium. She glanced about: There wasn't a clear way down, with the women and the children crowding the gallery, and the men in their neat rows of chairs below. *Please don't let me look a fool, tripping my way down there.*

Or actually perhaps that would be better. Anything to convince them she wasn't a threat.

Unless it's a test. Perhaps they expect me to fly down.

"Now," Adelaide had said after they'd spent several hours poring over the papers. Theodora felt vaguely as if she was in trouble. "There is the matter of a test. They shall almost definitely ask for a test –"

Theodora had groaned and shut her eyes. Her entire face wrinkled as if she'd eaten something very old and very rotten that wasn't very good to begin with. *That was it, then. It's over.*

Of course there would be a test. She'd known it, somewhere in her mind, all this time, but hadn't wanted to think about it. And as soon as they asked her to prove her witchery, well – she might as well just go home now. *Unless someone felt like pulling off an assassination again.*

Or John went chasing after her.

Yes, better to just pack it all up and go home.

She opened her mouth to say as much when Adelaide interrupted.

"Open your eyes, dearest. I was going to say, before you began to moan, that there will be a test unless we put on a sufficient show of force."

"Force?"

Adelaide bit her lip and assessed Theodora critically. "Perhaps force is not the right word. A show of mettle."

"Mettle?"

Adelaide rolled her eyes. "You're very intimidating when you want to be, you know," she said. "Plus the ministers will do anything to keep you from actually doing magic in front of all those visitors. If you act as though your powers are a *fait accompli,* no one will ask you to actually *accompli* anything. Plus it's the last day of session, so they'll need to vote on your inheritance tomorrow anyway. No time to deliberate. It's brilliant, really."

Theodora repressed another groan. "So all I have to do is be an utterly persuasive, all-powerful but not threatening, beacon of ancient witchcraft with absolutely no ulterior motives towards march of progress. With a speech. Of less than four minutes."

"I'd keep it to three, actually," Adelaide had said. "Attention spans aren't what they used to be, you know."

"We come to session!" the deputy shouted.

"Looks like he's trying to crack the damn thing," Adelaide whispered beside her. Across the way a stillness in the crowd caught her eye.

"Isn't that Victoria White?"

Adelaide scanned the crowd. "It is," she said, no longer glib. She shook her head. "Poor girl. I'm amazed she's out so soon."

Victoria sat very still on the other side of the gallery, surrounded by chatty spectators but very much alone. She was dressed in black and it made her look even younger.

"It's my fault," she whispered, though Adelaide didn't seem to hear. Theodora now felt nauseated in addition to nervous.

"I do believe everyone is looking at us," Adelaide said. "I mean they're probably looking at you, if I'm being honest."

"We come to session!" the Governor said again, this time as though he meant it. The men took their seats. The Governor put down his gavel.

"We come to session for the last meeting of our great Assembly before the break for Winter Solstice. Welcome esteemed members of the court, judges, ministers, assembled laypersons, invited guests."

And then he turned to look up at Theodora, as though she had a spotlight on. "And as our first item, to Mistress Theodora Ashe-Martin, a special welcome."

She'd practiced it a dozen times. Say that she wanted her mother's estate. Publicly renounce her claim to anything else.

State clearly that she was, had always been and always would be, a witch. Look imperious. Hope for the best.

She turned to Adelaide, who had frozen a smile on her face. "Stand," Adelaide said through her teeth.

The gallery seating angled sharply down and away from where they sat, and when she stood Theodora could no longer see any of the women around her. She looked straight down on a sea of combed hair and dark wool, expressions ranging from skeptical to amused to – damned if it didn't still surprise her, and hurt each time – angry.

Also not for the first time, Theodora felt a frisson of anger run up her own spine in response. *What have I done wrong, besides marry too young and too quick and be left behind? What besides be born possessing certain gifts and then losing them?* She wasn't sure which part was worse in their eyes.

But for the first time, she had a reason to talk back. Cowering would no longer save her; only loudness and blasphemy and confidence. She caught John's eye, staring up at her with an encouraging smile on his face. Beside her Adelaide squeezed her hand.

And what if this was her only chance? To tell them not just that she wasn't a threat, but that she could help them, maybe, still, if they'd let her be.

Her heart started to beat even faster, a bird panicking in a cage. She'd tell them that they'd treated her like an outcast and a traitor. That they'd run her mother out of her own home, and not they would do the same to her. Tell them that if she wanted to hold power, if she really truly wanted to bring a storm down upon all of them, she damn well would.

Theodora put her hand on Diana's head and took a deep breath.

"Thank you very much, Mistress Ashe-Martin," the Governor said blandly. "Your presence is noted and appreciated. You may sit down." He turned back toward the men. "For our first order of business, we turn to the bill proposed by Sir Stonewall for an expansion of naval oversight beyond the traditionally maintained half-mile border."

"Wait," Theodora said, but her mouth had gone dry and the words barely made any sound at all. Everyone had already turned away.

Except John. Across the room they locked eyes again and Theodora shook her head, not understanding. *What just happened?* John shook his head back, but his face was rigid with something approaching rage.

She felt a tug at her side and sat down so hard her skirt puffed like a cloud. Diana shoved her snout onto her mistress' knee.

"I don't understand?" Theodora said, turning to Adelaide, who looked nearly as mad as John.

"They trotted you out just to shut you up," Adelaide said, balling one gloved fist into the other. Her eyes were wide and wild. "Oh but don't worry, Ted, we'll see to it they know you've come for business. That you are open for business!"

"Addy, for the love of god, keep your voice down," Theodora whispered back. "And don't say it like that."

It was starting to sink in that she'd been had. To prove she was on their side, or worse. That she was completely controllable, to reassure the men weighing whether to write checks and invest in the island. No test, no questions. The fate of her home never even in question.

Her own fate. She thought of the cottage her father had spoken about and felt in place of her bird-heart a gaping, growing hole.

She found John again but he was staring at the podium now, the same grim look on his face.

The session droned on. One hour, then two, and Theodora was consumed by a numbness both mental and physical. It was poor form to get up while there were still items on the agenda, and when the Governor announced the final agenda item she nearly wept from relief.

"Our newly nominated Minister of Agriculture: John Dove!"

Blessed Hecuba. Theodora and Adelaide both started in their seats.

The Governor was grinning, holding out his gavel toward John.

The rest of what he said was drowned out by the banging of the men's heels on the floor, plus a surprising amount of whooping.

It brought her back to herself somewhat.

As he made his way up he was applauded and jostled and, again, touched as though something of what he was might rub off. She couldn't read the expression on his face. He leapt gracefully up the last few steps.

At the front of the room John placed his hands to either side of the stone. Theodora wondered what it felt like. He smiled at the crowd, his face nearly bashful.

"He's not shy at all," she said aloud. With a sudden drop in her stomach it occurred to Theodora that she might not know him very much at all anymore.

Surely he can't have known. Surely he would have told me. She realized both her hands were in fists and shook them out suddenly, only to see her fingers still shaking. *He certainly couldn't have known they were bringing me here just for show. He would have warned me.*

Surely he would have.

But then John found her eyes once more and settled there for a moment before turning back to the Assembly.

"Thank you," he said, and only for a briefest of moments glanced back up at her. "This is quite a surprise!"

Her chest rose, gasping for a breath she didn't realize she'd been holding.

A young man in front, leaning back with legs outstretched and his hat at a devilish angle, called out to scattered appreciative laughter, "About time, old boy! Take what's yours!"

John's facade cracked.

"Thank you," he said again. "It's an honor to stand here. Glad to know freezing my balls off this past decade has made you all proud. Or made you some money." He took a deep breath. "Don't know that I deserve it. Don't know that I did anything other than be born my father's son and wait until a good man was murdered.

"But here sits a woman who has been maligned and spoken ill of by the people in this room simply because she had the rare misfortune of being more talented than any of the rest of us and was used –"

Theodora flinched but could not look away " – and cast aside by an ignoble scoundrel. You should all be ashamed." He shook his head. "We should all be ashamed."

"Do not speak that way of a murdered man!" someone yelled.

Diana started to whine loudly. Adelaide had composed her face but was fanning herself with so much force she was apt to stir up her own small weather system. Theodore didn't know if she wanted to kill John or marry him on the spot.

"Not suggesting we go back to the dark ages, are you!"

"She's a damned radical!"

Some of the men stamped their feet once more.

"It's her or you!"

How quickly they turned, when afraid. It took seeing John up there, getting the brunt of their rage, to make her realize it was fear driving them.

John seemed very far away when he spoke again. *Tunnel vision.*

"Please stand, Mistress Ashe. Have your say." John held out a hand to her, as though she'd be able to take it from a hundred feet away.

As though she wasn't, in truth, totally alone.

Damn it, John. Murder it is.

Sweat broke out on Theodora's lip. She felt the pressure building, pulsing and whipping itself around the room.

Her dress felt two sizes small. She stood unsteadily and looked at John through tunneled vision. Everyone in the room had gone quiet. They stared at her while also angling themselves slightly away. Maybe that was the tunnel vision, too.

Being asked to speak was so very different from usurping the podium. Perhaps not for John but definitely, definitely for her. It turned what should have been straightforward into something that would scare people. Something akin to revolution.

John glanced around at the angry faces. One eyebrow went up. But he braced himself behind the podium and turned back to Theodora, half a smile on his face in an attempt to break the mood: "The floor is yours, Mistress Ashe."

Theodora turned to Adelaide, who gave her the tiniest of shrugs, her face a mask.

Theodora turned back to the unsmiling crowd and, looking upward to the gallery across the way, made eye contact with Victoria White. The girl's face was still and expectant. Waiting.

All right then, Theodora thought.

Feeling like she was underwater, she began to speak.

As she did another voice shouted from the assembly: "Don't you want what's owed you?"

That was when the ceiling fell in.

39

Botanical University District
Blessed Sirens-by-the-Sea Hospital
Just before rounds, December 12, 1947

"What in the name of hell is wrong with me?"

"A ceiling fell on you. You have a broken rib and two dislocated fingers. For starters."

John shot George a sidelong glare, which took considerable effort since George was helping him limp back to his hospital bed from the bathroom. It was so cold in here. A wind from somewhere kept blowing John's hospital gown open and everything had been painted a blinding white that became a sickly green in the glow of the algae lights spaced every ten feet along the wall.

"You know what I mean," John said through gritted teeth as they entered his room.

"Yes, I do. That's why I said for starters. Figured we should get the physical and political out of the way before we tackle the moral and metaphysical."

With a thud John fell back to the cot, aided not a little by George's slightly premature release. George stood back and assessed the patient, for all the world like his doctorate was in biology instead of geology. "It's a miracle you're not dead."

"I should be," John said darkly, and very gingerly lifted his legs to recline once more. Five other people had been buried in the collapse, three ministers, the deputy governor, and a page. All three ministers were still critical. The deputy couldn't remember the last three weeks but otherwise seemed all right, if that was the word for it. The page seemed all right, thank the skies, saved by his small size and a convenient gap made by the crashed pieces of granite. He'd been asking for updates on them all each hour.

"And on top of it, Theodora must want to kill me. Perhaps she should. As a public service."

"Are you sure she didn't try?" George asked, pulling out a cigarette.

John shot him an angry glance and felt the muscles in his neck scream in protest. "Fuck off, man. That wasn't her. She'd never hurt people like that."

George held his hands up. "All right, all right. Sorry. Anyway there's no time for that now."

"For what?"

"Being dead. Or dying. Or murder for that matter." George struck his match. "You and Theodora have far too much to clean up."

John raised an eyebrow. "You sound like you're auditioning to play a spy, Mr. Law." His leg was itching terribly through the cast. "Though you do wear it well, this beleaguered intelligence thing. Is that what won over Adelaide?"

"Play nice. You need me to help you if you want to take another piss, remember." George blew smoke a little too close to where John sat, but he also looked a bit as though he'd been punched.

"I'm sorry," John said, and leaned back against the pillows. "You're a good friend. I'm an idiot."

George threw the morning's *Sentinel* down on the bed. "They don't throw just anyone up on the podium, you know, despite all the foot stamping and all that. You're in it now."

John looked down and his stomach dropped. Fat letters bannered across the front page:

BLACK WIDOW WITCH STANDS ACCUSED OF TERRORISM, ATTEMPTED MURDER & DISAPPEARANCE OF HENRY MARTIN

Mistress Theodora Ashe-Martin Has Been Called to Account for Attack on Assembly

John Dove, Acting Ag Minister, Near Death in Hospital

Inquest Reopened into Missing Master Martin

Teddy had been his first thought upon waking on the rubble and dust that used to be the floor of the assembly. He'd seen the sky overhead and a dozen very concerned officials, but no Theodora, and he'd nearly hurt himself far worse trying to jump up and find her. It'd taken four men to hold him down, and three others to convince him that she'd been seen leaving, unscathed, with the Court Mistress.

He jabbed at the paper. "When the hell did this happen? When did the newspaper become a, you know —" he gestured at the uniform typesetting, the thick stack of pages, the professional photography (his own face, looking like a smug idiot at the podium moments before the collapse) — "a real newspaper?"

"New editor. Rumor was he was installed in anticipation of the harbors opening, to prime the pumps, editorially speaking." George shrugged. "Easier to read, at least."

John made to protest again but caught himself and picked up the paper. "I just wish they'd waited a little longer to get their act together. Next week even." He flipped to the editorial page: "Clearly The Time Has Come For An Inquest Into Mistress Ashe-Martin's Intentions In The South."

He groaned and rubbed the heels of his hands into his eyes. "I suppose circulation has gone way up?"

George grunted in affirmation.

John flopped back against the pillows. "How did I fuck this up so royally, George? It made such sense in my head. She deserves to speak!

You know it, and they know it, damn it! But she must think I'm like them, ignoring her and using her to serve my own purposes. Oh hell, George. Am I like them? I am like them, aren't I?"

"She should make herself known," George said, ignoring John's questions and walking to the window. It was a gray, heavy day without the relief of rain. He squinted. "Perhaps first we should focus on who's trying to off you? I'm not saying Theodora's tangled up in it, because they're obviously trying to frame her for it." He turned to John and exhaled again. "Unless –"

"Unless what!"

"I have to ask. You don't think she could be –? That she's using her magic to, uh," George waved his cigarette through the air so the lit end burned an X in the air.

"No! Teddy is not trying to kill me!"

George put up both his hands and ducked his head. "I had to ask." He smiled for the first time, a little abashed. "You're my friend, John. I'm trying to keep you alive for a bit."

John smiled grimly. "And I do appreciate it."

George stubbed out his cigarette and clapped his hands. "Right then. Shall we?"

"Shall we what?"

"You can't stay here. It's awfully depressing, and it's not secure."

John raised an eyebrow. "Now you're my head of security?"

George was already gathering John's coat and throwing him his pants. "Can you manage these? We'll get a cab to Adelaide's so you only need get to the front door."

John eyes went large and he couldn't help but laugh. "Adelaide's?"

"Mr. Dove? Is everything all right?" A nurse had appeared in the doorway, eyeing George warily.

"Quite all right, thank you," George said without looking over. He hoisted John up like luggage. "Yes, to Adelaide's." They began to move, quickly and inelegantly, out the door.

"Mr. Dove –" the nurse began as she jumped out of the way, but George steered them in the other direction with a sharp nod of his head to her.

John's mouth quirked. "Quite an elaborate ploy to get in Adelaide's good graces again, don't you think?"

George huffed and shifted John's weight. "I am serious! I will not be party to her throwing everything she has and could be away! Though she might make me deposit you on the front step. Damned stubborn, that one," he said admiringly. "And at any rate I can't take credit for the plan."

John's face lit up. "Teddy?"

"Your father."

John tried to pull up short but was dragged along by George. "My father!"

John winced as they hobbled down the white-washed stairs beyond the lobby. "One step, now, two, thank you. And please stop yelling, it's giving me an attack of nerves. I need a drink. And yes, your father."

"Why did you go see him?" They reached the front doors and George shoved them open with a shoulder.

"Ahh, that's better," George said, inhaling deeply." Several ambulance drivers milling about the doors nudged each other when they saw John. When he tried to pull his collar up further it only slipped further down his shoulder.

The hospital opened onto a busy thoroughfare of solstice shoppers, none of whom were too preoccupied with their holiday parcels to miss the opportunity to give John startled and appraising looks as George hurried them past. John attempted to tip his hat to them and nearly fell over. "I think it's actually warmer out here than in Blessed-Sirens," George said. "Very festive."

"Why did you see my father?"

"He requested to see me. In all things you give me too much credit, John. Maybe he's worried about you. With the attempted killing and whatnot."

"You believe that?"

A cab pulled up and George began to shove John inside. "Not really. I'll admit he seemed mostly fond of the idea that you'd be convalescing at the home of Magistrate. Looks good for your career. Outerbridge Estate, please," George said to the driver, and the ice horses trotted out into traffic.

"I seem to have very little say in the matter one way or another," John said, trying and failing to get comfortable with his cast and his bruised midsection as they bumped over the cobbles. He sighed resignedly and looked out the window. "Might as well make myself comfortable?"

Strings of multi-colored algae-lights were hung from lampposts. John hadn't been in Mooring for Winter Solstice in several years, and he'd forgotten how cheerful it was. Everyone making a fresh start, celebrating the end of the dark.

Something bumped his elbow. George proffered a flask.

"I do think your father is beginning to like me, though," George said as John took a long sip. "He said I had an excellent head for business."

John grimaced from the liquor and then laughed. "Well that's just patently false."

"I told him that, but he didn't seem to believe me." George took the flask back and sipped. "Maybe you're right to be cynical. Maybe he meant my head was literally good for his business, and I'm to end up stuffed on his library wall one of these days."

40

University District
City of Mooring
Dusk, December 12, 1947

THE BRICK STREETS around the Botanical University grew increasingly byzantine the closer you came to their source. Shops atop pubs beside apothecaries, all of them growing more specific: Ladies' garters and absinthe-only and cures for headaches that began behind one eye. Theodora hadn't spent much time in Mooring and now she was adrift in its sea. Like if she took a deep enough breathe she could dive down and never reach the bottom, encountering any variety of unknown creatures before her legs fused together and became a tailfin.

As though it was starting already, Theodora felt a chill run from the base of her spine up all the way to her ears, which began to burn in the cold wind. The university's clock tower loomed up to the northeast and Theodora turned toward it, pulling her hood closer.

Iron gates, molded all along the top like waves and thorny vines, surrounded the campus proper. The gate wouldn't be locked until nightfall but Theodora hurried beneath the archway anyway, feeling like someone would stop her.

At first the school had been only a collection of buildings clustered around a clock tower, and all they'd studied was botany, drawing on the skills and background of the first arrivals to survive. Geology, math, physics, theatre, archaeology, chemistry – those came later, as did larger and grander structures and a tower that eventually reached higher than any other building in the city and tolled not the hour but the rising of the moon.

The original name of the school had stuck. So had the thick vines that obscured every building on campus, so like the southern cliffs.

Theodora realized she hadn't thought of home much at all since she'd come up to Mooring. Of the entire point for her being here.

She shook that away. *Soon I'll be back for good*, Theodora thought. *Just need to save John first. And clear my name of murder.*

Murders.

She considered turning back around and heading straight for the headache shop.

At least the witchcraft ruse is going well.

Instead Theodora climbed worn, shallow steps to the library doors. They rose fifteen feet tall, made from a felled tree split lengthwise. She couldn't have opened it on her own even if she'd been allowed to. As it was she took a deep breath and banged her fist against the wood.

"May I help you?" Theodora's head spun. She couldn't tell where the voice came from.

"I wish to enter?" Despite her best efforts her voice wavered. There was no one else around, and the building seemed alive, like the voice wasn't behind the doors but the doors themselves, and if she failed they would swallow her up. All the building was made of wood, pale and glossed and unusual on an island where stone was preferred to save the trees for firewood and animals.

"Madame, you may not be aware, but women are not allowed in the library without a male – "

"I am not a woman. I am a witch." Witches were supposed to be able to get in. *Witches were supposed to get whatever they wanted.* She waited and then heaved a great sigh. *Fine.* She reached inside her coat.

"And I have a letter." She held it up and realized she didn't know where to hold it up to. She began to wave it around in as dignified a manner as possible.

A previously hidden mail slot banged opened to Theodora's right. She stared at it, half-expecting a very small doorman to emerge.

"Put it here, then," the voice said.

With a start Theodora dropped the letter into the slot, where it was whooshed inside. The slot banged closed.

Several seconds later she had to jump out of the way as the doors swung open. Adelaide had forged her husband's signature with confidence and at least three unnecessary flourishes, or so Theodora had thought, but apparently it worked.

Once her eyes adjusted Theodora could see that she was alone inside. *Perhaps it really had been only a voice.*

She stood in one cavernous room built like the outside of honey-colored wood, though in here it was delicate and arching like the ribcage of some massive, ancient beast. Windows at the back provided the only outside light. The stacks rose three floors high around the edges of the room, illuminated by sconces with pools of algae swirling slowly enough only to indicate they were still alive. Otherwise the low afternoon light shot through the latticework of the windows in a complicated, directed pattern that targeted each aisle, on every floor.

Theodora took a deep breath of dry, vegetal air, and began to walk up the grand spiral staircase to the first floor. She glanced back at the looming doors, shut once more, and walked a little faster.

She'd read her mother's books so many times she could not only recall the words on each spine and its place on her shelves, but feel the texture of every page under her fingers. She knew there was nothing in them to help keep John safe, and even if there was – if there was something, somehow that she'd missed – she couldn't go back south now, and she certainly couldn't ask her father to ship everything to Mooring.

But just because she and her mother had been the last witches didn't mean they'd had all the literature. She'd often heard her mother bemoan the books that had been lost, bought or commandeered by the university from the families who used to own them, before their power dried up one generation to the next. *Who knows we're missing!*, Marguerite would say, again and again, as she sought out answers to the problem of where magic had gone. Theodora had always felt so helpless then, like if she were truly worthy of magic she'd have been able to get all those books for her mother right then and there. Which was silly of course, she'd been just a girl.

She paused and ran her fingers down the numbers at the end of the first stack, on the first floor. If her mother had been so certain there were answers here, Theodora was willing to give it a try. *And what other options do I have?*

When the roof of the Assembly fell in, the room filled with stone dust and plaster and shards of glass from the light fixtures. Algae burst forth to land in infinitesimal specs that people would be finding inside their ears and in their waistcoat pockets for months, if not years, to come. Half the people inside Assembly rushed forward and half scrambled wildly for the exits. As at the Governor's, Theodora had remained frozen in place.

And in time. She imagined, so quick it was like remembering, what might happen if John didn't get up. What the world might look like then. What her world might look like.

Of course he did arise, or rather was pulled in a very inelegant way by far too many of the nearby men than was actually helpful or advisable. A cheer went up, though some people were still crying. Theodora realized Adelaide was again pulling at her sleeve.

"Coz! Coz, let's go! Now!"

Adelaide never called her coz anymore — she thought it sounded rural — and it had jolted Theodora back. In quick order they were outside, in the waiting carriage with its driver who had never more looked like a bodyguard, and then galloping through the streets.

"They're setting me up," Theodora gasped suddenly. She was surprised how sharp her voice was, when she still felt half like she was dreaming. Plus her ears were ringing. "They're setting me up."

Adelaide had been staring out the window, tapping her fingers fast and erratically against her thigh. Now she spun to face Theodora.

"Of course they are!" she nearly yelled. She sounded, for the first time in a long time that Theodora could remember, actually frightened, though she tempered it a little with a roll of her eyes. "Of course they are, Ted – do you finally believe it? They're trying to kill John, and they're trying to set you up to take the fall."

That was why Theodora was at the library, now at the end of the second balcony of books. She came to the staircase again on her loop and marched upward once again. But she hadn't found anything to help her yet, nor had anything made her any wiser as to what, exactly, she was looking for.

The third floor of the library seemed like an engineering mishap. The ceilings were too low and the shelves too widely spaced. Up here the floors were bare so that her footsteps rang out. The light was overly algaeic. Almost none of the light came through the window up here.

After she'd walked one half of the floor, Theodora walked to look over the edge. The sun was nearly set, and if she wasn't careful she'd get locked in by that anthropomorphized door. *Shouldn't there have been a librarian at least? Someone? Anyone who might be helpful?*

"What did I think I'd find, *Theodora's Guide to Getting By*? Where in the blooming organizational system would that one be, Teddy?" Her voice was getting louder but clearly there was no one around to hear. "Hmm? Tell me that!"

"I'd imagine Social Sciences."

Theodora only just caught the banister before she went over the edge in shock. Instead she spun round to find Victoria White, standing behind a table that had been obscured by the nearest shelf, her head only just visible behind a tower of books.

"Perhaps Philosophy? Anyway I agree it'd do well for these gents to get into the 20th century already," Victoria said. "Have you seen what's come in already on the boats? They have this Dewey system." She smiled crookedly, a little bit forced. Victoria's mourning dress was, Theodora saw now, very different than her own: Short and modern and fitted. But also severe, coated in buttons and large shoulders and pieces of sculptural jet jewelry that looked like armor.

She would defeat me in battle in a moment, Theodora thought, feeling suddenly very guilty and not a little intimidated.

"Victoria! I didn't see you. I'm sorry. I mean, I'm so sorry, I haven't had a chance to say that yet. About your father."

Victoria tipped her head just slightly. "Would you care to sit?" she asked.

Theodora opened her mouth to make an excuse but found her feet were moving forward.

"Only for a moment, I assure you. I don't want to interrupt."

"It's no trouble, I'm almost finished," she said. "I've been here all day. They don't actually know I'm here." She smiled a little, proud of herself. "I came in through the mail delivery ducts."

Theodora raised an eyebrow. "Clever. The best I could do was forgery."

They smiled at each other across the table, until Victoria pulled down sharply on her sleeves so the points of lace ended halfway across the back of each hand. Theodora looked away from the motion. The table was covered with textbooks.

"Are you studying?"

Victoria considered. "A sort of studying. I'm going to take my father's seat, Mistress Ashe."

Again Theodora found her mouth open. *Pulled along like a fish by this one. Wonder if that's what happened to John.*

"My father was a good person, Mistress Ashe. He did not deserve to die and I will most certainly not have his death be in vain. His work will not have been in vain." She paused and seemed to be composing not just her words but her entire self, putting herself back together in what Theodora took to be an ongoing, constant process. Something occurred to her.

"Victoria, are you a witch?"

The girl swallowed hard, like she'd been preparing for that question, and shook her head fiercely. "I am not. But I won't let that hold me back. I will not be in vain, Mistress Ashe. Do you understand?"

She sat back hard against her chair, still holding Theodora's gaze. Theodora blinked.

"My dear, I think that's —"

Victoria dropped her eyes. "I haven't been talking to many people lately, and I've been practicing that in my head. I really did think you'd understand, even given who you are." Her voice broke.

Theodora leaned forward and took Victoria's hand. "It's very impressive," she said. "I am very impressed."

Victoria smiled. "That means so much. Coming from you."

Theodora's waved away the words. "I'm nothing. What have I done?"

Victoria looked confused and, though Theodora was sure she must be mistaking it, hurt. "You're here, aren't you? You showed up."

"Is that all it takes?" Theodora asked, trying to smile, her voice a little weak.

Victoria gave no quarter. "Is that all you're planning?"

Who were they, these people who believed in her? Theodora remembered the dressmaker. How would they possibly know what she did at night, in darkened rooms where her breath showed for fear of lighting a fire and calling attention to herself?

Theodora found she didn't want to let Victoria down.

"I'm trying," she said, but she thought only of the ache in her fingers near the mountain, the fog that came when she couldn't control. *John.* "In fact, I've been trying all afternoon to find something that could help keep John safe." Theodora realized how alone Victoria might be. "Do you have other family?"

Victoria shook her head.

"If you would ever like to talk?" Theodora asked. "I did lose my mother, in a way."

Victoria seemed to wake up a bit. "I'm so glad you said that." She carefully pulled a book from the middle of the stack beside her and held it out. "I found this today."

Theodora took the book. It was thin, more a ledger or a diary than something professionally published. When she opened it the writing was her mother's.

41

Outerbridge Estate
Cocktail hour, December 12, 1947

"Came to your senses did you? Took you rather longer than I expected. Come in. Shall you have a drink?"

Adelaide greeted them at the door, dressed sensibly for dinner in a green silk dressing gown atop green silk pajamas, a martini nearly overflowing with olives in her hand. After she addressed them, or rather addressed George, she sashayed back into the house. John was still slumped over George's shoulder, both of them sweating from the exertion of getting from the carriage to the house but also shivering from the cold.

"There's no one else to carry him about, George, you've got to do it yourself," she called over her shoulder as she turned the corner.

"You heard Mistress Outerbridge," John said. "Heave-ho, mate."

George opened his mouth to protest and seemed to consider throwing John over the threshold. Instead he left him propped him up against the wall, went back for the bags, and shut the door behind them. George locked it in three places with quick, accustomed movements.

"Here," he said, and threw John a long pointed horn that a curved joint bone had been affixed to. "It's a walking stick," he said drily over his shoulder. "Adelaide's husband is a sea-hunter, didn't you know."

"Lovely," John said, holding it by two fingers. But he did need to lean on, and so John thanked the animal it had once belonged to and hobbled after George.

It was comforting to feel the support of a majestic creature under one's palm, actually. *Suppose that's how it starts*, he thought, and reminded himself yet again not to ever get too comfortable.

As he walked George ran his fingers lightly over the side tables and the framed paintings of sea battles and the Magistrate's constipated ancestors. The lamps had been turned down until the barest purple ember glowed – *brand new ore*, John thought, *and a very expensive one at that*. That they would leave the algae uncovered like this, barely casting any light and running out its lifespan for empty hallways, only amplified his awareness of the cost.

John stared at the wall above one of the sconces: the surface of the stone was faceted, a crystal dulled by time. It made the white walls feel alive, which he supposed was because something alive was giving them light.

"Adelaide chose that," George said, nodding toward the rock. "Didn't want anything to go to waste."

George pushed open the door Adelaide had left ajar, and John followed after. Inside his breath caught in his throat.

John lived very well: even on the ice, his house, though still drafty, had all the comforts of Wherewithal's modern age. He was fortunate, and in the future would probably only become more so. *Especially if I marry Victoria*. He shunted that thought to the corner of his mind.

But the Doves hadn't become rich until John was late in his teens, and before that they'd lived modestly. Struggled a little, compared to some. For a long time John's only exposure to wealth had been his summers with Theodora and Adelaide, and Theodora's family was a shabby sort of rich, people who'd meandered far enough down their own odd paths that the gardens had overgrown and everyone ate off tarnished antiques. Adelaide's family was more conventional, but her parents and their home always stayed on the edges of his world, probably on purpose.

So now he was very much caught off guard.

The room, which must have been the Magistrate's office, was the size of the ship he'd come down on, and it glowed with white-gold light that made the purple in the hall look economical. The walls were stuffed to the ceiling with every imaginable type of sea creature: preserved, mounted, and ready to splash down in revenge. A golden fire burned in the grates — John had never seen that done before, they must be heaping algae down upon actual flames just for the effect. A massive stone desk that reminded him very much of the Assembly podium sat to the right with barely anything on it, only a pen poised next to an inkwell. Every chair and couch and pillow was covered in shining embroidery that reflected back the golden algae's light and the flame until the whole place pulsed.

In the center of it all Adelaide sprawled across one of the couches. Her green outfit clashed against the light. Everything she did clashed against the light in this room.

"Refill, darling?" She held out her glass to George, who was already stationed at the wet bar. He moved familiarly among the bottles and turned to take Adelaide's glass from her with the beginnings of a smile at his mouth. *They've done this all before*, John realized. Not just the drinks and the trespassing but the arguing and the making up.

George positioned himself in an easy chair next to Adelaide, throwing the three hard pillows that had formerly occupied it to the floor. They both took long sips and then turned, simultaneously, to John, still leaning precariously in the doorway.

"You best sit down, dear, with that whole situation," Adelaide said, gesturing toward his various injuries with her drink.

"You know with any other couple this song and dance would be quite annoying," John said, as he moved to the fainting couch. The rug below him had once been a polar bear, and he gently moved his feet away from its head.

"But not with us?" George asked, more relaxed than John had seen him in some time.

"With you two I must admit I'm only jealous."

"My goal at all times," Adelaide said over the rim of her martini, but she glanced sideways at George with warmth in her eyes.

George, looking a little flushed, turned to John. "No drink?"

John gestured at his horn. "Must I do everything for myself? You were so solicitous when we were out in public."

"Oh!" Adelaide shot up from her languid posture, half her drink sloshing over the side of the glass. "Dammit," she said, glancing at her robe. "I nearly forgot!"

"Forgot what?" John asked, immediately nervous.

Adelaide paused. "The champagne. I know you prefer champagne to liquor, John."

"Adelaide, that's quite nice of you, but really not since we were very young –"

But she was already heading out a different door than the one they'd all come in, a doorway that gave the impression of leading to subterranean depths. "Come, Georgie."

George dutifully stood. "Don't run off," he called over his shoulder as he followed her out.

"Couldn't if I wanted to," John called back as the door shut behind them.

In truth he didn't want to move. It was good to be back among friends, even if someone was trying to kill him and he was sorely in need of a drink and surrounded by murdered fauna.

At least the drink he didn't have to wait for. He limped to the wet bar and grabbed the first bottle he came into contact with: Herbal, purple, high proof – *that'd serve*. He bent to pull a large, squat glass from the lower shelf and paused as he picked it up, partly because he was still a little dizzy from medication and partly because it was the heaviest glass he'd ever held.

Nearly a weapon. Looking over at the desk, he wondered when the Magistrate was due back.

From this angle he saw the desk wasn't empty at all. It was nearly covered, actually, by a sheet of vellum written over in fine dark blue markings. A map.

John took his drink and sat in the desk's overlarge leather chair to look closer. It took John a few moments to realize he was looking at the island, because the lines corresponded with nothing he could recognize, and the island's outline was bleeding and eroding all over the page.

But still, there it was. Ice to waterfalls, north to south, home to —

"Oh hello."

John looked up. Victoria stood in the doorway, glowing gold with purple outlines.

"Victoria!" He realized how absurd he must look behind the desk, and went to stand. Then a whalehound loped past Victoria toward the fireplace. She circled once and lay down, like a whale diving. *I know that dog.*

"John!" Theodora said, appearing beside Victoria. "What the devil are you doing here?"

He looked from Victoria to Theodora and back again, then down to the dog because she seemed the safest option. *Why in the devil are they arriving together? Are they friends? Actually they'd make good friends, come to think of it. What the devil am I thinking? I must get out from behind this desk!*

All his attempts at a calm, collected front evaporated as he miscalculated and shifted his weight too fast. His knee gave out and pain shot through his body, and as he went down his chin caught the edge of the table. The last thing John remembered was the watery outline of the Southern shore as the map slid down along with him.

42

Under the Outerbridge Estate
Just after cocktails, December 12, 1947

GEORGE FOLLOWED Adelaide at about the distance of his own body. He kept pace with her without ever drawing close enough to catch her, spin her around, and press her up against the stone walls, which was what he so dearly wanted to do.

How old is this passageway, he wondered each time. Adelaide didn't know, and it wasn't as though she could ask her husband.

George swayed as if he were drunk though he'd only had a few sips – he glanced down; *all right, fully half* – of his drink so far. Perhaps the feeling of drunkenness was a habit, too. Perhaps it was a consequence of being so near Adelaide. The two did seem to go hand-in-hand, unfortunately, which was part of the problem.

George took a larger step and lightly placed his hand on Adelaide's shoulder.

Adelaide spun and grinned at him as she continued backwards. She didn't falter or hesitate at all on the uneven cobblestones.

"Too much to do," she whispered before spinning back around. "You know that, love. Far too much to do for silly arguments getting in the way."

George cleared his throat. "Hmm. Yes. But you know we can't go on this way, Adelaide. As I said before, I did mean it, and I do mean it. I will not watch you throw yourself away on drugs and booze and, and – and on me, frankly – " His voice cracked and he cleared his throat again. "Things must change, Adelaide." He rolled his eyes at himself, at how ineffectual he sounded even compared to Adelaide's silence, even compared to the smile he knew was still on her face.

"No, of course I can't go on this way," she said lightly but like she'd made up her mind, like she was turning down a dessert course.

"You can't?"

"No, darling, you know that. I know that. But that's what makes us work so well together. Our fight to be on the bleeding edge of what's possible. To propel ourselves on the wave. Oh that's a pretty turn of phrase, isn't it? Anyway that's why I love you, and it's why you love me."

George felt increasingly absurd that they were having this conversation in a dark, damp hallway, and that he was having it with Adelaide's back. *She's not wrong, though.* She was hardly ever wrong, which was also part of the problem. He took a deep breath.

"I want us both to see that future, Adelaide. I need you in it. The future needs you in it. I need you in it."

Adelaide didn't respond as they turned a corner and rose up a little in the earth. The algae glowed brighter here and he felt exposed. They passed into a moss-covered passage.

"Adelaide?"

"I will be there," she said, her voice low and the words coming fast. George couldn't tell if she was embarrassed or lying. "I promise."

Then to his surprise Adelaide walked by the door that led to the wine cellars and began to trip up the stairs that wound to the back of the house and the kitchen gardens.

"No wine?" he asked, slightly embarrassed by his own concern about the matter.

"Oh yes do grab a bottle," she said. "Then come up to the kitchen door. We're meeting someone, and I'd like to show them both a proper hello."

43

Outerbridge Estate
Dinner is served, December 12, 1947

VICTORIA STOOD IN SHOCK. Theodora lunged for John and shouted at Victoria to get some ice, and then the girl jumped into the role of nurse quite eagerly. Theodora cradled John's head, grateful she wasn't alone and wondering if Victoria would rather be the lap supporting John.

He was breathing, and though he'd knocked himself out cold he looked very peaceful. His long eyelashes rose and fell and his hair swept down to brush against her arms.

John's head is in my lap.

It would have been very peaceful indeed if not for the fear he was in a coma. And, after Adelaide and George returned, the five other people and one very large dog who stood around them. Actually Diana wasn't a bother. Everyone else, though – they could leave.

There were five of them because Adelaide had invited the editor of the newspaper to dinner. She'd brought him and his secretary into the room with an air of triumph only to find John splayed out on the floor and Theodora splashing water on his face and Diana licking his hands.

Adelaide assured Theodora that John didn't seem to have slipped into a coma, that the drugs he was on for his various injuries had led him, with the help of the desk, into a very deep sleep.

The editors stood off to the side, murmuring to each other with a professional seriousness that made Theodora very uneasy. She sat up straighter even as she continued to stroke John's hair; she made her face as still and cold as she knew how. It had already been 20 minutes and the steadiness of his breathing could only do so much to alleviate her fears.

Meanwhile Adelaide bustled about the room.

"Here you are, then," she said, thrusting drinks into the editors' hands. "Shall we go through to the dining room?" Her voice was a little too bright.

"Adelaide!" Theodora exclaimed.

"Shouldn't we," said the secretary, a slight man with sandy hair, gesturing toward Theodora and John on the floor, "do something?" The editor peered over his glasses at them all.

"Oh him? He's fine!" Adelaide said, eyes very wide, and this time Theodora was sure she was putting on an act. She seemed to care overmuch what these men thought of her, which wasn't like her at all, and had gone into full society mode. Much to Theodora's surprise, George, though working at a much lower pitch, was helping.

George clapped the younger newspaperman on the shoulder, hard enough to cause them both to veer a little off balance. George laughed and the younger man smiled with slightly panicked eyes. The editor, meanwhile, assessed Adelaide with an amused, slightly superior expression. *He thinks he's already won*, Theodora thought. *Damn it, Adelaide, what were you thinking?*

Theodora looked down at John and held her breath to mark his breathing. She felt a warmth in her stomach spread upward through her chest and along the lines of her neck.

Had she and John ever sat like this, together, when they were young? No, of course not: John had never concussed himself that she could recall. But this level of intimacy – they'd been the best of friends, she'd been closer to him than anyone else, and she hadn't realized any of it until much later.

So why does it feel so familiar? Why did her body seem to remember something her mind did not? She was nearly annoyed: What right did her body have? She closed her eyes and tried to shoo it away, but all she felt was a deep calm.

Perhaps that was what she remembered.

"Oh hello, Teddy."

The words came out slurred. Theodora opened her eyes. John was smiling up at her.

Her breath caught. "Hello you," she managed after a moment.

"Oh fantastic!" Adelaide exclaimed with relief, and before Theodora knew what was happening George was lifting John off her lap and Victoria was helping Theodora to her feet.

"Thank you, Victoria, but excuse me," she said, adjusting her dress. "John!" The reporters had angled themselves in front of him, and he was rubbing his head in a way that seemed half ache and half confusion. "John!" she tried again. "Are you quite all right?"

He maneuvered his head around and flashed her an only somewhat dimmed smile. "This is quite a trend, eh? Maybe it's you after all," he said and winked.

It is far, far too warm in here. "Oh, well, glad you're all right! And if it was me I'd try to knock some sense into you along with it." She smiled back with pursed lips even as her stomach and chest felt like a herd of butterflies had taken root. *I should knock sense into myself, acting like a teenager,* she thought, and then noticed that the newspapermen were staring at her, noting everything she said and did. *How do they manage to blend in so much when they're standing in the middle of the bleeding room?* When she'd first seen her name in the paper after Henry had gone Theodora had felt ashamed, but unsure why. But she was much different now, and she knew exactly where that shame came from, and who it served.

"Excuse me!" she began, but then Adelaide took her arm and spun her round in a completely unnecessary circle that gave the rest of the party time to leave the room ahead of them and quite suddenly the butler had appeared from out of nowhere to help Theodora from the jacket she still wore and by the time she'd been extracted everyone was gone and all she could do was follow them into the dining room.

The table had been set with gold-tipped crystal that shone against the red algae votives lining the center of the table. Despite what Adelaide had told Theodora this morning, as Theodora hurried out the door on her way to the library, everyone hadn't been given the day off: The butler and the cook and the nanny had all been hard at work, getting overtime Theodora hoped. The nanny poured wine without missing a drop; the butler unfurled a napkin so thick it was nearly a sail; and the cook dropped a delicate piece of raw pink fish on her plate with surgical precision.

Adaptability, Theodora thought, *must be a requirement of working for Adelaide. Or befriending her.*

Including adapting to the sudden presence of Victoria. But her seat was fitted seamlessly among the others, a scripted name card above the plate. She'd been sat between the newspapermen but now stood frozen behind her pulled out chair.

John had already sat down but now he stood up smoothly and walked to Victoria's side. He whispered something in her ear that made her laugh, and then helped her into her seat. John let his hand linger on her shoulder for a long moment before he returned to her seat. Victoria glanced across the table at her and smiled, looking utterly relieved.

Theodora, embarrassed to have been caught staring, quickly looked down at her fish. It had been sliced up with the bones all exposed and turned upwards for easy dissection. *I know how you feel.*

How could I have been so stupid? Of course John had been the one to remember the shock Victoria was still in. John charmed; he delighted; he made you feel as though you were the only one in the room. It had always and ever been that way, and she'd let herself think that it was somehow different when he looked at her.

Everyone was taking far too long to sit down and get settled. Theodora focused on the red glow of the algae, which seemed to pulse in place of the usual, irregular ebb and flow in the glass. No, that was only her own breathing; she couldn't seem to get a breath deep enough into her lungs. Theodora thought of Roberta in her lab with that bright blue algae.

Did the algae feel anything in there, trapped and away from home, forced to put on a show for the illumination of others? How had she never thought of that before? *I'll have to ask Roberta. I miss her.*

I miss my home. I need to get home. Get my home back.

Victoria seemed largely recovered, if a little wide-eyed. *She can't be older than nineteen,* Theodora thought. Two seats down John looked a little drunk, smiling at his fish as though he was about to tell it a joke. *Perhaps that's the drugs. Perhaps that's what John looks like when he's in love.*

Not with the fish.

Perhaps they'll announce the engagement soon.

The red glow started to blur the edges of everything. Theodora blinked and looked to the head of the table, where Adelaide held a glass aloft. She beamed around the table, back in her element.

"Welcome and thank you so much for joining us tonight. Most of all, thanks to our honored guests from *The Sentinel*. This is Master Jack Greenwood, editor of *The Sentinel*, and Master Roy Hill."

The editor dipped his head at Adelaide, smiled benevolently. Master Hill nodded around the table at them all.

"I believe you're both newly arrived on our fair island? Welcome."

"Guilty," Jack said.

"You're not from here," John said, surprised.

Roy picked up his water glass and raised his eyebrows above the glass as he took a long gulp, and for a moment Theodora thought he wasn't going to say anything more. "New Zealand," he said by way of explanation, though that wasn't on any map Theodora had ever seen.

They looked alike, a little; Roy seemed like a version of Jack that someone had forgotten to water. *But how in the world had they gotten here so fast? How long had they been here?*

Knowing more about it seemed of the utmost importance: *What is it like, who lives there, is it safe? Why did you come here, of all places?*

Theodora was about to ask when Adelaide spoke again.

"Down to business, shall we? I think we know why we're here."

Theodora frowned around the table. Victoria was staring at all of them like she was studying an unknown species and George only stared at Adelaide adoringly. *He really is in deep.*

John, however, was looking right at her. When their eyes met he shook his head in a way that Theodora did remember from their childhood. It meant: *What the devil is Adelaide up to now?*

Theodora turned to Adelaide. "Enlighten me?"

"Why, we're here to set the story straight about Mistress Ashe-Martin," Adelaide said.

Theodora's stomach dropped. Her mouth opened in a way that made her feel, again, like the fish course.

Adelaide was still talking.

"*The Sentinel* has been running stories about my dear friend that are, I dare say, scandalously inaccurate."

"If not to say libelous," George added from his end of the table.

"If not to say that," Adelaide said significantly, glancing up through her eyelashes at the editors. "Which we shall not. For now. But I realized after my outrage had subsided over the most recent issue, that neither of you have had the opportunity to get it from the woman herself. An exclusive. A 'scoop.' Isn't that what they call it?"

Mr. Hill nodded. Mr. Greenwood smiled with only his mouth.

"You do have papers to sell," George said.

"And on the far side of international war, as Wherewithal has emerged as an outpost of unexpected technological progress, and trust me no one expected it less than I, perhaps you might agree that it would be prudent to position your paper as a beacon, if you will, of hope and truth, rather than fear-mongering, lies, and scurrilous backward-facing gossip?"

Adelaide sat back, taking her wine glass with her. Somehow she was not out of breath, and she bored her eyes into Jack Greenwood's face. "Now it's your turn to talk."

Theodora felt like she was floating above the table. *Tunnel vision again. But surely this was a bad idea, given how the press had always treated her, given how this trip had gone thus far.*

"Excuse me –" Theodora finally managed.

"Don't you think someone should have asked –" John began.

"Fine," Jack said. He picked up his glass and raised it to Adelaide as though a deal had been struck. It seemed that it had.

"Brilliant!" Adelaide said.

"Bravo," George said. "That's a relief, I'll say."

"Hold on! Aren't you forgetting someone?" Theodora asked, finding her voice. They all turned to her at once, and the tunnel vision got worse.

Jack Greenwood smiled at her. He had so many kinds of smiles, it seemed. This one was hungry.

"My dear," he said, and leaned forward while extending his arms out upon the table, so that his fingertips glowed red in the algae. "Do you know how many stories I've heard in the time I've been here, about the woman who lives in a backwater castle and killed her husband in the middle of their wedding night like some sort of tropical spider from I-don't-know-where jungle, and who's been sitting down south for the last nine years waiting for the clock to run out so she can steal her ex's money and spend it on who-knows-what sort of illicit and immoral goods and activities? Enough to know it's a good story, nothing more."

Victoria's eyes had grown very wide beside him.

"Sir, I do think –" Adelaide began.

"Right, hold on now –" George said.

Jack Greenwood held up a hand. "Mea culpa. I'm editorializing. I don't believe any of it," he said. "Neither tit nor tail. You did not murder your husband. You're not here to start a revolution. Am I correct?"

She hated it, the effect this man had just by forcing his voice on them. He assumed they'd acquiesce and they did. She did. She nodded.

"Good. I don't like to peddle in superstition and radicalism." He spread his fingers out wide on the table. "Now. I assume you've heard about what's happening in the south? With the drought?"

A charge ran up her forearms and landed, throbbing, at her temples. Her voice was hoarse when she spoke. "You can't be serious."

Another smile. Disappointment. "Ah. You haven't heard then. About the deal that's been struck."

Her mouth went even drier and she picked up her glass. "Deal?" she asked, as calmly as she could. *Get control of yourself, Teddy!* She felt like information was leaking out of her without her even realizing it. And with it, any power she might have had.

"There's been no deal!" John said, but he didn't sound sure, and Jack ignored him.

"Yes, the deal," Jack said, slower, as though she was a child. "The ministers drew it up today. Easier now that two more of them are dead."

A strangled sound came from John's throat. "No – they didn't – " But Jack didn't pause.

"They're going to sell off your watchtowers and your fisheries and your lighthouses to the highest bidder. Internationally, I mean, which probably means military. Probably weapons testing, too. Am I going too fast?"

Theodora had the most vivid image of slamming Jack Greenwood's face down into his china plate. He shrugged.

"You can read about it in the paper tomorrow. It's a great day for us, Theodora," he said, and slid one hand across the table toward her. She thought he meant to take her hand and she recoiled, which made him laugh. He tapped the table lightly instead. "A great day for you most of all. The pressure's off."

Her name in his mouth made her want to scream but screaming had never helped. "They can't just decide something like that, " she said hoarsely.

"They held a vote," Roy said gently. "There's a law that lets them do so in an emergency?"

She nodded. There was.

"But how could you both know and I—"

"Gentlemen talk amongst themselves," Jack said. "At any rate it brings us back to you. What do you want out of this situation, Theodora? What's your goal here?"

"This is absurd!" Adelaide said, who clearly had not planned things going this way and who hated being upstaged. She ticked items off her fingers, nearly sputtering: "Theodora Ashe-Martin is a witch and as such she deserves to inherit Henry Martin's estate, to have a vote in Assembly, and to inherit her family estate! If you're telling me that you're in league with these cloistered, backwards –"

Theodora had to lick her lips to get the words out. "I want to go home," she said.

Jack picked up his knife and fork and looked down at his plate before glancing back up at Theodora. "Listen. It's not going to happen. You're a threat. Even if you were a witch, which –" he smiled a little bit at himself " – you are not, the story is coming for you. The gossip, the charges of murder. All of it. It's too damned convenient. You should be on the next ship off, Theodora. Get away like your mother did. Like your man did." He began to scoop up food onto his fork and smiled at her again. No longer hungry. Satisfied. "Cause otherwise," he said, "who could ever forget a pretty little bitch like yourself?"

John made a sort of choking noise. He had tried too quickly to stand, or really to lunge himself across the table, and now he was breathing painfully and wine was spilling across his hands where he'd slammed them down to catch himself. George handed across a napkin without looking away from Jack.

Theodora cast down her eyes. She couldn't look at him. She spoke to the red glow that made her water glass reflect pink on the tablecloth. "Thank you, I –"

She stopped. *Thank you? What the devil is wrong with me?*

It was one thing to have these things said about her in print, or behind her back – but maybe it was all one thing and the same.

Except if someone said something to your face, at least then you had the option of saying something back. She'd spent so much time not defending herself, hoping that silence would convince everyone of her innocence, reward her with peace. Only to have people tell her when to stay and when to go, time and again.

She was no longer sure that peace was what she was after.

Theodora picked up her red-glowing glass. She held it high above the algae, and craned her neck to look at the underside.

"Teddy?" John said.

Tiny bubbles were collecting at the bottom of the glass. In her palm the glass felt warm. A bit unstable.

"Theodora?" Adelaide said.

Oxygen piling up on itself, shoving for prominence. A tower of bubbles began to form in the center of the glass, and the tower started to spin and whip into a frenzy. With an academic interest – *Roberta would be proud of me* – Theodora wondered if they'd keep their color when they reached the air. *Would the tower stand or fall? I suppose it's up to me. I'm doing it, aren't I?*

The tower climbed past the horizon of the water, small shimmering beads of air suspended inside the finest garnet-colored film.

It whipped round faster and taller until the crystals in the chandelier began to shake and glow red with the reflection of the liquid. Water drops were flying everywhere, covering her friends with the finest mist, but she hoped they would understand. *I am doing this. I'm doing it! And it's so beautiful.*

So she'd never get her home back. So John loved Victoria. So the world thought she was a murderer, not even because they believed it but because it served their purposes.

So what now?

A storm in a wine cup. A tornado in the dining room. A witch who wasn't done.

When the tornado consumed the chandelier entirely so that the crystals shook in a frenzy, she made eye contact with Jack, and smiled.

What did she have to lose?

"Cheers to that," she said. The tower collapsed back into her glass. Theodora lifted the goblet up slightly into the air. "Who'd want to be forgotten, anyway?"

"I will kick that man off the island myself if he ever says something like that to you again," John said. His face was bright red. "I should never have let something like that happen to you."

"You didn't," she said quietly. "It's not your responsibility. And nothing happened."

"I should have done more," he said. He was across the room but spoke to her as if they were the only ones there.

They might as well have been. The rest of dinner had passed in a rush of courses and forced jocularity, with Adelaide and George seeming to speak in code through half of it.

After the anemone course, fried and displayed so their long strands rolled over each plate – Roy ate heartily but Jack hid them beneath his potatoes – Jack stood up abruptly.

"Early deadline," he'd said, with a glance to Adelaide. Then he looked back at Theodora, at whom he'd been staring since the tornado. Her tornado.

She seemed to have become the de facto leader of their little party.

"Thank you for coming," she said. The magic had made her so tired she could barely lift her fork, but she summoned all her strength. "I hope you got what you came for?"

He pulled at his vest to straighten it. "Like I said, you can read about it tomorrow. Late edition." He jabbed a finger in the air toward her. "I'll tell them you're a witch because it's too good a story and I'm a businessman. But don't think it changes anything. They want you gone."

He clapped Roy on the shoulder so hard the younger man's elbow hit the table with a crack.

Jack strode out the door, Roy on his heels after a polite nod to Theodora and a stutter-step when he realized he was still clutching the white cloth napkin in his hand. When he threw it back to the table from the door it fluttered through the air and looked for all the world like surrender, until it landed on one of the red algae-lights. Then it looked soaked through with blood.

Dinner had wrapped up very fast after that. Now Theodora needed to have a long talk with Adelaide.

Soon. Very soon.

"Here you are, dear!" Adelaide said, and poured champagne into the glass Theodora had somehow come to hold. Small bubbles splashed back high into the air.

"Perhaps I can do it, too!" Adelaide laughed. "Just joking," she said, and patted her friend's shoulder.

Theodora took the bottle out of Adelaide's hand. She was in no mood for sobriety.

"That was amazing," Victoria said, coming to sit beside her. "I can admit now, I wanted so badly to believe but I had no idea you were really able to do it. What it looks like to see it!"

"Yes, me either," Theodora said, bringing the bottle to her lips and tilting it back. She wiped her mouth. "I barely remembered. Though I suppose water bubbles aren't the same as weather, are they?"

Adelaide plopped down on her other side, her dress frothing up around her. "Do you think it's due to the new wardrobe?" She playfully tugged at her Theodora's skirt.

"Is this the first time you've done it?" George asked, appraising her from across the room. "I mean since Henry left. Adelaide said –" He glanced at her for confirmation, and Adelaide in turn looked shyly at Theodora.

"I did tell Georgie about that. But also about when we were children! How you used to make snowstorms in the nursery." Adelaide's hands fluttered in excitement, her face lit up.

"Your timing is quite good," George said. He sat in a large embroidered armchair and Adelaide popped up to sit down again on his lap. "Having *The Sentinel* on our side really can't be underestimated. This will change everything," George said.

Theodora took another long swig of champagne.

"So you think he's on our side then? Jack didn't seem too happy with my performance." She remembered what he'd said as he left, and laughed bitterly. "In fact it sounds as though my bon voyage party is well under way."

She thought about her home. About never seeing it again. *Drink.*

"This was always the plan, don't you see?" George asked. "If you wanted people to believe you were a witch when you weren't one, how much better when it turns out you really are!" He sounded a little giddy.

"Right. Our 'plan'." Theodora's eyes felt hot, like she might start to cry, and so she drank a bit more champagne. There was something else behind her eyes, too: a little more than alcohol and a little less, right now, than a thunderstorm. "Why did this all have to happen behind my back?"

Adelaide raised her eyebrows at George. George coughed and sipped his martini.

"Yes?" John asked, putting down his beer.

"Was there always this much skullduggery amongst you?" Victoria asked, seeming slightly bewildered by all of them.

"Hard to say," Theodora said. "Apparently I'm nearly always in the dark."

Adelaide laughed. "Well you did seem to like it that way, dear."

Theodora's nostrils flared. "I think I'm ready for enlightenment. George?"

George coughed again, leaning over as though he was having a fit. When he peeked up everyone was still staring at him.

"Ahem," he said, sitting up. "It seems I've found a side project in intelligence work."

Adelaide gasped aloud. Theodora turned to her with a pursed mouth.

"Really, Addy! You obviously already knew."

"I know," Adelaide said, clasping her hands. "But it's quite dramatic still, isn't it?"

"You're a spy?" John said, squinting at George as though he could find the spy in there somewhere. "For whom? For how long?"

"Were you a spy, as well, then?" Theodora asked Adelaide, feeling inexplicably annoyed at the idea. "Are you still?"

Adelaide waved her cocktail around. "Of course not. Too many parties to throw and as many horrid invitations to turn down." She waved her arm at the desk looming in the corner, a dark swatch in the light. "That's how we met, though. I caught George snooping around my dear husband's desk during a ghastly cocktail hour. I was trying to escape, and lo and behold –" she smiled warmly at George " – I found him."

"Yes, it was rather terrifying before it was romantic," George said. "Adelaide would make an excellent interrogator. Of course at the time I didn't realize where her sympathies lay."

"I like to think I supported the war effort," she added, with a Cheshire cat smile that made Theodora blush and look away. "In my own way."

"She couldn't be court-martialed. I don't think," George said a little uneasily. "Perhaps you all could now. Interesting, that. I should check. Though perhaps better not to arouse suspicions…"

"George?" John said.

"Right, yes. Where were we?"

"War," John said, sounding extremely uneasy. "You mentioned war. Which war? What war?"

Theodora kept imagining George and Adelaide passing notes in dark tunnels.

"Is that why you set up this whole charade tonight?" she asked. "Spycraft? What use could a witch alienating an editor be?"

George cleared his throat again. "It wasn't because I expected you to suddenly evince yourself a witch," he said with a crooked smile. "The feeling among the intelligence community is that the current state of affairs on the island, ignoring our past and what we might offer the world, is a missed opportunity."

Theodora frowned and studied the carpet. "I wasn't aware that there was a current state of my affairs. Or that we had an intelligence community."

"What war, George?" John said again, more adamant.

"There isn't one. Not officially," George said carefully. "There isn't an intelligence community, either, officially. The men in Assembly, most of them, don't believe anyone's intelligence matters more than their own. Such as it is. Among the academic community, though, there's an awareness that we don't understand how the world works nearly as well as we should. That we've been left behind. So some of us came together to form a loose network of contacts. Shared allegiances."

"Only most of them?" John asked. "Who are you working with in Assembly?"

In answer George turned to Victoria. "Your father," he said. "Did you know?"

"No, I didn't know," she said softly, but then the corner of her mouth turned up slightly. "Well done, though, Dad."

"Very well done," George replied. "We miss him quite a bit."

John put his head in his hands.

"We're at a very important moment, Theodora," George went on. "In history. Wherewithal has been hiding for too long and now we learn the whole world's been broken apart. I'll be damned if I won't help to put it back together."

He spoke the last bit with an intensity that took Theodora aback. He sounded nearly angry. At her. "To have it bandied about on the international stage that we're a nation of gossipy backwater puritans – that's how people think of us. I'd thought to get them to take us seriously, so we might contribute our technology and not be taken over and turned into a military pawn of the great powers. But if you can actually do magic," he worked his jaw, looking for the words, "do you realize how much good you might do?"

Theodora's mouth was dry, somehow, and she took a sip of champagne without answering. She was staring at the head of the polar bear rug on the floor, and couldn't seem to look away from it.

"But Adelaide gets the credit for tonight," George said, beaming up at her beside him.

"Look at you, darling! You're a witch! A real one." She moved her hand through the air as if she was laying out a headline. Perhaps the title of a play lit up on a marquee. "A witch of the modern age. I know you've never been good at grabbing life by the horns. That's what we're here for."

"I see," Theodora said.

"And we're only just beginning," George said. He took a seat and leaned forward, deep in thought. "I'll contact the office in the morning. Or perhaps I shouldn't wait that long. Addy, can I use the house tube? I'll let them know things have changed. We'll want to alert the team about *The Sentinel* and draw up a strategy for what you'll say. A script."

"A script?" Theodora asked. "How convenient."

"Do you think he'll tell the truth? It's better for them, isn't it, if he just pretends it never happens?" Victoria asked. She seemed to have a much more naturally strategic mind than Theodora did.

Adelaide looked thoughtful. "I think we can trust it. I said they could have Theodora if he presented exactly what he saw, no matter what, and otherwise we'd deny any involvement, completely drag them through the mud. You know, Jack's new enough —"

"You told them they could *have* Theodora?" John asked. He was up as much as he could be in his seat with an expression on his face of anger and annoyance and utter frustration at being totally unable to gesture as wildly as he would have liked. *John did speak with his hands,* she recalled.

Theodora laughed aloud at the absurdity of it. She was also full of annoyance, and frustration and — *yes,* she realized, *anger.*

"I don't think it was right that you did this," she said quietly.

"I know it wasn't ideal," George said, "but it was too important to leave it up to whim."

"I am not whim," she said tightly. "I am not a pawn." She stood up, not quite knowing why. Now they were all looking at her.

"Ted, come now," said Adelaide. "This was best for you!"

Theodora swallowed hard and tried to focus on Adelaide. "Perhaps I should be in charge of deciding what's best for me." She was still holding the champagne bottle and she lifted it a little for emphasis. On her couch Victoria scooted away. "You had no right, Adelaide!"

Oh fuck. You're drunk, Theodora.

Adelaide stood up and swallowed her drink, as if for courage. "You had no right yourself," she said, a hard edge to her voice. "To settle for so little, when you could do so much."

Now Theodora stood. "I never wanted more, Addy!"

"I didn't say you should want more, Theodora," Adelaide said "I said you could do more. You owed it to us. You owed it to me!"

The fuzziness in her eyes, the feeling of almost-crying, had migrated to her fingertips now. *My palms are itchy. That's new.*

Theodora wondered what her own face must look like. *I wish I could see myself from very high above,* she thought. *I wish I knew what other people saw when they looked at me.*

Gods, I am quite drunk. Too late now. Best to commit. To everything.

"You're a folk hero, Theodora!" George said, grinning. "People love you!"

A loud scoffing sound emitted from Theodora's throat.

"They do," George insisted. "You're the last witch. You are reminder of why people came to this island in the first place, and that we were once able to do magic, and that, I don't know, maybe we could do it again. Or at least not completely destroy the island and make it into the refuge it was once meant to be." He grinned a little bit. "It was damned good for recruitment to drop your name, tell them you were on our side."

"You used my name?" Theodora said.

"Not as an 'endorsement,' per se," George said, making air quotes, "more as a reminder –"

"It was me," Adelaide said, folding her arms, daring Theodora. "Don't be angry at George. I knew you'd believe in what we're trying to do here."

"Addy, why didn't you just tell me? Why didn't you just ask?"

"You didn't seem very interested, did you?" Adelaide said, still angry but also near tears herself. "In anything. Or anyone."

Theodora shook her head, trying to clear it. "That's not the damned point, Adelaide!" They didn't understand, she'd hidden away to protect them. To protect herself.

She'd locked herself up in her father's house and seemed perfectly happy, eager even, to remain in seclusion the rest of her life.

My father's house. She laughed aloud again.

No one spoke as she brought the bottle to her mouth. The lights of the room were green through the glass. Like being deep underwater at the hot springs, though this was different. This was dark waves under a moonless sky.

Light broke into infinite pieces all the way to the horizon. They were going east on a very large ship. It smelled terrible, and she leaned over the rail for some relief. Beneath the waves there was deeper movement and — Theodora squinted — more flickering light? Very similar to what glowed in the light fixtures on the walls, except there were no walls.

I see hands. I suppose there must be mermaids, she thought. *How interesting. I had no idea.*

Theodora brought the bottle down and blinked.

"Mermaids," she said by way of explanation.

Adelaide took a deep breath, calmed her voice. "You need to rest, dearest. Perhaps you've had enough to drink?" She put one hand on the bottle and the other on Theodora's arm.

Theodora jerked her arm away. "Funny for you to say."

Adelaide's whole body tensed but she recovered. "Come. You'll feel better in the morning." She started to guide Theodora toward the door.

"I am not a child, Addy!" Theodora said loudly, snatching her arm away once more. *You sound like a child, though*, Theodora thought. *Never mind, no going back.* "Despite what you may think," she said to Adelaide, "despite what you have been led to believe," she said to the rest of them, "I am a grown woman! I am not to be picked up and tossed aside when convenient!"

She still felt like she was on a ship, the room rolling around her. *I'm going to be sick.*

"Ted, don't be silly," Adelaide said. "God's blood, you were talking of mermaids! Now please come to bed."

"No!" Theodora exclaimed, and she swung her arms away. The champagne bottle, much lighter than it had been, flew from her grasp.

And straight at George.

Theodora inhaled sharply.

He raised his hands to his face half a second before the bottle arrested its flight in mid-air. It spun drunkenly in place, like it was stuck upside down in a drain. Bits of dust and stray threads from all the embroidery whirled up to join it. Theodora twitched her fingers and a loose feather flew up from the floor to join the rest.

This feels amazing. Like regaining a limb. Like making love ought to feel.

George slowly lowered his hands and craned his head around the bottle. It spun just fast enough, with enough wobble in its revolution, that when he reached out a hand he quickly thought better of it and pulled back.

From across the room Theodora made a sound, somewhere between a gasp and a laugh and a gulping for air. In the second everyone blinked the bottle dropped to the ground; the glass turned to sand and skittered outward in a circle, as though a bomb had fallen.

By the time they'd all looked up again, Theodora had run out the door.

Water was leaking out of her soles.

By the time Theodora reached Adelaide's wing each hurried step she took was accompanied by a squelching noise that made her sound as ridiculous as she felt. By the time she reached the door of her own guest suite the puddles had become a stream and the water that she was calling up from the ground in lieu of frustrated tears was flowing under her like a moat of her own making. She was ruining the carpet.

In her room Theodora sunk down so her skirt puffed up around her like a parachute. Raindrops flew out from the hem in all directions.

"Enough!" she yelled.

There was a sizzle on the air, and the raindrops vanished.

"Thank you. Thank me. Oh dear." She collapsed into the folds of her dress. She wished she could drop deeper, deeper, into the earth until she was swallowed up. Or perhaps back under the sea, back to wherever it was she'd gone to, when she saw the lights reflected through the bottle.

A wail escaped her, loud and long, and it caught her so off-guard that Theodora's head shot up as though the noise had come from outside her. She held her breath and waited, but the stone walls hid everything, probably by design. For that, she was momentarily thankful. She did wake up Diana. Resentful at having been left out of the day's trip to the library, the dog trotted in and lay beside her but refrained from putting her head on her mistress' lap. *I deserve that*, Theodora thought.

She looked down at her arms, her waist, the lines of her thighs beneath the gown. Nine years of loneliness and gloomy outfits and rumors and suspicion.

Why the devil had Henry left? Why had John gone north and never come home again? Why did my mother teach me nothing at all about how I might help or how to survive when my heart was broken?

Not just because of John. Now, when it seemed she was finally a witch once more, half the island wanted her to leave and the other half wanted her to stand silent and let everyone else do the work. She was a burden or she was a symbol but the only thing that mattered was that she'd figured everything out far too late to help anyone at all, least of all herself.

She laughed out loud with a hiccup that became a cackle and ended with her coughing and shaking, wild-eyed. "Like a witch!" she hissed at no one.

That was the problem, then, the same problem she'd had for as long as she could remember. The same problem that kept coming up: She was alone.

Theodora took a deep, shuddering breath, and exhaled a wispy cloud. She stared at it as it dissipated, then wailed again and let her head fell into her lap. Her forehead hit something very sharp.

As soon as her hand brushed the pebbled leather she remembered not just her mother's book, but her mother. She remembered the feel of the back of her mother's hands and the smell of her hair, the sides of her mouth when she'd smiled and the cadence of her walk.

Theodora tasted tears, saltier than they ought to have been. *A bit like brine. Not a bad taste, actually.* She licked them away and laid the book on her lap.

It was small with a green leather cover, and the edges of the pages had been painted gold. In the same metallic the book's title was printed:

Meteorologica (Modern)
Marguerite Headwaters

She touched the book with one finger, as though it might be very hot or cold. But it was very ordinary. Surely only luck or diligence could have led Victoria to it.

So many years had passed since her mother left, and though only half as long since Henry had disappeared, even that was now a long time ago. She'd been living with both losses for so long as though they had just happened. Until she'd come here and forgotten for a little while, thinking she could be someone other than herself.

Theodora hiccuped. *Still drunk.*
Still a witch.
Shit.

She squared her shoulders and tried to make herself look as regal as possible while sitting with smeared mascara on someone else's floor. Then with a finger still salty and wet she opened the book.

✳

John's voice was muffled, because his head was in his hands and he spoke directly down into a carpet three inches thick.

"What?" Victoria asked. "Enunciate, John.

He lifted his head slightly. "I said: Victoria, I think I'm in love with Theodora. I think I still am. I am."

Several feet away Victoria laughed softly. She was examining the pattern the sand had made on the floor; for what, he wasn't sure, but it had been occupying her for the greater part of the last 15 minutes. He could still hear the scratch of her pencil as she wrote down notes. George and Adelaide were long gone, occupying themselves and each other elsewhere.

She tsk-ed softly. "A witch fetish isn't terribly unusual around here, John. I would've thought you'd be slightly more creative."

John looked up sharply, but it was less what she'd said — which was more or less in line with the tenor of their correspondence — than how. She didn't sound mad. She seemed amused, and not at all surprised.

"Did you, uh, hear me, Victoria?" She hadn't stopped measuring the nautilus the broken glass had formed on the ground.

"I wish I had a camera," she muttered before finally sitting back on her heels and turning to look at him. "Yes, I did hear you. You're in love with Theodora Ashe. Congratulations. I think the feeling is mutual. You're both, you know," she rolled her eyes and waved her hand like a particularly nauseating country road. "You're both fond of taking the scenic route to get somewhere." She turned back to what used to be Theodora's champagne bottle. "Yes, that's what we'll say," she murmured, and laughed a little.

"But –" He stopped himself and leaned back in his chair. John studied Victoria as he might a landscape, trying to work out the angles and how the colors fit together.

No, that's wrong, and that's how I've always looked at her: All wrong. He leaned forward again and looked at her as a person.

"You're not angry with me?"

"I am not, of course not. Though I do wish you'd help me take measurements. I wish we had a camera. Oh! Perhaps you could draw this? That would be a great help. Theodora's not thinking clearly, obviously, but she'll want a record of her early powers, I'm sure. Or history will. Those I suppose these aren't early. I suppose this is her renaissance?"

Victoria leaned back on her heels and stared dreamily into space. "Don't you feel like something great is starting, John? I can't say I'm surprised you're in love with Mistress Ashe. She's odd and very unexpected. And not a little intimidating. Yes, I do think that's your type," she said, and leaned forward with a triumphant look on her face, as if she'd figured out a puzzle that had long bedeviled her. "Now if we could figure out what my type of woman was, I might be in business," she murmured. "Anyway, yes, please do find some larger sheets of paper and perhaps some pens. Be useful. Stop sitting on your ass."

"Wait," he said. "Your what?"

She looked up through wide eyes, then spoke very slowly. "Your ass."

"No, no. The other thing?"

Victoria looked to be mentally reading back their conversation. "Oh, my type of woman?" She pursed her lips and cocked her head at him in her familiar teasing way, but there was a tightness at the corner of her eyes. "Took you long enough to figure it out, didn't it?"

John thought very hard for several seconds, until all at once he thought he understood.

"Victoria," he said, and leaned very far forward in his chair. "Am I right in saying that Theodora could, ah, be your type? If the stars aligned, shall we say?"

She clucked her tongue. "That's not how it works, John. It's not just any woman, you know, who I happen to be in the room with."

He was mortified. "I'm so sorry, that's not what –"

"But yes," she said, looking back to the pattern on the floor. "Theoretically. I could fall in love with Theodora, and perhaps more to your point, were she to be similarly interested in me, we would, perhaps, consummate our love. To my liking, if I liked her in such a way. Which I do not because, as I mentioned, it does not work that way."

John flopped backward. "Huh."

Now Victoria was trying not to laugh. "Yes. I really thought you knew."

"No, no," he said thoughtfully. "Undoubtedly my fault. Ego, you know."

"Mmhmm," she said. "I've heard of it, yes. Though I think everyone was helping you along in your assumptions. So was I, if I'm honest. I should've told you before. It's just that –"

John spoke in a low voice: "I only wish you'd trusted me earlier and it's my own damned fault that you didn't." He hesitated. You don't, erm, hear much about that these days, do you?"

Victoria's hands hesitated only a second in her calculations. "You do not, no. Funny how backwards a place founded by witches can become, isn't it? Though I suppose fashion –" she raised her eyebrows at the term " – does ebb and flow according to what's most useful or convenient. As we've seen with Theodora."

"Is that why you told me now? Because of Theodora?"

She nodded. "Not because you're in love with her – I mean that's really splendid, I do mean it. But because she's a witch again. A real witch with real power. It made me believe that there might be a different way forward. A different way to have a voice and some power of one's own."

"Other than marrying me?" John asked with a smile. Victoria looked up sharply but relaxed when she saw his face. "I'm so sorry you felt you had no other option."

"I would have, you know. Are you angry?"

He shook his head. "Of course not. You've just as much right to be mad at me."

Victoria shrugged. "You're a good friend, John. We would have had that, at least." She paused, and for the first time seemed truly unsure. "May we still have that?"

"The alternative never crossed my mind. Truly."

She smiled and turned back to her record-keeping. "Good."

John sat for a few seconds, staring into his palms. "Victoria."

"Hmm?"

"What you said about having a voice, and power? Does that mean you think you might also be a –"

"A witch?" She shrugged. "Anything's possible, I suppose. But no inklings so far."

"Hmm. Yes. Perhaps you're right." He was still staring at his hands, and now he looked up. "What were you referring to, then?"

Victoria was smiling again, hard at work. "Why on earth do you think I've decided to go into politics?"

44

Theodora Ashe's Guest Suite
Outerbridge Estate
Middle of the night, December 13, 1947

BY THE LIGHT outside it was around 3 a.m. She'd finished her mother's book and it had become clear about halfway through what she was going to have to do. Now she had to do it.

She had to sleep with John. If she wanted to keep him safe, there was nothing else for it.

That thought had sobered her right up, unfortunately.

The book hadn't offered any revelations about her mother or why she'd left. There was no, *beloved daughter, here's everything I never told you* on page 87; page 87 was one-third of the way through a lengthy discussion of geysers, and Theodora didn't know what that had to do with the weather, anyway. The whole book was like that: Part book-of-days, part grocery list, with bits of spells in the marginalia and coded in shorthand throughout. All of it in a rambling, stream-of-consciousness that scratched just enough at Theodora's memories of her mother to make them raw again, without offering any sort of relief.

It was dated long before Theodora had been born, long before her parents had ever married. Which made the advice Theodora was about to take even more suspect. And it was, Theodora reminded herself as she stepped out of Adelaide's rooms and into the wide sweeping stairway at the center of the house, quite suspect. *How much, at such a young age, could her mother have known about love and sex and power and protection?*

Probably more than me, Theodora thought as she climbed the stairs. All the lights had been nearly covered, only a small glow escaping at the bottom. That was why, despite the advice being very suspect indeed, Theodora was still going to take it. To save John.

Yes. That's why.

His room was on the floor below. She paused at the top of the stairs and adjusted her dress. *I should have snatched something from Adelaide's closet.* Or maybe – she raised a hand to her head; *damn it all* – checked her hair in the mirror first.

Never mind that, she decided. It was whether or not John would be alone she was most concerned with. She'd seen Victoria's carriage leave, but what if she'd sent it ahead?

Perhaps best not to think about Victoria now.

Or herself. She wasn't doing this for herself. No, not in the slightest, even if her pulse had quickened and her cheeks flushed. That was exhaustion.

She was doing it to save John. Her mother's book had been very clear, or as clear as it was about anything: *The surest way to save a lover is to send them far from you. To save a former lover bind yourself to them. To save any loved one, leave them.*

John was a former lover, in a sense. Wasn't he? And that meant sex, didn't it? It had to. What else could it mean?

She didn't know what else to do. He couldn't die.

Don't kid yourself, Theodora, she thought as she began down the hallway to the only doorway with a green lamp glowing outside it: You're doing this for yourself.

45

John Dove's Guest Room
Outerbridge Estate
Middle of the night, December 13, 1947

THE MOON WAS NEARLY INVISIBLE, the sky above the gardens behind Adelaide's house empty of clouds. John leaned out the window he'd shoved open, nearly falling out of it in the process, and saw every leaf illuminated with the strength of starlight alone. Every blade of grass, every stone along the pathway, every flower bud closed up and waiting for morning. He could see everything better at night than in the daylight, or at least that's how it felt.

"At least I don't need eyeglasses yet," he muttered.

He'd helped Victoria finish her work, the two of them working in easy silence. He really didn't know now what he'd been thinking all these months, except that he'd been cold and lonely and it was convenient to imagine something that had never been there at all.

He'd been tempted to fall into bed still in his clothes but didn't want anything to impede his sleep once he finally found it. But it had taken fully half an hour to maneuver out of his shirt with his injuries and bandages getting in the way. John let his fingers glance over the bump on his forehead and winced.

John turned away from the window. The bed was wide enough that he could have stretched out full length sideways, covered in dark green satin that looked like damp grass at night. It was an impression aided by the mural covering the entire wall behind the headboard: ruins and storm clouds and dark hills covered by sheep and shepherds who couldn't seem to tie their tunics right to keep them from falling off. It was absurd and beautiful, and John was certain Adelaide had stuck him here as a joke.

He laid down gingerly and noticed that the mural extended to the ceiling. Zeus appeared to be about to smite someone.

The door to his room banged open and he sat halfway up.

"Shit!" he said, wincing. "Teddy?"

"Sit down," she said breathlessly from the doorway. John had covered up the lights in the room and she was lit dimly from behind in undulating greens.

"What? I'm lying down, Teddy."

"Right. Sit up, then. Carefully!"

"What's happened?" he asked as she shut the door behind her. He propped himself up on the pillows. "What's wrong? What –" He stopped as she walked up very close to the side of the bed. So close that he could feel her breath and see the rise and fall of her chest. She lifted her chin and looked him square in the eyes.

"Teddy, you look ready for battle," he said, smiling, though he was quite nervous. "What's wrong?" Something must be wrong, to occasion such a late visit, but having Teddy so close to him, so close to his bed, was causing him to run through a full range of not entirely unpleasant sensations. Suddenly it occurred to him that there was nothing stopping them any longer, and it made his chest feel as though a sliver of summer had opened up inside of him.

She took a deep breath and screwed up her face in concentration, then leaned forward onto the bed and kissed him.

The summer sun burst full upon his chest.

As did her knee.

"Ow!" he said, trying to recoil while not breaking contact with her mouth.

She jumped back, looking him over immediately as though she might have broken him clean in two. Then her face grew annoyed, though not necessarily with him. Perhaps only slightly.

"Damn it," she said, folding her arms and appraising him again. "Are you all right enough, do you think? Able to withstand – you know." Her cheeks went red and she waved her hand about vaguely. John raised an eyebrow and tried not to smile, though it was damned difficult.

"I'm fine, Teddy. Considering a roof recently fell on me. But are you all right? This is, erm." *Shut up, John, shut up.* "I was not expecting to see you."

"I'm fine, John," she said, seeming a little distracted. Or rather very intent upon the job at hand. In one quick move she carefully lifted one knee over him again until she was sitting atop him. Or rather hovering there. John gasped and she took a deep breath.

"Except I haven't done this in quite a while so you might need to, you know. Assist. Not too much, though," she said, as she slowly lowered down. He blinked several times, checking to see if he was asleep. *Perhaps this is a wonderful coma.* "Otherwise," she said, "I think it might not work."

"I'm fairly confident it'll work," John said, smiling but still half-panicked. It had been quite a while for him, too.

She began to undo his pant buttons and he stayed her hand. "What are you doing here, Teddy?" he asked, and already he was embarrassed by how husky his voice had become.

She paused and glanced at him. "Isn't it obvious?" For the first time she looked really worried. "Is it not obvious? Is it – shall I go?"

John propped himself on one elbow and cocked a smile. "Please do not go. It's only – I'm unsure of why now?" He grabbed tight to her hand. "Which is very different from not wanting it to be now, I assure you."

They were so close. It had been so long since they'd been this close, or maybe they never had. This was not how he'd imagined he and Theodora would be together, and he'd imagined it quite a few times.

Conquest-while-nearly-maimed hadn't been one of the scenarios. But he wanted to stay this close to her forever.

John smiled wider. "What the hell am I saying?"

With all his strength, which admittedly wasn't much at this point, but aided a great deal by enthusiasm and something like desperation, John kissed her back. Theodora, caught off-guard and off-balance, nearly toppled off the bed.

John threw his arms around her to catch her.

"Oh!" she exclaimed, leaning backwards out over the precipice of the bed. John's face tensed but only for a moment. They stilled, Theodora leaning out over the precipice of the wide bed. John took a deep breath.

"I caught you," he said.

Theodora grinned madly and pulled herself back up to kiss him once more, and they tumbled back together, ever so gently, onto the bed.

Theodora opened her eyes to clouds, and angels, and also for some reason great ships being towed by dolphins. *Those gods are dressed very impractically for the storm coming in from over by the dressing table. Gods almighty: John's dressing table.*

She and John had had sex last night. *A few hours ago?* That might be more accurate, given how tired she could already tell she'd feel, after the adrenaline suddenly surging through her had subsided. Adrenaline and awareness of her physical self in this bed, in space, in time. She closed her eyes and retraced John's fingers in her mind and the places where he'd traveled lit up again like pins on a map.

It had been a very long time.

And this, of course, was when Henry had gone. Or rather, she supposed he'd gone at some point during the night, after the sex but before the rest of their lives. But this was when she'd realized it.

Now Theodora found she was nearly too terrified to look. Obviously, John would be gone. The magic would have worked in reverse, she'd have done away with him entirely instead of saving him as she'd intended. If she kept staring up at the ceiling and its absurd fresco, then she could delay the inevitable. *Perhaps I could spend the rest of my life here. Oh look, there's a mermaid riding a giant seahorse. Her hair looks marvelous. Oh no. Mermaids. Adelaide must be so angry with me. She'll never let me live forever in her guest bed.*

John gave a huge honking snore, startling Theodora so thoroughly she yelped.

"What?" John sat upright and immediately lay back, groaning. Theodora began to laugh until she realized John had thrown an arm across her chest. To protect her, she supposed.

She turned to him and he was smiling, his eyes darting over her face as if to assure himself.

When she decided to sleep with John, it was to be an isolated event. A spell she could cast that would build a crystalline wall around him and protect him from the world.

But that was not how John was looking at her. Like she was land after too long at sea. She realized she was smiling began to wonder if she was staring back at him the exact same way.

"Sorry!" Theodora slid out from under his arm. "I'd meant to be gone by now. I'm going now, it's quite all right, please go back to sleep." She continued until she'd slid all the way to the floor beside the bed. Completely naked.

He began to get up. "Go? Why? Now?" He was having a great deal of trouble – *perhaps I've only managed to hurt him worse than before; that'd be ironic, though fitting given my history* – and after a moment he stopped and instead flipped the sheets back. "Please come back?" he asked, smiling a bit sheepishly.

Nearly all at once what he was offering unspooled before her: the warm weight of the blankets, the balance of their arms around each other, what seemed for all the world like safety even though he was clearly in no shape to defend her from anyone.

But that's all shite. The day had begun and someone would find them and then everything would fall apart even if she did manage to keep John alive. Victoria would find out, and the newspapers, and she'd end up ruining John's life just as surely as she'd been trying not to. *Especially if he keeps looking at me like that.*

"Oh no!" she said, trying to smile. "Once was quite enough!"

John's entire face crumpled.

"Where is my damned stocking?" She dropped to her hands and knees. She wanted to hide from that look on his face and hide her own face in turn, so that he wouldn't see how completely and totally she didn't mean it.

Maybe she could just roll under the bed and stay there until spring came. *Perhaps John would think he dreamed the whole thing.* She gritted her teeth as she stretched to reach her slip, balled up on the floor behind the bedpost, and when she grabbed it she put her forehead down against the soft pile of the carpet. *I can't lie to him. At least not entirely.*

"Once was lovely," she said, half-hoping he wouldn't hear her. She pulled on her stocking and her slip. "I'm just afraid I feel rather foolish now."

Two bare feet plopped heavily down beside her, followed shortly after by a proffered hand to help her up. She followed the line of his calf up past the knee, closed her eyes without really meaning to, reopened them somewhere in the middle of his lightly furred belly, followed the line down the center of his chest all the way up to his neck, his mouth, his eyes.

"I don't feel foolish at all, Teddy. And I don't want you to go," John said, his face very serious. He took her hand gently. "I don't want to lose you again."

"I don't want to lose you either," she said, and though she'd meant to say it matter-of-factly her voice shook. In fact, her knees shook, too. *Magical hangover.*

Theodora decided to get it all out at once.

"John," she began.

"I'm not in love with Victoria."

Theodora paused, mouth open. Was she surprised? She was not, but that wasn't really the issue.

"And Victoria is not in love with me," John added quickly, as if he'd heard her thoughts.

Something like relief flooded through Theodora, that made her clutch the bedpost lest her knees give out entirely. Though that was silly. People married without love all the time.

"What I mean is," John was still saying, "she and I aren't together. There are no plans for us to be together. I found out last night. Earlier in the evening, obviously. When I told her I was in love with you and –"

Theodora hung on to the bed for dear life. "You're in love with me?"

"Yes," he said. "Of course I am."

Theodora pitched forward into the blankets. "I think I'm going to be sick," she spoke through the feather down.

"Teddy?" John sounded panicked. Theodora turned his head to find his face right next to hers. "I'm sorry, I shouldn't have sprung that on you. Damn it all, I'm not good at declarations, am I? You're white as the sheets. Here, come, I think we need to get you breakfast." He pulled her back upright and leaned her against the bed.

"It's not you, it's the magic catching up with me. Breakfast might be helpful," she said, keeping her eyes closed.

Or almost closed: John walked across the room to collect his pajamas, still hung neatly in the closet. Amid tangled sheets and low lights she hadn't gotten a good look at him last night. Though she'd felt her way around well enough. *More than well enough.*

The light through the window gilded the tufts of hair shooting every which way from his head as though he wore a crown in some old illuminated manuscript. All his hair shone, actually. *A very hairy man,* she confirmed. He moved easily across the room, as if he'd lived here all his life and as if he didn't mind at all if she was watching him.

"I didn't mean that what you said made me sick. It was unfortunately timed. I'm afraid I'm under the weather." She laughed loudly, and her head pounded. "Oh heavens," she said, and tried to fall backward onto the bed. John caught her. "I suppose the champagne didn't help matters."

"No, no. Breakfast. For both of us. That'll do the most good." He held out a dressing gown to her, long with blue pinstripes, and started to slide her arms into overlong sleeves.

"What is this? Stop moving me about, please, John. Honestly, I can do all that." But he was lifting one foot and then the other and sliding her into his slippers.

"There," he said, and pivoted her in front of the mirror.

She stared at their reflections, side by side. His arm hovered by her in case she might need it and she leaned very slightly into him, still dizzy. In return she put a hand tenderly around his arm, to support his injured leg.

"Thank you," he said softly.

"Come," she said, and steered them both toward the door. She held it open for him and he pretended to tip his hat to her as he passed through.

John immediately went flying onto to the hallway floor with a yelp.

At some point in the night Diana must have tracked her here and now sat wagging happily as John lay spread eagle on the floor.

"Oh no, Diana! John! So much for saving you," Theodora said as she helped him up. "I am so sorry. She really is a very good dog, extremely loyal. Are you all right?" she asked as she tried to brush him off.

"I'm fine," he said, taking a couple wobbly steps in the opposite direction of the whalehound. "She's an immoveable object, that one." Diana was carefully licking her right paw, paying him no mind. "What do you mean saving me?" John asked as eyed Diana a bit warily.

Theodora felt a tide of nausea again. She smiled through it and took his arm. "Isn't that what we're trying to do? Among other things, I mean. Keep ceilings from falling in on you and dogs from tripping you up? Though I don't think Diana is the enemy agent. Come, girl," she said, and clucked her tongue at the dog as they continued down the hall.

Probably not the time, Theodora reasoned, *to fill John in on magical reasons for late night trysts*. Especially given what he'd just told her.

And if there was never a time, so be it. She'd grown used to keeping things to herself.

At the foot of the stairs in the main hall, Theodora stopped dead. John tripped over his feet.

"Teddy, jokes aside, I would appreciate it if you could give me a bit of advance warning."

"Yes, I agree," she said absently. "It's just I forgot about Adelaide and George. They'll be at breakfast. They can't see us like this. It would be terrible for your reputation."

John stifled a smile. "I don't give a damn for my reputation, Theodora."

She turned to look at him. He couldn't mean that. "I'll never hear the end of teasing from her."

"Perhaps that'd be a nice change from people trying to kill us?" He patted her arm. "Besides, it's 2 p.m. darling."

"It is?"

"We don't have to worry about them until cocktail hour."

Theodora let out a breath and laughed. "Thank the stars."

John frowned. "Would it be that bad? If they saw us together?"

He never had seen the point in secrets and hiding, a privilege she'd never shared.

"You don't understand, John," she said. "What people will think of you, with me. You saw it a little bit at Assembly, but that was just rumor. Now it'll be real. You can't let your guard down."

As she spoke Theodora realized how true it was. It was one thing to play the part of a witch. *To really be one, after so long?* If people had been cruel and dismissive before, what would they be now?

Then he smiled at her warmly, and a much younger, more innocent version of herself felt her stomach flip. "I plan to let my guard down long enough to eat like a farm animal," he said. "Surely that's allowed?"

He pulled open the door to the morning room and Diana trotted inside around her, drawn to the smell of food. He looked so kind, standing there in the light, that she caught his arm suddenly, her grip tight.

"I'm not embarrassed. I am, in fact, so very thankful you're in my life again, John." Her voice caught and swallowed hard. *How to tell him? How to tell him 10 years' worth?* "I just want to make sure you stay in my life. Alive. Safe." *From me,* she thought. "Let's save you first, all right?" she asked softly.

John searched her face a long moment and she wished she knew what he found there. "All right. And thank you, Teddy," he said, smiling just a little, "for not holding my youthful idiocies against me."

"As long as you don't hold mine against me," she said. For a few seconds more they stared at each other in the doorway. The light coming through the open door was bright and low, and it lit up John's face. It made him look much older than the image she had in her mind. *Older and more beautiful.*

"I'll allow behaving like a farm animal for a brief interlude," she said, looking away quickly with a smile.

"It's about time."

John and Theodora both jumped and turned toward the room. At first they were only shadows, blending with the velvet chairs. But yes, there were Adelaide and George, sitting at a late breakfast or an early lunch with papers and notebooks spread out before them. They grinned at John and Theodora like schoolchildren.

"Hello, coz," Adelaide said, waggling her fingers. She held up a bottle. "Fancy a little hair of the dog?"

46

Island of Wherewithal
Dates lost, estimated early 18th century

SAFE, yes. Comfortable?

The canyons which had been so captivating from the water were, on land, like gaping mouths ready to swallow whoever tripped into one on a dark night. The ground was fertile and grasses grew abundantly, but the grasses were also sharp as razors and the river flooded regularly.

Differences which had seemed small and complementary on the ship now seemed huge and jarring when you considered that you'd have to live with these people for the rest of your life. That your children would have to marry into their families and you'd be stuck seeing these same tired faces every new and full moon until old age or a hole in the ground or one of the damned horned ponies that travelled in nervous and stampeding packs returned your soul to the earth.

No, they were not comfortable.

But they weren't desperate until winter came. Though the winds that blew over the island were mild, the nights still became long, and longer, and the witches found that all of their powers were insufficient to create enough light. How could they build enough homes, raise enough families, teach their children, if they couldn't see? No kindling would catch, which was a metaphor but also the truth: The island was too raw and wet for anything, even magic it seemed, to burn bright enough or long enough.

Until now they'd stayed in the southern part of the island. A mountain chain ran from eastern coast to west and, as none of them could fly, they hadn't yet dared to try to pass it. But the nights kept getting longer, and it was decided that the men would go north to see what they could find. Maybe a kinder landscape. Maybe the sun.

How did they decide? No one could remember later who suggested the idea, but a vote was held and the resolution passed. In those days everyone voted, clustered around a stone plinth dug up by the river. They'd all come here to save the witches, and it wouldn't make sense to send the witches on a suicide mission so soon after saving them. It made sense at the time.

Nine years the men were gone.

47

Outerbridge Estate
Early evening, December 14, 1947

AFTER A LONG LUNCH of cheese and toast and many, many loaded glances from Adelaide and George, Theodora and John had ever so awkwardly gone to their separate apartments. Now there wasn't any way to know whether it'd worked than waiting to see whether he lived. *The whole rest of my life, I'll be waiting to see if John Dove is all right, and I don't mind at all as long as he is.*

But there was still quite a bit to do right now, of a less scandalous sort. If the south really had been sold out from under her she needed to know more as soon as possible: Which farms and lighthouses were to be given over, which slot canyons licensed out to foreign ships and loading docks. Assembly didn't seem likely to give her any information of the sort but the Magistrate had his hands in everything on the island, and even more importantly, he had to sign off on it all. Which meant he'd have records.

And luckily, he was an uptight, fastidious ass, which meant he'd probably already had the paperwork sent ahead and filed away by his secretary.

With some difficulty Theodora zipped up one of the black dresses she'd brought from home. She ran her hands down her waist and across her skirt, smoothing nonexistent wrinkles. Strange, wasn't it, how she still felt such a responsibility to this place, after they'd all but run her out of the place. But if anything her zeal to protect these people and this land had only grown stronger. *Perhaps it's just stubborn pride*, she thought. *But there are worse reasons to get off one's ass after ten years.*

She picked up her notebooks, shook out her hair, and clucked her tongue at Diana.

She'd been to the Map Room once before, after Adelaide had married and Theodora had finally made it to Mooring. At that point her friend was so caught up in the glow of being married to one of the island's most up-and-coming that she hadn't even mentioned Theodora's absence at the wedding. Adelaide had thrown open the door and barely let Theodora get her coat off before starting the tour.

The Map Room was at the end of a hall on the second floor, and in truth it wasn't called the Map Room by anyone but herself. Adelaide had described it as her "dear husband's room for his navigational studies." Theodora had no idea then or now why a Magistrate needed to study navigation, but who was she to judge, a widow studying the clouds?

She paused outside the door but heard only her own breathing and turned the knob. It wasn't until she was halfway across the room that she noticed John in the tall-backed chair by the fireplace, lit by a pale green algae glow in the glass burner.

No one else could pull off that color. How aggravating.

He was bent low over a notepad, glasses on, which suited him. He frowned as he cast his eyes over the paper and she took a step back, thinking to retreat, when a breeze slammed the door shut.

John jumped fully out of his chair, moving his hands to cover the paper in his hands. He looked a bit like he was trying to be modest.

"I'll go? Didn't mean to interrupt, my apologies."

"No! No. Please stay. I'm –" he moved his hands behind his back.

"I'm nothing. I mean. This is nothing. Please sit." He nodded toward the chair opposite.

"You're sure? You're working on something top secret, it seems," she said, smiling a little, not sure if she could tease him any longer. "Plans for world domination?"

He looked even more embarrassed. "No, no, I'm – this is – I'm drawing."

She clapped her hands together and bounded across the room. "John, are you truly? How wonderful! May I see?"

He dropped the notebook into the chair and sat down hard atop it.

"Oh no, please don't sit on it, you'll ruin it!" She grabbed his hand and pulled him back upright almost as soon as he touched the seat. Together they half-fell, toppling backwards like the start of a dance until John ended up leaning over Theodora in the chair opposite, braced with his face several inches from hers.

"Oh," she said, suddenly breathless. *Too familiar.* "I became too excited, perhaps."

He repressed a grin. "I wouldn't say –"

She slid out from under him, and he twisted and fell into the space where she'd been.

"Teddy, honestly –"

"May I?" she asked, moving quickly to where he'd been sitting. When they were young she'd collected his scraps and sketches, telling him she was going to sell them all when he became famous. "I missed your work so much."

John sighed. "I suppose."

Theodora gently picked up the paper and turned it upright. "I didn't know you worked in – oh," she said softly.

"I don't. I don't really work in anything, to be honest."

He'd been sketching a building, and she recognized it immediately: The view from the street of the Navigators' Club and the window where they'd sat together. Snow piled up on the windowsill. Her face in profile, odd nose and all.

She shook her head. "You're too good, John. Here." She held it back out to him abruptly. "I'm sorry I intruded."

"Thank you," he said, and gently took it back. "I've become a bit skittish about showing people. And you know. I do value your opinion."

"It's perfect," she said, and hesitated. "Shall I leave you then?"

John smiled. "That would be much worse. Please sit. Do whatever you were planning to do. I'll keep working. It'll be nice to have company. Unless you wanted to be alone?"

Theodora shook her head. *No wonder we never got anywhere*, she thought, and walked over to the nearest shelf. She slid her hand into her pocket to feel her mother's journal, to reassure herself it was still there and still hidden. She felt better having it with her.

It was an atlas she'd come for, and there was a pocket version on the table next to her. I'm sure we'll find out everything we thought about the world was wrong now, she thought.

"Did you like doing it?" John asked.

Theodora nearly jumped out of her chair. "What?"

"Magic?"

"Like it? What a funny question."

"Seems rather important to me."

She flipped open a book, buying time to compose herself: *Northward Ho, a treatise on no-man's land*.

Bollocks. She shoved it back on the shelf.

"Can I admit I've never thought about it before? That's absurd, isn't it?"

"You have a lot on your mind as a general rule, Teddy."

She ran her finger along the spines. The Magistrate had topographical surveys going back 200 years at least, though nothing from the last five years. "It just always felt right to me. Even when it was driving me mad."

"And does it still? Now that it's back, I mean?"

"I guess it really is back, isn't it?" she said. "It feels more real to hear you say it, I think, than to do it." She blushed and looked down. "But yes, it still feels the same as it always did. Like the right thing to do, even when it drives me mad."

She looked over her shoulder to see him smiling at her, and she grinned back until a loud, excited squeak came from the direction of the door.

A mouse? But when Theodora looked down she saw shoes, attached to Adelaide's erstwhile nanny who stood in the doorway with a newspaper clutched to her chest. There was a look of utter joy on her face that bordered on mania.

"Hello, Rosemarie," John said lightly. "How are you this evening?

Rosemarie's eyes grew wider and lips formed a perfect moue. "Me? I'm quite fine, Master Dove." She took several quick steps into the room. "How are you two, then?" She held the newspaper so hard that it was crinkling; there seemed to be a rather large headline but Theodora couldn't read it.

"Is there something you needed us for?" Theodora asked, amused. Then she gasped. "Bleeding Nimue and Morgana. I'd forgotten! The paper, give it here! Please," she added, lunging forward for it. She couldn't believe she'd forgotten about the late edition, about Jack Greenwood and magic in the dining room.

Rosemarie thrust it forward to Theodora. "I'm so happy for you two," she said in a stage whisper. "It's a perfect match, I must say."

Theodora snatched it roughly from Rosemarie's hands and heard a strangled noise. *Perhaps a bird hitting a window?* Then she realized it had come from her own mouth.

John was staring at the paper. "What the devil?"

"Is this not – are we not meant to know?" Rosemarie whispered, taking a step back. Theodora read the headline again:

NOT A WITCH BUT A MANHUNTER
Mistress Theodora Ashe-Martin's "Witchcraft" Debunked by Our Eyewitness
Sets Her Sights on Noted Humanitarian-Businessman Master John Dove
Details of their affair, pg.5

Theodora smashed the entire thing into her fists. "What is this utter shit?" she fairly yelled.

Rosemarie backed up until she hit the wall. "I thought, perhaps – is it not true then?"

"No it is not!" Theodora shouted, at which point Rosemarie turned and nearly ran into a man-sized globe in her effort to flee the room. She spun and found the door and clattered down the hall nearly at a run.

"I'm sorry! Rosemarie! Damn it, now she's gone," Theodora said. "She'll tell everyone I'm a monster who rejected John Dove."

"No! Come back!" John called out, but he was – *is he actually laughing?*

Not just laughing. Crying with laughter. Shaking with it. Theodora felt heat rise in her stomach along with something else she couldn't quite place. It took her a moment to find her breath and her voice and to quell the storm inside her.

"Did you do this?" she asked, her voice very low.

John kept laughing. "What? Yes, Teddy, I was somehow able to engineer this between brunch and right now." She folded her arms and said nothing. "Teddy, you can't be serious! Why would I ever do that," he said, nodding toward the paper, still smiling, though a little less so. He stood and gestured to the paper. "We could sue if you like. One night hardly qualifies an affair. Perhaps it's libel. Come on, give it here."

She pulled the paper close to her. "No! Tell me you didn't do this. Tell me this isn't some ploy. To shame me or to win me or, I don't know, John! Tell me!"

She heard the quaver in her voice, the mix of anger and fear.

"Teddy," he said softly, sadly. He'd stopped smiling entirely. "I wouldn't make that choice for you, Theodora. Ever."

She exhaled, but none of the tension left her body. She couldn't look at him. She began to pace the room, muttering. "It must be the assassin," she said. "But why? Perhaps they're trying a different tack to delegitimize you, make it seem you're mad or under my control since all the murdering isn't hitting its mark." She stopped and looked up suddenly. "Is this Adelaide and George again? Do you think they did this?"

Her voice nearly broke and her breathing was coming in much too fast and shallow.

All those headlines, after her mother left. Then again after Henry had gone, accusing her of so many things. And now there was nowhere for her to go. She'd gotten so distracted here, by John and by her damned unreliable, unhelpful witchcraft, and now she had nowhere to go.

"Teddy! No. Stop it. Breathe." He came to stand very close to her and reached a hand, but stopped short of touching her. She wanted nothing more than to fall into his arms but for all she knew there were spies in the walls and damned if she'd get him caught up again.

"Who is doing this, John?" she asked again, now sounding near tears to her utter mortification. She could not cry. She could not make him want to save her. "Do something, John!" she said angrily, to get him to stop looking at her like that. Like he always had.

John frowned down at the paper. "Only one way to find out," he said and strode from the room.

Startled still for a moment, Theodora watched him walk away. "John?" She hurried after him.

He went directly to the house's gilded mail tube inside an equally gilded small glass cabinet. A large fern hung over the space in the house's entry hall, to enclose whomever was sending or receiving.

Not quite the post office at home, Theodora thought, pacing the floor as John scribbled on the pad in front of the cabinet.

He pulled the switch for the operator, shoved the note inside, and sent the tube flying. "Jack Greenwood," he said by way of explanation. "Might as well go to the source. So to speak."

She stood back, appraising him. "Will he really just take a message from you?" she asked. "Just like that?"

John looked away. "Yes."

Who could Theodora have reached out to? Where did her power lie? In parlor tricks and old women's magic. In other words, nowhere.

She spun about in the entryway. "All right. Where did they put the coats? Damn it, there are far too many closets in this forsaken place." Theodora began opening and slamming shut whatever door she could lay a hand to, finding two entire hallways she hadn't known existed. "Diana!" she yelled. "Diana, come! Come now! Where in blazes is my coat?"

Her long black woolen coat materialized, held out from the long arm of a long-faced butler, who had similarly materialized.

"Thank you, Ned," John said resignedly.

"You brought your own butler?" Theodora exclaimed.

"How many things are you going to be angry at me about, Teddy? And he insisted!"

Theodora snatched the coat from Ned and began to put it on in as inefficient a manner as possible. It had grown an extra armhole and at least three new buttons.

"Diana!" she yelled again, and this time finally there was the sound of claws clicking on marble. It was good to have back-up, and gentle as she was, Diana's appearance could be very convincing. Having finally gotten her coat mostly on, Theodora began to march toward the front door.

"Teddy," John said quietly.

Theodora stopped to look at him, hands on waist. "Well? What?"

"Mind if I join you?"

She ears reddened, but her embarrassment only made the fear rear up stronger.

"I'm not your mother," she snapped. "Do what you like, John."

She turned away before she could see his face, but that was the worst of it: She knew what the look on his face would be. She'd known in the split second she'd decided to bring up his mother. Diana came up beside her as Theodora walked out the door, held open by Ned. Theodora gave the dog two firm slaps on the rump to distract herself from the emptiness that had replaced the storm in her stomach.

48

Offices of *The Sentinel*
Nightshift, December 14, 1947

Roy Hill looked like he'd been vomiting.

Actually, he looked like he still might. He sat behind the editor-in-chief's desk, perched on the edge of the rolling chair. John and Theodora and Diana had burst into the building and stormed through what seemed an unusually quiet newsroom. But Jack wasn't there.

"Jack is dead," Roy said, saying each word as if still trying to convince himself.

"What?" John and Theodora asked at the same time.

"He was found early this evening. Almost everyone was at dinner. There was only a skeleton staff." He bit his lip. "Wrong word choice."

"Where?" John asked. Now he felt like vomiting, too. The whole ride over Theodora had stared stonily out the window of the carriage, as if she still really believed he might have orchestrated this. Or worse, that he hadn't but the very thought of people knowing about them had been enough to make her turn against him entirely.

Roy nodded at the far side of the room, beside the desk, and John and Theodora both leaned over to look. The space was notable only for how clean it looked compared to the chaos of the rest of the office.

"Not again," Theodora said, putting her hand to her forehead. She wavered a little. John steadied her with a low hand on her arm, trying not to be seen. But when he glanced back across the desk Roy was watching, though he looked away quickly.

"I was at dinner at the Navigators' and the evening edition came, and – I don't have to tell you that wasn't meant to be the front page." He swallowed hard. "We think it's connected."

"Do you have any leads?" Theodora asked. She sat down unsteadily. "Anyone at all?"

Roy raised his eyebrows at her before shaking his head and gathering his bearings. "Not yet, I'm afraid." He scooched backwards in the chair and sat up a little straighter. John didn't believe him.

"Someone must have murdered him after making him change the headline. So clearly it was to keep them quiet. Some sort of deal must have gone bad," she said thoughtfully. "Have you considered revenge? Did he seem to have been tortured? There were very few people who could have known –" She suddenly pressed her lips tight and sat back. "They obviously didn't want it getting out that I am," she dropped her voice, perhaps without even realizing it, "a witch."

Roy was nodding, not breaking eye contact as he picked up a pen and started to write down notes on the blotter.

"Or perhaps blackmail was involved?" Theodora asked. "What would it take, do you think, to have something like this retracted?"

"Oh, Teddy," John muttered. He had to restrain himself from knocking Roy out to keep him from hearing any further incriminating questions. How easily Theodora fit as the murderess: she wanted to shut him up or she wanted the story to see the light of day. It didn't matter did it, as long as the story got rid of her once and for all?

"Perhaps it could've been to get him to print it in the first place," Roy said thoughtfully. "They were worried he couldn't be trusted, maybe?"

Some color had come back into the younger man's face. *Murder perks a certain type of person right up,* John had noticed.

"He must have had other enemies, though?" John asked. "I mean, er, enemies? He was fairly vocal about Assembly matters in his editorials. Very pro-occupation, obviously. Plus, you know, he was a bit of an ass when we come down to it –"

"John, the man has just been murdered," Theodora muttered. "Because of us," she added in a whisper that Roy, most definitely, was transcribing verbatim.

"I don't think that gained him many enemies, that I could see," Roy said. "A lot of powerful friends, definitely."

"Right, it could be – you know – anyone in Assembly," John began. *At least I'll incriminate myself, too.* "How was it done? The death, I mean." *Oh, damn it all. Now even I think I sound guilty.*

Roy sat back and began to swivel back and forth in his chair. "Poison. In the coffee."

"So not magic then!" John asked. Theodora and Roy both looked at him sharply. "I mean nothing mysterious about that, I suppose."

"They'd also stabbed him," Roy said. "And we found a pile of money beside him."

"Mmm, an attempted bribe," Theodora said, and John nearly lowered his head between his knees.

"If you must know," Roy said, "we hoped to start international distribution very soon, via the wire. The world is ready for, uh, unusual stories. This is quite an untapped market." Roy glanced at Diana. "Is that dog quite necessary?"

"I promise she's harmless," Theodora said, reaching up to lay a hand on the dog's head. "Unless someone threatens me, of course," she added, and started to absently scratch the dog's head. Diana groaned.

"Where were we?" John asked.

Roy scowled at them both. He was beginning to look far too comfortable behind that desk for John's liking. Roy had seemed a more reasonable sort than Jack at dinner, but perhaps that had simply been better journalistic instincts.

"The myriad motives for Mr. Greenwood's murder," Roy said.

Dammit, John thought. *And he's alliterative.*

Roy sighed. "It's the same as everywhere else: Murder and gossip.

You, at least, live up to expectations Mistress Ashe," he said, smiling at her.

"Oh!" she said. "Thank you?"

"But apparently, I've got a newspaper to run." He laughed bitterly and shook his head. "On top of solving a murder and scooping the constabulary. What a way to get promoted."

That was enough for John. He stood up fast and tipped his hat to Roy.

"Mr. Hill, my deepest condolences and my heartiest congratulations. Long may you reign. Teddy? Shall we? Yes. Let's. Diana? Thank you, ma'am."

Diana jumped up as John led the way out of the office, her very large tail giving them a wide berth as they walked through the newsroom. That, and the full force of John's charm, turned to slightly mournful yet vaguely endearing, kept everyone away from them as they made their way to the elevator.

"John, what are you – damn it, Diana!" Theodora called as she hurried to catch up.

When the elevator doors closed Theodora turned to him, hands on hips. Diana immediately lay down and closed her eyes.

"Why did you leave?" Theodora asked. "We learned practically nothing! How will we help them?"

John pressed the button for the lobby. The lever to make them move was on a small metal plate with "Dove Hydraulics" pressed on it. *I didn't even know we did that.*

"We helped them quite enough. Did you know it's a popular novelistic convention that the criminal should return to the scene of the crime? Makes for good foreshadowing and such."

Theodora rolled her eyes and jabbed twice more at the button for the lobby. "Stop it, John. Stop doing that charming thing you do with your face."

"I don't seem able to," he muttered. The bell dinged and the doors opened. John walked out as quickly as before, patting his leg as he went to bring Diana to his side. A path cleared before them through the lobby; he was beginning to understand why Teddy liked having her around so much.

"Where are we going? John! Diana, heel!"

They were nearly running now, or as close as John could manage without attracting much attention and with several rather severe injuries still hampering him.

"John!" Theodora shouted from the top of the stairs that led to the newspaper's entrance. Below her on the sidewalk several people stopped to gawk but she didn't seem, for once, to notice. "I need to fix this! I need to fix everything!"

"For the sake of all that's good, Teddy!" he shouted back at her, looking up from the sidewalk. His voice was shaking. "You need to save yourself first! A man has died and you are quite obviously the one whom everyone will suspect!"

By now a crowd had gathered. *Well, let them. Better if they do.*

"What? You cannot be serious." It was damp and freezing out and when Theodora spoke the words collected in the air around her as a cloud, that nearly obscured her face.

"Teddy," he said, reaching up for her. "Come down?"

But then she laughed, a hollow, desperate sound. "You should stay far away from me, John," she said. "Clearly I'm a threat to your future."

That was too much for him. "Damn it! That's not what I meant!"

The crowd around them was such that the traffic in the street was backing up. Several reporters were hanging out the windows above them. *Good.*

He didn't want it to be this way, any of it, and he didn't want to force her hand. But he was going to anyway.

"I won't have you hurt, John," she said fiercely, but at the same time she bent partway over, supporting her hands against her thighs as though she had run a very long way and couldn't go any further. "I won't have anyone else killed because of my failings. I came here only so that I might be allowed to keep my home, John." Her voice broke. "But I came here and –"

"And you fell in love with me."

She suddenly seemed to notice the people around them. Theodora stood up very straight. Even Diana's ears perked up. "What the devil are you talking about, John?"

He cleared his throat and began to take a knee. Then he remembered his leg was broken and switched to the opposite knee. There were gasps and squeals around them. Flashbulbs.

"And I with you, Theodora Ashe-Martin," he said, projecting. He was very quite Diana was supporting her so that she didn't tumble down the stairs from shock. "So, I'll ask you now: Will you marry me?"

49

Outerbridge Estate
Late, December 14, 1947

"Yes," George said finally. "I do agree. A wedding is the only way."

Theodora threw up her hands. "How wonderful for you both! Where shall I send the gift?"

"Ted," Adelaide said quietly. They were back in the Magistrate's office. Adelaide was sunk deep in an armchair, legs tucked up beneath her, and Theodora was perched like a nervous bird beside her. Now she turned so far around to stare that she nearly slid into Adelaide's lap.

"Not you, too!"

"I think it might be the only way. Or at least the best way." Adelaide looked worried but also sober and serious, which made Theodora that much more nervous.

"Each one of you has lost your respective mind," Theodora said, jumping up to pace.

"Teddy, I swear," John said, "I wouldn't have suggested it if I thought there was any other way."

She was fairly certain she believed him. Generally John was quite wise about this sort of strange, political goings-on. But this was his entire future. His life.

"You didn't suggest it, John! You proposed. In public! And while my reputation went to shit years ago yours is bright, still. Even considering all the near-death. Do you really want to throw it away on me?"

"Damn it, Teddy, I do not care an algae bloom's ass for my reputation," John said, his voice rising in frustration. Adelaide snorted. John was pacing, too, so Theodora kept nearly bumping into him. She flounced down onto the couch in aggravation.

"There's no reason to think that I'm actually a suspect. At least not a serious one," she allowed.

"Dearest, *The Sentinel* has been printing salacious stories about you for years," Adelaide said. "You have every reason to hate them."

"But to murder! Over silly stories! That's an absurd leap to make."

John shook his head. "Stories aren't so silly when people believe them. You heard Jack. More importantly, so did Roy."

Adelaide laid a hand gently on her arm. "That's why we have to tell our own story."

"Whoever did this," George said, "is playing on what John's assumed reaction would be. John's supposed to swoop into the void left by the Ag Minister. They want him to cut you off, Theodora. They're trying to make you look desperate, which means they must be getting a bit desperate themselves."

John sat down next to her on the couch. "Even if they try to pin the murder on me, I would survive it, Theodora. My family's – my father's – business means too much to the island and the ledgers of a lot of powerful people. But, it seems, people would benefit from you being found guilty. For confirming that the past they'd like to forget is well worth forgetting. You could be banished or –" John's voice broke.

"John," Theodora said, and laid her hand over his on his knee.

"If, however," George said, "you call it an engagement, it's possible we might be able to, as Addy said, make it our own story." He cleared his throat. "I mean your own. Perhaps buy some time discover not only who broke the news about you two, and who's been trying to off John, but who might have a bit to gain from the death of a prominent figurehead for algaeic research and international cooperation."

"George, dear," Adelaide interrupted.

"If it's the same person," George went on, gaining steam.

"Darling," said Adelaide.

"Perhaps it's multiple people!"

Adelaide picked up a throw pillow.

"A conspiracy. Maybe worldwide!"

Adelaide hit him squarely in the chest, sloshing George's cocktail on the floor. "Try not to sound too excited, love."

George looked up from the wet spot on his shirt, noticing the gloomy faces around him.

"Sorry," he said, getting up to refill his glass. "I promise my enthusiasm is nearly totally about saving both your lives. What I mean is that you might both being doing a public good. A real one, in addition to the good of self-preservation."

Theodora turned back to John. "This is your life, John," she said again, more quietly. "Being married to me might be more dangerous than any other occupation," she added, trying to smile but knowing from the look on John's face that she must only seem very sad.

"I know what I'm doing, Theodora," he said. He searched her face, like he was looking for something.

He didn't seem to find it. "But it's not just me we're talking about," he said, jumping up. "I've a place waiting for me back on the ice in about a week's time. Ashe House passes to me if we marry. Which means it would pass to you," he said, quickly, "of course. You could go home."

Theodora felt something inside herself tighten. A resumption of the same reserve she'd cultivated over the past nine years. Maybe longer. *Pity. I didn't even realize I'd been feeling any different until it was gone.*

"Right," she said, taking a deep breath. "You'll go to the glacier. I'll go south. Home. A marriage of convenience."

John looked like he might say something, and for just a moment Theodora felt a crack, a dangerous crack, in her veneer.

But then he nodded and resumed pacing.

Theodora looked at Adelaide. "You think this is best?"

Adelaide took a few seconds to answer, frowning as she did. "I believe it is," she said carefully. "It removes at least one motive for Greenwood's killing. Furthermore why would you try to kill John if you were going to go ahead and marry him?"

Adelaide looks so very tired, Theodora noticed, but at that moment her face also lit up . "And dearest, you'll get your house! You'll be safe there."

"I suppose," Theodora began, looking to John, but he'd started pacing again.

Adelaide cleared her throat. Now she looked rather pained. "There's just the one thing, dear. You'll have to give up being a witch."

"What?" said John, stopping dead. "No! That wasn't the plan at all."

"I don't understand," Theodora said. George was silent, which she took to be a bad sign.

"If you're not a witch," Adelaide said, "then you're just a silly woman. Caught up in city politics and caught up in love. But if you're really a witch," she took a sip of her drink, then another, "anything might be possible of you. Plus, if you're not a witch you can't inherit Henry's fortune so there's no trouble there, either. Everyone wins," she said, trying to smile.

They all looked at Theodora, waiting.

"Theodora, I never meant for this part of it, you must know that!" John said. But even he didn't deny that it was necessary. And even Theodora could see that it was.

It shouldn't have mattered. It was always a game she was playing, and for so long she'd thought she was no longer a witch at all. It was just, to be so close to who she used to be –

But she couldn't leave John alone now. He was in too much danger.

"Fine," she said firmly, to convince herself as much as them. "I'm no longer a witch. But John, may I speak to you? Alone?"

"Good idea." George grabbed Adelaide by the hand. "Ta, then," he said. "Let us know what you need, lovebirds!"

Adelaide called back over her shoulder: "We'll make you a beautiful bride, darling!"

The door shut behind them.

John turned to her. "Drink?"

"Please."

John poured two and handed her one as he sat down in a chair beside the couch.

"I have to tell you something," she said. "I had sex with you."

He smiled suddenly, and he looked so sweet and like her John that she nearly started to cry. "I recall," he said. "Quite well."

Theodora bit her lip. She didn't want to do this. Maybe, if they weren't to be married – married! – it could have come out in good time. Naturally. Or maybe she would have never needed to say it. But she didn't want to marry him without him knowing. She didn't want it to be any more false than it already would be.

"It was for a reason," she said.

John raised an eyebrow.

"It was to save you. I read in a book –"

"A book?"

Theodora looked away. "A book my mother wrote –"

"You wrote to your mother about – wait, no – she wrote to you – hold on. What?"

"I thought if I had sex with you I could keep you from dying."

She'd thought this would be only embarrassing, but now it seemed cruel, too. John's face had gone totally blank. Not angry, not even displeased. Just thoroughly professional. "I thought it would work a spell that would bind you to me and let me keep you safe. I read it in my mother's spell book, that Victoria found – well you know she was a witch! My mother, I mean, not Victoria."

John opened and shut his mouth several times. "Victoria?"

"I ran into her at the library. She'd found the book, and the book had a protection spell," Theodora said, staring at the carpet, her voice trailing off. *You sound ridiculous*, she thought. *You don't even know if you did it right! Any of it, actually.*

"That's why you came to my room?"

Theodora opened her mouth to answer. She closed it.

"Was it?" he asked again, his voice gone lower.

The book had said to bind herself to the person she wished to save.

Didn't that mean sex? Mustn't it? But what if it meant any number of other things, too, and she'd just picked the one that she really, truly wanted?

"I don't know?" she said in a whisper.

He gave her half a smile. His eyes were shining in the glow of the fireplace, but the problem with algae-light was that it absorbed as much as it reflected, and now Theodora couldn't tell if there were tears at all or what those tears might mean.

She swallowed hard. "I had to save you, John. I have to. You must be safe."

He took her hand again, and then quickly let her go, and then took it again. "You are a good, dear friend," he said. Now her own eyes were shining. "But I won't lie to you. It meant more to me than that. I've loved you for quite a while, Teddy. I'm not sure how long, actually."

Something inside herself burst open. She couldn't tell if she was hollow now or if the sun was shining on her for the first time.

"John –"

"Let me say this. I never say enough. Teddy, it'd be wonderful to be married to you, even as just part of a ruse. It'll be wonderful because it's you, and that's partly because you're a wonderful friend, and always have been. Even when we didn't talk for nearly ten years," he said, and the corner of his mouth went up.

"Nine," she said, smiling a little, "and that was your fault, too."

"Either way," he said, raising an eyebrow, "I never want it to happen again. If afterwards, when you're safe and we've figured out who's after us, or after me, you want to leave and never see me again, that's fine. I care deeply for you, and what you want, we will do. You never need doubt that. But I love you, Teddy, and always will. You never need doubt that, either."

"I care for you, too," she said softly. "You great bloody idiot."

The problem was that she didn't just care for John. She loved him. She loved the twitch of his lips and his artist's hands and she loved the world with him in it.

But even as she thought it, she saw what would happen as good as if prophecy had been her talent instead of a meteorology that came and went as it pleased: He would leave. She would make him. She'd driven her own family away, hadn't she?

John squeezed her hand in his. "Damn it, Teddy, you deserve more than they want to give you. And I suppose I don't deserve to have a ceiling fall on me. Another one."

"I agree," she said, with just the hint of a smile. "Once was enough."

"Good. George seems to think this will throw whoever's after us off the trail enough to buy us some time or information. So let us protect each other. And you can have your home and I can have – well, the ice is quite beautiful actually. All right?"

Theodora nodded. "All right."

John smiled when he let go of her hands she felt the pull of him like a magnet, each finger stretching out toward him once more. She put her hands in her lap.

"Good," he said. "But promise me you'll always write?"

50

Diviners' Club
Commercial District
Luncheon, December 15, 1947

"When someone of John's stature is married, it is nearly always done in the Assembly. It'll be early, probably at 8 a.m., and in addition to the full component of old families and Ministers the bride and groom's family and close friends are, of course, invited."

Adelaide made another note in her notebook. This was the most serious Theodora had ever seen her. Like she was preparing for battle.

The wedding was a week away. Theodora and Adelaide had gone out to breakfast to the Diviners' Club, headquarters of the Women's Society, the Youth League, the Botanical Medicine Organization, and so many other groups listed on a placard by the front door that Theodora hadn't had time to read them all.

Adelaide acknowledged nearly everyone they passed as they made their way through white wicker and heavy perfume toward the cafe. A hundred inside jokes and bits of gossip hung in the air, charged with significant looks and half-smiles, and Theodora was surprised she hadn't needed a passport to enter. It had been easier, somehow, to be sequestered like an outcast in the men's' club.

Ostensibly Theodora and Adelaide were here to plan the wedding, though it seemed to Theodora that nearly the whole thing had already been determined by yet another committee of which Adelaide was probably the president.

Theodora twisted to look over the lists Adelaide was making in her fine fountain-pen hand, and the drawings from the wedding designer Adelaide had already hired. "It's all perhaps a bit staid, isn't it?" Theodora asked carefully. "Not that I care overmuch," she added quickly.

"Oh certainly," Adelaide said. "Terrible business. Rather like my own wedding! Which of course you weren't there for," she added lightly, with a laugh that became a sigh. "Unfortunately."

Theodora's first wedding had been orchestrated by her stepmother, a mix of traditions gleaned from back issues of *Seasons*, the island's ladies magazine. Henry's mother felt that the dress was all wrong – though Theodora thought the real problem was the person wearing it – and alterations were still being made the morning of the ceremony.

That was one of Theodora's most vivid memories of the day: Her own reflection, barely balanced atop a small velvet stool, white silk pooling on the floor as several older women pinned and tucked fabric. She'd kept blinking, trying to recognize herself. Whenever she tried to move any more than that the women scolded her to keep still.

Adelaide's wedding was only a few weeks after Theodora's, a much grander affair but done in a rush. Theodora had watched the rest of her family leave for the ceremony through a dark haze. She wasn't even sure she'd ever officially declined the invitation.

They'd never spoken about it. Much like they hadn't spoken about their argument the night that Jack Greenwood and Roy Hill came to dinner.

Much like Theodora had barely spoken to John since the engagement was made official with an announcement in *The Sentinel*. Repression was beginning to seem a theme, though Theodora supposed that wasn't terribly new for her or for the island. They were largely descended from Puritans after all, even if they had been witches.

Now Adelaide waved her hand. "Anyway, I tried to get Oiseau to draw something up but she's much too avant-garde." Adelaide rolled her eyes. She picked up a scone and started to spread a thick layer of yellow butter. "Which won't do. Marrying a Minister is quite different from trying to look like a scandalous witch," she said through a large bite. "It's a pity we couldn't get you something new and unusual."

Theodora gave her friend a teasing smile. "You do love new things."

"I love beautiful things," Adelaide replied sharply. "There's a difference."

Theodora's face went hot. "I didn't mean to imply you were frivolous, Addy."

"Like these women?" Adelaide asked, a little louder than Theodora would have preferred, though no one looked up. "There's a lot you can achieve working within strict confines. It forces you to be creative. We're not such silly women, and I'd remind you that you're about to join our ranks."

Theodora was thoroughly taken aback. "I would never say that!"

"Oh? I am a wealthy, kept woman, not even a housewife, barely a mother. Is that what you meant?" Adelaide began to butter more bread, a little more roughly this time.

"What? No! That's not at all what I think of you! No one could. Look at me, please," Theodora said, taking her friend's hand, trying to meet her eye. "I'm sorry."

Adelaide put down the scone. She took up her cocktail and after taking a sip leaned back in her chair. When she finally looked at Theodora again there was a much younger girl there, frustrated and angry.

"I'm sorry, too," Adelaide said, sighing. "I know you don't think that of me. Perhaps I think all that of myself."

"You're the smartest person I know, Addy." Theodora lowered her voice. "You're also apparently a spy, so as far as I know you are instrumental in the triumph of good over evil." Adelaide pursed her lips. "You're not a silly woman! None of you are. You keep the city running, as far as I can tell, while your husbands are off doing who-knows-what."

She sat up and sipped. "But you think we could do more in the light of day."

Theodora considered the centerpiece, a purple and pink flower that would surely die if it ever left this room. "Yes," she said finally. "I think you could do a lot more."

Adelaide nodded. "Then I would say the same to you."

Theodora waved that away. "I'm different."

Adelaide twisted her head so she could catch Theodora's eye. "Yes, you are. Brilliantly so. And a witch, so every door is open to you if you want to walk through it. You're shackled to nothing."

"Not shackled yet, you mean," Theodora said lightly.

Adelaide flopped backward in her seat. "Not shackled yet. You know I didn't want this for you, Ted. John is different, but — I wanted more for you." She swallowed hard.

"John is different, Adelaide," Theodora said, willing herself to believe it. *He was, though. He had to be.* "

Adelaide toyed with her hair a moment then smiled brightly. "Yes. I'm sure he is. And as I was saying, beautiful things can be quite powerful. If they're the right things, used the right way." She smirked and unhooked her hand from Theodora's. "So please prepare yourself for the adventure of a lifetime: paper stock!"

51

Assembly District
Teatime, December 15, 1947

To GET from George's apartment to his father's house John had to cross nearly the entire university campus, full of students so strung out by studying for finals that John feared if two of them collided a small explosion might result. He cut east across the river against a bitterly cold northern wind that had been blowing everyone upside down and sideways all day. The bridge was snarled with noonday traffic of carriages and the automobiles that seemed to be reproducing daily, a new batch on every ship. John didn't mind the walk, though. He wanted to rehearse a little more what he was going to say.

But once he was across he had to navigate the shopping district, full of last-minute Solstice crowds, and then he was only at the very north of the Assembly plaza. Black hats and robes swarmed in advance of the holiday break, and somehow even more people wanted to talk to him than had before the engagement was announced. It took him nearly half an hour to get across the large cobbled square to his father's house, down several small twisty lanes that belied the expense of the real estate. As he got closer the wind beat against his back harder, nearly lifting him off his feet.

"Subtle," he said to it, and the words flew away.

The weather was so bad that his father's secretary had sent a note that morning, care of the pub, asking John if he'd like to reschedule. John was surprised his father had noticed the weather, since he never seemed to leave the house anymore. But John didn't want to put this off.

At Dove House John lifted his hand to knock and the door opened. His father's secretary stepped back into the dark hallway.

The door closed with a bang, and the sudden absence of wind made John dizzy. The events of the last weeks had altered his equilibrium.

"I can find my own way, thanks," he said, and when the secretary lingered, looking as though John had spoken a made-up tongue, John gave him his most winning smile and stepped off forcefully in the direction of his father's study. When he turned the first corner he looked back, and found he was alone.

The house was darker and warmer than the last time John was here. *More diseased.*

As a child John had treated this entire section of this house with awe and suspicion. Even now he felt like he was getting away with something every time he entered, and he hesitated before knocking. Finally he turned the knob and entered unannounced.

His father sat by the window, in a tall-backed chair with his legs under a blanket. A cup of tea sat neglected beside him as he stared out at the river. *Perhaps he's sleeping.* John took a half-step closer. *Or –*

"John," his father said, smiling but not looking away from the window.

"Thank you for seeing me," John said, and closed the distance between them.

"Sit, please. Would you like some tea?"

"No thank you." John perched on the edge of the low chair opposite. He didn't take off his coat, and his father lifted one white, wiry eyebrow.

"In a hurry? I told you we could reschedule. Did Mr. Grove not call? This damn wind is a disgrace, no one should be out in it. Time for staying home and doing work, instead."

"Staying home, yes," John said. "Sounds nice." Archibald was distracted and John needed to present his case coherently. Strongly. Not more than once, because his nerves couldn't take it. "Father," he said, "I've come to tell you something." He swallowed, his mouth having gone completely dry. *Damn, tea would have been a help.* "Victoria and I are not to marry." *Strong, strong tea.* He swallowed again, hard. "Theodora Ashe and I are."

Archibald's face changed only slightly, in ways no one save the most loyal household staff would recognize. Or his son. His gnarled fingers twitched and his wild silver eyebrows drew together and his gut expanded with a deep breath taken in advance of a dressing down.

"So the witch then?" he asked.

There it is, John thought: *No longer a grandfather, now an avenging God from ancient times with lightning in his veins.*

But just as quick came another thought: *Or just a mean, sad old man sitting here like an angry elephant seal.* He'd never thought that before and now, at completely the wrong time, John couldn't help but smile very broadly. Or perhaps exactly the right time.

Archibald's stomach deflated, like he'd been punched or was preparing to launch into a tirade. His eyebrows retreated. He folded his hands on his lap.

"I'm glad this makes you happy," he said evenly. He leaned forward and patted John on the knee twice.

John was unsure what to say. It was true. He was happy. He was happy to have declared, out loud and to his father for the first time, what he truly wanted to do.

He was also completely, utterly confused as to why his father didn't seem to care. *Could it be he never cared?* Could it be John had spent the last – *no, best not to think of the exact number of years* – living in anger towards this man who only wanted his son to be happy?

Strangely the thought made John want to scream.

"Thank you?" was all he said.

John and his father stared at each other across four decorous feet.

Perhaps they would be there still had not a large broken branch banged against the window, carried by the wind.

The bang was followed by a crack. The glass splintered like a web.

"Shit!" John said, jumping toward the window. "It's liable to shatter." His father would never be able to shield himself or survive such an assault. "We've got to move away and get something against the glass. Mr. Grove!" John turned back to help his father. "Come get away from –"

His father was smiling at the window. He looked at the broken glass with the same benign, vaguely curious face he'd had when John first entered the room. Not unseeing or unaware but as though he looked out and saw only a world entirely of his own making.

"Father?" John asked weakly, sounding like a boy again. Just when he was close to stepping closer and reaching out, his father turned his head. "Call Mr. Grove. We'll be sliced to pieces any moment, and that's not the sort of corpse I thought to leave."

Half of John's mouth went up, hoping that was meant to be a joke. He really couldn't tell. Archibald just turned away.

John went to fetch Mr. Grove, who seemed deeply relieved to have a crisis to deal with. He stood staring into the dark hallway to his father's rooms, wondering if he should go back.

Then John went straight to the front door and into the wind.

52

Office of the Pneumatic Post
Assembly North
Just before closing, December 15, 1947

THEODORA WENT STRAIGHT FROM THE DIVINERS' Club to the post office to write Roberta. The conversation with Adelaide, and the long list of tasks she'd been given to complete before the wedding, made her realize she needed the help of one person specifically.

She paused in front of the grand building, dark and ominous like an approaching storm and just as welcome to her right now. Each stone step was worn down in the middle to a gentle bow. The doors opened and closed before her, a pre-holiday rush of mailings, and everything about the place spoke of familiarity and connection and hope.

She hadn't been in touch with anyone back home. Not that anyone had reached out to her, either. By now they must've found her note. *Certainly! Or at least noticed my seat was empty at dinner?* And then of course they would have already learned of the wedding in the worst way possible, reading about it two days late in *The Sentinel*. *Well at least that should make Father pleased. Even if Roberta'll kill me for not telling her first.*

But there was no denying she needed her sister's help. And it felt good to be out alone again, doing something routine like checking the post. Adelaide could be a bit oppressive when she got her mind set on planning a party.

Maybe there'll be a letter from Henry, Theodora thought absently.

She laughed aloud. Then ran up the stairs with more lightness than she'd felt for some time.

A tall young man held the door for her with great ceremony. "After you, Mistress Ashe-Martin. Or should I say Mistress Dove. Almost, that is." He winked as she went by.

"Oh!" Theodora laughed – *was that a titter?* – in a way she'd never heard from herself before. *I supposed Mistress Dove does have a nice ring to it. A bit better than Murderess Wench or Widow-Witch or –*

She pulled up short. The same young man ran smack into her back.

"Oh my, I'm so sorry," she said, only half-looking at him and helping him pick up his hat. Most of her attention was focused on the room, as much as she could. It was so dark and so large it seemed night had already arrived in the far corners, the walls only evident by the pulsing glow in round frosted orbs in brass holders.

A tall brass gate that was really more of a wall ran the length of the room before her. Long lines had formed in front of it, queued up behind shadowy workers visible mostly by the hands that reached out for packages and mail. She'd be lucky to mail the letter before closing.

She took a step forward only to have her foot slip sideways on something. Catching herself, just barely, she took a step back to scuff out the offending patch, and as she did the octopus became visible for the first time.

It was made of tiny, glittering squares of tile. Only one tentacle was visible, a few suction cups. But even in that small area was blue, green, and pale pink, each square no bigger than her thumbnail. *It must have taken months, maybe more.* Theodora stepped lightly to the side and in the mosaic bubbles surged toward the surface. The edge of a tail fin flicked away from a long, sharp tooth in cold water. She scuffed her foot along the floor like she was dancing and revealed a winding green plant. *So much life.*

"'Scuse me, ma'am," someone said from behind, and Theodora was nearly lifted from her feet by a sudden wave of people. She was deposited in one of the long snaking lines, the mosaic obscured again by feet and darkness and filth.

Theodora scowled. On top of it all she had no idea if she was in the right line. She sighed loudly, and the woman one line over turned with a look of concern, replaced quickly with wide eyes and a small step away.

"Sorry," Theodora said, unsure if she was apologizing for being loud or for being herself. "Is it always like this?"

The woman shifted her bags. "Only at Solstice, Mistress Ashe-Martin."

Theodora groaned, then tried to put on a bright face. "Well. I suppose it's nice to be out amongst people."

The woman smiled and shifted her bags to her other shoulder. "Quite," she said, winking "I have eleven children, so for me this counts as alone time!" She chuckled as she turned back to face the front.

"Quite," Theodora said, blinking rapidly. *Eleven! Bouddica save her.*

When it was finally her turn, Theodora folded the letter with a sharp crease and set back her shoulders. She strode forward to reach the woman behind the gate, who was busy reshuffling items on her particular square of counter. She didn't look up.

"Good morning," Theodora said. "Excuse me, that is, good afternoon. I have one letter to mail to Ashe House."

A brass slot banged open in front of her. The woman tapped her nails twice against the marble, and the sharpness of the sound cut through the dull din of the crowds.

"Riverside?"

"Yes, that's Riverside," Theodora said, but gripped her letter a bit harder. "Unfortunately – I mean not unfortunately, just that I'm sure you're busy, it's just that I'm meant to ask to speak with the Postmaster General about hand delivering invitations –"

For the first time the woman looked up and squarely at Theodora, eyes narrowing. "Oh," she said, drawing it out so it was almost an accusation, "hello, Mistress Ashe-Martin."

Her tone was not nearly so solicitous as that of the man who'd held the door. This woman was young, probably much younger than Theodora, and wore bright red lipstick, and even through the murky glass Theodora could see the perfect curls and coils of her upswept hair.

"Yes, hello," Theodora said, squaring her shoulders and lifting her chin.

The two women stared at each other a long while, until the younger shrugged.

"Here," she said, waggling her fingers through the slot again. "Give me your letter then, and I'll let you write out a note to the Postmaster. I'm sure he'll see to it when he's back from lunch."

Theodora opened her mouth to insist, then screwed up her lips to the side. She glanced at the skylight. *Lunch at 4pm?* She didn't have time for bureaucracy, but this woman seemed frighteningly competent; she hadn't stopped sorting the entire time they'd been talking, except for when she'd knocked her talons against the glass. Theodora didn't feel she'd get very far arguing. She also wasn't sure she'd win.

"Fine," she said, and relinquished her letter. "Please send it First Class Overnight, with receipt."

"Whatever you say, Mistress Ashe-Martin," the woman replied, exchanging a pen and a notepad of pale pink paper for the letter. She looked up over her glasses and raised an eyebrow. "Congratulations on the engagement by the way."

She had to get used to this: The entire point was that people should know.

"Thank you very much," she said, feeling her lips move into a smile but feeling unsure of the result. Like she was in a terrible actor in a play.

"Did you know," the clerk began, still filing as she went, "that woman before you in line has eleven children? Eleven! Comes in every week to send mail along to other widows, too."

"Mmhmm," Theodora said, trying to write as quickly as possible. But then she looked up. "She's a widow, too?"

"How many do you think you'll have?" the girl asked. She lowered her voice. "D'ya think they'll be witches, too? Don't know which one the Dove Dynasty would prefer, but more's the pity if you're the last, dontcha think? Can you imagine little witchettes running about?" She clucked her tongue. "How adorable."

Theodora's pen drew a jagged line across the page which she tried to save by scrawling it into her signature. *Deny, deny, deny.* She shoved the note back under the grate.

"You still believe I'm a witch?" she whispered, and the clerk finally stopped sorting her mail to look Theodora in the eye.

"Didn't stop believing it for a minute," she said, all seriousness. "There's a lot of us that do. Can't believe everything you read, can you?" She winked and then pressed a lever next to her station. "Have a lovely day! Next!"

A dusty keyhole flipped open above the window, revealing green light, and a man in a porter's uniform staggered forward under the weight of a dozen packages. Theodora barely dodged out of his way and turned to navigate back through a crowd which had only grown more disorderly.

A witch. Eleven babies. Surely John didn't expect that. He'd said as much, that they'd go their separate ways after the wedding. And if, at times while planning the wedding Theodora had let herself wonder if separation would really be necessary, that was still a far cry from wanting eleven babies.

Eleven witch babies?

In the time she'd been inside her eyes still hadn't adjusted to the gloom, and the crush of people waiting made it slightly hard to breathe. As Theodora approached the exits even the low light of the early winter evening seemed warmer than she felt here, trapped. *If I could just get through this damned crowd —*

When she was young, Theodora had gone to the mineral pools on the eastern coast with Adelaide's family. "Tacky," her own father always grumbled when he declined the invitation to join them, though as she grew older Theodora wondered if the scene at the pools had in fact been too cosmopolitan for her father. So much potential for saying the wrong thing or being judged in poor taste himself.

None of Adelaide's family actually went in the pools — apparently that was considered a bit tacky, after all — including Adelaide, who by age fourteen spent all her time artfully draping herself across the chairs so that the steam hit her like a someone in a novel standing on a train platform. Theodora, though, could never resist the water.

It had felt like this. The air around her was so thick she felt she could fall back and it would catch her. Or that she could dive down into it and disappear. Her limbs were weightless, like she was dissolving.

Her skin was dissolving.

Oh hell.

The people are her began to gasp as the dissolution became more evident, as a gust of icy-cold air burst into the humid warmth of the post office.

The first thing she felt was panic.

But as Theodora wafted out the open doorway of the post office, as she slid out the cracks in the windows and blew past the people on the stairs, she realized that it was a very good sign that she could still feel anything at all. *Not dead then. That's a good start.*

And once she realized that not only could she still feel, but could think as well, the panic began to subside. Then, as adrenaline or its molecular equivalent stopped coursing so strongly through whatever it was she was, Theodora began to feel, wonderfully, the whole world, all at once.

She blew down the stairs and onto the street.

Forget the post office girl! There, she's already forgotten! Theodora whipped up dry leaves and they turned to dust in her midst. She felt each one disintegrate along ever smaller cracks until they disappeared altogether and blew off onto another breeze. *No, not disappear, that's wrong. Only becoming something else again.*

Theodora blew down Post Office Land, ruffling women's skirts and pulling men's satchels from their hands as she went. At the first intersection she flew upward into the gray sky, smooth like metal but charged like it, too, ready to spark if she was too soft or too warm. *Hold steady, girl.* There was Assembly, full of ministers closing up shop for the Solstice. Doubtless plotting. *Should probably check in. Blow up a few arses.*

Theodora laughed and it emerged as a shimmer in the gray light, like heat in summer. *Maybe this is what I'll be missing when I marry*, she thought. *Maybe this is why my mother left.*

She shot higher into the air and out over the river.

How high might I go, then? She had to work a little harder now, the way she might have taken a deep breath to dive. Instead she shot higher into the air, where it was less gray but more electric and unstable.

Theodora was being pulled south, past the factories and into the forest where the temperature sank and with it her own altitude, so that she felt the long dry needles of the trees brush against her. She was only at the very edge of the forest but the change from the city – the silence and the fullness of the world away from people – worked on her like a drug. It occurred to her that she shouldn't stay too long like this, in case she was unable to change back.

Theodora blew towards Adelaide's, holding her hands out to guide herself. *I have hands again*, she thought, still very calm, all her panic blown away on other winds. *Perhaps I ought to hurry, though, before I'm spotted stark naked among the treetops.*

Adelaide's garden was ornate enough to provide both cover and a decently soft landing as Theodora half-fell, half-lowered herself through the trees onto a bed of tall grasses. It was itchy, but otherwise very accommodating, and Theodora splayed out, staring up at the sky she'd just been part of. She wiggled her fingers and toes to count them. *All here.* The stars were starting to come out, and everything was turning from gray to violet.

Theodora opened her eyes very wide so the cold evening air came back into her bloodstream. I wonder what this is what it's like to have died. *I wonder this is what it's like for Henry and my mother.*

If death is like this, she thought, *perhaps it's not so bad at all. Perhaps they're all right.*

"Theodora! Why on earth are you naked in the garden?"

Theodora sat up so fast her vision spun. Adelaide stood staring with hands on hips, half-outraged and half-immensely curious, and Theodora began to laugh.

53

Outerbridge Estate
Mid-day, December 17, 1947

"Are you sure she'll like this? Damn it. This beast weighs twice as much as me. Is she made of lead?"

"I'm sure she'll like it. As much as I'm sure of anything. Hold still. I don't even know that you're necessary, really, George. Roberta seems to have it covered."

"That's because Diana likes me," Roberta said. She'd arrived two days ago. John had wasted no time recruiting her help.

They were in the back garden at Adelaide's, in a corner shielded from the house and the wind by spiked bushes. John was painting his wedding present.

He didn't know exactly when the idea had occurred to him. Perhaps it was more that he'd been waiting for an excuse to make something for her. But painting Theodora's willful, very giant dog might have been a challenge he had not fully anticipated.

"I'm more than happy to leave you three to your artistic pursuits, trust me," George said.

"No, on second thought I think it would throw off Diana's balance. I'll buy you several drinks, George, just put your back into it. Recall your wrestling days at university. Pretend she's a particularly hirsute opponent."

In response George grunted and leaned his weight further into Diana's shoulder. He'd gone a little paunchy around the middle but underneath was still solid and muscular.

"Several drinks and a new suit, perhaps. I'm sweating right through this one."

"Consider this my stag party?"

"Done. A whalehound party. Perhaps it'll catch on. Society wedding of the season and all."

"Then perhaps I'm the one that should leave," Roberta said. "I don't think dognapping was why my sister asked me to come up early, you know. And while you're buying George a suit, I do think I'll need a new dress after this, John."

He decided to give up convincing either of them that wrangling Diana was worth it. Which it would be. He was fairly certain, at least, just as certain as he was that neither of them really minded. Surely George had done stranger things in the name of friendship and the future of the nation, and according to Teddy, Roberta was always off digging around in the dirt.

"Perhaps I should include you both in the painting," John said. "Greek hero and heroine struggle to hold toppling mountain upright. Echoes of Sisyphus."

The larger question was not whether Theodora would like the painting — her feelings for the dog were obvious, and she seemed to like his art — but whether or not she would ever speak to him again after the wedding. They'd barely spoken since the engagement was made official. John had been kept quite busy with wedding preparations and George's cloak-and-dagger crew and Dove family business, but at every hour of the day, and oftentimes at night, he was wondering about Theodora. Not simply missing her, though it was that, too. He wanted to be there for her, just in case she needed him.

Which it didn't seem she did.

Diana, in response to George's most recent shove, leaned sideways against him with all her weight. She did really seem to like Roberta better.

Or actually – has the dog fallen asleep again?

He knew it wasn't a real wedding. Of course he knew that. But he hadn't felt like painting, or drawing, or finishing anything in so long, and now that he finally did he wasn't going to let it go to waste. No one had ever seemed to appreciate his art quite so much as Theodora. Frankly he could use the encouragement.

John stepped back from the canvas. *Not terrible, thus far. Clearly out of practice.* And for whatever reason he couldn't get the lilac bush behind the dog to come out right. He kept making it too blue, too dark, as if he was painting night instead of the brief blinding bit of sunlight they got this time of year. Diana, at least, looked good: near-iridescent grays with enough of the sea in the color to do her breed proud.

"Excuse me," someone said from behind.

John turned so fast his brush, loaded with white, sent paint splattering through the air looking exactly like bird shit. Luckily the man who'd come around the holly jumped out of the way fast enough to dodge it, which John found rather impressive. When he'd recovered the man surveyed John's painting with squinting, discerning eyes. He wore a long dark coat and excessively shiny shoes.

"Good reflexes there," John said.

"Yes," the man said. "I'm sorry to interrupt, but –"

"Hello, Master Salt!" Roberta said. She hadn't gotten up from the ground, and she looked very amused to find the apparent Mr. Salt in the garden.

"Mistress Roberta," he said, lifting his hat, his face gone pale. "What an unexpected surprise."

"Aren't they all?" she said, half a smile on her face. "What called you away from your studies?"

Salt's mouth twitched like he was trying out several answers or had bitten into something not yet ripe. "I'm here to see the Magistrate."

"How exciting for you."

"Quite. Is he in?"

"I don't believe he's been in for several months," Roberta said. "I'm staying here, you know. My sister is the Court Mistress's cousin by marriage."

Salt frowned briefly. "I believe I do recall that." He turned to John. "And you are Mistress Ashe-Martin's betrothed? Or she is yours. I am speaking to the famous John Dove, am I not?"

John laughed very loudly but Mr. Salt only raised an eyebrow. John stuck out a hand, nearly splattering Salt with paint again before switching hands. "Not famous. Not by any means. But we are to be married. And I am John Dove. How do you and Mistress Roberta know each other?"

"I was in the south doing research."

"Migratory patterns, wasn't it? Mr. Salt is a scientist, as I am."

"Hmm? Yes, a scientist. As well," he said. He clasped his hands behind his back and glanced around the bushes, as if someone else might be inside them.

"Did you find anything of note?" Roberta asked, stroking the dog's head. "Migratorily speaking?" Diana was definitely asleep by now, and George appeared to be trying to blend into the shrubbery out of intense embarrassment at having been found in these circumstances.

"Of note? No, nothing of note," he replied. He seemed to consider turning away from her, then stopped and cleared his throat. "Science is quite a long game, my dear. One cannot expect to make great discoveries every time one sets out of the house."

"Not every time, no," Roberta said back, smiling widely.

"Hmm. Yes. Will the Magistrate be back soon?" he asked, turning to John. "I really do need to speak with him."

"I'm afraid I don't know," John said. "My apologies. I'd thought he was gone for quite a while."

"I'm afraid we must return to the pursuit of art," Roberta called out. "Don't want Mr. Dove to lose the light."

Mr. Salt looked upward and squinted as if he'd been caught off guard by the presence of the sun. He put his hat back on and nodded to John before turning away. He did not say goodbye to Roberta. He did not seem to have noticed George.

"What an odd man," John said, looking after him, once he heard

Mr. Salt's rather loud footsteps crashing through the bushes. "Thanks, Roberta, for getting him out of here. We really are going to lose the – oh, come now."

"What do you think of him, George?" Roberta and George were standing. Only Diana's tail was visible as she retreated into the undergrowth.

"Not a politician," George said, thoughtfully. "He seemed barely able to put a coherent sentence together, let alone lie professionally. Do you believe he's really a scientist?"

"I do," Roberta said, looking after Salt through the holly. "When I stumbled upon him near home, he seemed to know what he was about, though he definitely wasn't looking for birds. For one thing he was on his hands and knees and seemed as interested in what was below ground as I was. Knew enough to fake his way through the conversation though. And he's had enough of a certain kind of schooling to assume that I can't possibly keep up with him."

George chuckled. "Military? Off-island, sent over in advance of the harbors opening?"

John stood there, arms folded, nostrils flared, paintbrush rapidly drying.

"That's the conclusion I came to also. Did you see his shoes?"

"Dead giveaway," George said. "Actually, perhaps John can be of assistance. Oh, John?"

John raised his eyebrows. "'Oh John,' is it? Feel like including me, do you? This is becoming a pattern," he said, but he was also making his way over to them. "How may I be of service to the nation? Or is it to science?" he asked, turning to Roberta. "Unless. You aren't a spy, too, are you?"

She pursed her lips. "I'm far too busy with my own research, frankly. But I do have eyes."

John pursed his lips back at her.

"Right," George said. "John, how much access do you have to your company's records?"

Now he was annoyed. "All of it! It's my damned company!" *For now*, he thought, though it didn't seem the time to mention it.

"Sorry," George said. "What I mean is, your company – er, you – have been doing quite a bit of business with Assembly. Correct?"

John nodded. "And you want me to see if I can determine who Master Salt really is, and what he was really doing in the south related to the soil. From what you said, Roberta, and the way he was eyeing my painting like he was looking for clues inside it, I'd wager that man is an archaeologist, and I've seen that sort of discomfort with the sun in men who've spent weeks beneath the ice. And what might he have learned of such great and immediate importance that he was desperate enough to show up unannounced when everyone knows that the Magistrate has been traveling for months? He's obviously been kept out of the main flow of information, which means whatever he's doing can't be on the public record, which also explains why he didn't write first."

George and Roberta stared at him, amused and a bit stunned.

"Why would you be friends with me if I was completely useless," John muttered.

George repressed a smile. "Next time we'll ask you earlier."

"Shall I fetch the whalehound?" Roberta asked brightly. Without waiting for an answer, she turned and skipped off into the bushes. "Can't lose the light!" she called back over her shoulder. "Even with all the spies about!"

54

Merchants' District
Afternoon, December 17, 1947

THEODORA SPENT the rest of the week shopping.

It was so easy, once she was no longer a spectral cloud of condensation, to find people willing to take her money. Not her money, specifically. Adelaide's, and if they were being technical about it, Adelaide's money was really the Magistrate's. John could have paid, surely, but she had told him not to involve himself in that part at all. It would have seemed worse, somehow.

Theodora didn't want to think about money, or her future, or why she'd agreed to go along with the wedding at all. Or what it meant that the last time she'd considered any of that she'd turned into fog.

But after the post office clerk, no one in any of the shops asked her about the role of women in the island's future or property ownership or ancient magic or fixing the drought, even after the newspaper led with eyewitness accounts of the "Black Widow Smoke Witch-to-be-

Wed in Postal Puff of Paranoia." Roy was still getting the hang of headlines, clearly.

They had to make the wedding seem as real as possible, Adelaide said, if they wanted to buy Theodora's innocence with a pair of signatures on a marriage certificate. It seemed to be working. The shopgirls and store owners smiled and seemed thrilled she was there, then handed her another small ledger book to sign when she was done. Adelaide seemed to have accounts nearly everywhere, and everyone knew she had a trousseau to fill.

There were fittings for her own dress and visits to the dressmakers for Adelaide's gown, and to the men's store for suits for John and George. There was the hair salon and the beauty salon, the haberdashers and the shoe store. She tried small bites of entree and dessert until she'd had a full Solstice feast two weeks before Solstice, and all the food ran together into one vaguely fishy, vaguely frosted substance that nearly turned her off eating entirely.

There were, too, meetings with George and an assorted cast of his underworld associates. The men who came in patched-elbow jackets and fedoras brought stern instructions about how Theodora should carry on and gave every indication that they were deadly serious about their mission. Theodora figured it was best to simply trust the whirlwind around her.

Wednesday afternoon Theodora stood on a small white pedestal holding up a bouquet of dyed flowers to her heart. Her eyes were closed.

"So?" the florist asked. The florist had many strong opinions, all of which were telegraphed almost exclusively with raised eyebrows and deep sighs and "so?" uttered like a test Theodora was sure she was failing.

"Beautiful," she said, not remembering what the flowers in her hand looked like at all. She breathed in deeply: At least they smelled good.

Pretend you're in a greenhouse, she thought. *Breath is scent and memory. Pretend you're part of the earth, growing roots and thorns. Pretend you can make it rain and make yourself grow.*

"Yes? But which ones would you like, Mistress Ashe-Martin?"

Theodora opened her eyes. She took the proffered price list.

"These," she said, and selected several combinations of blooms for herself, for Adelaide, and to decorate the aisles, the bower, the carriage that she and John would take to – wherever they would go afterwards. She chose the most expensive flowers, because that seemed expected.

When Theodora stepped outside she was momentarily dizzy from the shock of switching climates. The driver of her carriage opened the door.

"May I take those, ma'am?" he asked, and Theodora realized she still held the last flowers in her hands. She wasn't even sure if these were among the ones she'd chosen.

"No," she said, and pressed them tight against her chest.

The car crawled back to Adelaide's, the roads full of commuters and shoppers. And some people, she realized with a start, who might be newly arrived in the city for her wedding. Who knew how long the guest list for the reception had grown?

The car turned into Adelaide's neighborhood, where the vegetation was dense and well-fed. Trees and tall grasses, spiky, thorny and flowering, grew in vast lawns around the houses. All the buildings were tall, in the newer style.

The world hushed as the car continued deeper inside. *Maybe this is why Adelaide likes it here. If you're one of the lucky ones, it's definitely a refuge, even if it's never a home.*

The driver let Theodora out before pulling the carriage around to the back with her purchases and samples. All except the flowers, which Theodora was still gripping as the butler let her inside and her coat was taken away. She'd give them to Addy. Theodora looked at the flowers. Perhaps they were quite garish, actually. At least they'd be further evidence that every choice Theodora made about her wedding was entirely inept.

Adelaide sat in the middle of her drawing room, leaning against an ottoman. She looked quite pale beneath her makeup. *Almost as if she'd been crying.*

Theodora couldn't remember the last time she'd seen Adelaide cry. She took another step into the room, but Adelaide didn't seem to notice. If Adelaide hadn't been crying whatever she was doing was worse: bottling everything up and turning herself into stone.

"Addy?"

Adelaide startled.

"What is it?" Theodora dropped the flowers. "Is it the children?"

Adelaide's face crumpled. "It's always them, isn't it?" Her voice broke and she looked away. "My husband has come home."

Theodora stopped where she stood. "Oh no."

Adelaide laughed and it caught in her throat. "Apparently he's coming to perform your wedding ceremony."

"Aunt Ted!" A tornado of children came into the room via the side door. Theodora gasped and dropped to her knees. She opened her arms wide.

"Hello, my loves! Look at you, look how you've –"

The boys knocked her over, giggling, and she fell to the floor with them. When Theodora looked back at her, Adelaide's face was turned to the wall.

"It's so good to have them back, Ted," she said, and when her voice broke again she clapped a hand over her mouth. Robert, the eldest, turned away from Theodora and looked at his mother with concern. He unhooked himself from his aunt and slung his arm over his mother's shoulder, looking at eight very much like the man he'd be one day.

"Do you know for how long?" Theodora asked quietly. Adelaide shook her head.

Theodora hugged Bill and Michael tighter; they seemed engaged in an elaborate game with their aunt as home base, so they didn't need much distracting. But Robert looked between Theodora and Adelaide with great concern: Half-fear and half-responsibility.

Robert spotted the flowers Theodora had dropped, and his face lit up. He nearly ran to pick them off of the ground, collecting the petals that had crumpled off.

"Here you go, Aunt Ted," he said, holding them out to her so enthusiastically Theodora nearly laughed, then nearly cried.

"Thank you, darling," she said, "but actually they're for your mother." She looked at Adelaide half-apologetically. "I picked out your matron-of-honor flowers," she said sheepishly. "It's so stupid. This might not even be them, I was so turned around. Do you like them?" Theodora realized that now both she and Robert were staring at Adelaide like small, hopeful children. Adelaide looked from one face to another, and then to the flowers.

"Right," she said, and took a shuddering breath as she began to stand. "Very nice, Ted. You didn't do badly at all. I have notes, of course. But that's to be expected, isn't it?" Adelaide pulled her oldest child back to her, looking at him with a mix of thankfulness and military rigor. "Robert, go run and put these in water, will you? Then make sure your brothers don't get far advanced in burning the house down. Bill, Michael, unleash your aunt. She and I will be along shortly and we'll all have a good lunch. Go ahead now."

Robert flashed a smile at them, looking very much like his father, which would serve him well. He ran off toward the nursery wing.

Adelaide turned with her hands on her hips. "Right," she said again, only a hint of shakiness left. "As I was saying, I have some notes on the flowers, and also on the dress fabric we spoke about earlier. I don't think it's going to work."

Theodora put up her hand and Adelaide stopped talking, which Theodora also couldn't remember ever happening before. But Adelaide had the strangest look on her face.

She was staring at Theodora's hand.

Then Theodora felt it. The air around her fingers was pulsing with increasing speed, turning into a rumble. There was a frisson high in the air around the robin's egg blue ceiling, and then whatever it was – light, power – chased the molding around the edges of the room.

Theodora put her hand down and grasped it tight in her other palm.

"Sorry! Sorry."

Adelaide raised an eyebrow, looking a little bit impressed and a little bit scared.

Theodora shook her head in frustration. "Not about you. Not directed at you, I mean." She lunged forward and grabbed Adelaide by the arms, ignoring her friend's wince. The words left her like the lightening would have. Theodora had always thought of Adelaide's finery, her cosmopolitan nature and her way of putting on airs, as though it was all a game, but in truth Adelaide had always been much the more adult of the two of them. As much as Theodora hated to admit it that was part of why this was so damned upsetting: Theodora didn't know how to be in a world where her friend had been so obviously broken down.

"It's directed at your damned husband, Addy, or at least I wish it could be. What can we do? What can I do? Finally, after all this time. Please. Please, tell me what I can do."

Adelaide shook her head. "Nothing. Except carry on. That's our lot, isn't it? Marriage is a necessary evil. You know that, obviously."

Theodora shook her head again. "No! No, that's wrong in every way. Weren't you the one telling me things can be different?"

"I was wrong. Do they seem different to you? You're the only one that's any different, you're a witch and it all ended up the same anyway."

"You don't mean that," Theodora began. But her heart wasn't in it. Here she was, marrying to escape the nearly ceaseless grip of her previous marriage by marrying another. If Adelaide didn't believe Theodora could still be something more, then Theodora certainly didn't think so herself.

"You know," Adelaide said, her voice a little distant, "you're why I married him. It seemed so glamorous. To fall in love and marry so quickly. It seemed glamorous when you did it. But so did everything." She shook her head too hard, frowning. "No. Everything seemed beautiful when you did it. When Samuel came along, and mother and father seemed to like him so much –" Adelaide had tears in her eyes. "I'm sorry. I'm terrible, still! So terrible. Listen to me. Blaming you. It's not your fault. It's my fault. All my stupid, silly fault."

She balled up her fists in her dressing gown, slamming them against her thighs. She hit herself again, and again, before Theodora could catch up her fists and pull her close.

"Stop it! Stop. You're not silly, you're brilliant and beautiful and I only ever wanted to be like you and I'm so sorry. I'm so incredibly sorry, Adelaide, that I left you behind."

"You're here now," Adelaide snuffled against her shoulder.

"I am," Theodora said fiercely. "I'm not leaving you again, either."

She wouldn't. She wouldn't just run and hide again and ignore her friends. She wouldn't run away from this wedding either, or pretend it wasn't happening, or that she wasn't marrying her oldest, best friend, even if the circumstances were – well, not what she would have preferred. Feeling Adelaide lean against her, with her children liable to be taken away at any moment, Theodora knew that she couldn't ignore what little power she still had remaining. Even if only by reputation.

They leaned against each other until they started to sniffle through their tears.

"We're both quite disgusting," Adelaide said finally, pulling away and laughing.

Theodora wiped her nose and laughed. "This is how I'll show up to the wedding, just to show them all."

"You should! I'll come dressed as Medusa. Lady Godiva. Both, perhaps."

Theodora frowned and took Adelaide's hands. "I will help you. I promise. John and I will help you. We'll get the children to you for good and get you some bit of freedom. All right?"

Adelaide swallowed hard. She nodded.

"But Addy, will you help me do one last thing? Something a little different? It's not much at all, but it would mean the world to me. Then I'll never ask anything of you again, I promise."

Adelaide rolled her eyes. "Yes of course, silly. We can go with your flowers, if you like."

"No, no. I mean, I don't know, perhaps I do like them after all? But it's more than that."

Adelaide cocked her head.

Theodora took a deep breath. "We have a lot of planning to undo."

55

Greenhouse of the Botanical University
Sunset, December 22, 1947 – Winter Solstice

THEODORA WALKED into the staging room with Roberta a few minutes before she was due to be wed, and found her father there waiting. He held a package out to her, and she wondered how long he'd been standing like that.

The room was normally where cuttings were taken before being sent out for further study. All the bits of plant and flower had been pushed to the margins for now, though the tile floor was coated with a little bit of dirt that couldn't be scrubbed away.

Mr. Ashe had frozen a nervous smile on his face, looking as though he was trying to avoid any unnecessary emotional interaction. Roberta squeezed her sister's hand.

"I'll head out to the aisle," she said quietly, "and wait for you there. See you there, Father," she added, with a warning glance. "Try not to make Ted more nervous, eh?"

Theodora watched Roberta go then turned toward her their father. She smiled tightly as she walked toward him.

"Thank you, Father," she said, taking the package from him. It was much lighter than she'd expected and she ended up waving it around a little without meaning to. "You shouldn't have."

"Of course I should have." He seemed so relieved to be rid of whatever it was, it made her a bit nervous. He coughed. "You look beautiful, Theodora."

She looked down at her dress and smoothed the front. It was a beautiful dress, she had to admit: old-fashioned with a flat bodice and a full skirt and a collar that came up behind her upswept hair. "Thank you. Adelaide helped pick it out."

"No you, you look beautiful," her father said, and when she looked up he was staring at her very intently. Blushing and sad. "Your mother should be here. She should see you like this. She would have liked to."

Theodora raised an eyebrow. "Would she have?"

Instead of answering he looked around the room. "Ah," he said, and half-stepped, half-fell onto a metal stool a few feet away. "That's better."

"Father, are you all right? Do you need water?"

"Fine, fine." He smiled at her, then gestured to the package. "Open it now, would you?"

Theodora eyed it. "You didn't have to bring this here."

Her father threw up his hands. "You needn't be so suspicious! It's a wedding present for the sake of baba yaga!"

She got the impression he'd wrapped it himself. She pulled a peach ribbon tied in a bow and the thin paper fluttered to the floor. There was more paper underneath. A deed.

She imagined what she must have looked like, dressed in white with her hair done up, a princess being handed a lit fuse. Theodora frowned at him a long moment, then laughed in spite of herself.

"Damn it, father."

She'd known it was going on behind the scenes, the transference of the property to John on occasion of their wedding. If Theodora had been able to convince anyone she was a witch – or rather convince them it was worth acknowledging her as such – then she'd have been able to inherit. But with her marriage, John would become as good as an heir. Plus he had the money, and the influence, to convince Assembly it'd be worth it to cede the sale.

She hadn't wanted to think much about it after all.

Her father smiled. "It's yours," he said gruffly, with a nod at the paper, "officially. It was your mother's. Now it's yours." He shrugged. "Didn't want to wait for a hearing or any of that nonsense."

When she looked back at the paper her vision was blurred. "You really didn't have to bring it here," she said.

He wiped his hands against his pant legs. "Glad to be rid of it. Quite a relief really. Couldn't afford to just give it you outright before, of course."

She shook her head in disbelief. "Was that all it was? Money?"

He went a little red in the face. "No, no, now calm down. That was part of it, but also – where did Roberta get to, you think?" he asked, peering around her toward the open door.

"Father, honestly!"

He pursed his lips and looked back at her. "Well, fine. I didn't think you knew what you were getting into. The responsibility that comes with witchery. Nearly broke your mother. Drove her away in the end. I didn't want that to happen to, erm, ahem –"

Theodora's eyes went wide. Never in all her years had she seen her father cry or come close before.

"The house seemed to be a way to keep that from you, I suppose. Seems silly now," he said, staring at the pattern of tile on the floor. "Do you remember," her father asked suddenly, "that your mother used to say a poem to you, to help you fall asleep? To make you fall asleep really. Maybe it was more a song?"

Theodora blinked away tears. "I don't recall it." It was true, she could never remember it in the morning, but more than that it was all she had of her mother, just to hold to herself.

"I could never remember it after she left. Pity, it used to help you so much. Such a comfort it seemed. I haven't slept well in years, if I'm honest. Not since she's gone."

Theodora opened her mouth to reply but he kept speaking.

"Anyway. What I mean to say is. She loved you so much, Theodora. Too much."

Theodora looked away. "Convenient. To love too much, I mean."

"Not convenient at all. It's what made her leave you, and she hated to do it." He tapped his chest, much harder than the wistfulness of his voice would indicate, so hard she thought he'd bruise himself. "But I believe she meant to come back. And that she would have taught you then, just like her mother taught her. I believe it truly, my Theodora."

She shook her head. *He doesn't mean it. He doesn't believe it. He doesn't know.*

"She always said you were the most capable child."

Her breath caught. She remembered her mother saying it. Once, or maybe many times. *Such a strange thing to say*, she'd thought at the time.

"Do you think she might come today?" Theodora whispered before she could stop herself.

He smiled halfway. "Anything's possible, isn't it?" he asked, gesturing to Theodora, and she laughed.

"Apparently."

"Good, good," he said, looking away. "That's settled." He coughed and held out his arm. "Shall we?"

Theodora folded the thin sheet first, and tucked it inside the front of her dress, next to her skin. She took her father's arm and gripped harder than she meant to.

He patted her hand. "John is a good lad. I always liked him."

They began to walk. "He is."

"Nervous?"

She shook her head. "Perhaps I should be? Perhaps there's something wrong with a bride who's not nervous on her wedding day."

He gripped her hand as they walked up the stairs. "Don't doubt yourself, Theodora," his voice thick once more. "Promise me that? You know your own mind. Always have."

She glanced sideways at him. It was closer than she'd been to him since she was a child. He looked both like her father and like a man she barely knew at all, but he looked kind. Infuriating, but kind. A little bit sad, still.

"Good, good," he said again, holding her more lightly. "And if you remember it, tell me that song, would you?"

The doors opened and they walked forward into sunlight.

John was very damp.

The drought plus the exceptional cold meant the greenhouse was bursting with plants and specimens Wherewithal's scientists were afraid wouldn't otherwise survive. And despite Adelaide's very vociferous protestations, the keepers of the arboretum hadn't been convinced to temporarily move their stores elsewhere. So now he was standing in a three-piece suit in a room that felt like a sauna and smelled distinctly of earthworm refuse.

John itched his sweaty leg through his wool pants and tried to concentrate on everything around him. There were upwards of 200 people here and he smiled out at them mechanically, the last stragglers picking up handfuls of petals from the font and taking their seats. Everyone smiled back. It seemed true, what George and his father had been telling him: He existed in a new sphere of influence. People would forever be trying to catch his eye, for one reason or another.

One of the things John loved about algae-light was that its glow was contained. The blue globes hung from the trees and lining the aisle didn't block the stars or blind one's eyes, and when John craned his head past the bower he saw a hundred thousand stars through the clear glass of the roof. It seemed very cold out there. Very clear and straightforward: If you were a star you burned. If you were a planet you revolved.

It's so damned hot in here.

"You're doing a great thing for our island, my boy."

A hand – a battering ram – clapped John on the shoulder, bringing him back to Earth. He spun, startled, and found the smiling face of the Magistrate. "A truly great thing," the man repeated, not having let go of John's shoulder.

John grimaced.

It was ridiculous that the Magistrate had offered – or rather demanded, since there wasn't much chance of turning down a man that powerful – to conduct their wedding ceremony. John had in fact only met him once before today, to advocate for opening the harbors. John had been there for show, and they'd barely said two words to each other. No matter how much of a show the whole wedding was, it still mattered to John, and he resented this man's intrusion.

But the Magistrate smiled with the smug confidence of someone who had long ago convinced himself that he was firmly on the side of righteous truth. He was a true believer, though in what, John wasn't sure. Surely not his wife.

John knew how this man had treated Adelaide. How he treated her still, if the ghostly pallor on her face the last few days was any indication. At least he'd brought her children back to her, for a time.

But everyone was watching, so he shook the man's hand gamely. "Thank you so much for coming," he said.

Then he realized how they would look, if Theodora were to come in right now: Both of them smiling widely up here, as though they'd won some contest. Conquered a mountain. John suddenly felt a little bit ill.

The Magistrate's smile only grew bigger and his teeth, if possible, whiter. "When I heard the news of your union, I had to come back," he said. "Had to bestow my authority upon it. It only seemed right. As I said, a truly great thing for our nation."

Don't ask, he commanded himself, but a lifelong curiosity in what made people do and say the things they did got the better of him. "I thank you. Though I'm not sure I understand the sentiment? Flattering though it is, Master Magistrate."

The Magistrate leaned back on his heels and opened his mouth wider; the action of laughter with none of the sound of it. "Please, call me Samuel! You've been living too long up north, son. Away from women," he silently laughed again. "While you've been bringing us into the future with technology and progressive ideals, do you know some people down have been trying to thrust us back into the past? The ancient past, John. A past of witchcraft and hysteria."

It sounded a bit like a sales pitch, though for what John couldn't be sure. *Perhaps a new religion.*

John kept his face blank. "Is that so?"

"It's crucial, John," the Magistrate said, and his voice took on a lower register, a parental whisper though in fact the Magistrate was only ten years John's senior. "That we form these kind of alliances."

"What kind? You mean me and Theodora?" John said, his voice loud with surprise.

He waved his free hand. "No, John. You and me! Dove Holdings and the Assembly, industry and the state. You and Mistress Ashe-Martin, well, she's just like the rest of them when it comes down to it. Even with all the stories and the dead husband, she's just another woman."

"Is she then?" John asked coolly.

"Yes, you see, women have powers, that's a fact, despite how some people would like to stick their heads in the sand about it." He gripped John's arm in a fraternal way, though squeezing rather hard. "Don't believe them when they tell you witchcraft is gone, John. Don't believe your wife is she tries to tell you that." He squeezed harder. "But we have power, too! The island was founded so that men would be the equal of witches and none would have to live in fear but now, finally, is our opportunity to see that power come to fruition. For the good of all. You understand, I'm sure, given your record on the ice."

John shook his head, wishing the damned man would let his arm go.

"What have women's powers gotten us, John? An arid island, devoid of hope!"

John did not understand. He did not understand, though he felt hollow inside to think that the work he'd done had given this man the impression he might agree with him. Furthermore dehydration and the effort of maintain some sort of civility were making John a bit dizzy, and the Magistrate's face had become truly one of the most fascinating John had ever seen. Weathered but unlined, tanned but with hair gone prematurely white.

Perhaps I should try painting him. John began to lean a little closer in, trying to get a better look, growing a little unsteady on his feet.

The Magistrate didn't seem to notice. "Damned hot in here, isn't it?"

John jerked backward. "Thank you so much for coming," he said again, and turned back toward the aisle, where George was running toward them.

He was already apologizing as he ran up the few steps to stand next to John on the dais.

"So – sorry – friend." George clapped John on the back as best he could while bent over panting. He was meant to have spent the entire morning with John, helping him with – John wasn't sure exactly, but whatever it was, he hadn't been doing it.

"It's fine," John said, very relieved to no longer be standing alone with the Magistrate. "Just buy me a drink at the reception, would you?"

George laughed, or wheezed, still bent over. John bent to join him. "Are you all right? What's happened? There's not another war on is there?" he asked, only half-joking.

"Oh not yet," he replied, which was not terribly reassuring. But his voice had gone completely normal again, like he wasn't out of breath at all. George reached into his jacket pocket and began to pull something out.

The music began to play. They both popped upright.

Standing so quickly, plus not eating anything all day – *damn, yes, that was what George was meant to help with* – made all the blood surge to John's head. His vision telescoped and he nearly swooned into a prickly, night-blooming hedge that formed the backdrop for the ceremony. But as he began to be swallowed up by shrubbery, a hand reached out and pulled him roughly upward. George clapped him hard on the back to get the blood flowing.

"Don't worry, no one saw," he whispered to John. "Everyone's looking right where you ought to." He nodded down the aisle. John followed George's glance, noting that Adelaide had arrived beside them.

Then he nearly swooned again as Theodora came down the aisle.

"I had a speech prepared. About honor, and patience. Duty, and the future. But it seems I won't be giving it."

The Magistrate shrugged and the corner of his mouth curled up. There was polite and happy laughter from the crowd – *who the hell are all these people*, Theodora wondered – but from up close it seemed much more likely that the Magistrate was displeased at having his performance altered.

Fine. Even if the man wasn't an ass, Theodora felt some things were sacred. And a woman's wedding, even her second wedding, even one done out of political convenience in the hopes of drawing out a murderer and proving oneself innocent of same, was one of those things. She'd be damned if it wasn't going to go just the way she wanted it to. Just as when, very gently, she'd unhooked her father's arm from her own and sent him scooting down the side of the room beneath the ferns and the birds of paradise to find his seat beside Theodora's stepmother.

That part, at least, hadn't been planned. When Theodora saw John at the front of the room, waiting for her, she realized she had to walk past all these strangers with her head held high, alone. Confront not only anyone who might be hiding in the wings waiting to spring upon them both but also everyone from Mooring and the south, every member of her family who hadn't vanished into thin air, everyone who'd ever read a cruel word about her and laughed. She would let them know that she chose this path with her own free will and her own free mind.

John and Theodora hadn't been seen together since the engagement, such as it was, and the consensus was that if someone was still trying to kill him, they'd use this occasion. As Theodora walked down the aisle she had to remind herself to breathe, so afraid was she that the ceiling was about to crash in on him, or a shot come through the glass walls, or his boutonniere turn man-eating, for all she knew.

This time they'd be ready. George's associates were stationed throughout the crowd, and Assembly had insisted on extra security besides. But still she had to keep reminding herself to breathe.

She'd been coached thoroughly in the right set of her mouth: happy, but nervous. Grim, but overjoyed. Nothing at all like she actually felt, which was that if she looked away from John for even a moment her whole body would shatter into molecules of water and light.

That she wasn't really alone at all and had never been. That all that mattered was keeping him safe. That he'd been waiting for her the whole time.

She took the last few steps to stand across from him.

"I love your dress," John whispered. He didn't seem to realize there was anyone there besides the two of them.

She'd gasped when Adelaide had shown it to her, because of course she'd left it up to Adelaide: palest blue brocade, a skirt so full that if she leaned back it would probably catch her. The lace overlay on the sleeves ran all the way to the back of each hand, where it ended in a point below her knuckles. Adelaide did know her, better sometimes than Theodora knew herself.

"Thank you," Theodora whispered back. "Bit different from black, isn't it?"

"They all suit you."

Theodora blushed. The Magistrate was still going on about something.

"Are you nervous?" she whispered.

"About getting married?" John asked.

"About –" Theodora waggled her eyebrows at the edges of the room, where George's men were stationed.

He shrugged. "I trust you."

"To continue," the Magistrate said loudly, "our bride has requested a very old rite of marriage replace the common words and ceremony. I'm not one to buck tradition," he chuckled, "though it does make me something of a figurehead at the moment."

John glanced down at his watch and then raised an eyebrow at her; she barely kept from laughing.

"So now I will hand over the reins to Master Dove and Mistress Ashe-Martin. At the end of the ceremony, I will need to sanctify the union," he added, leaning toward them. "To bind it."

Theodora wished he'd step slightly back from them. Then over a bit and straight into the fish pond. Instead of helping him in, she turned back to John, who was looking toward the ceiling. Theodora followed his gaze: The sun was gone.

With nightfall it had been nine full years since Henry had gone. He was officially dead and his inheritance, if she both wanted it and wanted to proclaim herself a witch, would be hers. Moreover for this one moment she was free: Untethered from Henry or anyone else. Alone. She could run down the aisle and not stop until she got to the river, dive into the icy water and let it take her to the cliffs and out to sea. She could catch a boat to one of those mysterious continents to east or west, or maybe just turn back into fog.

Stars appeared in the purple sky as she watched, faster than she could have imagined. Theodora looked down to see John with one eyebrow raised. A question.

"It's beautiful," she said.

"It is," he replied.

It had been such a last-minute request, to change the venue of the wedding from the Assembly building to the botanical gardens, to change from the common ceremony to the one that had married the first settlers. Adelaide had managed it, though.

Theodora and John clasped their right hands together, then left hands over top. She could feel a current running between them. If whoever was after them wanted to make the greatest impact, this would be when they'd strike. *Especially if they want to keep us apart.* Theodora looked at their hands and realized exactly what they were about to do.

She held her breath. The moon emerged from behind a cloud. Someone coughed, and a baby squealed with delight at some unseen thing.

John squeezed her hands, Theodora exhaled, and together they began to speak.

"Together on the darkest day, the longest night. We begin."

She found the words at the back of her mother's book along with a notation that according to laws still on the books – albeit dusty books shoved to the back of shelves, moth-eaten and moldering and requiring another forged letter from the Magistrate to obtain – these words would make them wed.

"By the bottom of the ocean and the deepest of its trenches. By the ice and the waterfall. By vines that encroach and encircle and fires that burn our feet and warm our hands; and storms that wreck and ravage and cast us on familiar shores."

Admittedly, it was a little bleak. But staring into John's eyes, Theodora didn't mind the darkness at all. She supposed that was the point.

He'd memorized them, too, though she was sure he wouldn't. She couldn't remember why now.

Adelaide and George stood witness. Adelaide knew they'd be staring into each other others' eyes as the words were spoken.

"If tomorrow we collapse into the frozen sea, splinter against the rocks, run out of light to show us our way, let us clasp each other's hands in the dark and move forward together."

Theodora gripped harder.

"Let us from this day forward search for the shore, the light, our place to build." "Together," said Theodora.

"Together," echoed John.

The birds had stopped calling to each other or flying from perch to perch. Theodora could barely feel where her own skin stopped and John's began.

"Finished, then?"

The Magistrate's voice was loud but melodic, and after only a beat there was scattered laughter in the crowd and then a moment later boisterous clapping. It was done and Theodora looked at John, waiting to see regret on his face. He was beaming.

"Then I suppose it's my duty to announce you Master and Mistress John Dove! You may kiss your bride, Master Dove."

For a moment Theodora thought she might throw up or faint. *Damned but it's hot in here.* She focused on his face: His brown eyes had gone very wide, and his face was no longer smiling. *Perhaps a bit panicked? Maybe we'll both be sick,* she thought. *How romantic. Perhaps I could aim for the Magistrate's shoe.*

It was ridiculous really. It's not as though they hadn't done it before. She stifled a laugh and it came out as a snort, and at the same moment John closed the space between them. He paused, pulled back, looked at her with a question in his eyes once more.

She broke free from his hands. Then she put her palms to his face, and kissed him.

"I suppose we're meant to sit for a portrait now?" John said, breathless. He and Theodora stood very close, just beyond the doors at the end of the aisle they'd crafted in the arboretum.

There were other people still around, he was sure. George and Adelaide, attendants from the gardens, all those many guests they'd just walked by. But all he saw was his wife.

"I suppose so?" Theodora replied. She looked a little stunned. They were standing quite close, truly. "To keep up appearances, I mean."

He searched her face. *Blessed mother, she looked incredible.*

"John," she said.

Maybe we could sneak away, for a little while? Not to consummate, per se, but –

"Ready?" someone asked, and a burst of burnt algae went off to light the picture.

Then it was more lights, a long line of hands to shake and cheek kisses, and then the band began to play and it was time for their dance. A ballroom floor had been installed at great expense.

"Holding up all right?" Theodora asked, as he spun her back to him amid polite applause.

"Oh marvelously," he replied, trying to sound droll and dry, as if it wasn't the truth. He spun her outward. "You?"

"The same." He pulled her close. "Espionage is so boring, isn't it?" She whispered into his ear, and he resolved to keep their turns much tighter going forward.

Dinner was served, at least for everyone else. Theodora and John had to do the rounds, say hello, make themselves a target for both potential assassination and the society pages.

Because that's what all this was for, John had to remind himself throughout the evening. Theodora wouldn't be safe from suspicion, not truly, until they apprehended the assassin. *Would-be assassin*, John corrected himself.

"Very romantic, isn't it," he said to her as they made yet another circuit, nodding yet again, "the bride and groom as sitting ducks?"

"Perhaps this is what George and Adelaide like so much," Theodora said out of the side of her mouth, smiling politely at the minister for herbs. "The constant anxiety and tension. A bit like foreplay."

John's mouth went very dry.

"Here," Theodora said, and handed him a passing glass of champagne. "Wait," she said at the last moment, and pulled it back toward her. She took a sip and grinned. "Now here," she said, handing it over.

The evening went on like that, always waiting for the roof to cave in again but the crash never coming. After a while John began to imagine that perhaps this was an ordinary wedding after all. *Almost.*

"Spare a moment?" George asked.

"Unless this is some sort of newlywed hazing?" John said, clapping him on the back.

Theodora wagged her finger at George. "I've sworn to come after you if you lay a hand on my husband. Blood oath and all that."

George raised an eyebrow at John and smoothly took three champagne flutes from a passing waiter.

"Here you go, Mistress Dove," he said, handing her a glass. He threw his own drink back and held onto the other. He sounded too serious for John's liking. "No, not hazing. Come on over here, would you?"

He led them through the crowd, somehow managing to avoid all the well-wishers who'd been swarming them all evening, fading into the background in what must be a professional technique, and then onto a veranda.

Entering the cold was like walking into a wall. John's vision blurred for a moment from the shock. "Hurry it up, please," Theodora chattered. John took off his coat and draped it over her shoulders. She pulled it tighter and pulled closer to him.

"Here," George said, and thrust out the paper he'd tried to give John earlier.

"This keeps happening," Theodora said as she took it from him.

"Can you sum it up?" John managed to get out as Theodora unfolded the sheet and held it up in the dim glow of two hanging lanterns. "This is a long document for sub-zero."

"Henry's mother," George said. "She's dead."

Theodora's mouth opened but no sound came out. She'd gone white as marble.

"Holy hell," John said to George. "Why didn't you come out and say it if you were going to be so blunt in the end?"

Theodora gasped, like coming up from under water.

"I'm so sorry, Theodora," George said. "I'm so, so sorry. We only got news of it this afternoon."

John put his arm around her, but Theodora felt suddenly rigid.

"How?" she asked.

George looked at John for some sort of instruction, but John only nodded. George took a deep breath. "There was a fire."

She looked back at the paper with something between devastation and hysteria. John looked it over, too; it was a notice from the constable in the Martin's district. "Why? I don't understand," Theodora asked, her voice rising. "Why would anyone hurt her?"

George stood like a soldier on a fatal mission but he faced her squarely. "It happened last night, Theodora. The house is so damned isolated no one saw the blaze, and in the drought, it went up like kindling." He sucked in his breath, realizing what he'd implied, but apparently decided it was too late to turn back. "She died before the wedding. Henry's inheritance is yours. There's no one else left."

Theodora's eyes went wide. She laughed, nearly a cackle, then slapped her hand over her mouth. Her eyes welled up as she began to shake her head.

"Teddy," John began, but she wasn't listening.

"Diana!" she yelled. Or tried to but her voice was hoarse and thick.

"Whatever is the matter, coz?"

Adelaide spun into view, the circle of her skirt continuing on around her like she was an unstoppable force, a body in orbit. She put an arm on Theodora's shoulder and took a sip of her drink with the other hand. The presence of her husband had turned Adelaide's countenance sharper, her eyes more hollow and dashing every which way.

Theodora shook her head, near tears. "It's Electra Martin. She's died." She shook her head and clasped a hand over her mouth.

Adelaide's face fell. "No," she said, and roughly pulled Theodora close to her. She looked at George and John with something like accusation in her eyes. "They wouldn't," she said. But George nodded.

Adelaide pulled back from Theodora, searching her face. "This is not your fault," she said firmly.

Theodora pulled away roughly. "Everything is my fault!" she hissed, clutching her arms around herself. Everything about her was collapsing inward. She looked so alone.

"Teddy, you can't save everyone yourself," he said. He just wanted to touch her but as he reached out she pulled away like his touch would burn.

"Who has been saved at all, John? And all this?" She swept her arms up and around. "For what?"

He winced at the pain in her voice. At something that sounded like regret.

"I don't act and people get hurt," she said. "I act and people get hurt. Another person dead. Another lie told. Widow Martin didn't deserve this. None of us did!"

John stepped back, feeling a peculiar pain in his chest. *Worse than a ceiling*, he thought. *Losing her.*

Because that's what was happening.

"Especially not you. I'm sorry," she said. "I'm so sorry. But I should be alone." Theodora turned and ran back towards the party, but at the last moment swerved away from the guests. In her retreating shadow Diana loped into view, following after.

John's jacket slid from her shoulders and landed softly just beyond the algae glow.

He walked over to it slowly, picked it up and slung it over his shoulder. He turned back to George.

"I'm sure she'll be fine. The truth is she's always been fine." He paused and looked after the space where she'd been. "I'm not sure what help I could be, anyway."

George threw up his hands. "You're her husband! Damn it, man, she didn't seem fine. In fact in this one, very particular regard," he held up his hands in defense, "I think you might be overestimating her capabilities."

John spoke sharply. "She's not like everyone else. You don't know her as I do. You don't know how the responsibility weighs on her, how no one else can understand what she goes through."

"I know she's still human. I mean mostly. I think. And she's still allowed to grieve. The least you can do is offer her some sympathy." George smiled with half his mouth. "You're not so useless as that. You're actually quite good at bolstering people's spirits. You know, you can offer a handkerchief or something."

John felt a mixture of panic and despair rising up in him.

"John," Adelaide said quietly. She was clutching her drink as though she'd crush the crystal in her hand. "It's not true that no one understands her. You always have."

He looked from one of them to the other. She might be halfway south by now. Halfway to the moon. He turned and ran.

Theodora had gone in the direction of the experimental gardens. He ran through glassed-off laboratory rooms full of clippings and multi-colored algae lights, turned a corner sharply and came into the rose room.

Vines with thorns like talons climbed to the ceiling and then across it. Roses wrapped around the irrigation system and the metal supports for the windows. There were fantastic colors, whole blooms the size of fingernails and individual petals the size of a fist. *Maybe the botanists had allowed them all to run riot, afraid of the thorns. Maybe it was awe, not fear.*

The smell was dizzying and John slowed in spite of himself.

"Theodora?" John's shirt snagged every few steps. "Teddy?" He stopped and held his breath, but couldn't hear anything. No steps, no breath except the warm exhalation of the flowers.

Flowers don't breathe. At least none that he'd ever known. He looked down.

The thinnest fingers of fog were curled around his left ankle, pulling him onward steadily, lapping like the tide.

"Can we go home, please?"

There was a car waiting for her, or rather waiting for her and John. A big, beautiful car, pale blue and curved like a whale, with an entire back wing, two-thirds of the whole structure dedicated to her privacy and personal space. Theodora climbed inside without waiting for permission or assistance and spoke through the still-open dividing window.

The driver only paused a beat. He'd been reading, waiting for them to emerge. Both of them.

"I just need an address, Mistress Dove," he said, slipping his book away into a private space.

"It's Ashe-Dove," she said, and then wanted to smack herself, though it was true now. "And we're going to my home. Ashe House." She held out the letter her father had given her. "It's all here," she said.

The driver scanned the letter and handed it back. "It'll take all night, Mistress Ashe-Dove."

Theodora dropped her head into her hands briefly, then moved to get out of the car. "Damn it. Of course it will, I'm sorry, I wasn't thinking –"

But the driver was already starting the engine. "I was just letting you know. It's no trouble."

"Oh. Thank you," she replied, a little embarrassed. She was pressed back into the seats as the car pulled out into the empty night. Everyone was at the wedding still.

They crossed the river and went south along it. She watched Adelaide's neighborhood pass. *This was what I wanted, wasn't it? My home back. This is where I would have ended up eventually anyway. I'm just speeding it along.*

The trees grew thicker, acting more like they were in charge, and then the car turned away from the river. Theodora was already asleep as they entered the forest via the old road, and well before they reached the base of the mountains.

56

**Southern edge of the forest
Morning, September 23, 1933**

NOTHING LIKE GOING *by foot to remind you how big an island is.*

Marguerite Headwaters-Ashe was nearly numb with exhaustion and soaked through with the storm that had started the moment she stepped beyond her threshold. But she wasn't lost. Things hadn't gotten so bad yet that she couldn't see far enough into the future to tell where her next footfalls should land. Even in the darkness of the forest, where it was nearly always night, she knew exactly how far she had to go, how to keep well away from the train tracks, what steps to take and where they'd lead her.

She knew, too, that no one had come after her.

That was the part that surprised her, that had only revealed itself after she'd burst into her husband's study, interrupted him putting a ship into a bottle and told him that she had to go. She had to find what was destroying the witches before it destroyed the island entirely. By which she really meant, before it destroyed Theodora.

Her husband had been surprised at first, but only for a moment. Then he'd stood and taken a large purse from his cabinet and put it heavily into her hand. And turned away.

She could live with all that. She'd lived with not being understood for very many years.

A bird swooped low and Marguerite jumped.

"First one in half a day and you choose to be an omen about it," she yelled, and began to walk quicker, looking up through the trees at clouds so low and heavy being inside the mountain might actually be a relief.

I should have brought Theodora, she thought for the thousandth time. *Explained it to her, at least. I'm too damned selfish, is what it is.*

She'd always known that about herself, everyone had told her so since she was a child. It was why she hadn't ever revealed that she could see into the future, to Theodora or to anyone else, even as her daughter's only teacher and her mother besides. Marguerite wanted something that was only hers. People had always approach her slowly and cautiously and hungrily. *Fuck them all*, she'd begun to say to herself as a refrain, *ever since puberty*.

Maybe I was wrong. But Theodora had fits in the form of tornadoes, temper tantrums that ended up tropical storms. Marguerite was only just barely able to contain the storm systems to the living room. Giving her more responsibility had seemed cruel. *Maybe now I'll never know.*

Marguerite set her jaw and drove her walking stick deeper into the ground. She couldn't think about not seeing Theodora again. That was why she'd let her sleep, though she'd told herself it was mostly to spare her daughter pain. It had also been to spare Marguerite.

It was when they started drilling down into the land around her family's home, requisitioning mailtubes, inserting torturous-looking metal instruments deep into the sides of slot canyons in the search for more algae, that Theodora began to get sick: Sweating through her sheets, nearly manic during the day, thirsty always, huge welts on her body that withered away hours later. It couldn't be a coincidence. It had started the very same day! Though certainly her husband and all the doctors they'd consulted had tried to say it was only the natural progression of things: *It happens to all girls this age,* he'd said. *That's why boys are so much easier.*

Her husband was a good man. He'd asked almost nothing of her during their marriage, and he loved Theodora.

"But damn he is an obtuse man," she whispered, the words lost in the rain.

And since that bastard Archibald Dove had denied all Marguerite's requests to investigate under the ice, Marguerite was going to the one place that remained untouched. Not that she knew what she'd find there. Not that she knew whether she'd be able to fix the witch-sickness or stop it. She had to try.

Marguerite stopped to catch her breath in the suddenly thin air. She'd arrived without realizing it.

57

Island of Wherewithal
Dates lost, est. mid-18th century

THE WITCHES MADE DO with what they had. The days became longer and their magic, tightly knit together, grew strong enough to scratch at the earth and make something grow. They gave up hope that the men would come back, but found there's a dull peace in giving up hope, too.

Until one day a man stumbled back into the settlement. His eyes were too wide and shone too much. They couldn't tell who he was, or rather who he'd been, so changed was he: His hair was thick and sleek and he filled out the furs he wore.

Where had he gotten furs? He seemed half-seal but he spoke with the fervor of the recently converted.

"There's even less sun there!" he proclaimed, like it was something good.

"Maybe he's crazed from all the sunlight here," someone whispered.

"Maybe he ate the rest of them," someone else said. They examined his fingernails and teeth, his clothes and his boots.

"No, no, listen," he said, "there's less light from the sky but there's light under the ground!" He stamped his foot, wearing a broken shoe wrapped in scraps of cloth. "There's light in the ice. You can eat the light! It's a whole world beneath the ice!"

"Come get rest," the captain's wife said, because she was in charge of this sort of thing. "Everyone else, quiet now. We'll ask him more later."

The man who came back from the north let himself be led to a bed by the fire.

"And there were people up there," he said over his shoulder, his eyes looking glassier the nearer he got to the hearth.

Everyone hushed, even the woman who'd been hacking because of the smoke.

"People?" the captain's wife asked calmly, like they were talking about the weather instead of something that might threaten this entire sanctuary they'd found. She helped him lie down and pulled off his boots.

"People live on the ice. We've sent the men away and taken their women as wives," he said, and if it was possible for silence to grow deeper, to pull several more layers over itself and bury itself underground, it did now.

"You'll have to tell us more when you have more strength, won't you?" She patted him on the shoulder. "But get some rest now. Shore up your strength."

She brought the fire down to embers with a movement of her hand and turned to the rest of the women with her face gone white as the moon. She hurried them all outside before she lost the ability to breathe entirely.

The cold was bitter and everyone clumped together so their breath formed a cloud.

"They killed the men!"

"They took the women!"

"It's just like before."

"Well not *just* like. The opposite, really."

"It sounds like they have food."

"Maybe the men were violent. Who knows what they were like, living on the ice like that. Maybe it had to be done."

"You might be right. It was about survival."

The words were moving too fast, catching and growing into something dangerous. "We know nothing about them," the captain's wife began, "so first we must –"

"We know enough, don't we?" one of the others asked. "Weren't you listening? Warmth. Light. Food."

"And they don't have magic. How could they?"

"So we're safe. We're still in charge, aren't we?"

The captain's wife pursed her lips, feeling as though she was talking to her children when they were being silly and scared and cruel.

"Now hold on," she began. "We can't just go agreeing to murder and forced marriage! Isn't that what we came here to escape? And to dig up the earth like it isn't all we have? Where will we be then, when there's nothing of the ground left beneath us?" She grabbed one of the women, the closest one, and shook her shoulder roughly. "Don't you realize what you'd be playing with?"

But then she was speaking only to a cloud of warm air, quickly dissipating. The women looked to each other in agreement with each other and then turned away. They began to walk to the new building by the river, where the islanders held their meetings.

"Finally, this damned place will give us something," one of them said, her words carried back on the wind. The captain's wife was left staring at the wall of women as they walked away, heads huddled together against the cold.

58

Ashe-Dove House
Quite late, December 23, 1947

"Teddy!"

John gasped for breath, but though he leaned over with his hands on his knees he didn't take his eyes from her face. She'd been walking across the entryway with purpose when he burst in upon her, and now he felt absurdly embarrassed that he hadn't written first.

"John?" She stared at him for a moment as if he might be a ghost.

"Am I interrupting?" he asked.

She blinked and shook her head, then rushed to his side. "Bleeding Circe, John, of course not. I was just going out to post you a letter. Are you quite all right?"

"I thought you'd gone," he said.

"Gone?" She put a hand to his back. "Did you run here?"

John tried to laugh. "I thought you'd left – left me." He stood up, his face red "You know. Since you ran away. From our wedding reception."

"And you came after me?" She hadn't thought he would.

"I did," he said. "I'm sorry it took me as long as it did. But," he waved vaguely to the floor, seeming a bit embarrassed. "Did you not want me to come? I thought maybe you did."

She cocked her head, not understanding until John gestured behind him, out the still-open door. A trail of fog wound across the gardens to the front door, where it pooled and curled like a contented cat.

"Oh," Theodora said, suddenly seeming embarrassed herself.

"Do you know that it has a, uh, quickening effect? I was in a coach but we made it in half time. Oh fuck, did you truly not want me to come?"

"No! I mean yes." Theodora reached out and took his hand, sweaty and damp. "Yes. It's lovely to have you here. In my house," she said, and laughed though it almost turned into a sob. "Our house."

"Your house, Theodora," he said.

"I'm sorry I ran away. Hearing about the Widow Martin, after everything we did to try to stop people dying. I needed to come here. To prove it wasn't for nothing." She sobbed again and half-stepped, half-fell closer to him, though she held back from going into his arms. "As if a house could be worth someone's life."

John looked up and Theodora followed his gaze. The entryway opened to a faceted glass roof, and though the evening was grey, the ceiling had been designed to amplify the light. A billion dust motes were caught in the air above them.

"It's not your fault, you know," John said, both of them still looking up. "You wanting a home didn't lead to this."

Theodora shook her head. "I cannot now let it go to waste."

They were silent a long moment, holding hands, looking up, until John spoke: "Do you think I could get a look up there? It's always fascinated me, how they built it."

She smiled and tugged his arm so he looked at her. "Monsieur artiste. Of course. But first come inside properly, let me get you some water. You're still half-maimed, you know. An entire ceiling fell on you, and a witch has you in her clutches. Or did you forget?"

"Never," he said, breathless once more.

※

She led John to a chair by the fireplace in the sitting room, tender and brisk and for all the world as if this was where she was always meant to be. John couldn't stop looking at her.

"There," she said, fluffing one pillow behind him and another under his knee. "Better?"

He raised an eyebrow, amused. "Yes. Thank you, nurse."

She stuck out her tongue.

He looked into the fire and took a deep shuddering breath, though he'd recovered from the trip and the run up the hillside to the house. *But what point was there in holding anything back now?* "I thought perhaps the news about Henry's mother – I thought it had reminded you of who I'm not."

"You're not a victim," Theodora said firmly, though not looking at him. "And you're my John. That's who you are." She moved to the floor in front of the fire and held out her hands to the blaze. Just as John was about to comment how odd it was to see her in white, she reached behind an old ottoman and pulled a large black cardigan out of a bag of knitting.

"They left my things right where they were, though they took the rest," she said, pulling it tight around her with a small smile. "Do you mind?" she asked, and he knew she meant the black.

He shook his head. "Thank you for saying that, Teddy."

She shrugged. "Though I suppose I'm officially a widow now. A widow and a wife."

"And a witch," John said. "Don't forget."

"Never," she said, with a small smile to herself. "I wonder if he wanted to die."

"You think Henry killed himself?"

She shook her head. "No. But I don't think he'd have ever stopped until he gave all of himself."

"A saint, then."

"A martyr," she said. "Not just women get to do it, you know."

He slid down onto the carpet next to her. "I'm so sorry, Teddy."

Finally, she looked at him. "I made my peace with him being dead a long time ago. Pathetically I think it took me longer to make my peace with him not wanting me. Stupid youthful vanity. But I haven't loved him for a long time."

John raised an eyebrow.

"It's true. I did once. But John –" She was looking in his eyes so intensely that he was afraid to blink. "For so long I truly did believe I killed him."

If he hadn't known her so well he'd have understood why people found her so uncanny. Nearly frightening. As it was he only saw how sad she was, and how afraid she'd been.

"Teddy," he said, softly. "No, never. How could you?"

"There's a lot I've never understood about myself, John. A lot I still don't understand. Who knows what I'm capable of."

"You don't still believe it, do you?"

"That I killed Henry? No. I've been angry, and I've been scared, but I've never wanted to hurt anyone, not really." She dropped her head. "But do I hurt everyone, don't I? It's just that I do it without trying or meaning to. I certainly drove him away. My mother, too. And –"

"Stop," he said, firmly. "All you did was love. It would be a hell of a lot easier if love could make someone stay or make them go, but I truly believe it can't. That's why it's such a gamble, but it's also why it's good."

He reached out and intertwined their hands. "I'm sorry for leaving, years ago. No one should ever leave you again. Look what they'd be missing."

She furrowed her brow, eyes tracking over his face. He had the feeling she saw things he didn't even know about himself, and the heat in his cheeks spread through the rest of him until any embarrassment had burned away entirely. If she didn't say something soon he was going to have to kiss his wife.

Theodora pulled her hand away, unfolded herself, and stood in one smooth motion. Then she held out her hand again.

"Come to bed, will you, Mr. Dove?"

John had never been to Theodora's room before. Rather, he'd never been to the room she had growing up, at the side of the house beside the copse of ash trees. But he'd certainly never been where she was leading him now, to her mother's wing, which had clearly become Theodora's own.

She pulled a set of keys from the pocket of her dress, beneath the cardigan, and unlocked the door to the house's west wing. Inside here, everything had been left as it was, and John noted the open door to what must be her study with a jolt of excitement. It might as well have been the inside of her brain.

At the end of the hallway Theodora reached around her neck to pull out the key he'd seen before, on the night she came to his room. From deep inside the door he heard the heavy shifting of metal workings, and then Theodora jammed her shoulder against the wood with unexpected force.

"Old wood," she said by way of explanation. Then the door gave way and they were in her bedroom.

Theodora stopped in front of the bed, the biggest he'd ever seen, and turned to face him.

"It smells awful, doesn't it? I've been a month away, I suppose." She hurried to the window and threw it up to let the night air in. "We should start a fire." She scurried from the window to the fireplace.

"Theodora."

"Damn this damp wood!"

"Theodora," he said again. "It's lovely. It's the biggest damn bed I've ever seen, but it's lovely. Was it a wedding present? From your first one, I mean. The other one." He put his head in his hands and started to laugh. "Damn it."

Theodora started to laugh, too, kneeling before the fireplace. "Is that terrible? I'd almost forgotten somehow."

"It's not," he said.

"I'm quite tired," she said, standing up. "Are you?"

He nodded. "It was a long trip down."

Theodora began to walk across the room and looked back over her shoulder at him. "I'm afraid I might need your help with the dress."

When she woke everything was white.

The sun came through the windows with the strength of a late winter afternoon and Theodora blinked against the brightness. Everything felt fresh, like after a snow.

She sniffed. Even though, yes, definitely, it did smell.

She'd have to update everything. She'd gotten lazy. Modernize plumbing, a hook-up to the pneumatic post, get hot water running beneath the slate floors that had felt like ice last night through the thin soles of her wedding shoes.

She smiled at the thought: *Theodora Dove, angel of modernization. Avenging angel. Wedding shoes.*

"It does smell, you were just being nice," she whispered. Theodora ran a hand over the coarse fabric, stretching toward John.

Stretching on and on.

She rolled over, stomach lurching. He was gone.

Surely he'd only gone to the bathroom. Perhaps he was making breakfast. Wouldn't she seem like a crazy woman, jumping out of bed in search of him as if every man she married would bolt immediately?

Theodora jumped out of bed.

The floor was so cold it made her bare feet ache, and goosebumps broke out across her arms. *Damn it. Where are my clothes?* Theodora grabbed John's pants and shirt and threw them on. Either he was impervious to the cold or he hadn't gone very far. Or he was desperate.

Theodora stomped out of the room, trying to bring blood into her toes and summon up anger to stave off fear. *He couldn't have woken me up?*

This was too much like before: the naïve waking, the hopeful searching, the growing realization. Panic. *What did I do? What did I do this time?*

She breathed deep. She had to trust him. John would not leave.

"Damn it, this is too traumatic to happen twice!" she called out. "I'm going to kill you if you haven't started breakfast! And coffee!"

Halfway down she saw him, standing beneath the entryway ceiling, staring up. He wore his suit jacket and his boxer shorts, barefoot.

She was so relieved she laughed and when she did John looked toward her.

"Maybe I won't kill you after all," she said, slowing to a saunter with her hands on her hips. Seeing him made her realize how much she wanted to see him. Again and again and again.

John was shaking his head.

She slowed.

His face was ashen, and he looked about to speak when from behind him Archibald Dove stepped into view.

Holding a gun. Pointing it at John. Looking at her.

"Archibald, holy hell, what are you doing?" she yelled, startled by how loud her voice was in the hallway nearly emptied of her family's things.

"Good morning, dear," he said. "I suppose I call you daughter-in-law, now?"

He'd been too sick to come to the wedding. That's what he'd said, anyway, though here he was and she couldn't tell at all if he was well or not. His eyes shone even at this distance, though from illness or madness or tears Theodora wasn't sure.

John's back was arched a little against the point of the gun. She wanted to vomit.

"Get away from my husband." Her voice vibrated with rage. And fear.

"I'm simply taking what is mine," Archibald said.

He didn't seem angry or vengeful. If anything he looked relieved to finally be at this stage of the game. It was so wrong to see a man be so calm while holding a gun to the heart of his own child. He'd thought things through and still, somehow, this was the course of action he'd decided upon.

"None of this is yours, Archibald," she said. "Not by rights or by reputation. Now put down the gun and get out of my house."

"Teddy," John said. "Turn around, walk away." Theodora didn't look at him, for fear she'd falter.

"Of course he's mine," Archibald said, scorn in his voice. "I made him, didn't I?"

"You never made anything," John said through gritted teeth. "You just took whatever you wanted and left a hollow core."

Archibald ignored him and beckoned Theodora with his free hand. "Come along. Family meeting time."

"Shut up!" John suddenly screamed, and Theodora flinched as Archibald stabbed the gun harder. John kept talking. "I am your legacy," he spat, "leave her out of this."

How far away was she? Fifteen steps? Twenty?

She took two steps closer. "Your father has always blamed me for his perceived shortcomings."

"I wouldn't give yourself too much credit, dear. Your mother is largely to blame."

"Stop calling me 'dear,'" Theodora spit, and the old man's veneer cracked the tiniest bit.

"Fine. Mistress Theodora Ashe-Martin-Dove, is it? Very melodious. Comprehensive in its reach. Tell me, how many men will you fuck and murder before you're through? How many names will you steal?"

Theodora felt the words like a punch but took two steps closer still. "I haven't decided yet. It's a new world. Perhaps I'll take a new name entirely? Or maybe the one I've always had will do." She started walking, hand gripping the edge of a tabletop for all the world as if it were her mother's hand and she was once more a scared child.

Archibald was getting impatient, looking up to the sun through the glass ceiling. "No. I can't take credit for that much."

"I think you want me to keep all those names I've acquired. Including your own. All those titles and land."

She didn't say the rest of what she was thinking: That if Archibald had orchestrated their marriage it would feel like some cruel summer-borne illness come over her life.

"He was testing me, Teddy," John said. He sounded so very tired.

"So it wouldn't go to waste!" Archibald said, his voice coming for a moment to an unsteady pitch. "So our name wouldn't go to waste! I wanted what was best, if that is a crime."

"It is a crime, in fact," John said drily. "Several of them."

"You could have killed him," Theodora said, disbelieving still. "He is your son."

John's eyes fluttered shut. "He's insane. Teddy. Leave. I'm begging you."

Archibald's eyes had become a little more wild. "You do not become great without being tested, and no test matters if it does not have stakes! And if you failed one of those tests –" He shrugged. "For the good of the island I had to protect the future of our work and our name."

Theodora said nothing. She imagined what her mother might do if she were here. She took another step forward, into the light.

"Good, good. Keep coming along, please." *Definitely impatient.*

She folded her arms, strengthened by the warmth of the sun. By her nearness to John. "What's the rush? We're married. Consummated, too. Can't this wait 'til after the honeymoon?"

John laughed in surprise. Archibald's face went nearly purple.

"What's the plan, Archie? Get me to leave the country? Kill me and claim self-defense?" She cocked her head. "Actually, why don't you just kill me, after all? This seems a lot of trouble. You're not a young man."

Archibald shifted his weight and sighed in exasperation. "I don't want you dead! A dead woman is a martyr. A dead woman is no trouble at all. It's alive that you were dangerous. Useful.

"Your name was to be dragged through the mud even more than you'd managed on your own. Accused of attempted assassination and murder. The half of the island that still thinks you a witch would realize your powers are no good to us at all, and the half that believes you nothing but a dried-up hag would do the work of throwing you out or stringing you up. Turn the tide against your kind once and for all and let the Dove come into what is ours free from superstition and speculation about what this island might be." He shoved his son with the gun once more. "I took care of Victoria White's father for you, boy. Truly I couldn't have made it easier for you."

John's jaw clenched so hard she could hear it. Archibald shook his head.

"But when John made it clear his feelings for you hadn't changed, the story had to." He shrugged. "Perhaps it's better this way. Less messy in the end." He raised one hand as if writing the headline across the air: "John Dove Saves Own Life, Magically Transforms Widow Witch into Lovely Wife."

Panic rose in her chest, a familiar sense of being trapped.

"Headlines don't rhyme, father," John said grimly.

Archibald grinned. "My son, mine, will be the man who made magic safe. Brought us into a bright new world of energy and free commerce and open harbors. And now you'll sign over your home and all the Martin's land and all your mother's land and the mining rights therein to Dove Holdings for perpetuity, because if you don't you know I'll end his life. You've seen what I can do. What I will do."

"Father, please," John said, his voice angry and desperate. "Leave Theodora alone."

"Come now, John. The Doves! Can you believe it?" Archibald nudged his gun into his son's back, for all the world like he expected a thank-you. When John didn't speak Archibald looked back to Theodora. "Let's go to your father's study, then. Get everything signed."

"He will destroy everything you love, Teddy," John said. "Don't do it."

She couldn't let him die. He *was* everything she loved.

Archibald took the gun away from his son's back only to point it at her. "I'd like to get this squared away before the evening edition," he said.

She looked at him helplessly and took a step toward her father's wing of the house. But John was staring at her so hard it made her own eyes ache.

Like it was the last thing he'd ever do.

"Oh no," she said softly. "Oh no, please no."

Then everything happened at once:

John lunged sideways at his father, putting his body between Theodora and the gun.

Archibald didn't hesitate, and a shot rang out.

Theodora, though she didn't remember doing it, raised her arms in a V above her head, fingers wide.

Then the wind. More than wind: a hurricane.

Light burst in upon them as the glass ceiling shattered. The dying sounds of metal and wood and plaster being wrenched apart as the ceiling ripped away to reveal the entirety of the sky.

Archibald Dove and his gun carried up into it, twisting every which way so that his shot was thrown off course and the old man spun like a bottle stuck in a drain.

John slammed into the floor and lay groaning. But he rolled over and looked up at her, stunned like a bird who's run into a window. Theodora stood nearly hyperventilating as a rain of cement dust and obliterated glass particles rained down around her.

"When the time comes," she said, "do what I tell you?"

He opened his mouth but the wind took his words away. It was whipping up again, lifting her hair into the air like a water spout and blowing his shirt around her. Bits of dust and broken tile and scraps of greenery from outside whirled through the air. John feared she might not be able to keep her balance.

Instead she seemed to find it. Theodora rose, too, and when she got to the jagged glass of the broken roof she stopped, buffeted lightly like a ship at port, itching to get to sea.

"How are you doing that?" Archibald screamed.

He'd landed on the blown-out edge of the roof and was leaning a little too far out, one hand stretched toward Theodora in accusation. The gun was still in his other hand.

Despite himself John sat up and called out. "Father, stop! You'll get yourself killed!"

Though of course Archibald wasn't listening. If Theodora was trying to ride the wind, he was attacking it like a boxer.

"You could do it all along!" he screamed, jabbing the air. "Unnatural beast! Witch! Hellish bitch!"

Silly that it should matter, after his father had seemed ready to murder him, how he spoke to Theodora. But matter it did.

John looked at his wife. *Give him your best*, he thought.

Though she was getting farther he could tell, very clearly, from the arch of her brow that she was rolling her eyes. He nearly laughed.

"Yes, I'm a witch!" Her voice carried everywhere at once on the wind. "Isn't that what you really wanted, Archie? All this power, harnessed to you?"

"Everything I built and made. You will destroy it all!"

"The opposite of everything is not nothing!" John screamed, as loud as he could so his father would hear him from far below and through the wind. How long had he fooled himself that the way things were was the way they should be? "You would have seen how much you had if only you weren't so damn scared of losing it!"

John screamed so loud that whatever he'd done to his head when he'd the floor reared up again like a dark black wave crashing against his eyelids. He fell backwards and felt the stone crack. *Fuck it all. I suppose I am a hard-headed bastard.*

John closed his eyes.

Hope Theodora doesn't mind. Perhaps she'll want to redo the entryway anyway. Why am I thinking about redecorating? Oh shit. Perhaps I'm cracked, too. He almost started to laugh. Archibald had started yelling again.

Of course he trusted her, on a level deeper than he could explain. His brain instructed his lungs to do as his wife told him. He shut his lips together tight against the urge to scream.

Maybe it wasn't a scream. Maybe it was only her name.

Suppose now I'll never know, he thought.

Archibald began to raise the gun again, fighting the wind. She flinched, but

Archibald wasn't pointing the gun at her. He was pointing it at his son.

John lay on the floor besides a crack in the tile. His eyes were closed.

"No!" she screamed and tried to direct a burst of wind toward John's father. "You have so much! I don't want any of it, please, believe me!" Her voice broke and Archibald held on. "He is still your child!"

"We all have a responsibility to act," Archibald said sadly, though his hand did not waver.

"John! Hold your breath!" she yelled. *Please trust me*, she prayed. But she didn't even know if he'd heard her.

She pushed her hands downward to shoot higher into the air, and for a second she tottered and spun. But she never lost sight of John until the moment she closed her eyes.

That was when she thought of Widow Green. The Widow's appearance at this moment was nearly as annoying as it was every damned time Theodora went to the post office. But now Theodora thought of the letters the widows sent to each other, speeding along tunnels dug all throughout the island.

All the connections and all the entry points. She could see it, or perhaps sense it: Lines illuminated from the bleeding edge of the glacier down through Mooring, under the forest and the mountains, spreading throughout the south like a root system or an arterial network. The lines burned bright blue in her mind, and Theodora asked for help with eyes still closed.

The line of blue came up through the rock of the earth, the dirt, the foundation of the house, the basement. It scratched against the stone of the floor.

Brilliant blue light geysered up as the crack in the floor split open wider. It rose so high it hit Theodora's bare feet in a flash of pain and color; it wasn't just light, it was flame and it rose so high and wide it shattered the remains of the roof that Archibald clung to.

Into the crevasse John Dove toppled, his eyes suddenly open as he fell. Theodora watched him gasp for breath one last time as he fell into the earth. Then the stone tumbled on top of him.

Theodora felt her skin start to burn away. She couldn't escape if she wanted to keep it rising up around her, pushing Archibald away from the edge. His mouth formed an O – surprise or pain, Theodora wondered, not sure which she hoped for. He was tumbling down the roof, and she tried to catch him on the wind and pull him upright.

But he lunged away from her grasp and toward the flame with what must have been the very last of his strength. For a moment he was surrounded for a moment in a sphere of blue light. The bubble burst and he was gone.

Far below them the bullet hit the shards of shattered floor and rolled until it hit the wall. No one saw it. Theodora had turned into the storm.

59

Ashe-Dove House
Dinnertime, March 20, 1948

"Hello, darling! Gardener? Yes, you! Hello there!"

John smiled into the radishes. The layer of sweat and dirt built up on his face cracked. He'd been out here all morning and afternoon.

When he stood the low sun was in his eyes, coming through the still-gaping hole in the line of the roof. But it would have been easy to tell it was them even if Adelaide hadn't shouted out her calling card. Her forward bouncing gait – the least graceful part about her, really, in the best of ways – and George's nearly backwards saunter cut distinctive shadows across the dry lawn behind Theodora's house. The three smaller shadows of Adelaide's boys danced across the field along with their shrieks.

"Hello there!" he called out.

Besides, they came to visit him nearly every week, though each week he was sure they'd be too busy, what with George's ever-increasing work at the university, and Adelaide having the children again. The Magistrate's travel plans had been delayed, it seemed, though if possible he and his wife saw each other even less than when he'd been gone.

One of the children got to him first. "Hello, Uncle John! Goodbye, Uncle John!" he screamed as he ran past.

"Careful of the workers!" John shouted. "Please do swing around again soon, sir!"

"Hello, darling," Adelaide said, and kissed him on the cheek.

"Dinner already?" John asked. He wiped his hands against his pants. "Come then, I suppose something's been set up on the patio." Ned, recovered but limping, would have gotten lunch out when he'd seen them all arrive.

"You're beginning to sound a bit crotchety, darling," Adelaide said, taking his hand.

"You would too if you had to deal with this damned rocky soil all day," he began, but she squeezed his hand and when he looked down her eyes were kind.

John blushed and cleared his throat. "Just trying to play the part of the lonely widower. Keep up appearances. You know."

"Hello, sir," George said, chuffing him on the shoulder as he broke into a sprint. "Can't talk!" he called. "I believe I'm 'it'!"

He and Adelaide continued through the grounds, each shielding their eyes with their free hand. The gardens and the pool were in a much better state than they had been last winter. Aided by correspondence with Theodora's stepmother, who was busy building up a new garden on the western coast, bulbs and seeds lay in wait. *Spring might be quite beautiful,* John thought. *Especially if it rains.*

Since Archibald and Theodora had disappeared there'd be plenty of stories about what might have happened. Good or bad, nearly all the stories involved Theodora being a witch, and that meant soon speculation started about whether her disappearance would bring the rain. Certainly, it had worked with her mother, for a time.

He cleared his throat. "Adelaide, there's something I should say."

She looked at him with one eyebrow raised as they continued to walk.

"I've been meaning to say for a while now. I'm sorry, that I was so distant these last years. I should have been there for you and I wasn't. There's no excuse."

Adelaide was silent. She looked over at George and the boys, running on the lawn, then glanced up at John again. "I did miss you. So thank you for saying that. But we all should have tried a little harder." She squeezed his arm. "And you're here now. We all are, almost, and we will be again."

Lately the papers talked about Theodora as though she was a warrior-queen out of an ancient story, someone whose reappearance would make everything right again. John sympathized with the sentiment. Perhaps Adelaide did, too.

"Thank you for saying that, too," he said. "And I'm very glad you have George."

"Me, too," she said simply.

They walked in companionable silence until they reached the little patio by the edges of the forest park, where George and the boys had ended up and now waited for supper.

"I saw they postponed open bidding again," John said. Recluse he might be, he still got the papers. With the death of his father and several prominent ministers, a vacuum had opened up in the fight for control of the southern coast. John found the occasional suggestion, via editorial and pundit, that it was somehow his responsibility to jump in betwixt foreign powers and the Assembly and his own company utterly laughable.

But wasn't that he didn't want to do something. He just wanted to make sure it was the right thing this time.

"Yes, and in fact they're sending me up north again," George said. "For a little while," he added with a glance at Adelaide. "Alternative investment opportunities, though I'll be damned if they've actually given up on selling coastal rights. Too much money to be made."

"Too little rain," Adelaide added, with a glance to the thick gray-pink sky that had lain over the island for the past few days. The latest in a series of empty promises.

"Roberta wrote me that she's still trying," Adelaide added brightly. "Digging through Ted's notebooks."

"Her handwriting is terrible," John said, smiling. "Completely illegible. She should have been the doctor, Addy, not you. I mean of course either of you should have been."

Adelaide didn't answer but looked over at her boys with something like contentment.

"Adelaide's said she'll visit me on the ice," George said. "You should come with her, John. It's still your company. Still your name on it, anyway."

"I'm sure it's in fine hands," John said, but the fate of the family's business was another thing keeping him up at night. He couldn't very well shut down operations: Too many jobs, plus the island still depended on algae and, increasingly, the ice. But while business was better than ever, public opinion was far less favorable. Archibald Dove had never been a popular man, and his legacy couldn't compete against the story of a martyred newlywed witch.

Damn it. She would have hated being called that.

"Oh no, please come," Adelaide said, leaning forward. "Can you believe I've never been to the glacier? I think I'll be able to bring the children. You really should come, John! We could whisk you out under cover of night, no one need know."

John raised an eyebrow. "Taking to the spy life?"

Adelaide sat back and folded her arms. "I think I'm an asset to the nation, frankly." She smiled across the table at George.

They stayed in the garden until their shadows grew long, dessert and coffee were finished, and John became self-conscious.

"You must be getting back soon," he said gruffly.

"Is that a question or a command?" George asked. He looked very full and very comfortable.

These visits always left John in a better mood than before, but it was a mood that declined precipitously after they left. Sometimes it seemed better to get it all over with, or to never see them at all.

"Thank you for coming again," John said, pushing back from the table. "I know you're both very busy these days."

George shrugged and gestured to the few visible stars above. "Today of all days? We couldn't let you be alone."

John grunted into his coffee. "Is today anything special then?"

Adelaide pursed her lips. "You know very well what today is."

John shrugged. "The equinox is really just another day. When you're not out in the shops or being dragged around to services of one kind of another, it's nearly identical to what comes before and after."

"She may still come back," George said quietly. "She's very powerful."

John was silent. Adelaide stared hard at her boys, playing in the field adjoining, and nodded her head.

John didn't think she would come back. He knew she would. He just had no idea when.

But he knew he would wait.

John showed them out, carefully steering the children around the gaping hole in the entryway. Then he locked the door and leaned hard against it. He wasn't used to talking that much.

He wandered the house slowly, checking windows and the general progress, and then began to make his way back to the entryway. Adelaide had been teasing, of course, but it really was remarkable how quickly he'd taken to living by himself and staying out of company. Perhaps not so surprising, given how he'd adapted to living on the glacier. He wasn't sure if that was a good sign or not.

The workers and architects and engineers were making progress, but slowly. Materials were still in great demand with all the investment flowing into the island, and John was being very particular about the rebuilding. He wanted it to look as it had, but also better. More like Theodora.

At least the lack of rain was good for building, if nothing else. John had put off rebuilding the roof far longer than was at all prudent or respectable. And this was where he wanted to sleep, closest to where he'd seen her last, disappearing into the blue morning.

He covered the globe of algae-light so the room only glowed with starlight. He unrolled the blankets he kept hidden beneath the sideboard, pulled out a pillow from where it was wedged at the bottom of a bookshelf, and kicked off his shoes. He lay down and closed his eyes, tired from a day outside. Even here, sleeping on the floor, he felt at home and breathed deep.

Dog shit.

Ever since Teddy had gone Diana had been roaming the house and the grounds, scaring the carpenters and overturning paint cans. John never saw her, let alone caught her, but from the very fresh smell she'd been wandering around the front of the house instead of Teddy's wing, where she usually slept. It wasn't as though the dog couldn't take care of herself, but John did worry she'd be mistaken for a mythological beast one evening and inspire some errant knight to take up a quest. Or at least a constable to attempt a net.

"Diana-girl?" he called. There was a scratching at the front door, and when he pushed open the front doors there was the dog for the first time in months, wagging politely on the mat.

And there was Theodora.

"Diana!" John gasped, forgetting himself.

Theodora smiled with half her mouth. "Glad to see you've grown so attached, John. Sorry to scare you. Were you worried about her?"

Theodora was still wearing his clothes, though they'd been scorched and blackened throughout. *Black really does suit her.*

She was so near he could see her chest rising and falling even in shadow, like the chest of a real live woman would. He stepped closer.

"You didn't scare me," he said. He would have been sure he was dreaming if it wasn't for the dog: Diana laid down across her mistress' feet like a moat to be crossed, and he'd certainly never have dreamed such a roadblock.

"I'm glad," she said slowly. She didn't seem used to talking to people, either. "How are you, John?"

He braced himself against the doorway to keep from running toward her. "I'm fine. Are you fine? Have you been fine? Where have you been? You look fine. You look wonderful. I missed you so much. Damn it, Teddy. What happened to you?" His voice broke.

She crossed her arms so her hands rested on her forearms. She clasped and unclasped her own skin like she was trying to prove something to herself. "I feel all right. I think."

"I missed you." The words came out of him in a rush. "So much."

He'd had so much time to think of everything he wanted to tell her – *and nine years before that, too* – and he couldn't help but feel she'd be gone again on the next stiff wind. *Why didn't I fix the bleeding roof?*

She smiled slowly. "I missed you, too. I'm sorry I had to – you know. All of it. Leave. Evaporate your father. I never meant to. Truly. I had no idea that would happen."

She looked very cold standing there, and he gripped the wood beneath his hands tighter. He didn't want to go to her before it was right. "Don't apologize. You saved me."

She swallowed hard. "I'm so glad you're still here." She laughed and John saw that her eyes were shining in the darkness. "And that you've been fixing up the house."

"I've quite a ways to go still." His hands broke free and he took a step toward her. Diana stood to attention. "Damn it all, Teddy! Where did you go?"

She looked away, shaking her head, and he pulled back.

"I'm sorry. You don't have to tell me."

"No, it's not that. I don't know. I don't know where I went. I was here and then I was elsewhere and now," she held up her hands, palms up, "I'm here again. I remember the force of the energy hitting me, and then there was only blue. I thought I'd died. It seems I was mistaken," she added with a dry laugh.

John laughed. Theodora stood just beyond the threshold as though she was the one who'd opened the door. Looking up at him as if the entire world was her home and she was inviting John in.

"Come here," she said.

He stepped through the doorway, closer to her, ignoring the dog.

"Did you really think I wasn't coming back, John?" Her voice was a whisper.

I am a witch and I have a home, she thought. *I don't need him to believe in me. I don't need his trust and his belief and his love.*

But she wanted it. So desperately it felt like she might disappear again without it.

"I wouldn't have blamed you. I promised you legitimacy. Status. Power. A good name," he said, and his voice was more bitter than she'd ever heard from him before. He seemed a few years older, not months. "My name is no good now."

Theodora patted Diana on the head to shoo her aside and took the final two steps to bridge the distance between them. She wrapped her hands around John's forearms and he gripped hers without hesitation, so that they stood braced to catch something that might fall from the sky. *Something other than myself.*

Up close he saw how different she looked. Not younger but – there was no other way to put it: She looked exceptionally well-hydrated.

The corner of his mouth went up.

Theodora frowned. "What is it?"

"No," he said, gently adjusting his hold on her. "Teddy, I always believed you'd come back. That's why I left the door open," he said, with an upward glance.

She laughed and then, so fast he almost didn't see it happen, moved her face towards him. He opened his mouth and closed his eyes and to his disappointment felt her breath as she bypassed his mouth entirely.

"Don't worry about your name, John," she whispered into his ear.

He pulled back a little and cocked his head at her, confused.

She raised an eyebrow and smiled. "You can take mine."

ACKNOWLEDGMENTS

Thank you to Erin McRae and Racheline Maltese for an invaluable and encouraging first round edit. Thank you to Emily Martin for an equally important edit late in the writing. And thank you to Amy Harwood for designing the cover of my dreams.

Thank you to my parents, Maureen Mahon and Jim Sharp, for their encouragement of my writing and enthusiasm for it, basically since birth. Thank you to my aunt, Peggy Mahon, for my first typewriter (which I still have).

Thank you, Joe, for every day.

ABOUT THE AUTHOR

Alexandra Sharp lives in Portland, Oregon, with her family. This is her first novel.

Made in the USA
Middletown, DE
31 October 2020